WAGONS WEST THRILLED MILLIONS OF
READERS WITH ITS STUNNING DEPICTION
OF THE AMERICAN WEST—AND THE MEN
AND WOMEN WHO TAMED IT: NOW,
AUTHOR DANA FULLER ROSS TURNS BACK
THE CLOCK TO PORTRAY THE FOREBEARS
OF FAMED WAGONMASTER WHIP HOLT
. . . AS THESE EARLY HOLTS LIVE
THROUGH THE MOST RUGGED ERA OF
AMERICAN EXPLORATION, FOLLOWING
THE WIDE MISSOURI, CROSSING THE HIGH
ROCKIES, AND FIGHTING FOR THE FUTURE
THEY CLAIM AS THEIRS.

WESTWARD!

AN ALL-NEW HEROIC SAGA OF PASSION, DE-
FIANCE, AND ADVENTURE WITH THE RUG-
GED MEN AND SPIRITED WOMEN WHO
VOWED TO CARVE A FUTURE FROM A WILD
AND PERILOUS LAND

CLAY HOLT—

Buckskin-clad and bronze as an Indian, this older
son needed to live free, roam far, and leave the past
behind . . . because lies had destroyed his good
name and a feud had made him a violent man.

JEFFERSON HOLT—

His flintlock rifle held at the ready in his strong
right hand, this younger son is as solid as the Ohio
hickory tree . . . a man who stands tall, loves
hard, and strikes out for the frontier leaving all he
cherishes behind.

MELISSA MERRIVALE—

A calico coquette, she had her sweet, young heart
set on marrying Jeff Holt, not knowing that their
wedding day would end in tragedy . . . and their
separation might prove to be permanent.

ZACHARIAH GARWOOD—

Evil eyes glinting with malice in a handsome face, this Ohio Valley lad took the crooked path in life, walking it with whiskey in his gut and a pistol in his hand . . . aimed at the Holts.

JOSIE GARWOOD—

Men came to her like bees to honey, but it was Clay Holt she wanted, and when she couldn't have him, she told the world that he had sired her child . . . and doomed them all.

SHINING MOON—

This proud Sioux woman of forest and stream was fairer than the wild rose, softer than the dove, braver than the she-bear . . . and the only wife Clay Holt wanted . . . even if their marriage shocked the world.

DUQUESNE—

Cruelty in a human form, this French trapper was a secret agent with a plan to incite the Indians against the Americans . . . by killing without mercy and framing Clay and Jeff for the slaughter.

ELK HORN—

Wearing his arrogance like a badge of honor, this hotheaded young Sioux intended to take the woman he wanted with no regard for her wishes . . . but that woman was named Shining Moon.

MANUEL LISA—

A paradoxical scoundrel with a brave and loyal heart, the Spaniard saw the profit in the furs of the New World and founded an empire that would make him rich . . . and make others envious enough to want him dead.

JOHN COLTER—

The archetype of the mountain man, he went west with Lewis and Clark, and then struck off on his own with a pack on his back, a knife in his belt, and a vision of absolute freedom in his heart.

PROUD WOLF—

Quick-witted rather than brawny, Shining Moon's young brother embraced two white men as his friends, Jeff and Clay Holt, only to discover that he would pay the price in blood and tears.

WAGONS WEST
FRONTIER TRILOGY
VOLUME 1

WESTWARD!

Dana Fuller Ross

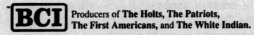
BCI Producers of **The Holts, The Patriots,**
The First Americans, and **The White Indian.**

Book Creations Inc., Canaan, NY • *Lyle Kenyon Engel, Founder*

BANTAM BOOKS
NEW YORK • TORONTO • LONDON • SYDNEY • AUCKLAND

WESTWARD!

A Bantam Book / published by arrangement with Book Creations, Inc.

Bantam edition / July 1992

Produced by Book Creations, Inc.
Lyle Kenyon Engel, Founder

ISBN 0-553-29402-4

Published simultaneously in the United States and Canada

Bantam Books are published by Bantam Books, a division of Bantam
Doubleday Dell Publishing Group, Inc. Its trademark, consisting of
the words "Bantam Books" and the portrayal of a rooster, is
Registered in U.S. Patent and Trademark Office and in other
countries. Marca Registrada. Bantam Books, 666 Fifth Avenue, New
York, New York 10103.

Dear Reader:

When *Independence!*, the first book in the *Wagons West* series, was published in 1979, I was tremendously encouraged by its success and hoped for a series that would run through perhaps half a dozen volumes. Never did I dream that the response of the public would be so great that twenty-four of these books would ultimately be in print, taking the family of Whip Holt through almost forty years of changes and challenges.

I was even more gratified when Bantam Books asked me to continue the saga of this American family in *The Holts* series, and I have enjoyed seeing where these diverse and energetic characters would take me—for the process of getting their stories on paper has been as much an act of discovery as one of creation. Now an idea that has always held a great appeal for me has been realized: With the publication of *Westward!* the story of Whip and Toby Holt's ancestors is finally being told.

Whip Holt's background was never revealed in the early *Wagons West* books, partially because the addition of background material would have slowed the pace of the books—something I knew my readers wouldn't appreciate. Yet as I wrote the two dozen books about Whip and his descendants, a rich and varied past was taking shape in my mind regarding his forebears, people who carved a life on the edge of the American frontier. Many readers sent me letters asking about the man and woman who brought Michael "Whip" Holt into the world. Finally the good people at Bantam Books asked me to respond to the numerous inquiries by putting the story of the first Holts on paper. What you hold here is the result, the story of Bartholomew and Norah Holt and of their five children, especially Clay and Jefferson Holt, brothers whose treks into the frontier opened a new land full of promise and danger.

But this is only the beginning of their story. I hope you enjoy reading *Westward!* and the two upcoming books in *Wagons West * The Frontier Trilogy*. I sincerely appreciate the loyalty and encouragement of my readers over the years, and I hope to offer new worlds of entertainment in the future.

DANA FULLER ROSS
Azle, Texas

AUTHOR'S NOTE

Westward! is a work of fiction grounded in fact. Quotations drawn from the journals of Meriwether Lewis and William Clark appear in the three-volume *History of the Lewis and Clark Expedition*, edited by Elliott Coues and reprinted from the 1893 edition by Dover Books. Along with the journals, this excellent reference source also includes Meriwether Lewis's lengthy "Essay on Indian Policy." Also of great assistance were *The Trailblazers*, published by Time-Life Books, and *Give Your Heart to the Hawks*, by Winfred Blevins, a fellow member of the Western Writers of America, Inc., and one of the leading authorities on the mountain men and their era. Any inaccuracies or misinterpretations that have crept in are solely the responsibility of the author. In addition, certain minor details may have been changed slightly for dramatic purposes.

Thanks are due to Greg Tobin of Bantam Books and Paul Block of Book Creations Inc., who helped immensely in shaping the early history of the Holt family. Pamela Lappies of Book Creations Inc. did a marvelous job of editing the manuscript, never failing to improve it with her diligent eye and intelligent suggestions; thanks, Pam. George Engel and Marla Engel of Book Creations Inc. made the whole thing possible, and of course the Holts would never have come to life in the first place without the late Lyle Kenyon Engel. Finally, friend and fellow author L.J. Washburn was the best sounding board any writer could ever hope for, and if anything in this book moves or entertains you, the reader, some of the credit should go to her for her unfailing inspiration and assistance.

The pioneer spirit embodied by the Holt family has carried this country farther, perhaps, than even her founders ever dreamed. As long as that spirit lives, there are no limits.

WESTWARD!

Following the return of the Lewis and Clark expedition, trappers intent on making their fortunes filtered into the new territory. The weapons they carried were their lifeline, providing them with food and protection. (1) The U.S. M1799 North and Cheney pistol was a .69 caliber flintlock with an eight-and-a-half inch barrel. (2) The tomahawk, or 'hawk as it was often called, was used by both whites and Indians. (3) The U.S. M1803 .54 caliber rifle, made at the government armory in Harper's Ferry, Virginia, was carried on the Lewis and Clark expedition. (4) Hunting knives came in a variety of styles, but most had handles made of antler or bone. (5-6) Hunting or "possibles" bags carried ammunition and were slung over the shoulder, along with powderhorns, in which gunpowder was stored.

RON TOELKE '91

American Indians used bow and arrow, shield and lance as weapons long after they had obtained guns. Unable to produce gunpowder and ammunition, they had to rely on white suppliers. Also, gunpowder could get wet and firearms could break, whereas the traditional weapons were reliable under any condition. (1) Shields were made of buffalo hide stretched over a frame and then decorated. (2) Lances were fashioned from bone, flint, or metal for the head and wood for the shaft. The length depended on the lance's purpose, the shorter ones used for hunting and the longer ones for war. (3) Many types of war clubs were used, some made from a rock lashed by rawhide to a handle, others carved entirely from wood. (4) Most prevalent were the bow and arrow, used for hunting as well as fighting.

RON TOELKE '91

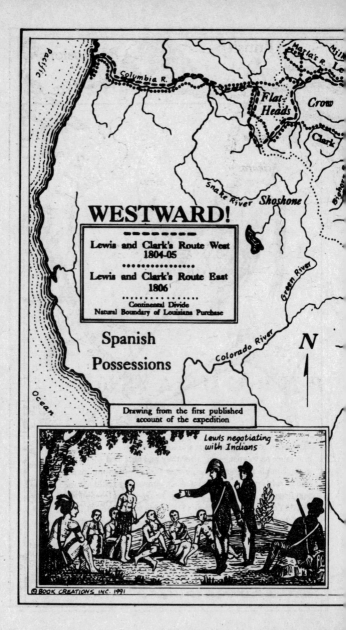

Pacific

Columbia R.

Maria's R. Le

Mi

Flat-
Heads

Crow

Clark

Snake River

Shoshone

Bighorn

WESTWARD!

- - - - - - -
Lewis and Clark's Route West
1804-05

• • • • • • • • • •
Lewis and Clark's Route East
1806

Continental Divide
Natural Boundary of Louisiana Purchase

Green River

Spanish

Possessions

Colorado River

N

Ocean

Drawing from the first published
account of the expedition

Lewis negotiating
with Indians

© BOOK CREATIONS, INC. 1991

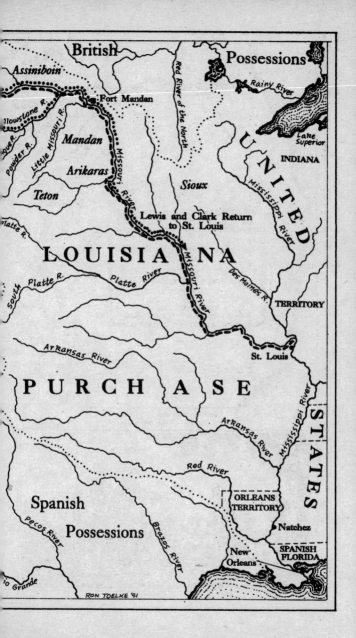

PART I

The object of your mission is to explore the Missouri river, and such principal streams of it, as, by its course and communication with the waters of the Pacific ocean, whether the Columbia, Oregan [sic], Colorado, or any other river, may offer the most direct and practicable water-communication across the continent, for the purposes of commerce. . . .

Your observations are to be taken with great pains and accuracy; to be entered distinctly and intelligibly for others as well as yourself; to comprehend all the elements necessary, with the aid of the usual tables, to fix the latitude and longitude of the places at which they were taken; and are to be rendered to the War Office, for the purpose of having the calculations made concurrently by proper persons with the United States. Several copies of these, as well as of your other notes, should be made at leisure times, and put into the care of the most trustworthy of your attendants to guard, by multiplying them against the accidental losses to which they will be exposed. A further guard would be, that one of these copies be on the cuticular membranes of the paper-birch, as less liable to injury from damp than common paper.

—PRESIDENT THOMAS JEFFERSON, from a
letter to Captain Meriwether Lewis,
June 20, 1803

CHAPTER ONE

The tall man in buckskins and coonskin cap paused at the top of a rise and looked out across a broad valley with awe-inspiring mountains on the far side, the craggy, snowcapped heights reaching high into the bright sky. The man carried a .54 caliber flintlock rifle produced at Harper's Ferry in 1803, a brace of 1799 North and Cheney flintlock pistols, a heavy-bladed hunting knife, and a tomahawk. He was armed for war, but at the moment, he felt utterly at peace.

Clay Holt was quite possibly the first white man ever to stand on that hill and survey the magnificent vista. He rested the butt of the flintlock rifle on the ground at his feet and leaned on the barrel. His beard and the hair that hung almost to his shoulders were a deep black, the color of midnight. His keen blue eyes searched the distance, scanning the thickly wooded hillsides, the meadows of lush grass and wildflowers, the lines of brush that marked the course of creeks. Far across the valley an eagle wheeled through the sky and then began to climb, seeming to ascend above the very peaks of the Shining Mountains themselves.

"It is beautiful, is it not?"

The voice came from behind Clay. He glanced over his shoulder and smiled at a young Indian woman carrying a baby. "Yes. I don't know why anybody would ever want to leave it."

"This land has been my home for many years. I would never be happy anywhere else."

"Reckon I can understand that," Clay said.

The woman deftly transferred the baby from the carrier on her back to her arms. The boy had been sick recently, but he seemed to have recovered his health. "Good, Pomp," she murmured to him and then looked up at Clay. "You will go back to this place you call St. Louis." There was no question to her words.

"Aye. But I'll be back here someday, Janey. You can count on that. I've never seen people who live a simpler life than yours. I don't reckon I've ever seen any who were happier, either."

Clay was happy, just about as happy as he had ever been. Almost from the first moment he had seen the Shining Mountains, he had recognized their strong pull; he felt as if he had come home. The freedom he experienced was unlike any he had ever known. He enjoyed Janey's company, too. There was nothing romantic between them; she was another man's wife. But she was Clay Holt's friend, and they had spent many long days talking about this country where she had lived her life.

"Well, I guess we'd better be getting back," he said. "The others'll be expecting us."

Janey took a few steps but then froze. "Clay Holt," she said in a soft voice fraught with urgency.

Clay heard her warning tone but managed to retain his casual attitude. He turned toward Janey, looked past her, and saw two warriors standing near a grove of pines a short distance down the ridge. He had seen a great many Indians during the past months —Shoshone, Sioux, Minnetaree, Crow, Blackfoot—but

from their markings he could not recognize the tribe
these two belonged to. They were unusually tall for
Indians, well over six feet, and they carried bows almost as tall as they were. Their dark hair was woven
into braids, and Clay thought he saw rattlesnake rat-
tles adorning each tip. As the two men regarded the
white man, the young Indian woman, and the baby,
their expressions were fierce. Clay sensed that he was
in more danger now than he ever had been since coming to these rugged mountains.

"You know who they are?" he asked Janey in a
quiet voice.

"Their tribe is not known to me. I think they are
enemies of the Shoshone, though."

"How can you know that?"

"Do they look like friends to you, Clay Holt?"

He had to admit she had a point. After a moment
he said, "Well, are we all going to stand here and stare
at one another for the rest of the day?"

"Perhaps they are just curious and will soon
leave," Janey said, but she did not sound as if she held
much hope of that happening.

Certainly Clay did not expect that to be the outcome. Yet he was not overly worried. His Harper's
Ferry rifle was primed and loaded, as were the two
flintlock pistols tucked underneath his belt. That gave
him three shots, affording him one miss if the Indians
attacked. Besides, he was confident in his abilities
with knife and tomahawk, and he had always been
able to hold his own in any kind of rough-and-tumble.

"Ask them what they want," he said, taking
Pomp from her arms.

Janey glanced dubiously at him. Then, using the
sign language understood by all Plains tribes, she
moved her hands gracefully to form the question.
When the strangers gave no response, she repeated
the movements, but again they failed to answer.

"Come on," Clay said, handing the baby back to
her. "Let's get out of here." Boldly he walked down
the slope toward the Indians, thinking that perhaps he

could bluff them into getting out of the way. If not, at
least he would be in better pistol range.

To Clay's great surprise, one of the Indians suddenly said in English, "This is not your land, white
man. You should not be here."

Clay stopped and, though he felt anxious, calmly
regarded the Indian who had spoken. Keeping his
voice level, he said, "I come in peace. I do not wish to
bring harm or trouble to any of your people."

The second Indian spoke. "This may not be your
wish, but it will happen. The white men will come,
and there will be great weeping and sorrow among
the lodges of the people. The plains will be littered
with the bodies of the dead, and the streams of the
Shining Mountains will run red with blood." The
words were not spoken harshly in anger but rather
with sorrow and resignation.

"How do you know this?" Clay asked.

"The spirits have spoken. They have told us these
things. Just as they told us where to find you."

Clay knew better than to scoff when Indians
spoke of the spirits and the messages they brought.
While he did not share such beliefs, he had come to
respect them. "Are you saying that if I leave this land,
the things you just told us won't come to pass?"

"We wish that it were so. But you are one among
many. Killing you will not stop what must happen."

Clay smiled tightly. "Then let us pass."

Both of them shook their heads. "We cannot,"
said one.

"The killing must begin somewhere," said the
other.

And with that, they reached into the quivers on
their backs.

"Run!" Clay barked at Janey. "Take the baby and
get out of here!"

"No!" she cried. "I will stay—"

The roar of Clay's rifle drowned out anything else
she had to say. He had always been a good marks-
man, and his eye and his nerve did not betray him

now. The lead ball smashed into the chest of one of the Indians, and he fell backward, dead. The second man managed to loose his arrow. Clay dove desperately to the side as the feathered shaft cut through the air, the arrow plucking at his sleeve, tearing the buckskin and leaving a painful gash in his arm. As Clay hit the ground, he yanked one of the pistols out from his belt and cocked it. The Indian already had a second arrow nocked, but before he could release it, Clay pressed the trigger of the flintlock. The pistol bucked in his hand, and acrid smoke from the exploded black powder filled his senses.

As had his companion before him, the second Indian died without a sound. He fell, the breast of his buckskin shirt turning crimson from the spreading bloodstain.

Clay came up on his knees and lifted his other pistol, holding it ready just in case either man was only wounded and not dead, although he was fairly certain that wasn't the case. He glanced up at Janey, still standing nearby cradling the baby. She was slightly shaken but seemed to be unharmed.

"Are you and Pomp all right?" Clay asked.

"Their arrows did not touch us," she said. "But their words . . ."

Clay got to his feet as the young woman's voice trailed away. He understood what she meant. The grim prophecy pronounced by the two Indians had disturbed him, too.

"It doesn't have to be that way," he said. "Just because they thought some spirits told them—"

Janey shook her head. "I do not think the spirits told them of this vision. I think they themselves were spirits."

"They're flesh and blood," Clay insisted, looking at each warrior to make certain he was dead. "They're men, and they died as men."

"Then how did you know what they said?"

Clay stared at her. "They were speaking English. I admit, that's sort of strange—"

"They spoke Shoshone," Janey said softly. "I heard their words in my tongue, just as you did in yours."

For a long moment Clay did not answer. Then he said quietly, "I reckon at least one of us is mixed up. We'd better get moving."

"Your arm is hurt. Let me look at it first."

Clay held out the arm that had been grazed by the arrow. The minor wound had hurt like blazes at first, but now it seemed strangely painless. His eyes widened as he examined the buckskin sleeve and found no tear. Quickly he shoved the sleeve up over his forearm.

The skin was unmarked.

Clay took a deep breath. "Maybe you've got something there with your spirit talk." Looking around, he saw the arrow lying on the ground nearby and stepped over to it. He reached toward it gingerly, and when his hand grasped it, he was instantly reassured. The arrow was real, all right. Maybe he had just imagined that it hit him.

Janey stepped closer and looked at him intently. "You must give me your word, Clay Holt. You must pledge to me that you will do what you can to see that there is peace in this land. I know that you and the others will come back." She smiled sadly. "You will not be able to stay away."

There was truth in what she said, Clay thought. The lure of the mountains was too powerful. He could speak for no one but himself, but he knew that whether he went back East or not, someday he would return to these mountains.

"Let's make tracks out of here and get back to the others," he said. "These two could have some friends close by."

"Your word," the young woman insisted. "You must promise me, Clay Holt."

"All right," he said, facing her squarely. "I give you my word, Sacajawea." At a moment like this, he felt it was better to use her real name, rather than the nickname Captain Clark had given her. "Now, come on. Cap'n Lewis and Cap'n Clark just sent us out to scout ahead. They're bound to be wondering what happened to us. And if they heard those shots—"

"Tell them you fired at a deer and missed." She looked at the dead men and shuddered slightly. "This is not something the captains need to know."

Clay agreed. With all the talk about spirits and prophecies, he thought it would be best to keep his mouth shut. If he told the others about it, they might think he was crazy.

"Do not forget your pledge," Sacajawea reminded him as they left that place.

"Don't worry," Clay Holt said, his hand tightening on the arrow. "I won't forget."

For all the signs of civilization they could see, the men might have been alone in the millions of square miles of trackless wilderness around them. Their camp in the Rocky Mountains was so isolated from the rest of the growing country, in fact, that they might as well have been on the far side of the moon.

In the summer of 1806, a trip to the moon would have been inconceivable, of course, but no more so, to most people, than a two-year journey across the Rockies, to the Pacific Ocean, then back over some of the most rugged terrain known. But that was precisely what the so-called Corps of Discovery had done under the joint command of Captain Meriwether Lewis and Captain William Clark.

Clay crouched near one of the campfires, looking around at his companions. Fewer than three dozen in number, they were mostly clad in buckskin tunics and trousers, with raccoon-pelt caps perched on their long, shaggy, matted hair. The ringed tails of the animals had been left intact, to dangle down the back of the wearer's neck or be pulled forward over his shoulder. Some of the men had left the heads on as well, so that the creatures almost seemed alive, ready to swing their sharp little faces toward the first scent of danger.

Clay had removed the head of the raccoon from whose pelt he had fashioned his cap. Now he pushed the headgear back on his shock of thick black hair and sipped tea from a battered tin cup. It was not real tea, such as the English drank, but had been brewed instead from the roots of a plant that grew in abundance in that area. The tea was strong and had a bite to it, and it helped wake a man up on a chilly morning. That high in the mountains the mornings were cool, even though it was the middle of summer.

Nearby, both Lewis and Clark were writing in their journals, the scratch of their pens audible in the clear mountain air. Unlike most of the frontiersmen who had accompanied them on the trip, the captains wore blue uniform jackets and heavy tan breeches, with high-topped black boots that had survived the journey well. Nearly all the other men wore moccasins.

Captain Lewis looked up from his journal and said to Clark, "Have you written about our parting?"

Clark said, "Aye. Would you like to hear it? It will be easier to understand than trying to read my poor spelling."

Lewis laughed. "Yes, yes. I'd appreciate that."

Clark lifted his opened journal and read:

> "We have formed the following plan of operation: Captain Lewis, with nine men, is to pursue the most direct route to the falls of the Missouri, where three of his party are to be left to prepare carriages for transporting the baggage and canoes across the portage. With the remaining six, he will ascend Maria's river to explore the country, after which he will descend that river to its mouth. The rest of the men will accompany Captain Clark to prevail on some of the Sioux chiefs to accompany him to the city of Washington."

"You haven't mentioned the Indian woman."

"Oh, yes. Sacajawea will be traveling with me. Perhaps I should amend it."

Lewis held up his own journal. "Here is what I've written concerning the natural surroundings." He cleared his throat and began:

> "We were successful in procuring a number of fine large deer, and the Indians assert that there are great numbers of the white buffalo or mountain sheep, on the snowy heights of the mountains west of Clark's River. They generally inhabit the rocky and most inaccessible parts of the mountains; but they are not fleet, and easily killed by hunters.
>
> "The plants which most abound in this valley are the wild rose, the honeysuckle with a white berry, the seven-bark, serviceberry, elder, aspen, alder, chokecherry, and both the narrow- and broad-leaved willow.
>
> "We prevailed on our Indian friends to accompany Captain Lewis on part of his route, so as to show him the shortest road to the Missouri, and in the meantime amused them with conversation and running races, on foot and with horses, in both of which they proved themselves hardy, athletic, and active. To the chief Captain Lewis gave a small medal and a gun, as a reward for having guided us across the mountains; in return the customary civility of exchanging names passed between them, by which the former acquired the title of Yomekollick, or White Bearskin Unfolded."

Captain Lewis snapped his journal shut. "Well, that's that," he said. "I suppose we'll be ready to push off shortly."

"Aye."

Both men seemed rather casual, considering that the expedition was about to split up for the first time since it had left St. Louis in 1804. Roughly a third of the men would accompany the tall, dour Meriwether Lewis, while the others would continue on with William Clark. The commanders had reached the decision together, and there was no animosity involved. This was, after all, an expedition of discovery, and by breaking up into two groups on the return trip, they could cover more ground. That meant more information and more maps to be taken back to President Jefferson in Washington City.

Clay Holt respected both Lewis and Clark. They were excellent soldiers—although Clay did not really know much about soldiering as such—and their record spoke for itself. The group had been to the Pacific and had come this far back with the loss of only one man. And Sergeant Floyd had died as the result of a sudden illness, something that could not have been prevented. So far, although the Corps of Discovery had encountered hundreds, perhaps thousands, of Indians, they had had no trouble with the "aborigines," as Captain Lewis called them.

At least no trouble that the rest of the group knew about. Clay had not forgotten the encounter Sacajawea and he had experienced with the mysterious warriors a couple of weeks earlier. As they had agreed that day, neither said anything to the others about that strange meeting. Sacajawea had not even told her husband, the French wastrel Toussaint Charbonneau.

Clay had made his choice of which captain to accompany strictly on a whim. He would go with Lewis, who intended to head north to the Great Falls of the Missouri River, and from there explore along Maria's River—named by Lewis for one of his lady friends in the East—before turning back and rejoining Clark's party farther south along the Missouri. The trip would be considerably longer that way, but Clay did not mind.

After all, he was in no hurry to get back to civilization. Hell, he thought as he drained the last of the root tea, he would not really care if he never got back.

Roaming the wilderness for the past two and a quarter years had changed Clay Holt. He had left the family farm in the Ohio River valley a restless young man, quick-tempered and seldom satisfied. In the mountains, for one of the few times in his life, he had found contentment.

Several days earlier he had overheard two of the men talking about the possibility of staying in the mountains and living with the Indians. That idea held some appeal for Clay, too, but it would mean deserting. He had signed on to make the entire journey with Lewis and Clark, and he was a man of his word. At least he liked to think of himself as one.

Nothing would stop him from coming back later, though, after the Corps of Discovery had returned to St. Louis and disbanded. He could make a quick trip to the Holt family home near Marietta, Ohio, then find some excuse to head west again. That was exactly what he would do, Clay decided as he stowed away the empty cup in his buckskin possibles bag.

Captain Lewis called out, "You men who are going with me, prepare to mount. We'll be pulling out shortly."

Clay went over to his horse, a sturdy Indian pony like the ones ridden by the other men. The horses had made this part of the journey easier, Clay thought. In the roughest stretch of mountains, the corps had been forced to travel most of the way on foot, using the horses only as pack animals. Here, they could ride.

Clay slung his possibles bag over his shoulder, grasped the pony's mane, and swung up agilely. They had no saddles, only buckskin pads to protect the backs of the animals. The pads did not offer much protection for the rear ends of the riders, Clay thought, but they were better than nothing.

He looked at the other men going with Captain Lewis: Sergeant Gass, Frazier, Warner, Drouilliard, McNeal, Goodrich, Thompson, and the two Fields

brothers. Good men, all of them. They had been experienced frontiersmen to start with, and the expedition
had seasoned and toughened them even more. Clay
was proud to have them for companions. Several of
the Shoshone men who had attached themselves to
the expedition as guides would be coming with them,
too, although Sacajawea and Charbonneau would continue on down the Yellowstone with Clark's party.

Lewis rode up to Captain Clark, who was on foot
beside Clay's horse. As Lewis reined in, he leaned
over to take the upraised hand of his fellow commander. "God willing, I'll see you in a few weeks, my
friend," Lewis said as he gave Clark a firm handshake.

"God willing," Clark repeated.

Although neither of them made much of their
parting, Clay could hear the concern in their voices. So
far, the mission given to them by President Jefferson
had met with remarkable success—but that luck could
change at any moment. Disaster could lurk around the
next bend in the trail.

Captain Lewis lifted an arm and waved his hand
forward, signaling for his men to depart. The small
group rode away from the clearing, leaving their former comrades behind, striking out into virgin territory
on which it was quite possible no white man had ever
laid eyes. They were following a stream they had
christened Clark's River on their westbound journey.
Even though it was summer, the waterway was still
somewhat swollen by the spring runoff from the
mountains. The Shoshone guides, seemingly tireless,
trotted alongside the riders.

Mountains that remained white-tipped with snow
year-round loomed above them. Thick stands of timber covered the lower slopes, and the grass beneath
the hooves of the horses was thick and lush. Wildflowers in colorful profusion dotted the meadows
through which the party rode. This was beautiful
country, Clay thought as he lifted a hand to rub his
black-bearded jaw. Beautiful country indeed. He did

not look back at what he and his companions were leaving behind, preferring instead to look ahead.

Yes, he would return once he had paid a visit to his family, he vowed. But not just because of the landscape's wild beauty and the appealingly simple life led by the Indians. Clay had reasons other than his growing love of the frontier for not wanting to remain in the Ohio River valley.

The image of Melissa Merrivale's lovely face, framed by her flowing dark hair, was in Jeff Holt's mind as he strode down a woodland road on an Ohio summer evening in 1806. The sun had set only a few minutes earlier, and a red glow still suffused the sky to the west. A cooling breeze had sprung up to carry off some of the heat of the day, and it felt good as it plucked at Jeff's linsey-woolsey shirt. He was tired, having worked in the fields all day, as usual, but the thought of soon seeing Melissa made his step lighter.

Jeff had never been affected by the wanderlust that had gripped his brother Clay. Even if he had not enjoyed the work on the family farm, had not experienced the satisfaction of tilling, planting, and weeding and finally being able to see the results of his labor and hold the harvest in his hand, he would have been perfectly content to remain in the valley. With Melissa here, he thought, he had no reason to go traipsing off to God knew where, as Clay had done.

That thought made him pause in his stride. Shielding his eyes with his hand, he looked over his shoulder to the west, where the red of the sunset was deepening to purple.

It had been well over two years since Clay had left, heading for St. Louis and leaving bitterness and bad feelings behind him. Some people had been glad to see the oldest Holt son go, but Jeff had not been among them. He missed Clay to this day, and he found himself wondering if his brother was still alive.

Though life in Ohio could still be a rugged existence, Jeff knew that it was not the wild frontier terri-

tory it had been when Bartholomew Holt had brought
his family there almost two decades earlier. Then the
vast lands to the northwest of the Ohio River had been
almost as unexplored as the great mountains that divided the continent. The Northwest Territory, as the
area was known, had been wrested from the French by
the English in the French and Indian War, and with
the end of the American Revolution, it became the
property of the ambitious new republic.

One of the problems that had faced the fledgling
United States government was how to pay the thousands of troops who had served in the war to liberate
the colonies from England's grip. General Rufus Putnam and Timothy Pickering, the quartermaster general of the army, had hit upon a scheme that in one
stroke solved that problem as well as promoted the
expansion of American settlement into the Northwest
Territory. Simply put, the soldiers were to be paid in
land.

The plan, supported by General George Washington himself, was eventually shepherded through Con-
gress and became a reality. On April 1, 1788, a group
of hardy New Englanders set out down the Ohio River
in the *Mayflower*, a bark named after the ship that had
brought their forefathers to the New World. The destination of the settlers was Fort Harmar, a military post
established by General Putnam at the junction of the
Muskingum and Ohio rivers. There, under the protection of the troops, they intended to found a township.

Among those bold immigrants had been Bartholomew Holt, his wife, Norah, and their young sons,
Clay and Jefferson. Tucked securely in an inside
pocket of Bartholomew's coat was the document
granting him land in the Northwest Territory in return
for his service during the war. As he stood at the railing of the *Mayflower*, his arm around his wife and his
sons beside him, Bartholomew had watched the heavily wooded banks of the river glide past and had
known the rightness of what he had done. He could
have stayed in Massachusetts; such a course would

have been safer for his family, he knew. But it would not have satisfied the growing urge in him to move on, to begin something that would last and perhaps one day grow into more than his mind could even imagine. That had been Bartholomew Holt's dream, and he was determined to make it real or to die trying.

The first settlement, across the river from Fort Harmar, had been known as Campus Martius, the "place of arms." Indeed, the area had a distinctly Roman look to it, with its great mounds, its vestiges of roads, and its earthworks and causeways heaved up in ages past by some vanished, unknown people and then abandoned for centuries. Soon, though, people took to calling the community Marietta. It was the first white settlement in the Northwest Territory, later the state of Ohio.

And it was here that Clay and Jeff Holt had grown to young manhood.

Jefferson Holt had been named for the great patriot who was helping found a new nation about the same time Jeff was born. Jeff Holt did not remember living as an infant in Massachusetts with his mother and older brother. Instead, his memories were wrapped up in the fertile valley of the Ohio, where he not only learned the skills needed to make a living from the land but also how to hunt and fish and survive in the woods. Like Clay, Jeff had done his share of the work in the fields of the family farm, strengthening his muscles by guiding the crude, mule-drawn plow, but there had usually been time for the more pleasant activities, too. He'd had a good shooting eye and had been able to bring down a squirrel at fifty paces with a musket by the time he was ten, although the barrel of the weapon had been longer than he was tall.

Jeff had known how to take care of himself in the rough-and-tumble battles with Clay and the other lads in the vicinity, but for the most part he did not seek out trouble. He usually tried to find a way to settle things short of violence. He lacked the stature of his father and brother, having grown only to medium height, but his shoulders were broad and his muscles as hard as the rocks he carried out of the fields being cleared for cultivation. By the time he had reached his early twenties, his handsome features and curly, sandy-blond hair had won him no small number of female admirers.

Jeff was only interested in one woman, though: Melissa Merrivale. He had been paying court to the pretty young eighteen-year-old for several months now, and before much longer, he told himself, he was going to kiss her, even if he got his face slapped. He had a feeling, though, that Melissa would not object much.

Jeff walked on down the road that led to the cabin where Melissa lived with her parents, not far from the Holt house. With each stride he thrust his nagging concern for Clay out of his mind. The plain and simple truth was that a body could get killed any number of ways on the frontier; no point in worrying about Clay. Someday, if Clay was still alive, he would come home. Of that Jeff was sure.

He had only gone a few feet farther when a sound behind him made him pause. Frowning, he looked over his shoulder. Tall oak trees lined the road, their shadows deep and thick. Jeff's eyes could not pierce the growing gloom, but he was certain he had heard hoofbeats behind him.

Seeing no one, he turned and resumed walking, his pace a bit faster now. But after a moment he again heard the same sounds. He stopped short; the noise ceased as well.

Somebody was back there, all right, Jeff thought. And likely up to no good. Any normal traveler on horseback would have overtaken him by now. The rider's stopping every time he did boded ill.

Thieves had been known to haunt the roads around Marietta, lurking in the darkness to waylay unwary pilgrims. Men had been hit on the head, their purses stolen. Occasionally a body was found when some hapless victim had put up too much of a fight to suit his robbers. But such violence was rare.

Jeff was not worried about Indians either. Those were shod hooves he had heard behind him, and that meant white men. The Lenape, who had been pushed into the area by the eastward expansion of the fierce, warlike Iroquois, had dwindled in number, and only a small tribe remained. They had been at peace with the settlers for years.

He darted a glance at the thick growth of trees beside the road. If the rider or riders gave chase, there was no way he could outrun them on the road. But he could dash into the woods and elude them there.

Jeff's tongue slid across dry lips. If the strangers in the twilight were highwaymen, they were taking their own sweet time about striking. Perhaps they were just toying with him, trying to make him nervous. He could think of only a few individuals who would do such a thing. . . .

As if they were aware of his thoughts, the riders began to speak, their harsh voices floating out of the gathering dusk as they called to him.

"Who's that up there on foot?"

"Don't rightly know," another voice answered. "You sure he's on foot? I figured he was crawling on his belly!"

"Like a worm, ya mean?" Jeff heard a loud sniffing noise. "Shooo-eee! Stinks worse'n a hog, too!"

"Crawls like a worm and stinks like a hog? Must be a Holt!"

Jeff's jaw tightened angrily as he recognized the voices, confirming his suspicions. They belonged to two of the Garwood brothers, probably Zachariah and Peter from the sound of them. Zach and Pete were the oldest of the brood, close in age to Jeff's brother, Clay. There were two other brothers and a sister, and they all made their home with their widowed father on a farm not far from the Holt land.

So far, Zach and Pete seemed content to hang back in the twilight and shout insults at him. Jeff stalked on down the road, trying to ignore them. There was bad blood between the Holts and the Garwoods, and this was not the first time one of Jeff's family had been harassed by the Garwoods.

Walking along the road, Jeff heard the clip-clop of hooves as Zach and Pete put their mounts into a walk again. The shouting continued, becoming more profane and more direct. The Garwoods were not trying to be funny, now. Instead they heaped obscenity after obscenity on Jeff and his family.

Finally, after a particularly vile comment concerning his little sister, Susan, Jeff stopped and wheeled around to face them. His good mood had completely vanished. Clenching his fists as he stood in the middle of the road, he called out, "Dammit, Zach! If you and Pete have something to say to me, come up here and say it!"

Zach and Pete rode out of the growing darkness. "All right, Holt," Zach Garwood replied. "We'll do just that!"

With those words Zach drove the heels of his boots into his horse's flanks, kicking the animal into a gallop—directly at Jeff. Pete rode beside him, leaning over the outthrust neck of his horse as he urged it on to greater speed. Both riders raced at Jeff, the sound of hooves suddenly like thunder in the early evening air.

For a few seconds Jeff's mind could barely credit what his eyes saw all too plainly. The two men on horseback were sweeping out of the darkness at him, intending to ride him down. At the last instant he regained control of his muscles and flung himself to the side, just in time to avoid being trampled. He landed in the shallow ditch at the side of the road and felt the earth shake under him as the horses thudded past only a few feet away. The harsh laughter of the Garwoods raked at his nerves.

As he lifted his head, his teeth clenched in rage, he saw Zach and Pete reining in and turning their mounts. They rode back toward him.

"What's the matter, Holt?" Zach asked. "Somebody like you ought to feel right at home wallowing in a ditch."

Despite his leanings toward peacefulness, Jeff wished at that moment he had a pistol or a rifle or some other sort of weapon. He would wipe that smirk right off Zach's face, he told himself.

Then he realized he would do no such thing. He was not a cold-blooded killer and never would be, no matter what the provocation. But if he left the ditch and went after the Garwoods with his fists, tried to drag them off their horses, they would hand him a severe beating. All they were looking for was an excuse. Jeff took a deep breath and tried to will his anger away. He would stay where he was.

"You got yourself all dirty, Holt," Pete said. Jeff couldn't distinguish their features in the darkness, but it was easy to make out Pete's larger form and recognize his voice. Pete gave a burst of dull-witted laughter and went on, "Maybe next time you'll stay in the ditch when you see the Garwoods coming."

"That's where all the goddamn Holts belong," Zach said, a vicious edge to his voice.

This had gone beyond mere horseplay, Jeff realized, and his muscles tensed. It was impossible to predict what Zach Garwood might do. He might even whip out a gun and take a shot at Jeff.

But then Zach added, "Let's go, Pete. I'm tired of this." He pulled his horse's head around and sent the animal off in a gallop toward Marietta. Pete followed him closely.

Jeff waited until the sound of the horses had completely died away, then pushed himself onto his feet and trudged out of the ditch. His hands, knees, and the front of his shirt were stained with dirt and grass. In addition, one shirtsleeve was torn from being caught on a root in the ditch. He wiped his hands on his trousers as best he could, then stepped into the middle of the road and again started walking toward the Merrivale farm. For a moment he considered turning around and heading home; he hated for Melissa to see him in this state. But the Merrivale place was closer than the Holt farmstead, and Melissa would not mind his appearance. Her father, old Charles Merrivale, might be a different story, however.

As he walked along, Jeff listened closely to make sure Zach and Pete were not returning. All was silent, however, except for his plodding footsteps, the night cries of birds, and the rustle of small animals in the woods on both sides of the road. Jeff's anger grew. That anger was directed not only at Zach and Pete, but also at the situation that had caused the hostility all the Garwoods felt toward the Holts. It just was not fair.

He was angry at one other person, too—his brother, Clay. If Clay had not left Marietta when he did, making it look as if he were running away . . .

Such thoughts would not do any good. Besides, the Garwoods had disliked the Holts as long as Jeff could remember, and they hadn't caused Jeff and his family any physical harm in the two and a half years that Clay had been gone. They had relied instead on insults and humiliation.

Jeff saw the warm yellow glow of a lamp up ahead, and he knew that he was nearing the Merrivale cabin.

Charles Merrivale had paid dearly to have glass windows brought down the Ohio on a freight boat. Even in the town of Marietta itself, few houses had glass windows. Among the farms outside the settlement, such a luxury was unheard of. But Merrivale was determined to have only the best for his family, no matter what the cost.

That desire for the best extended to his daughter's suitors. Jeff knew Merrivale did not exactly approve of him, but that knowledge had never deterred him. The old man could frown and stomp around the cabin all he wanted to; Jeff was still going to call on Melissa.

Showing up in such a disheveled condition, though, would lower Merrivale's opinion of him that much more, Jeff thought. But it could not be helped, and he forgot that worry as he saw the door of the cabin open. The light from inside silhouetted a slender form, and Jeff felt his heart beat a little faster. Melissa was looking out at the night while the family dog stood near the cabin, barking.

"Budger!" Melissa called to the dog. "What is it, Budger?"

"Get out of the door, girl!" Jeff heard the command from Charles Merrivale. "What if it's a savage the dumb brute is barking at? You want an arrow through your gullet?"

"Charles!"

Jeff smiled slightly at that shocked exclamation, which carried clearly through the night air. Melissa's mother, Hermione, might have been married to Merrivale for over twenty years, but she had never grown accustomed to his surly manner.

Melissa stepped out into the yard in front of the large cabin. "Oh, Father!" she said. "You know as well as I do that the only Indians around here are the Lenape, and they're as peaceful as kittens."

Jeff might have argued that; the Lenape did not go hunting for trouble, but neither was it wise to cross them. However, Melissa could say almost anything she wanted to without having to worry about being contradicted by Jefferson Holt, and she knew it quite well. Perhaps too well.

"Hello, Melissa," he called softly.

"Jeff!" she exclaimed. Turning her head, she said into the cabin, "You see, Father, I told you. It's Jeff Holt."

"Hmmph!" Merrivale snorted, his tall form appearing in the doorway behind Melissa. "I'm not sure I wouldn't have preferred the savages." Jeff stepped into the long rectangle of light that spilled through the door, and Merrivale went on. "Good Lord! What happened to you, lad? You look as if you'd been in some sort of fight."

Merrivale's words made Jeff tense with remembered anger as he thought of Zach and Pete Garwood.

"I had a mishap on the way over here, sir," he said, carefully keeping the anger out of his voice.

"I can see that," Merrivale said acidly.

Hermione Merrivale came to the door and stood beside her husband, inquiring solicitously, "Are you all right, Jefferson?"

"Yes, ma'am," he replied. "I'm fine, just a mite the worse for wear. I'm sorry to cause trouble—"

"No trouble at all." Melissa took his arm. "Come along with me. There's a bucket of water in back. You can wash your hands and brush the grass out of your hair, and then I'll see about mending that sleeve for you." There was a merry little smile on her face.

Conscious of the warmth of her fingers through his shirtsleeve, Jeff let her lead him behind the sturdy dwelling, where a large wooden bucket full of water for washing sat on a bench. Light from inside spilled through one of the windows, allowing him to see what he was doing as he sank onto a three-legged stool beside the bench and began washing his hands. Melissa picked grass from his hair and brushed it off his back.

He looked up at her as her hand rested on his neck for a moment. Her rich, dark brown hair flowed over her shoulders in waves, and it gleamed with auburn highlights in the light coming from the window. He had always thought Melissa had the most expressive face he had ever seen, but now as her brown eyes crinkled in a knowing smile, he felt that he was only beginning to perceive her beauty. And the burgundy dress she was wearing with its lace-edged square bodice only intensified her attractiveness.

"What really happened?" she asked in a quiet voice, now that they were out of earshot of her parents. Melissa had no brothers or sisters, and as an only child, she was something of a rarity in that time and place.

"I had a run-in with a couple of the Garwoods," Jeff replied. "Zach and Pete tried to ride me down. I had to jump into the ditch to get out of their way."

"Perhaps they didn't see you in time to slow down," Melissa suggested, but she did not sound convinced of the likelihood of her theory.

"It was no accident. They wanted to trample me —or at least scare me good and proper. Which they did."

"But you're really all right?"

"I'm not hurt." He left it at that.

"Someone should do something about the Garwoods. They're always causing some sort of trouble."

"They don't break any laws, at least not when the constable's around," Jeff said with a shrug. "I suppose we'll just have to put up with them."

"I suppose so." Melissa smiled down at him, her dark eyes glimmering with reflected light. Jeff thought he had never seen such warm, beautiful eyes before in his life. He gazed at her a moment, and then they both broke out in self-conscious grins.

"Well, come inside," she said at last. "A cup of hot cider will make you feel better."

That did sound good, Jeff thought. Hermione Merrivale was known throughout the community for her apple cider.

Most of the farm cabins in the area were built of logs, solid enough dwellings but rather crude in appearance. The logs used to construct the Merrivale cabin, however, had been split and then planed to give them a more finished look. The roof was covered with wooden shingles, rather than lengths of clapboard, and the windows, of course, had glass in them instead of canvas or oiled paper. The cabin was larger than most of its neighbors, too, with a large main room, an attached kitchen, and a storeroom, along with the downstairs bedroom, shared by Charles and Hermione. Melissa's room was in the loft, and it was reached by climbing a staircase rather than by the more common method of using a crude ladder of pegs driven into the wall.

The main room was furnished with a long table flanked by benches, a pair of armchairs stuffed with straw, a couple of side tables, and a brocaded eight-legged sofa that had been freighted down the Ohio from the East. Most of one wall was taken up by a massive stone fireplace, an impressively carved hickory mantel above it. Two muskets hung on pegs above the fireplace, and a Kentucky rifle was mounted over the front door. The puncheons—split logs—that formed the floor had been planed like the logs of the walls, so they were smoother and fit together better than most.

A man could stand inside the cabin and know that its owner had plenty of money—which, Jeff supposed, was exactly what Charles Merrivale had intended.

Merrivale had not made his money from farming, that much was certain. He was an indifferent farmer at best. But he had been a successful merchant in North Carolina, Jeff knew from things Melissa had said. Jeff was not sure why Merrivale had ever given up that business and decided to move to Ohio. He was glad, however, that Merrivale had made such a decision. Otherwise, he never would have met Melissa.

She brought him into the house and led him toward the sofa. Her father was already seated again in one of the armchairs, a pipe with a large bowl and a long curved stem clenched in his mouth.

"Not there," Merrivale snapped. "I don't want dirt all over that fabric. One of the benches is good enough."

Good enough for a Holt. Merrivale did not have to finish the sentence for Jeff to know its meaning. Ever since Bartholomew Holt had come to the Northwest Territory, his family had enjoyed a good reputation, but in recent years that reputation had taken a beating, an undeserved beating in Jeff's opinion. He could not deny that things had changed. Most of their old friends had stood by them, but Charles Merrivale hardly fell into that category. He was a relative newcomer to the vicinity, and he seemed willing to believe any evil lies that the Garwoods and others might spread about the Holts.

Merrivale was an impressive figure, tall and broad shouldered, with a shock of white hair. His ruddy features were often set in a stern frown, and he comported himself rather like an Old Testament prophet. He seemed to fancy himself one, too, judging by the way he would lay down the law to his wife and daughter. He was quick to anger, quick to condemn, and absolutely convinced of the rightness of whatever opinions he held. How he had fathered a sweet, lovely girl like Melissa was a mystery that Jeff could not fathom.

Merrivale must have some good qualities, Jeff thought, or surely Hermione never would have married him. Petite and still very attractive, with only a few strands of gray in her red hair, she came bustling in from the kitchen, a pewter cup of cider in her hand. A faint British accent could be detected in her voice as she handed the cup to Jeff and said, "There you go, my dear. That will fortify you."

Mother and daughter thought alike in some respects, Jeff concluded as he took the cup. Sipping the steaming brew gratefully, he was aware of Melissa sinking onto the bench beside him, close but not close enough for their bodies to touch.

Jeff said to Hermione, "Thank you, ma'am."

"Oh, you're welcome, Jeff, quite welcome."

Jeff knew she liked him and welcomed his courting of her daughter. He also knew it was highly unlikely that Merrivale would be won over as easily.

Puffing on his pipe, sending a cloud of smoke wafting toward the ceiling, Merrivale said, "I heard what you told Melissa about Zachariah and Peter Garwood. You're mistaken about them, Holt. They wouldn't try to harm you—though the Lord knows they've reason enough to hate your clan."

Jeff felt a quick surge of anger. He controlled it with an effort of will, aided by the soft touch of Melissa's hand on his as he placed the cup of cider on the table. The smile vanished from Hermione's face, replaced by a look of concern, but she ducked back into the kitchen, unwilling to dispute what her husband had said, at least to his face.

"I've never done anything to hurt the Garwoods, sir," Jeff said, striving to keep his voice level. "I want no trouble with them or anyone else."

Merrivale pointed the long stem of his pipe at Jeff. "Well, you can't deny this wouldn't have happened if not for that no-account brother of yours, Jefferson," he said sternly. "You can't blame the Garwoods for being upset with your family after what Clay did to poor Josie. And then to run off as he did!" Merrivale shook his head in disapproval.

"No, sir," Jeff replied. "I reckon I can't blame them."

"No good will come of it," Merrivale said darkly. "No good at all."

Jeff could not argue with that, either. But whether or not the Garwoods' anger was justified, Jeff knew that there was going to be real trouble sooner or later —unless they learned to leave the Holts alone.

CHAPTER TWO

Near the place where we crossed Clark's river, we saw at a distance some wild horses; which are said, indeed, to be very numerous on this river, as well as on the heads of the Yellowstone.

—from "The History of the Lewis and Clark Expedition"

As Captain Meriwether Lewis, Clay Holt, and the other members of the party drew rein on the banks of Clark's River, Clay turned around on his horse and looked behind him for the first time since the group had split up that morning. Clay estimated they had been following the river for some ten or twelve miles. Their former companions were long out of sight and might as well have been across the continent in Washington City.

The Shoshone guides were talking to Lewis, gesturing at the river and spouting a bastard mix of English and their native tongue. Clay could follow it well enough to know that the Shoshone were suggesting they cross the river there. The water, perhaps a hundred and fifty yards wide at that point, was flowing rapidly, and to Clay the spot did not seem well chosen as a ford. The Shoshones had not yet steered them wrong, however.

Captain Lewis turned to the company and said, "The natives claim that crossing the river will be more difficult farther along and propose that we cross here. I'm inclined to agree with them, gentlemen. We'll camp here tonight and make the crossing tomorrow."

The sun would soon be dipping behind the mountains to the west. Once it had done that, night would fall quickly, so Clay was in agreement with Lewis.

"Sergeant Gass," Lewis said, "take Holt and Warner and see if you can find us some fresh meat. Look sharp now; the Shoshones tell me that we'll soon be approaching Minnetaree territory."

The sergeant gestured for Clay and Warner to follow him. Clay shouldered his rifle and set off with the other two on foot. They waded across a creek and slid like shadows into the woods on the other side of the narrow stream.

The Shoshone and Minnetaree were traditional enemies. The Corps of Discovery had encountered several bands of Minnetaree braves on its westward journey, and the Indians had seemed friendly enough. But as long as the group was traveling with Shoshone guides, it was better to accept their prejudices, Clay decided. Later, if the party encountered the Minnetaree again, the white men could pretend agreement whenever the Minnetaree began their harangues about the evil Shoshone. Diplomacy had never been Clay Holt's strong suit—plenty of folks back in the Ohio River valley would laugh at such a notion, in fact —but he had learned quite a bit from observing Lewis and Clark during the expedition.

Most of the day's light was gone now, and it was the time when animals came to the creek to drink. Clay and Warner froze as Sergeant Gass suddenly motioned for them to stop. Up ahead, through a screen of brush, several deer were visible on the bank of the stream. With hand signals, the sergeant indicated targets for himself and the other two men. Clay lifted his .54 caliber rifle, already primed and loaded, and slowly cocked it, then seated the brass butt plate against his shoulder. Laying his cheek against the stock, he tightened his grip on the weapon and sighted on the deer that had been assigned to him by Sergeant Gass—a fine buck with an impressive set of antlers.

"Now," breathed the sergeant, and Clay gently squeezed the trigger.

All three long rifles blasted as one, and two of the deer went leaping into the air only to crash headlong on the bank of the creek. Clay lowered the flintlock and smiled in grim satisfaction. He took no joy in killing, but he knew it would be mighty good to have some fresh meat tonight.

Later, when Clay and the others had taken the deer back to camp, Lewis made a show of presenting half of the meat to the Shoshone guides. Early in the journey Lewis had discovered that the Indians appreciated such gestures. Some of the venison was roasted over the campfire, and the men ate gratefully, hunkering around the flames, gnawing on the tough, slightly gamy meat. It tasted fine to Clay.

One of the guides, kneeling next to Lewis, gestured toward the east when he had finished eating. "That way, short walk, find trail," the Shoshone said. "Take you to Cokahlarishkit—River of the Road to Buffalo, in white man talk. Follow to Medicine River. Take you to big falls."

Clay knew the Shoshone was talking about the Great Falls of the Missouri. That was where Lewis intended to head north into unexplored territory. Lewis said to the Shoshone, "I'm sure we can locate the falls.

But it would be much simpler for you and your braves to show us the way."

"Minnetaree land." The Indian's mouth twisted as if the name of the rival tribe tasted bad. "Some Blackfoot, too. Not good for Shoshone to go there." He thumped his chest and then pointed northeast. "We go find Shalees. They friend to Shoshone. Not like Pahkees."

Clay was not sure what *Pahkees* meant, but he knew it referred to the Minnetaree and knew as well that it was used in a highly uncomplimentary manner. The Shalee, he remembered, had also been dubbed Flat-Heads because of their custom of flattening the tops of their children's heads in infancy. Clay grimaced at the thought of the barbaric custom. The Shoshone could seek out the Shalee if they wanted to; he would just as soon not encounter them again.

The same held true for the Blackfoot. They were some of the fiercest fighters in the mountains, making war for the sheer joy of it at times, and if the expedition was going to have Indian trouble, it would likely come from the Blackfoot.

"Are you certain I can't talk you out of leaving us?" Lewis asked the Shoshone leader. The man shook his head emphatically. "Very well. In the morning, before you leave, some of our men will go hunting again. I would like to present you with more meat before we part."

The Shoshone gravely accepted Lewis's proposal.

Clay lifted a hand and swatted at a mosquito that had landed on his neck. The bothersome insects were starting to swarm, as they did every night about that time, and Clay was not the only one being annoyed. The horses danced around in agitation as clouds of mosquitoes settled on them. Lewis ordered more fires built. Woodsmoke kept the insects off to a certain extent, and while the thick smoke made the men cough, it was better than being sucked dry of blood. *Some of these 'skeeters*, Clay thought, *are probably big enough to*

do just that. Hell, some of them might even carry off a horse
or two.

He was still grinning at that idea when he rolled
himself in his blankets a little later. Through the haze
of smoke that hung over the camp, he could see the
stars floating overhead in a sky blacker than anybody
back East could ever imagine. The light of the stars
was more clear and brilliant, too, than those folks
dreamed. He had thought many times, especially in
the winter months, that the stars were close enough to
reach up and touch. That was one more reason he
liked the mountains and would have enjoyed being
able to remain in the wilderness.

But every day, every step toward the east,
brought him that much closer to civilization, and the
time would come when he would have to live around
settled folks again, even if only for a short time.

He hoped he could stand it.

The next morning, after the Shoshone guides had
departed, the men scattered along the bank of the
river, felling small trees with axes and tomahawks.
Clay joined in without complaint, chopping down
several saplings with the tomahawk given to him in
one of the Shoshone villages, where the weapon was
called a 'hawk.

He and his companions worked quickly, staying
with the task until three rafts had been constructed.
Lewis called a halt, and the group ate a quick cold
meal, then began loading their extra food and supplies
onto the rafts, taking the packs from the backs of the
extra horses.

Some of the men mounted the pack animals and
swam them across first. The horses breasted the current with little difficulty. Several more members of the
group made the crossing in similar fashion before
Lewis started the rafts across, laden with the valuable
supplies. The current carried all three craft downstream, where men were waiting to retrieve them
when they came ashore.

The man called Thompson approached Lewis while the captain was watching the rafts float across the river. He rubbed his beard-stubbled jaw and said hesitantly, "Cap'n, I ain't much of a swimmer. I ain't sure about goin' across that there river on the back of a horse."

"Very well," Lewis replied. "I don't see any reason why you can't ride across on one of the rafts. Once all the supplies have been taken over, of course." He looked around at the men who were still on this side of the river. "Would any of the rest of you prefer this method?"

Clay had never learned to swim very well, but he trusted his pony and would have been willing to risk the crossing on its back. Still he knew from Thompson's expression that he was embarrassed at having to make such a request. It might make him feel better to have company.

Clay caught Lewis's eye and said, "I'll ride on the raft, if it's all right with you, Captain."

"Certainly, Mr. Holt. I believe I'll join the two of you. Our horses can make the swim unburdened."

Several trips were required before all the goods had been ferried across the river. Clay frowned as he watched the swiftly moving water. The current seemed to have grown stronger in the few hours they had been there. Looking downriver, he saw white water and knew that meant rocks just under the surface. He was beginning to wish he had not volunteered to ride one of the rafts, but it was too late to change his mind now, since the remaining horses had already been sent across. Lewis and Thompson and he were the only ones left on that side.

The constant downstream drift of the rafts had caused the men on both sides of the river to move more than a mile from where they had started out. Lewis was waiting when the empty raft sent back across by the others came to ground. He splashed into the edge of the stream and grasped the makeshift craft.

"Come along, gentlemen," he said briskly, gesturing for Clay and Thompson to climb aboard.

Clay stepped onto the raft, not liking the way it sank a little under his weight. He moved to its center and was joined there by Thompson. Lewis was the last one to step on. The three men used the butts of their rifles to shove off, pushing against the bank until the current caught the raft and carried it toward the center of the river. Once it was under way, the passengers knelt in the middle of the raft.

Clay looked toward the opposite bank and saw the rest of the company mounting up to ride downstream in an effort to stay even with the raft. He grasped his rifle tightly in one hand and rested the other on the raft, struggling to keep his balance. Lewis and Thompson were doing the same thing. Water sloshed over their feet, and Clay could feel how cold it was, confirming his guess that the river was still being fed by melting snow, even if it was July.

The crossing seemed to take forever. They had no way of steering, of course; they had to go where the current took them. Clay looked toward the nearby rapids. They should have gone back upstream before starting out, he realized now. If the raft collided with one of the rocks, it would probably fall apart, and they would be in trouble. Some of the other men would have to swim horses out to them, a tricky task in the swiftly racing waters.

Clay glanced at Thompson and saw that his complexion was ghastly pale. Beads of sweat stood out on the man's forehead. He was terrified, and Clay could not blame him. Thompson would have faced marauding savages or a blood-crazed grizzly without flinching, but being adrift on this fragile raft was another matter entirely. Only Captain Lewis seemed calm and unconcerned, as always. The commander was looking at the far shore as he coolly judged their progress.

"Past halfway, men," he called to his two companions over the roar of the water. "We'll be there shortly."

It could not be soon enough to suit him, Clay thought.

In minutes the raft was within thirty yards of the bank. But it was in rougher water now, bounding into the air and then dropping sickeningly as it bobbed on the current. Even Lewis was looking worried. Clay spotted something just under the surface of the water ahead of them and recognized it as a jagged rock. He started to let out a shout of warning . . .

Too late. With a jolt and a bone-jarring crunch, the raft smashed into the rock and fell apart.

Clay felt it dropping away beneath him. Thompson howled in fear, and Lewis tumbled to the side. Clay lunged toward the captain, reaching for Lewis's arm, but he came up short. All three men fell into the water with a huge splash.

Clay swallowed some water before he could get his mouth closed. Gagging and coughing, he felt the chilly stream close over his head, and desperation made him stroke strongly downward with his free hand. His head popped back up. He took a deep breath of air and began kicking his feet as hard as he could.

Shaking his head and blinking to clear the water from his eyes, he looked around in time to see Thompson nearby, in the grip of panic and thrashing frantically. The river whirled Thompson crazily, and his head suddenly cracked against one of the rocks. Clay saw him go limp and sink.

There was no sign of Captain Lewis, but Clay didn't have time to wonder where he was. Thompson would surely drown unless Clay could do something to save him.

The weight of his sodden buckskins and the rifle dragged him under, but Clay fought against them, swimming awkwardly to the spot where he had last seen Thompson. Over the roar of the river, he was vaguely aware of shouts coming from the bank and knew that the other members of the party had witnessed the catastrophe. Some of them might be swimming their horses into the stream to try to help, but they were too far away to do any real good.

Clay's free hand, stroking through the water, brushed a buckskin jacket. Closing his fingers over it, he hauled up with all his strength, and Thompson's limp form came to the surface again. Clay slid an arm around him and struggled toward the bank, trying to keep both their heads above water. He was not entirely successful. In fact, it looked as if both of them were going to drown.

But then Clay felt a section of the raft underneath him again. Its buoyancy brought it back up from the depths of the river. Clay wrapped his legs around it and held on for dear life. He was able to pull Thompson onto the wreckage and balance the unconscious man there.

Twisting his head to look behind him, Clay felt a wave of relief when he saw that Lewis had been swept even closer to shore by the current. The captain kept his wits about him, as usual, and reached up to grasp one of the bushes that grew from the bank and overhung the water. Still holding his rifle, he pulled himself out of the river, his uniform sodden and dripping.

Clay turned to Thompson, who was beginning to choke, moan, and come around. "Hang on! We'll be all right now!"

Thompson sputtered and moaned again.

"We're back on part of the raft," Clay told him. "Look, we're getting closer to shore!"

Sure enough, even though they had already been carried more than a hundred yards downstream from the spot where the raft had broken apart, they were much closer to the bank now. A few minutes later they went aground with a jolting thud. Thompson rolled off, and for a second Clay thought the other man was going to kiss the ground under him. Clay also disembarked, shaking water from his soaked buckskins as he stepped onto the bank.

Two of the other men, Drouilliard and Joe Fields, pounded up on horseback. Fields grinned at Clay and asked, "Are ye all right, Holt? Ye look a mite like a drowned rat!"

"Feel a little like one, too," Clay replied. "How's the captain?"

"Seemed fine when we rode past. Some of the lads stopped to tend to him."

Drouilliard and Fields dismounted and checked Thompson's head injury. He had a small cut and a good-sized lump that was already turning black-and-blue, but Thompson insisted he was all right. Now that he was back on solid ground, he was not going to worry about a bump on the head. All four of the men walked upstream toward the spot where Captain Lewis had pulled himself out of the water.

As they approached, Lewis was holding his large pocket watch next to his ear and shaking it. "Blast!" the captain exclaimed. "I've gotten my chronometer wet. It still seems to be working, however, so there's no harm done, I suppose."

That was true in more ways than one, Clay thought. All three of the raft's passengers could easily have drowned. It was sheer luck that the raft had bobbed up again underneath Clay and Thompson.

Luck seemed to be following the expedition, though, despite plenty of hardships.

Lewis hung his watch from its chain again and cast a glance toward the sun. "Still some daylight left. Have the supplies been put back on the packhorses?" One of the other men said they had been. "Well, then, let's push on, shall we? Our clothes can dry as we ride."

The men mounted up again and rode northeast, still following the river. Clay's buckskins were uncomfortably wet, but they dried fairly quickly in the warm sunshine. By the time Lewis called another halt, three more miles had been covered, and Clay's clothes were only damp. The river crossing was already just a memory. But not one Clay would forget any time soon.

Marietta had become a prosperous settlement in the years since its founding as Campus Martius, across the river from Fort Harmar. The original log stockade, with its watchtowers at each of the four corners, was still standing, but now it was surrounded with houses and shops, which lined the several streets of the town. On a slight hill just outside the settlement was the school, one of the first buildings erected. Docks had been built along the Ohio to accommodate the river traffic, mostly goods being brought down from Pennsylvania, a hundred miles away, to stock the stores that supplied the farmers in the area. One such store was owned by Rathburn Steakley, and it was with Steakley's establishment that Charles Merrivale did business. In fact, Steakley had recently received a keg of nails ordered by Merrivale for the construction of a new barn. The nails were quite expensive, but Merrivale preferred them to the wooden pegs usually used to hold such structures together. In the same shipment with the nails had come a bolt of cloth for Hermione Merrivale.

Melissa did not mind picking up the cloth for her mother, she thought as she walked down the road toward Marietta, but she was certainly not going to lug a keg of nails back home with her. Her father could take the wagon for it later.

She smiled and pushed back a lock of dark hair that the summer breeze had blown in her face. When Jeff and she were married, she would do errands like this for him, she mused, to give him more time to work on their farm. He would be very glad he had chosen her for his wife.

Of course, Jeff himself was not yet aware that he had made such a choice.

Melissa's smile widened. It would be good to be married to Jeff, to cook for him and care for his house and raise his children. That thought made her face warm. She could imagine him coming home from the fields and taking her in his strong arms, folding her into his embrace, bringing his lips down on hers as he drew her to him. A delicious little shiver ran through her as the fantasy played out in her mind.

So caught up was she in her thoughts that Melissa almost didn't notice she had reached the town. Steakley's Trading Post was ahead on the left, and as she looked toward the large, solidly built log structure, she saw a young woman climbing the steps to the store's porch. The woman was attractive in a coarse, earthy way, with hair as black as midnight and a lush figure tightly encased in a thin dress. She was holding the hand of a small boy, a two-year-old toddler who, as they reached the top of the steps, pulled away from her and darted into the store. "Matthew!" the woman called after him. "Don't you go getting into your usual mischief!"

The woman had not glanced in Melissa's direction, and Melissa hung back a moment to let her go on into the store. Catching at her bottom lip with her teeth, Melissa pondered her course of action. It would be easier to pass by Steakley's and return to the trading post later. That way she would not have to confront the woman.

But that would be cowardly, and no one was going to accuse Melissa Merrivale of cowardice, least of all one of the Garwoods. Having made her decision, Melissa squared her shoulders, marched down the street to the store, and went up the steps to the porch.

The interior of the place was rather dim; the building had only a couple of windows, and they did not admit much light. Across the rear of the store ran a long counter, and perpendicular to it were aisles formed by rows of rough shelving. Barrels of flour, sugar, beans, cornmeal, and other staples lined one wall. The opposite wall was piled high with furs, which Steakley had bought from trappers to ship upriver to buyers in Pennsylvania. The shelves in between were loaded with cheese, hardware, saddles,

guns, pots and pans—practically anything a settler
might need. The first pioneers in the Northwest Territory had of necessity been almost completely self-suf-
ficient. Anything they could not grow, build, or kill
they did without. Now, however, that was changing.
Ohio had been a state for three years, and most of the
recent settlers had no inkling of what it was like to
survive on their own in the wilderness. Thus the need
for trading posts such as this one, which would probably make Steakley a wealthy man someday.

The proprietor himself, a tall, stoop-shouldered
man with spectacles and a balding head, was standing
at the rear of the store behind the counter. He was
talking to the young woman with black hair while the
child ran up and down the aisles with a toddler's awkward gait. As Melissa entered the store, Steakley
looked over at her, caught her eye, and gave her a big
smile. Melissa was well aware that the store owner's
friendliness was due in large part to Charles Merrivale's valuable patronage. The black-haired woman
noticed Steakley's lack of attention to what she was
saying and glanced over her shoulder to see whom he
was smiling at. She frowned when she saw Melissa.

"Help you, Miss Merrivale?" Steakley called.

"No, you go right ahead with what you're doing,
Mr. Steakley," Melissa said quickly. "I can wait."

"You're sure?"

"Of course," Melissa replied, wishing he would
just ignore her and go on about his business with his
other customer. The young woman was still glaring at
Melissa, her eyes almost searing a path up the main
aisle of the store. Melissa went around the shelves and
started down one of the side aisles, where the goods
stacked on the shelves would block the view of the
other woman. After a moment, Melissa heard the
voices resume.

"I don't know, Josie," Steakley said dubiously.
"Your pa and your brothers owe me quite a bit of
money already. I ain't sure I ought to let you start
getting in debt to me, too."

"Don't you worry, Mr. Steakley," Josie Garwood told him, her husky voice carrying to Melissa even though the young woman was speaking quietly. "I always take care of my obligations—and you won't have any cause to complain."

"I, ah . . . well, maybe . . ." Steakley's voice dropped even more, and now Melissa could no longer make out the words. She did not want to hear what he was saying, anyway. She knew quite well what he would be proposing to Josie. Charles Merrivale would have a fit if he knew some of the things his supposedly sheltered daughter had heard around town about Josie Garwood. Josie was no better than a strumpet, and everyone knew it.

What else could be expected, though, of a woman who had a baby—but no husband?

Melissa pushed those thoughts out of her mind and tried to concentrate on a small contraption on the shelf in front of her. She had heard all the rumors about Clay Holt and Josie Garwood, and she had no wish to think ill of a man who would someday be her brother-in-law—if, indeed, Clay was still alive. Melissa picked up the object she was studying and turned the little crank attached to it. That turned a thin wooden shaft, and the strange-looking arrangement of wooden spokes at the bottom of the shaft began to revolve as well. Melissa frowned. What in the world . . . ?

"That's an eggbeater, Miss Merrivale," Steakley said from beside her. She jumped a little; she had not heard him come up. "Newfangled gadget from back East. I don't know if folks'll have any use for them or not, but I thought I'd get a few and give them a try."

"Oh." Melissa put the eggbeater back on the shelf.

"What can I do for you?"

"I came to get that bolt of cloth for my mother. And my father said to let you know that he'll be by later for his nails."

"That's just fine. I'll go get that cloth for you. It's

in the back room." The storekeeper went toward the rear of the building.

Melissa turned around, thinking that Josie and her son had gone, but she stopped short when she saw the woman standing only a few feet away. Josie stared coolly at her for a moment. Then without turning her head, she called, "Come here, Matthew."

She had to repeat the summons before the boy went to her. He caught her skirt, pulled it partially in front of him, and shyly regarded Melissa. He was a handsome youngster, with dark, curly hair and skin already bronzed from being out of doors a great deal.

Josie reached down and stroked her son's hair, and as she did so, she said, "How are you, Melissa?"

"I—I'm fine," Melissa replied, angry with herself for stumbling over the words. She lifted her chin. She had no reason to be embarrassed or feel awkward around Josie Garwood. Josie was the one who should be ashamed. "And you?"

"Oh, I reckon I'm all right." Josie smiled, but the expression did not reach her eyes. "So's Matthew."

"That's good."

"You ever hear anything from Clay Holt?"

The question caught Melissa by surprise. "Clay . . . Holt? Why would I hear anything from him?"

"His brother's courting you, ain't he? I thought maybe Jeff had said something."

Melissa shook her head. How did Josie know about Jeff and her? "Jeff doesn't talk much about his brother," she said.

"Reckon he's ashamed of Clay. He's got reason to be, the way Clay done, getting me with child and then running off like that. But Clay'll come back someday and put things right. You wait and see."

Melissa doubted very seriously that such a thing would ever happen. Clay Holt might return to Marietta, but he would not marry Josie Garwood. Melissa was certain of that, just as she was sure that Clay was not the father of little Matthew.

Of course, not everyone believed that. Folks did

not want to think the worst of Clay, since the Holt family had always been well respected in the area, but when Josie had turned up pregnant and blamed him for it, all he had done was make one halfhearted denial and then leave for the West. That was the last anyone heard of him. Melissa had to admit it looked as if Clay had run away from his responsibilities. And she supposed it was possible. After all, Josie was attractive in a sluttish way, and Clay could have had a moment of weakness. . . .

She was casting around for something else to say to Josie when the sound of heavy footsteps on the porch outside made both young women look in that direction. Zach Garwood appeared in the doorway, his tall, broad-shouldered figure almost filling the opening. "You about through, Josie?" he asked.

"In a minute, Zach," Josie said. "I've got to get some sugar." She took Matthew's hand, gave Melissa one more hard stare, then turned away and went across the store to the barrels along the far wall.

Zach Garwood grunted in acknowledgment, then looked at Melissa. A grin spread slowly across his face, and she looked away quickly, repressing the shiver that ran through her.

Zach was a handsome man, there was no denying that. He was tall and brawny and had thick dark hair that flowed to his shoulders. He was clean-shaven, and his features had only just begun to show signs of dissipation from drinking. The Garwoods were known around Marietta for the whiskey they made, and no one had a greater appreciation for it than Zach himself.

Melissa glanced toward him as he walked into the store. Behind him came his father, Alfred Garwood. A slender, silver-haired man, Alfred had once stood proud and erect, but now he was bent and looked even older than he actually was. His wife had died several years earlier, Melissa knew, and her death had dealt Alfred Garwood a blow from which he had not yet recovered. It was beginning to look as if he never would.

Melissa moved toward the rear of the store as Zach ambled toward her. She knew his reputation as a brawler and a troublemaker, and she wanted nothing to do with him. His attempt to hurt Jeff a few nights earlier made her despise him that much more.

Zach seemed to be paying little attention to her, but Melissa nevertheless felt increasingly uneasy as he gradually worked his way closer to her. Where was Mr. Steakley? she wondered. He should have been back by now with the cloth for her mother. She ducked around the end of a shelf and found herself standing by one of the piles of hides. It was rather shadowy in that corner, and suddenly she knew that she had made a mistake: Zach loomed between her and the light. He moved so that he could block her flight with a quick step in either direction, all but pinning her against the stack of furs. He leaned closer to her, the grin on his face now a leer.

"Howdy, Melissa," he said, near enough to her that she could smell the whiskey on his breath, even though it was not quite the middle of the day. "How're you doing?"

"Quite well, thank you," she replied, making her voice cool and trying not to let it quaver.

"That's mighty fine," Zach said. "And how's Mr. Jefferson Holt?"

"I wouldn't know. I'm sure he's all right."

"You mean you ain't seen him lately?"

"Not for several days."

Zach chuckled. "That's funny. I figured he'd be over at your pa's house just about every night, sparking you." His voice lowered. "Or have the two of you been doing some spooning—or more?"

A surge of anger mingled with Melissa's fear, and she said sharply, "That is none of your business, Zachariah Garwood."

"Maybe not." He was close enough now that with one more step forward his body would be pressing against hers. "But if Holt ain't been getting something off you, he's a damn fool—like his brother."

"Please . . ."

The leer on Zach's face was replaced by a savage look of hatred and anger. "It'd serve the goddamn Holts right if somebody they cared about wound up in the same situation as my sister. How 'bout that, missy? How do you think Jeff Holt'd feel if you had a squalling brat just like Josie? Reckon I'd enjoy planting the seed—"

Melissa's senses swam. Zach was pushing himself against her now, crowding her into the pile of furs, and she felt as if she would pass out at any moment. She opened her mouth to scream for help, but no sound emerged. It wouldn't have done any good anyway, she realized desperately. No one was around except Mr. Steakley, and he was no match for Zach Garwood. She told herself that Zach was just trying to scare her to get back at the Holts, but she knew that if he wanted to, he could take her right there—and she would be helpless to stop him.

"Zachariah!"

The stern voice cut across her fear. Zach straightened and looked over his shoulder. "What is it, Pa?"

"Where are you, boy? Come along, we've got to get home. There's work to be done, dammit." Alfred Garwood's voice came from the front of the store, and Melissa was sure he couldn't see what was going on in the shadowy rear corner.

"I'm coming, Pa," Zach called. He turned back to her and whispered, "Remember what I said!" He brushed one of his big, rough hands across her lower belly and clutched her for a second in such a mortifying manner that she let out a gasp.

Then, abruptly, he was gone. Melissa heard him stomping out to the porch. She sagged against the hides again, all of her strength deserting her as she drew in several deep, ragged breaths to calm herself.

"Miss Merrivale? Where'd you go?"

That was Steakley's voice. He had finally

emerged from the storeroom at the rear of the store and come out from behind the counter, looking for her. Melissa forced her muscles to work and stood away from the furs. She managed to smile, and her voice sounded only slightly strained as she called, "I'm over here, Mr. Steakley." She could not let the storekeeper see that anything was wrong, she thought, because if she did, word of what had happened might get back to Jeff.

And she had already made up her mind that Jeff must never know what Zach had said and done to her. If he found out, he would go looking for Zach in order to avenge her honor—and then someone would die. Melissa was sure of that. She was just as sure that the someone would be Jeff. He would not stand a chance against a vicious brute like Zach Garwood.

She couldn't bear it if anything happened to Jeff. She would never forget Zach's crude words and his even more repulsive touch. But she could live with that memory; she could not allow Jeff to be hurt or killed.

Melissa took the bolt of cloth from Steakley and carried it out of the trading post. She paused on the porch and looked up at the sky.

The sun still shone brightly, but for Melissa Merrivale, the world had grown a little darker.

CHAPTER THREE

*Indians are not the only plunderers which
surround camp; for last night the wolves or dogs
stole the greater part of the dried meat from the
scaffold.*

—from "The History of the Lewis and
Clark Expedition"

The party led by Meriwether Lewis had not run
into any trouble since the nearly disastrous
crossing of Clark's River. True to the prediction
of their guides, they had easily found their way to the
falls. From there, they would take Maria's River and
follow that tributary north for several days before cir-
cling back. They had passed this way on the westward
journey, and Lewis had been intrigued by the smaller
stream, thinking it was actually the Missouri itself and
following it for several miles before realizing his mis-

take and turning back. Now he would have a chance
to indulge his curiosity.

Well provisioned with fresh buffalo meat, the
group set out after a couple of days' rest, leaving behind Goodrich, Thompson, and McNeal to prepare for
the journey back. The iron wheels of the carts used by
the party when it had headed west were buried there,
along with a cache of other supplies. It was the task of
the men left behind to build new carts to fit those
wheels and load the party's gear on them, including
the many boxes of plant specimens the expedition had
gathered to take back to Washington City.

With waves to their comrades, Lewis, Clay Holt,
and the others rode northwestward, following the
course of Maria's River. In the distance they heard the
bellowing of buffalo bulls, the noise constant since it
was mating season for the great beasts. Fierce clashes
over the cows went on day and night, but the explorers had grown so accustomed to the sound that they
scarcely noticed it anymore.

The party made good progress in the next several
days, Lewis never allowing the pace to slacken; he
wanted to see as much new country as possible during
that side trip. To many people, Clay supposed, riding
all day and eating cold, jerked meat on horseback
would have seemed arduous, but he was enjoying
himself.

The only problem they had encountered so far
was waking up one morning to find that some of the
horses had gotten loose and wandered away during
the night. Lewis sent out search parties in an effort to
locate the missing animals, and that slowed the group
down for a time. Eventually, they found all but a few
of the horses, and as the expedition continued north-
ward, Lewis kept a man out sweeping through the
country around them to look for the strays.

Drouilliard had that duty one day, as the rest of
the party rode through the hills above the river. Earlier, Clay had seen Drouilliard ride off toward the water, and he was glancing in that direction when he

suddenly spied something from the corner of his eye. "Cap'n! Better take a look over there!" he called to Lewis.

Lewis brought his horse to a stop and followed Clay's pointing finger. "My word!" The captain whipped his spyglass out of his coat and brought it to his eye, training it on a rise ahead of them. After a moment he said, "There must be twenty savages on that hill."

"Nearer thirty, I'd say." Clay grunted. "They've got their eye on something, too."

Lewis glanced at him. "Drouilliard."

"He went down to the river to look for those horses," Clay said. "What do we do, Cap'n?"

Lewis closed up his spyglass and tucked it away, then looked at the grim-faced men who were waiting for his decision. "The Indians don't appear to have noticed us yet. We could turn and ride back the way we came."

Several of the men, including Clay, expressed their displeasure.

"But that would leave Drouilliard unaware of the savages and at their mercy." Lewis shook his head. "We cannot do that. Mr. Fields, break out that flag I gave you to carry."

Joe Fields reached into his pack and took out a flag, which was furled around a telescoping staff. Its bright red, white, and blue colors immediately caught the eye. Fifteen stars adorned the field above the stripes. The flag flapped placidly in the breeze as Fields raised it above his head.

Lewis lifted a hand and waved the party forward. The horsemen went down the hill at a slow walk. Clay saw a sudden scurrying among the Indians and knew that the expedition had been spotted. The natives, turning their attention away from Drouilliard, stolidly watched the approaching explorers from the backs of their ponies.

When the two groups were within a quarter mile of each other, Lewis called a halt. He sat there, again slightly ahead of his men, and waited to see what the Indians would do. For a few moments nothing happened, and Clay could feel the tension mount. Then, abruptly, one of the warriors rode out from the band, racing his mount toward the white men. Lewis calmly swung down from his horse.

Clay's hand tightened on the stock of his rifle. The captain was taking a chance. That Indian might ride up and murder him.

Instead, the man jerked his horse to a stop when he was still a hundred yards from Lewis, who lifted a hand and gestured for him to come closer. Ignoring Lewis's summons, the Indian wheeled his horse and rode back to his companions. Even from this distance Clay could tell that the Indians were having a lively discussion.

Quietly he said, "Captain, one of us could slip down to the river and find Drouilliard. Then we could all make a run for it whilst those savages are arguing about what to do with us."

"No, Mr. Holt, I think not," Lewis said without hesitation. "I doubt that our mounts could outdistance theirs, and they most certainly know the country better than we do. This show of strength is the best thing we can do."

At that moment eight more Indians galloped down the hill toward the explorers; the others disappeared. Clay uttered a silent prayer that Meriwether Lewis knew what he was doing.

"Stand ready, men," Lewis said as the party of Indians approached. "But don't make any threatening moves. These natives could be friendly."

They did not have any real reason to believe otherwise, Clay thought. Most of the Indians they had encountered on the expedition had been nothing but helpful. He was convinced, in fact, that they wouldn't have made it to the Pacific without the help of the Shoshone woman, Sacajawea, who had served as their guide for a good part of the journey. Maybe their luck with Indians would hold now, too.

When the Indians were close enough for the
white men to make out the markings on their clothes,
Lewis said, "I believe these to be the Minnetaree. Stay
alert." With that, he strode away from the main body
of the group.

Clay glanced over at Gass and saw the concern on
the sergeant's face. All of them knew better than to
argue with Lewis; the captain did as he pleased. All
they could do now was wait and see how it worked
out.

The advancing party also stopped, and one of
them dismounted. This was the same man who had
scouted them in the first place, Clay realized. The man
walked toward Lewis, who extended his hand in
friendship. Evidently the Indian recognized the gesture because when he reached the explorer, he responded by reaching out and grasping Lewis's hand.

When they had shaken hands, the Indian walked
toward the rest of the white men, deliberately turning
his back to Lewis to show that he was not afraid.
Lewis did likewise, briskly striding over to greet the
remainder of the Indians. As the first native approached, Sergeant Gass said quietly, "Dismount,
men," then shook hands with the Indian.

Gradually, the two groups came together and
merged into one, everyone shaking everyone else's
hand. The Indians' goodwill was obvious, but Clay
was still suspicious. It could be that the natives were
trying to lull the whites into letting down their guard.

That was not likely to happen with Lewis in command. He and his men remained alert as he used the
sign language he had learned from other tribes to ask
their identity.

After the leader of the band had signed back at
him, Lewis said, "Just as I thought, men. These are the
Minnetaree. I don't believe any of them speak English." He paused while he looked around at the Indians, but there was no reaction from them. "So I'm
going to warn you to be careful. Even though they
profess to be friendly, I'm sure they would not hesitate

to steal from us if they believed they could get away with it. Watch your guns and your horses at all times."

The Minnetaree headman made more sign talk. Lewis replied in kind, then continued, "They've invited us to share their camp at the river bottom, and I've accepted. As I said, be on the lookout, but don't forget that part of our mission is to establish friendly relations with any Indians we may encounter."

Both parties mounted their horses again. The Minnetaree led the way to a steep bluff overlooking the river with a path carved down one side of it. Clay felt nervous as his horse descended the trail with the others, but he took some reassurance in the relative ease with which the surefooted Indian pony negotiated the path. When they reached the bottom, the horses and riders gathered on a broad beach alongside the stream. On the bank were three large trees, and a crude shelter made of skins had already been erected nearby. Clearly, this was one of the usual spots where the Minnetaree camped when they were in this area.

Lewis sent a man with one of the young Indian men to fetch in Drouilliard. When the two returned, Drouilliard spoke French to the Minnetaree, as Lewis had hoped he might. The Indians had learned the language from French-Canadian fur trappers who had made occasional forays into the mountainous region. Lewis and Drouilliard sat down with the Minnetaree headman and talked for a long time while the other men busied themselves setting up camp.

One of the Minnetaree brought out a pipe, as usual, and Lewis spent the evening sitting crosslegged in front of the fire, passing the pipe and telling the Indians about the great expedition to the Pacific. Clay gnawed on some jerky as he watched the natives. They seemed skeptical at first, Clay thought, but eventually they accepted the story, as well as Lewis's claim that he had been sent to the Rockies by the Great White Father in Washington City. That was the first these Minnetaree had heard of a Great White Father, and Clay couldn't tell if they were more impressed or amused by the idea. Lewis presented them with a small flag, a medal, and a handkerchief, and they seemed well pleased with the gifts.

For their part, the Minnetaree explained that they were part of a much larger band hunting buffalo up and down Maria's River. That news did not sit very well with Clay; the idea of several hundred more Indians nearby was a little unsettling. Besides, the more he looked at the natives, the less sure he was that they were telling the truth. For one thing, he had run into Minnetaree before—and something about these Indians struck him as different.

Sergeant Gass settled down beside him and lit his own pipe. Out of the corner of his mouth, the sergeant said in a low voice, "I ain't sure about this, Holt."

"Me either," Clay replied, not looking at Gass. "There's something wrong about it."

"Don't let your gun get very far away from you."

Clay's expression was grim. "I wasn't intending to," he said.

Gass stood up and moved on, issuing more low-voiced warnings to the other men. Clay felt fairly confident that they could handle any trouble the small band might give them. If a hundred more Indians showed up, however, it would be a different story.

The Minnetaree—if that was what they were—seemed affable enough as they sat up long into the night talking to Lewis and Drouilliard. Eventually the Indian men began to roll themselves into their furs for the night, and the white men did the same. As Clay rolled into his blankets, he made sure that his rifle was close at hand. His fingers were resting lightly on the stock as he dozed off.

There was nothing like riding hard all day to make a man tired, and Clay slept soundly. As was his habit, he woke early, when the sun was barely up. Blinking his eyes, he looked around the camp in the reddish light of dawn and saw that the rest of the explorers, with the exception of Joe Fields, were still asleep. Fields was hunkered beside the campfire, holding out both hands to warm them.

Clay frowned. Where was Fields's rifle?

He saw movement behind the man. One of the Indians was bent over a sleeping figure, and Clay immediately suspected treachery. Sure enough, when the Minnetaree straightened, he had two rifles in his hands, one no doubt stolen from the careless Joe Fields, the other from one of the sleeping men.

"Fields!" Clay shouted as he threw his blanket aside and sprang to his feet. "Watch out behind you!"

Startled by Clay's warning, Fields whirled around awkwardly, losing his balance and sitting down on the ground next to the fire. A few feet away his brother was fighting out of his blanket and looking around for his gun. The thief broke into a run, sprinting away from the camp with the two stolen rifles clutched tightly to him. Finally both Fields brothers gained their feet and raced after him.

The commotion had roused the other white men. Lewis stood up and looked around for the source of the trouble. Nearby, Drouilliard had opened his eyes to see one of the Indians trying to make off with his rifle, and he jumped up to confront the man. Grabbing the weapon, he shouted, "Damn you, let go of my gun!"

Clay heard hoofbeats behind him. He jerked his head around and saw several more of the Indians hazing some of the ponies ahead of them. "The horses, Captain!" he cried.

Drawing a pistol from his belt, Lewis ran after the stolen mounts. "Come back here, blast you!"

One of the Indians stealing the horses turned to confront Lewis, lifting a stolen rifle as he did so.

Clay saw what was about to happen and stooped to snatch his own rifle from the ground, but even as he raised the weapon, he knew he was going to be too late. The rifle in the Indian's hands went off with a roar of black powder. The ball screamed close to Lewis's head, just missing it.

As coolly as he did everything else, Lewis stopped and aimed his pistol at the Indian. The pistol cracked sharply, and the Indian was driven back a step by the impact of the lead ball. He dropped the rifle and clutched his belly where the shot had struck him, then fell to his knees, folded up, pitched forward, and died.

The Fields brothers had caught up with the man who had stolen their rifles, and a frenzied struggle was going on between the thief and one of the brothers. They were rolling over and over on the ground. As Clay turned toward the fight, he saw the early morning sun flash on the blade of a knife, and then Fields stood up, blood dripping from his weapon. The Indian remained on the ground, motionless, as the brothers picked up their rifles.

Clay was starting forward to meet them when his eye caught a flicker of movement. His instincts screamed a warning, and he turned quickly, just in time to use the barrel of his rifle to block the downward sweep of a stone tomahawk. The Indian wielding it crashed into him, and both men went sprawling. Clay's flintlock slipped from his grasp.

Still on the ground, the Indian chopped at Holt again with the tomahawk. Clay caught his wrist and twisted savagely until his opponent grunted in pain and dropped the crude ax. The man, not wasting any time, lowered his head and butted Clay in the face, and the stench of the buffalo fat in the man's long hair made Clay gag. Rolling away, the Indian got to his feet, holding a knife he had snatched from the sheath at his waist.

Clay jerked his legs out of the way as the Indian slashed at them with the blade. While the man was slightly off-balance from his thrust missing its mark, Clay kicked him in the side, staggering him that much more. Seizing the opportunity to regain his feet, Clay rolled away and then sprang upright as the Indian closed in on him again. At the last instant Clay used his left forearm to block the enemy's knife. He felt the blade slice through the sleeve of his buckskin shirt and draw a thin line of fire across his flesh. Cursing, Clay slammed his right fist into the Indian's face.

The man's nose pulped under the blow, and blood spurted onto Clay's knuckles. Driven back several steps by the punch, the Indian dropped his knife as he brought both hands to his face. Clay yanked out his own knife and started toward the man, but the Indian turned and ran. Clay went after him, swearing, but a strong hand caught his arm and stopped him.

He spun toward this new threat, only to see the stern face of Meriwether Lewis. "Wait, Holt!" the captain commanded. "Let him go!"

A red haze seemed to have descended in front of Clay's eyes as rage engulfed him, and the sight of Lewis's face and the sound of his words barely penetrated Clay's maddened brain. His muscles trembled with the need to strike out at someone—anyone!—but he took a deep breath and forced himself to calm down. As he regained control, he saw that the rest of the Indians were in flight. They had even left their horses behind.

"The fight is over, Holt," Lewis said. "We'll have no more trouble with those savages."

Clay jammed his knife back in its sheath. "I hope you're right, sir," he said, his voice still a little hoarse and shaky from the emotions that had almost overwhelmed him.

"Two of them are dead. That's a higher price than they intended to pay in order to steal a few rifles and horses." Lewis frowned in thought. "Still, they said there were many more of their band nearby. We should leave this vicinity as quickly as possible."

Drouilliard spoke up. "They could've been lying about that, Captain. They lied about being Minnetaree."

"How do you know that?" Lewis demanded.

"I heard them hollerin' to each other in their own tongue when the fighting started. I'm no expert on Indian talk, Captain, but I know enough that I could tell they wasn't speakin' Minnetaree. I'd say they was Blackfoot."

That made sense to Clay. The Blackfoot were the most warlike of the tribes in the area, and these Indians had not hesitated to fight when caught in the act of stealing.

"We'll still push on as quickly as possible," Lewis decided. "Some of these ponies will do as replacements for the ones we lost earlier." He lifted his voice. "We'll be breaking camp in ten minutes, gentlemen. Please be ready. Until then, Holt, you and Warner act as lookouts, just to make sure those savages don't come back with some of their kinsmen."

"Aye." Clay picked up his rifle and turned to face the bend in the river where the fleeing Indians had disappeared.

The Blackfoot warriors—if that was truly what they had been—did not return, either alone or with reinforcements. The expedition moved out quickly, still following the river.

As usual, the captain turned out to be correct. They were not bothered by Indians during the rest of their journey, as they traced the river for several more miles and then swung around to make a big circle back to the Missouri. In fact, the natives seemed to be steering clear of them.

The party encountered only two problems during the next two weeks. One day, while several men were hunting, a rattling in the brush and a sudden growl were all the warning the explorers had before a huge grizzly bear lunged out of the undergrowth at them. Clay's rifle was primed and loaded, and he reacted instantly, throwing the weapon to his shoulder and pressing the trigger. With a roar of black powder, the flintlock's heavy recoil pounded against him, a haze of smoke obscuring his vision. When the powder smoke cleared away, he saw the bear's massive form stretched out on the ground, only a few feet from Captain Lewis. Clay's ball had entered its right eye and gone on into the brain, the only sort of shot that would have dropped the bear quickly enough to save Lewis's life. The other men congratulated him heartily on his marksmanship, but Clay considered the shot a matter of luck as much as anything else.

When Lewis investigated, as he always did, he discovered the reason for the bear's ferocity: In the thicket were two cubs, roly-poly balls of fur whose mischievousness delighted the party. "We'll take them along," Lewis declared. "The president charged us with the responsibility of providing specimens of the wildlife we encounter, whenever possible."

Clay and the men were amused at the idea of sending bear cubs back to Thomas Jefferson. As one of the men put it while he watched the cubs, "Them little fellas ought to fit right in, back there in Washington City."

The second dangerous incident occurred when one of the explorers, shooting at an elk during another hunting foray, accidentally planted a musket ball in Captain Lewis's left buttock. The wound was fairly serious, but the ludicrousness of the situation had all the men except the culprit smiling behind their hands during the next few days while Lewis recuperated from the injury. But the captain's strong constitution stood him in good stead, and he quickly recovered, although at times the healing wound pained him so that he had to be carried on a litter.

The expedition pushed on and, in the early afternoon of August twelfth, rendezvoused with Captain William Clark and his men near the juncture of the Missouri and Yellowstone rivers.

Three days later, as the reassembled Corps of Discovery was making ready to break camp, they were surprised by a hail of greeting. Clay Holt was sitting by a fire with his friend John Colter, a lean Virginian who had been an experienced Indian fighter and frontiersman before signing up with Lewis and Clark. Colter turned his keen eyes toward the east and muttered, "Who the devil's that?"

Clay followed Colter's gaze and saw two white men trudging into the camp, leading a couple of packhorses. The strangers had evidently been in the wilderness for a while, judging by their bushy beards and the wear shown by their clothes. If they intended to stay out here, Clay thought, they would do well to replace those store-bought duds with buckskins. He and Colter stood up and ambled over to where the strangers were greeting Lewis and Clark.

"Name's Joseph Dickson," one of the men said. "This here's my partner, Forrest Hancock. We didn't expect to run into a bunch of white men out here."

"I'm Meriwether Lewis," the captain replied. "This is Captain Clark, and these men are—"

"We know," Hancock interrupted. "The Corps of Discovery." He let out a low whistle. "Everybody back East has heard of you boys. Most folks figured you were dead by now, though. Thought sure either the savages or the mountains would get you."

Lewis smiled faintly. "Well, as you can see, Mr. Hancock, here we are, little the worse for wear. Now you might be good enough to explain what the two of you are doing here."

"We're going after beaver," Dickson said. "We've heard 'bout how the Rockies are swarming with the varmints. Their pelts'll fetch a fine price back in St. Louie." The man scratched his beard. "Say, I'm getting an idea. You fellas are the first white men to traipse through this part of the country, so you know it better'n anybody else. What say some of you come with us?"

Lewis and Clark exchanged a quick glance; both men frowned. For more than two years, they had maintained strict discipline among their party, and now these would-be fur trappers had come along and dangled the possibility of quick wealth in front of their men.

Nevertheless, several members of the expedition were private citizens, not members of the army, and they had done everything that the captains had asked of them, enduring long months of suffering and privation. It would not be fair to deny them the opportunity to seek their fortune. After all, they were special men. They had gone where no Americans had ever gone before.

"I'll go with 'em, Cap'n," John Colter remarked.

Lewis and Clark swung around to look at him. "Are you sure, John?" Clark asked. "Think, man. You've been out here in the wilderness for over two years already. Don't you want to go back and sleep in a real bed, live without danger constantly at your elbow?"

Colter smiled a little. "No, sir, not really."

Clay Holt caught his breath. He was about to speak, to declare that he wanted to be part of this, too, when Lewis said firmly, "Very well. But you're the only one who will be allowed to leave, Mr. Colter. After all we've been through, we can ill afford to have the expedition fall apart now. We'll need all hands to accompany us until we reach St. Louis."

Feeling a surge of disappointment, Clay clenched his fists. He might not like the decision, but he was not going to oppose Lewis and Clark. Not, as the captain said, after all they had been through. He heard a few mutters from the other men, but by and large they seemed willing to abide by the ruling. Clay was not the only one who watched with a bit of jealousy as John Colter gathered his gear and got ready to leave with Dickson and Hancock, heading west again.

"Thank you for understanding the situation, men," Captain Clark told them when Colter and his two companions had said their farewells, waved, and then disappeared around a bend in the river. "I know many of you would have liked to go with them. But remember, the beaver will still be in the mountains next year. Colter and his new friends can hardly trap all of them in that time."

That was true enough, Clay thought. Yet as he turned toward the Rockies and gazed up at their majestic, blue-shrouded heights, he wished he, too, were heading west again. It would be a hard life, and just as Clark had said, danger would be constantly at a man's elbow. The encounter several weeks earlier with the Blackfoot had proven that.

But it was better to have enemies who would meet you head on, Clay Holt thought, than ones who would sneak around behind your back and spread lies.

"Look there! Indians!"

Zach Garwood reined in his horse in response to his brother Pete's whispered warning. Leaning over in the saddle to peer through the screen of trees and brush at the edge of the trail, Zach snorted in disgust as he spotted the single bare-chested figure walking down a nearby hill. He was wearing a deerskin breechclout.

"Hell, that's just one brave," Zach spat. "And a young one, at that. Quit wasting my time, Pete."

"Well, there could'a been more than one," Pete grumbled. "Do we go on to town or not?"

Zach watched the Indian lad move steadily down the hill toward the road. There was a Lenape village in the direction the boy was coming from, and the inhabitants of that village sometimes went into Marietta. Newcomers might get spooked at the sight of a native walking down the street as bold as brass, but most folks quickly got used to them and knew that if the Lenape were left alone, they wouldn't cause any trouble.

"Come on," Zach said with a sudden grin. He clucked to his horse and got it moving again, but now his pace was slower. "We'll have us a little fun."

Pete's moon face broke into a wide smile. Zach knew that his younger brother counted on him to come up with entertainment now and then. The fact that the victim was going to be an Indian was sure to make Pete even happier. He did not like Indians and never had.

Neither did Zach. As far as he was concerned,

those heathens should have moved out when white men had moved into the Northwest Territory. And if the savages wouldn't go peacefully . . . well, that was all right with Zach, too. They could stay if they wanted to—buried six feet under the fertile Ohio soil.

Zach and Pete should have been back on the family farm, working in the fields. The Garwood farm was a failure, and the family desperately needed whatever crops they could harvest for simple sustenance. The week before, they had found out that the property would be confiscated by the authorities if the back taxes they owed weren't paid in full within the next six months. So they really couldn't afford to spend time—or money—gallivanting in town. But Zach reasoned that Luther and Aaron, their younger brothers, were taking care of their share of the work on the farm. They didn't particularly like it, but both knew better than to argue with the two oldest brothers. As long as their father didn't find out, Zach and Pete could slip into town, down a few ales at one of the taverns, maybe even take a serving girl out back for a little fun. It beat the hell out of working, Zach thought.

But so did tormenting Indians.

Zach glanced over at his brother. Pete was the biggest of the Garwood clan, even taller and heavier than Zach. His hair under the battered hat with the wide, floppy brim was wispy and pale, and his small, deep-set eyes had always reminded Zach of a pig. Anyone looking at him could tell that he was not particularly intelligent, yet when they had been growing up, Zach had handed a beating to any youngster foolish enough to refer to Pete as feebleminded. There might be some truth to that assessment, but Zach was damned if he was going to let anybody talk about a Garwood that way.

Right then Pete looked happy at the prospect of harassing the young Lenape whose path was about to cross theirs, and Zach was glad. Pete deserved a little happiness.

The youth emerged from the woods about twenty

yards ahead of them and stopped short when he saw the two white men on horseback. He had to be pretty dumb for a redskin, Zach thought, or he would have heard them coming. The boy tensed, and for a second Zach thought he was going to turn and dart back into the woods.

"Hold it right there!" Zach shouted, driving his heels into the flanks of his horse and sending it forward in a gallop.

The Lenape stayed where he was as Zach and Pete rode up. He was even younger than Zach had thought at first, no more than twelve or so. He watched the white men with wide eyes as they reined in.

Zach put a friendly grin on his face. "Howdy, son. Where you headed?"

The boy lifted a hand and pointed gravely toward Marietta. "Town."

"Good, you understand white man talk." Zach rested his hands on the pommel of his saddle and leaned forward. "Maybe you can help me."

The youngster just shrugged, his face giving away nothing. Zach thought he saw a hint of fear in the boy's eyes, though.

"You can show us where your village is," Zach went on. "We need to pay it a visit."

"Why do white men go to Lenape village?" the boy asked.

Zach laughed harshly. "Why, to get us some redskin women, of course! You got any sisters, boy? How 'bout your ma? She like layin' with white men?"

The Lenape caught his breath sharply, and his eyes glittered with rage. "White men stay away from village," he muttered as he turned away.

"What's the matter?" Zach demanded. "A couple of white men ain't good enough for your filthy squaws?"

The boy's hand started involuntarily toward the knife sheathed at the waist of his breechclout. That was the move Zach had been waiting for.

"Get him, Pete!" he shouted.

Pete sent his horse lunging forward as the boy broke into a run, fear overcoming the anger he felt toward the two white men. He was too slow, though, and Pete was on him in an instant. Zach thought his brother was going to trample the boy, but at the last moment Pete swerved his horse and bent over in the saddle to wrap his fingers around the youth's upper arm. The boy cried out in pain as Pete lifted him off the ground.

Holding the boy aloft as if he weighed almost nothing, Pete turned his horse around and returned to his brother. "What do we do with him now, Zach?"

"Bring him over here," Zach ordered, turning his horse toward an opening in the trees beside the road. "We don't want to be disturbed." He rode into the gap and followed a faint path to a clearing some twenty yards off the trail. The heavy brush surrounding the open space screened them from view. Pete rode along behind, the Indian lad still dangling from his grip.

Zach swung down from his horse and let the reins drop to the ground. As he turned, Pete flung their captive down. The boy bounced back up, his hand reaching for his knife, but Zach was right there to backhand him across his face. The boy staggered backward. Zach followed, plucking the youngster's knife from its sheath and throwing it to the side, into the brush.

"Pull a blade on me, will you, you filthy heathen?" Zach growled. He balled his hand into a fist and drove it into the boy's jaw.

"Teach him a lesson, Zach!" Pete said enthusiastically as the boy fell again.

"Damn right, I'll teach him a lesson," Zach snarled. The toe of his boot thudded into the boy's side, causing him to curl up in pain. "One even a stupid redskin can learn!"

He kicked twice more, but the boy did not make a sound. In fact, he had not cried out since Pete first jerked him up off the ground, and that cry had been startled out of him. Now he regarded his white tormentors in cold silence, his eyes filled with hate.

"All you Indians are nothing but vermin," Zach went on. "Ought to exterminate you." He whipped his long, heavy hunting knife from its sheath. "I'll teach you to talk smart to me, boy. You know who I am?"

Still the lad said nothing. Since he could not fight back, he would take whatever came in stoic silence. It was all he could do.

Zach leaned closer, brandishing the knife. "The name's Zach Garwood, you little red son of a bitch! And I'll make sure you never forget it. I'm going to carve it right into that red hide of yours!"

Bartholomew Holt reined in his horse, sure that he had heard shouting. He listened, waiting to hear the sound again.

He was a tall, rather spare man wearing homespun trousers, a linsey-woolsey shirt, and an old tricorn hat pushed to the back of his head to reveal dark hair streaked with silver. His skin had been turned a permanent brown by sun and wind, and despite his middle age, a life of hard work had kept him strong and vital. His eyes wore a permanent squint, and now they narrowed even more as he heard a threatening voice that was all too familiar.

Bartholomew spotted an opening in the trees and remembered the clearing back there. Hardly a square foot existed in that area that he had not explored back in his younger days, when he and Norah had first come to the Northwest Territory. Until their farm was established and the crops began to come in, the family had counted on Bartholomew's skill as a hunter to put food on the table. He had tramped through the woods many times carrying his Pennsylvania-made long rifle, its maple stock and brass mountings polished to a sheen.

That day, though, he had only a flintlock pistol tucked into the waistband of his breeches. He slid it out and reached for the powder horn slung over his shoulder.

As he primed and loaded the pistol, he eased his horse off the road and onto the narrow path through the woods, guiding the animal with his knees. The voices grew louder as he advanced, and soon he could make out the words. He felt his blood grow cold as he heard Zach Garwood threaten to mutilate some poor victim of his wrath.

Bartholomew took the loaded pistol in his right hand and gripped the reins with his left, pulling his mount to a halt. Leaning forward in the saddle, he peered through the brush and saw one man on horseback, another on the ground nearby standing over a boy.

Bartholomew recognized Pete Garwood's broad back, as well as his brother Zach, who was lowering his blade toward the terrified Indian. Bartholomew caught his breath as he recognized the boy. He was the son of one of the Lenape chiefs.

As one of the first settlers in the Ohio River valley, Bartholomew Holt had also been one of the first to make peace with the Indians. He regarded the chief as an old friend, and he was well enough acquainted with him to know what would happen if Zach Garwood carried out his threat.

For the first time since the founding of Marietta, war would erupt between red man and white.

Bartholomew knew he would have to act quickly, taking the Garwoods by surprise if he wanted to save the boy's life. So far the brothers had not noticed him, so intent were they on their vicious sport. Bartholomew drove the heels of his boots into the flanks of his horse and without hesitation sent the animal crashing into the clearing.

Pete turned to see who was interrupting their fun, but Bartholomew was too quick. He lashed out with his pistol, the barrel thudding heavily against the side of Pete's head. The blow sent the big man sprawling out of his saddle.

Bartholomew wheeled his horse around as Zach howled an oath. Training the pistol on him and cocking the flintlock, Bartholomew said sharply, "Release that lad, Garwood, or by all that's holy I'll blow out what few brains ye've got!"

Zach had a pistol tucked in his belt, but he wouldn't have time to reach it, let alone load it. Bartholomew could put a ball through his head with the merest squeeze of a trigger. And no matter how much Zach hated the Holts, he was not going to underestimate their skills as marksmen.

Bartholomew could almost see those thoughts going through Zach's head. "Drop the knife, too," he said.

On the ground nearby, Pete let out a groan and tried to push himself to his hands and knees. He failed, slumped back to the earth, and moaned again. It was obvious to Bartholomew that Pete was not going to be a factor in the confrontation.

Zach's features twisted with hate and rage as he looked from his brother to Bartholomew. Abruptly he threw the knife aside, the force of his toss burying the blade several inches in the ground.

The Indian lad, seeing that Zach was no longer a threat, rolled over and climbed to his feet. From the stiff way he moved and held himself, Bartholomew knew he was hurt, but with luck the injuries would not be too bad. The boy glared at Zach for a second and then turned away.

"Hold on, son," Bartholomew said. "You know me—Bartholomew Holt. I'm a friend of your father's. I'll take you back to your village."

The boy hesitated. At that moment it had to be difficult for him to trust any white man.

Zach bared his teeth. "I'll see you in hell for this, Holt!" he vowed. "That's what you deserve for defending a stinking red heathen!"

"I'll take my chances on winding up in the same place as you, Garwood," Bartholomew replied. "Now

put your brother on his horse and get out of here, the
both of you!"

As Zach went over to Pete, Bartholomew turned
in the saddle so that he could keep the pistol trained
on Zach. The man helped his brother to his feet. Pete
sagged in Zach's grip, and it took several minutes and
a great deal of grunting and heaving before Zach got
him onto the back of his horse. Pete, still only half-
conscious, wrapped his fingers in the animal's mane
and held on tight.

Zach mounted his horse and glowered at Bartholomew, then caught hold of Pete's reins and rode out of
the clearing, leading his brother's mount beside him.
Bartholomew waited until they were gone before he
lowered the flintlock.

Turning to the boy, he said, "Come along, son. I
want to get out of here in a hurry, before Garwood
decides to come back and take a potshot at us from
cover." He held out a hand to the youth.

The lad hesitated briefly before taking Bartholomew's hand and letting the white man help him onto
the horse. As the boy settled down behind the saddle,
Bartholomew urged the horse into a trot, then headed
deeper into the woods instead of returning to the
road. He knew that it would be a quicker way to reach
the Lenape village, and they would also avoid any
possible ambush by Zach Garwood.

After a few minutes the youngster said, "I am
called Raccoon. I thank you for helping me."

"You're welcome," Bartholomew told him. "And
I'm glad to meet you, Raccoon. Reckon I've seen you
around the village before, but we've never been introduced. Your pa is Bear Slayer, isn't he?"

Raccoon said, "He is known by that name to
white men. In our village, he is sometimes called Catfish Eater."

Bartholomew had to grin. The man he knew as
Bear Slayer was strong and proud, and the Indians
would have the same opinion of him no matter what
he was called. White folks might not be too impressed

by the name Catfish Eater, though, and Bartholomew could understand why the chief preferred the other name. "If it's all right with you, Raccoon," he said, "I reckon I'll go on calling him Bear Slayer. Might be best all around."

The boy laughed, and Bartholomew had to admire his resilience. The danger was over, and Raccoon had already put it behind him almost as if it had never happened. For his part, Bartholomew was still a little shaky. He had seen his share of violence, in the war and afterward, but that did not mean he had to like it. As distasteful as it would have been, he would have shot Garwood without hesitation if Zach had forced him into it. Just what had gotten into the Garwoods to have turned them so vicious lately? he wondered.

After riding over a couple of hills, Bartholomew and Raccoon approached the Lenape village, an irregular grouping of long, low lodges constructed of poles and bark and chinked with mud and moss. Bartholomew had sat in those lodges more than once to smoke a pipe with his Indian friends, and he knew the dwellings were more comfortable than they appeared to be. A fire was kept burning in the center of the lodge almost constantly, the smoke escaping from a small hole in the pinnacle of the roof. The flames were extinguished only when it was raining or snowing and the smoke hole had to be covered. The entrances were covered by bearskins that could be tied back in good weather, such as this. Dogs ran out and yapped at the heels of Bartholomew's horse as Raccoon and he reached the outskirts of the village, the commotion drawing several men from the lodges, including Bear Slayer, the boy's father.

The chief was a short, solidly built man whose dark eyes watched intently as Bartholomew rode up, dismounted, then assisted Raccoon off the horse. Bartholomew turned to Bear Slayer and lifted a hand in the universal gesture of peaceful intentions.

"Good day to you, Bear Slayer," Bartholomew said. "I have returned your son to you."

"I did not know he was lost," Bear Slayer said solemnly.

Raccoon spoke up. "Two white men attacked me. This man Holt drove them away."

Bear Slayer looked down at his son and asked, "Were you harmed?"

Raccoon replied in the Lenape tongue, gesturing at his arm as he did so. Bartholomew understood enough of the language to get a rough idea that the boy was explaining how Zach and Pete Garwood had jumped him. Bartholomew also understood when Raccoon repeated the things Zach had said, and he was not surprised to see Bear Slayer stiffen in anger.

The chief looked up at Bartholomew and asked, "Do you know what my son has told me?"

"I savvied enough of it. On behalf of the settlers around here, I want to apologize, Bear Slayer." Bartholomew could tell from Bear Slayer's expression that he was furious, and the other Lenape who had gathered around were muttering angrily.

"I know of these men called Garwood," Bear Slayer said. "They hate our people and wish to see us all dead."

"Well, that might be putting it a mite strong," Bartholomew said quickly, hoping to forestall any thoughts of revenge the chief might be having. "You know old Alfred Garwood. He has nothing against the Lenape. His sons are young and have much to learn."

Bear Slayer drew a deep breath, and then his mouth formed a tight line as he considered Bartholomew's words. Finally, he said, "You are right. The Lenape have always lived in peace with our white friends. But when our children are threatened and our women insulted . . ." The chief's hand went to the knife at his waist. "This cannot continue. These young Garwoods must be taught that they cannot harm our tribe."

"I'll see to it," Bartholomew said, his pulse beginning to race. He was dancing on the edge of war and bloodshed, and he knew it. "I'll speak to their father."

Bear Slayer took his hand off his knife, and Bartholomew sensed a slight easing of the tension around them. "See that you do," the chief said. The anger on his face was replaced by an expression of great sorrow. "This land is not what it was when you came here, friend Holt."

"Aye," Bartholomew agreed, thinking of the Garwoods and all the trouble that had plagued the Holt family over the past few years. "I'm afraid some people have seen to that."

CHAPTER FOUR

September 23rd. Descended to the Missis-
sippi, and round to St. Louis, where we arrived at
twelve o'clock; and having fired a salute, went on
shore and received the heartiest and most hospita-
ble welcome from the whole village.

—from "The History of the Lewis and
Clark Expedition"

The noon sun shone brightly on the half-dozen
canoes as they glided along the tranquil waters
of the broad Mississippi River. Earlier in the
morning, when the travelers had followed the Missouri into the great Father of Waters, several of the
men had spotted cows on the shore and let out a
cheer. Over the past few days they had seen various
signs of civilization—trading boats, a small village of
French settlers called La Charette, army patrols
mounted on horseback—but it had taken the sight of
the placidly grazing bovines to convince the Corps of
Discovery that they had indeed come home.

73

Civilization . . .

Clay Holt plied the oar in his hands with practiced ease as the canoes slid ever closer to St. Louis. He
was smiling, but inside, his emotions were confused.
The part of him that had grown up in the Ohio River
valley, on the farm near Marietta, welcomed the return to the world of civilization. But another part of
him had sprung into being in the Rockies, nurtured by
that wild, dangerous, beautiful frontier. That part of
him wanted nothing more than to go back to the land
of snowcapped mountains and towering pines and
laughing brooks that ran so cold their waters took a
man's breath away. He wanted that glittering blanket
of stars over his head again at night, and he wanted a
morning breeze to carry to him that crisp, clean air
gently touched by the smell of wildflowers. A man
could breathe in the mountains.

Soon, Clay told himself. Soon, he would go back.
But first there was civilization to deal with.

In the lead canoe Captain Clark rode with the
Mandan chief, Sheheke, whom they had brought from
his village upriver. The chief, who also went by the
name Big White—probably because of his large girth,
Clay thought—was accompanied by his wife and
sons. Dressed in ceremonial attire, the trio was sure to
attract even more attention to the party when it took
to shore. Clark planned to take Chief Sheheke, who
was more talkative than fierce, to Washington City,
where he would introduce him to Thomas Jefferson in
what amounted to a meeting of two heads of state. As
the canoes neared St. Louis, Clark turned around and
called, "Let them know we're coming, boys!" Several
of the men lifted their rifles, firing in the air, while
others threw back their heads and howled like timber
wolves. Clay had to grin at their antics, and he threw
in a few whoops of his own.

The buildings of the settlement came into sight
ahead on the left bank of the mighty river. As the
canoes drew closer, the explorers heard bells ringing.
Word of their impending arrival had reached St. Louis,

and the citizens were welcoming them with a peal of
bells from every church steeple in town.

Following the lead of Lewis and Clark—as they
had been doing for more than two years—the men
sent the canoes angling toward the shore. Docks had
been built along the riverbank, and now they were
lined with settlers—men, women, and children, who
had gathered to witness the return of the intrepid pioneers who had journeyed all the way to the other side
of the continent and back. People shouted, cheered,
and applauded, and dogs yapped frantically. The tu-
mult floated out over the river to the ears of the corps
members.

Clay leaned forward to Sergeant Gass, who sat in
front of him in their canoe. "Looks like they knew we
were coming," Clay said dryly.

"Reckon so," Gass replied over his shoulder. "I
expected as much, as many folks as we've run into
during the last few days. Word'll reach Washington
City 'fore you know it. Jefferson ought to be happy."

The president's satisfaction with the outcome of
the expedition was not Clay's foremost concern; he
had not gone along with Lewis and Clark to make
Thomas Jefferson happy. Yet Gass's mention of the
president made Clay think of another Jefferson—his
brother, Jefferson Holt. It would be damned good to
see Jeff again, Clay thought.

As the canoes glided up to the docks, a multitude
of hands reached down to help the explorers disembark. Clay stepped up onto the dock and, along with
the other men in Lewis and Clark's party, found himself surrounded by well-wishers. People crowded
around, slapping him on the back, and the uproar being raised by the citizens of St. Louis seemed almost as
loud as the bellowing of the buffalo bulls they had
heard weeks earlier and hundreds of miles away. Clay
smiled wearily and tried to ease his way through the
press of humanity. At the moment, he would have
almost preferred the buffalo.

Gradually the voice of Meriwether Lewis grew

audible as he called out for quiet. When the crowd had finally settled down, he summoned the men of the expedition together in front of him. Clay stood shoulder to shoulder with the other explorers. Lewis and Clark were standing with Sheheke and several well-dressed men who occupied positions of importance in the town.

Smiling, Clark put his hand on the shoulder of one of the townsmen and said, "Lads, this is my old friend Major Christy. He's retired from the military now and owns an inn here in St. Louis. He has kindly offered storage room for our gear, and he also has quarters for as many of you men as want to take him up on his invitation. He'll take good care of you—won't you, Christy?"

"Aye," shouted the innkeeper. "Nothing's too good for the heroes of the Pacific!"

Heroes, Clay repeated to himself. He had never thought of himself as a hero. He had simply done the job he had signed on to do, like everyone else in the party.

"Captain Lewis and myself, along with the chief and his family, will be staying with Mr. Peter Chouteau," Clark continued, turning to another of the prosperous-looking citizens. "We'll be preparing our reports for the president, and while we're about that task, the rest of you men are free to do as you wish. I'm sure you'll be welcome here for as long as you want to stay."

Another roar of appreciation from the crowd confirmed Clark's statement.

Lewis spoke up. "Those of you who are enlisted in the army will, of course, be required to remain in St. Louis until Captain Clark and I are ready to depart for Washington City, and you will accompany us there. As for you private citizens . . ." Lewis paused, his eyes sweeping the group of explorers and lingering on those men, like Clay Holt, who had joined the expedition for reasons of their own. The captain's stern voice was a bit warmer than usual: "Your country owes you a great debt of gratitude, gentlemen, as do Captain Clark and myself. Without your aid, this expedition might not have been a success. On behalf of the United States of America . . . thank you."

A cheer went up for Lewis and Clark, and this time it was from the men who had followed them to the Pacific and back, against all odds. Clay joined in, lifting his rifle over his head as he shouted. No matter what happened in the future, no matter where his fate led him, he knew he would never forget Captain Meriwether Lewis and Captain William Clark.

And he doubted that the country would ever forget them, either.

"What about the beaver? I hear there's millions of them up there in the mountains!"

Clay Holt leaned back on the bench, thrusting his legs straight out and resting an elbow on the table behind him. He used his other hand to lift a mug of ale to his lips, then swallowed thirstily before he answered the question of the eager settler who had bought him the drink.

"Aye, there's beaver, all right." Clay turned enough to set the mug on the table, then wiped the back of his hand across his mouth. "Plenty of pelts for the taking. A man could get rich."

He was feeling the effects of the ale. Not this mug, particularly, but the four or five he had already consumed that evening. No point in denying it, he thought. He was drunk. But he deserved a little relaxation. Hell, he was a hero, wasn't he?

The settler crowded closer to him. "Are you going back, Mr. Holt? I've heard talk—"

"So have I," Clay interrupted sharply, growing a little impatient. In the two days since the Corps of Discovery had arrived in St. Louis, he had heard so much talk that his head seemed to be ringing.

In every tavern in the settlement—and there were quite a few, as Clay had discovered—there was someone willing to buy a man a drink in exchange for being told about the West. The members of the expedition had found that their money was unnecessary in St. Louis. And the main thing that everyone wanted to talk about was fur trapping. As far as Clay could tell, the subject was on the mind of every store clerk, stable hand, and bartender in town, as well as farmers who had come into the settlement to greet the returning explorers. All of them were planning to head off to the mountains and become rich men, Clay thought. But none of them, not a one, had any idea what they would be getting into. Only a handful of white men really knew those mountains—and Clay Holt was one of them.

Fur trappers had penetrated the Rockies before, of course, but most of them had been Englishmen and Frenchmen who operated in the Canadian mountains to the north. Only a few Americans were trying their hand at trapping, the way being led by John Colter and the two men the expedition had encountered before their return to civilization. As Clay drained the last of his ale, he wondered where Colter, Hancock, and Dickson were at that moment, indeed, if they were even still alive. The Rockies were a hazardous place.

"I was wondering," the settler pressed on, "if you might consider taking on a partner when you go back to the mountains."

"Didn't say I was going back," Clay said. "Hell, mister, I just spent better'n two years out there. What makes you think I'm in a hurry to go back?"

"Well, I just thought a man like you . . . I mean—"

"You mean what else am I good for except to tramp around in the wilderness," Clay finished for him in a hard voice. "Right?"

"Well . . ." The settler was starting to look nervous.

Clay laughed harshly. "Don't worry about it, friend. I take no offense. Hell, you're probably right. What else am I good for?"

The man did not answer. Instead, while Clay was staring broodingly down at the planks of the tavern floor, he slipped off the bench and hurried away.

After a moment Clay looked up and realized he was alone. The talking and laughter inside the tavern continued, however. Several other members of the expeditionary party were standing at the bar, surrounded as usual by men eager to buy drinks for them. A haze of pipe smoke floated in the air of the low-ceilinged room. Serving girls in scoop-cut dresses moved through the crowd, delivering trays of drinks to the tables made of rough-hewn planks. Over the doorway was a magnificent spread of antlers taken from a deer shot by the proprietor on his way to St. Louis and now displayed as a symbol of luck. On the far side of the room was a large fireplace, the crackling flames dispelling the chill of the autumn night. Near the table where Clay sat, a narrow staircase ascended to the second floor. He had not been up there, but he imagined there were rooms where the serving girls plied their other trade.

Major Christy's inn, a building solidly constructed of bricks and massive timbers, was in a better section of town than this, the ale Christy served in the attached tavern of a better quality than the swill Clay drank here. But Clay's mood had grown steadily darker since the expedition had left the great river, and he had sought out this shadowy dive thinking it better suited his state of mind.

Seeing his frown, most of the patrons had the good sense to leave him alone, especially after the man who had been talking to him about fur trapping had left so hurriedly. Clay was not the only one in the place who had been drinking heavily, though, and a few minutes later a burly red-haired young man wearing the clothes of a farmer came over to him, mug in hand.

"Yer one of them explorer fellas, ain't ye?" the man asked as he stood over Clay. He took a long, noisy drink from his mug.

Clay, no longer in the mood to talk, heard the question but ignored it. After a moment the young man said impatiently, "Hey! I'm talkin' to ye, mister." When there was still no response from Clay, the man frowned in drunken anger and kicked the sole of Clay's moccasin. "Wake up, mountain man!"

Slowly, Clay lifted his head. He had cut off his beard the first day back but had not shaved since then, and his cheeks and chin were black with stubble. His heavy eyebrows lowered, and he rumbled, "Leave me be, boy."

"But I want to talk to ye. Want to talk about trappin' some furs." A smile spread over the young man's thick lips. "And about them Injun women. What'd ye think about them redskin squaws? They as tasty as white women?"

Clay heaved a sigh. The young fool, who was too besotted to realize that he was treading on dangerous ground, was not going to leave him alone. Too bad, Clay thought; it was not his mission in life to watch over all the fools in the world.

In one smooth motion Clay rose from the bench beside the table, his hand sweeping to the hunting knife on his hip and sliding it from its sheath with a whisper of cold steel against buckskin. The room quieted abruptly as Clay's free hand struck aside the mug of ale the man was holding. The mug fell to the floor, shattering with a crash, the spilled ale staining the planks. Before the man knew what was happening, Clay's fingers caught the front of his muslin shirt and jerked him forward.

Clay put the tip of the razor-sharp blade just under the man's chin and pressed hard enough to release a bead of blood onto the knife. "I reckon you're too stupid to live, boy," Clay said coldly. "But I don't feel like wasting the time to clean up after killing you. Why don't you get the hell out of here and go bother somebody else?" He gave a humorless chuckle. "I swear, you civilized folk are about as bothersome as those Rocky Mountain mosquitoes."

Terror had sobered up the red-haired farmer in a hurry. His features were as pale as his shirt. He tried to find his voice and was finally able to croak, "I—I'm sorry, mister! I didn't mean no harm. I'll go, I'll leave ye alone—"

"See that you do." Clay took the knife away from the man's throat, and another drop of blood welled out of the tiny wound. Clay gave him a shove toward the door.

The man spun and ran out of the tavern, the other drinkers getting out of his way. Every eye in the place was turned toward Clay as he wiped the blood from his knife onto his trousers, then slipped the blade back in its sheath. He turned and sat down, then took off his coonskin cap and dropped it on the table. He let his head sink into his big, callused palms.

He sat like that for several minutes as the noise in the tavern gradually built up to its previous level. The place had seen many brawls and more than its share of knifings and shootings. The brief encounter between Clay and the drunken, persistent stranger had been nothing in comparison. Nobody had died, and only a few drops of blood had spilled. The whole thing was quickly forgotten.

But not by everyone, Clay discovered a few minutes later when a soft hand came down on his buckskin-clad shoulder and a voice quietly asked, "You all right, mister? Can I get you something?"

Clay started violently at the touch, and the hand was hastily withdrawn. He looked up and saw one of the serving girls standing beside the table, a frightened but determined expression on her face. She was not particularly pretty, he thought—her jaw was a little too prominent, her nose a bit too large—but her dark hair was thick and lustrous, and her dark eyes were friendly, if somewhat cautious. She wore a blue dress and clutched a wooden serving tray in front of her.

With a grimace Clay said, "I'm sorry, lass. I didn't mean to scare you."

The young woman smiled. "That's all right. The customers in here, they can be pretty rough. I—I reckon I'm used to being a little scared."

"Nothing wrong with that," Clay told her. "When you're out in the mountains, you'd damned well better be scared. Keeps you awake. Keeps you alive, sometimes."

Her smile widened. "I don't think I'm very likely to ever go to the mountains. Can I get you something to drink?"

"I've had enough." He shoved the empty mug away from him. "More'n enough. Just want to be left alone."

Without being invited, the woman perched on the bench next to him, close but not too close. "That's not good," she said earnestly. "When a man's got dark things on his mind, he oughtn't be alone. It's too easy to start thinking bad thoughts when you're alone."

"You sound like you've got some experience with bad thoughts," Clay commented, his interest in her growing despite the pounding in his head from too much ale these past two days.

She shrugged. "A serving girl like me, we're usually alone, even when we have a . . . a gentleman with us."

Clay threw back his head and laughed. Several people threw glances his way before they went back to their own concerns. "Not bad, lass," he said. "You play the poor, helpless waif quite well. It's not necessary, though. If you want me to take you upstairs, you don't have to put on an act."

The smile vanished, and she glared at him as she leaned closer. "You bastard!" she hissed. "What do you want me to do, act like some cheap trollop?"

"That's what you are, isn't it?"

Her hand came up and flashed toward his face, but Clay's reflexes, even slowed as they were by drink, were sufficient to let him grab her wrist in midair. He laughed again as she struggled against his grip and then gave an oath of frustration.

"That's more like it. What's your name, girl?"

For a moment she did not answer him, but then she said in a surly voice, "Janey."

"Janey," Clay repeated. "That's what Captain Clark called the Shoshone woman who went with us. . . ." He shook off those memories. "Well, Janey, what say we go upstairs, since that's what you wanted all along?"

"You're damned sure of yourself, mister," she snapped.

Clay laughed again. "'Course I am. I'm a hero, remember?" His voice was tinged with more than a little bitterness.

He stood and picked up his cap, not wanting to prolong the discussion. His iron grip on Janey's wrist persuaded her to follow along after him, leaving the serving tray on the table. Clay headed toward the stairs, half dragging the young woman behind him. Maybe he should have played her little game, he thought; it would have made her feel better about herself, and she would have been more cooperative. He was in no mood for deception, though, the sly games men and women played being just one more aspect of civilization that he had come to despise. In the wilderness it was different. There, men and women knew what they wanted, and they took it.

The hallway at the top of the stairs was lit only by a small candle in a holder attached to the wall. Clay paused on the landing. "Which room is yours?"

"Any of them that's not occupied." She sounded more tired now than angry.

"Then come along." Clay headed toward the nearest door that was partially ajar.

The chamber inside was small and narrow with a bare wooden floor. Against one wall was a crude bunk with a thin straw mattress covered by coarsely woven ticking. Under the bunk was a slop jar. A small pail of water and another candle sat on a tiny table against another wall.

Clay glanced around the room in disgust. He would have much rather slept under the stars, on a carpet of thick grass in a mountain meadow. But then, he reflected, he had not come here to sleep.

He kicked the door shut and let go of Janey's wrist. "I've only a quarter eagle on me," he said. "I trust that'll be sufficient."

"It's fine," Janey said sullenly. She slid the sleeves of her dress down her arms, exposing her breasts. Clay watched expressionlessly as she took off the dress, then stood before him nude. Her waist was slender, almost girlish, but her breasts were full and heavy, tipped with large brown nipples. As she walked over to the bunk she said, "You can put the money on the table, next to the water."

Clay dug the small gold piece out of the pocket of his buckskin shirt and tossed it onto the table, where it rang against the pail. By the time he turned back to the bunk, Janey had stretched out on the meager mattress. Her breath misted in front of her in the chill air of the room.

"Come on, hero. It's getting cold."

Clay's hand clenched into a fist, and he took a quick step toward her, anger flaring inside him. He stopped short and lowered his hand when he saw that she was watching him impassively. No doubt she was accustomed to rough treatment in her line of work, but Clay Holt had never struck a woman in his life, and he was damned if he was going to start now. He watched her breasts rising and falling as she breathed, and he saw the nipples hardening. From the cold, no doubt. Yet her lips were parted slightly now, and he thought he saw a rosy flush spreading over her features that would indicate her heart was beating faster. He felt a quickening of his own and reached for the bottom of his shirt to pull it over his head.

He stripped his clothes off quickly, being careful to put his sheathed knife and his pistol on the table. Janey was ready for him when he came to her, and

neither of them wanted to waste any time on prelimi-
naries. Their lovemaking was brief but intense, and
Clay was glad to see that all the ale he had consumed
had not affected his potency. Unexpectedly, Janey
cried out beneath him in what seemed to be real passion, and as the act reached its crescendo, Clay felt like
shouting. Instantly, in the small part of his brain not
overcome by heat and flesh and sensation, he remembered the bellowing of the buffalo bulls that had
served as constant accompaniment to the expedition's
progress for weeks.

He collapsed in laughter, sagging onto Janey so
that her breasts were pressed against his chest. His
weight pinned her to the bunk. She grimaced and got
her hands on his shoulders, pushing. "Get off of me,
you great bloody ox!"

That drove Clay into more gales of laughter, and
he managed to say, "Not ox, lass. Buffalo!" He
whooped again while Janey cursed.

Tightening his arms around her, Clay lifted himself off the bunk and then turned over, taking her with
him, so that he was lying on the bottom with her
sprawled on top of him. He put a stop to the stream of
profanity issuing from her by raising his mouth to
hers and kissing her as he stroked her back. Within a
matter of moments her tense muscles relaxed, and she
returned his kiss.

"Better?" he asked in a hoarse whisper a few minutes later.

"Much better," she replied. Her hips moved
slowly and sensuously.

Clay was barely drunk now. Most of the liquor's
effects had fled, leaving his brain only a little fuzzy
around the edges. An immense weariness was stealing
over him, however, and he was more than content to
let the pace of their lovemaking remain tantalizingly
languorous. When they were finished, Janey rested
her head against his shoulder, the surprisingly clean
scent of her hair filling his nostrils. Surrounded by the
warmth of her body, feeling the beat of her heart

against him, Clay realized he was slipping into sleep. A whore's crib was no place to doze off, he told himself.

But that was exactly what he did.

A witch haunted his dreams, a beautiful witch with dark hair and eyes. She was trying to seduce him, dancing nude for him with wanton abandon. But even though he wanted her, wanted her as desperately as he had ever wanted any woman, he knew he did not dare to take her, for if he did, she would use him and then discard him, sending him spinning down into the bowels of hell, screaming as he fell into the eternal flames. . . .

Clay Holt's eyes snapped open, and his head jerked up off the mattress. His mouth opened wide, but he caught the cry before it escaped.

The room was dark, the candle long since burned out. He knew he was holding a woman in his arms, and enough moonlight came through the room's single grimy window for him to see that her hair was even blacker than the night outside.

The woman stirred a little, snuggling closer against him, and Clay recoiled. "Josie!" he exclaimed. "Damn you, girl!" He tried to pull away more, but the wall stopped him. His heart pounding, he put a hand against the woman's shoulder and pushed her off the bunk.

She let out a cry of pain and surprise as she fell to the floor. "You bastard!" she said. "Why did you do that?"

Clay rolled off the bunk, barely noticing how cold the floor was under his bare feet. He had no idea how Josie Garwood had gotten there, but he remembered that he had left his pistol and knife on a small table against the wall—there it was! His fingers closed over the bone handle of the knife and jerked the blade from its sheath.

"I should have killed you a long time ago, Josie," he growled as he swung toward the woman again.

She panted with terror as she scuttled backward on the floor. Moonlight glinted on the long, heavy blade of the hunting knife. "I-I'm not Josie," she stammered as Clay advanced toward her. "My name's Janey!"

"Lying won't do you any good. I know what a good liar you are, Josie. Well, we'll see how good you are at spreading lies with your tongue cut out of your mouth!" With that, he lunged at her, reaching for her long, dark hair with his free hand.

The woman twisted away from him and gave a shrill, piercing scream. Clay cursed and reached for her again, and once more she managed to elude him. The next few moments they played a deadly game in the shadows of the squalid little room. She kept shrieking as Clay tried to trap her.

"Scream all you want, Josie," he told her with an ugly laugh. "It won't do you any good."

Suddenly the door burst open, and dim light spilled in from the hall. A tall, bulky shape loomed in the entrance, and a man's voice boomed, "Here, now, what's this?"

"Save me, Mort!" the woman cried. "He's gone crazy!"

Clay turned toward the newcomer, recognizing him as the bartender from the tavern downstairs—at the same moment he became acutely aware of his own nakedness. He still had a knife in his hand, though, and that mattered more than clothes.

"Get out of my way, you son of a bitch!" Clay threatened as the nude, frightened woman darted past the bartender. "I'm going to teach that damned hussy a lesson she'll never forget!"

"You're not going to do anything, mister," the bartender said grimly, "except put your clothes on and get the hell out of my place. Understand?"

Clay drew himself up and glared indignantly at

the man. "You can't talk to me like that! I'm a hero, you stupid oaf!"

"I don't care if you're the goddamned king of England. Nobody mistreats my girls."

Clay swung the knife toward the bartender, but he was still logy from sleep, his reflexes not as fast as they usually were. The man easily blocked the knife thrust and drove his right fist into Clay's jaw.

The blow knocked Clay backward, and the room was so small that he ran into the opposite wall with stunning force. Following up on his advantage, the bartender closed with him, chopping the side of his hand down against Clay's right wrist. That arm went numb to the elbow, and the blade slipped from Clay's hand and clattered on the floor. The bartender hooked two devastating punches to Clay's belly. Clay doubled over, and the man brought clubbed fists down on the back of his neck.

Clay was only vaguely aware of hitting the floor. The lingering effects of the ale, combined with the beating, had left him grasping at consciousness. As if from far away he heard a voice asking, "What the hell's wrong with him, Janey? What'd you do to set him off like that?"

"I swear I don't know, Mort," came a female voice, so faint that Clay could barely make out the words. "He just woke up sudden-like and went mad."

"Well, he won't bother anybody else here. Get his clothes—and put something on yourself."

Clay felt himself being lifted and slung over a brawny shoulder. His head swung from side to side as he was carried downstairs, and with each pendulum-like rocking, he felt as if he were drifting closer and closer to an engulfing darkness that might never end. He willed his muscles to work so that he could escape from the bartender's grasp, but his body refused to obey.

A moment later a door creaked open, and Clay suddenly realized he was falling. The bartender had dropped him. He crashed into a hard surface, and the breath was knocked from him, making him gasp for air. He inhaled a stench so foul that he gagged and rolled onto his side, retching.

Someone tossed his clothes onto his naked body, and the bartender said, "You're damn lucky I don't keep this knife and pistol to square the trouble you made, mister. But Janey tells me you were with Lewis and Clark, so I'll let you have your weapons back. Just don't ever show your face in my tavern again, understand?" A booted toe prodded his side. "I asked if you understand."

Clay nodded his head jerkily and rasped, "A-aye."

"I'll take that as a yes." The bartender spat in contempt, and a second later the door slammed.

Slowly Clay's brain began to work again. He realized he was probably in the alley behind the tavern. They would not have pitched him naked into the main road—at least he hoped not. He was shivering with cold, and the smell of whatever he had landed in was still making his belly roil with sickness. He had to get out of there and get his clothes on before he froze to death.

His hand moving shakily, he reached out, and his fingertips brushed a stone wall. Scrabbling for a handhold, he pulled himself into a sitting position and leaned against the wall, resting a moment before trying to climb to his feet. He gathered his buckskins and held them close to him as he struggled upright.

The smell was a little better now that he was off the ground. After bracing himself against the wall, he stepped awkwardly into his trousers. He got his shirt over his head, then began looking around for his socks, moccasins, and cap. He found them nearby and drew on the socks and moccasins with great difficulty. The cap stank too much even to consider putting it on his head, and he tossed it away in the darkness of the alley.

His knife, back in its sheath, and his pistol were lying on the sill of the tavern's back door. Despite his anger, the bartender had been kind enough not to throw the weapons into the muck. Clay owed the man for that.

Lifting a hand to his face, Clay worked his jaw back and forth painfully, knowing that it was already starting to bruise and swell. He owed the bartender for that, too. Yet he could not blame the man for defending the serving girl.

As he tucked away his weapons, he started toward the end of the alley, marked by faint light from the street. Now that his mind was functioning better, he remembered enough of the last half hour to realize he had been in the wrong. Awaking from a nightmare, he had been convinced that Josie Garwood was in the room with him, instead of the trollop called Janey. The names were slightly similar, and Janey had the same dark hair and eyes as Josie, but the resemblance ended there. Clay knew he would have never made the mistake had he not been drinking and brooding for two days.

He wiped his hand on his trousers and rubbed his aching temples. His neck hurt, too, when he moved his head back and forth. *Damned lucky the bartender didn't hurt me even worse*, he thought.

His stumbling steps brought him to the end of the alley, and he emerged onto one of St. Louis's side streets. Most of the buildings on the street were dark. He looked up at the stars. They seemed dimmer in the city than in the wilderness, but they were still bright enough for him to estimate from their positions in the heavens that the hour was long after midnight. He needed to get back to Christy's inn and get some more sleep—after he had washed some of the mud and garbage off him.

He had gone less than a block, having just passed the mouth of another narrow, twisting alley, when a voice behind him said, "Well, what's this?"

Clay halted as he heard men moving closer to him. A second voice said, "I don't know, but he smells like he's been wallowing in offal."

Turning slowly, Clay saw two men standing a few feet away. He assumed they had come from the alley he had passed. He was not sure what they wanted from him, but he was in no mood to deal with anyone or anything. "Go away," he growled.

One of the men laughed. "Oh, he's a mean 'un."

Clay thought he recognized the voice. It belonged to the red-haired farmer he had humiliated earlier in the tavern. The words were slurred; the man was still drunk, Clay realized. He and his companion, who was taller and darker, were probably lurking out there, waiting for someone to rob.

Given the way he had been stumbling along, they had probably taken him for an easy target.

"I've got no money," he said. "Go away."

The taller man stepped closer and shoved him. "Don't talk to us like that, sot! And as for valuables, we'll be the judge of that. Hand over what you've got."

Clay's headache was worse, a pounding inside his skull that reminded him of a buffalo stampede. But he was able to smile grimly as he said, "All right—you son of a bitch!" He drew the pistol up, cocking the flintlock as he centered the muzzle on his assailant's face, a pale smear in the dim, shadowy street. The man gasped in sudden fear, and Clay chuckled. "You sure you still want it?"

"Look out, Otis! He's got a gun!" The red-haired man shouted the warning as he dove to the side, away from the pistol.

Clay pressed the trigger, and the flintlock clicked down harmlessly; the pistol was not loaded. In his near stupor he had forgotten that crucial fact. With a harsh laugh, he threw himself forward, slashing with the gun at the dark-haired assailant.

The barrel thudded against the man's head and sent him staggering to his knees. The red-haired man leapt at Clay, windmilling punches at him, one of which struck home, grazing Clay's temple. Clay grunted in pain and caught his balance as he started to fall. The farmer was closing in on him, obviously thinking he was about to go down, but Clay surprised him by driving the barrel of the pistol into his belly. As the man gasped and doubled over, Clay shoved him away.

The other would-be robber had recovered enough to lunge at Clay again. Ducking under a roundhouse swing, Clay dropped his flintlock and took out his knife, then slashed it at the dark-haired man, who was crowding him. For a second the blade caught in the man's shirt, then tore through and cut the flesh underneath.

"I'm hurt!" the man screamed. "Oh, God, my guts are spilling out!"

Clay seriously doubted that; the knife had not cut nearly deep enough to disembowel him. He drove his shoulder into the man and knocked him aside. The farmer was standing nearby, still gasping for breath. Clay brandished the knife at him and shouted, "Come on, you bastard! Come get a taste of cold steel!"

The man turned and ran.

Clay laughed. The wounded man was limping away, but Clay decided to let him go. He had no wish to kill either one of the fools. All he wanted to do was get back to the inn. He put away his knife, searched around for his pistol until he found it, and resumed his course.

He was never going to drink ale again, he vowed. And as soon as he had paid a short visit to his family, to let them know he was still alive, he was heading back to the West.

Considering everything that had happened since his arrival in St. Louis, he came to one inescapable conclusion: Cities were not the best place for him to be.

CHAPTER FIVE

April 4th. The day is clear and pleasant, though the wind is high from the N.W. We now packed up in different boxes a variety of articles for the President, which we shall send in the barge.

—from "The History of the Lewis and Clark Expedition"

Even though he held the most important position in the country, President Thomas Jefferson was having a difficult time keeping his mind on his work. Ever since he had received word that Meriwether Lewis and William Clark, his handpicked men, had returned safely from their expedition to the Pacific, he had been consumed with curiosity. Captain Lewis, formerly Jefferson's personal secretary, had already sent the president a long letter giving some details of the journey. Jefferson, however, wanted to hear

Lewis's report in person, and he was especially eager to see the botanical specimens the explorers had brought back from the mountains.

For years, even before the so-called Louisiana Purchase had made exploration of the West a necessity, Jefferson had been intrigued by the idea of finding a passage from one side of the continent to the other. His first attempts in that area had come years earlier when, as the American minister to France, he had met a man named John Ledyard. Ledyard was an adventurer, inclined to recklessness, true enough, but something of an eccentric genius in Jefferson's eyes. Acting in concert, Jefferson and Ledyard had come up with a rather bizarre plan: Traveling alone, Ledyard would cross Europe and Asia to Siberia, then sail across the Bering Sea to the western coast of the New World. An inland journey from there, Jefferson was convinced, would enable Ledyard to locate the headwaters of the Missouri River, which would then take him back to civilization.

Even though Ledyard managed to penetrate three thousand miles into Siberia, the Russians put a stop to the plan before he could continue farther. Thinking the adventurer to be some sort of spy, the Russians summarily booted him from the country.

By the time Jefferson became president in 1801, a transcontinental crossing had been accomplished, but not by an American and not over land owned by the vigorous new nation. A Scots fur trader named Alexander Mackenzie made a pilgrimage across northwestern Canada to the Pacific in 1793. Upon hearing this news, Jefferson had felt a mixture of envy and concern. Mackenzie might try again, this time farther to the south. That would extend the influence of the British into territory that the United States might someday wish to control, Jefferson feared.

Until Lewis and Clark's daring foray, though, his efforts to explore the Rocky Mountain region and beyond had come to nothing. All that had changed now, and Thomas Jefferson felt a deep satisfaction in having played a part in the expedition.

As he sat behind the large desk in his office in the President's House, trying to concentrate on the never-ending stream of documents requiring his attention, his thoughts kept straying to the West, and finally he put down his pen. He was more distracted than usual that day. The first crates of specimens from the expedition would be arriving any time now in Washington City; that was why he was so restless, he supposed.

Jefferson swiveled around in his chair and looked out the large window. Autumn had arrived in Washington City, bringing periods of cold, drizzle, and gray skies, but today was glorious, with bright sunshine. Earlier the president had strolled in the garden behind the mansion, enjoying the crisp, cool air.

A brisk knock on his office door made him turn around in his chair again. "Come," he said, none too enthusiastically. Chances were, the visitor, whoever he turned out to be, would only add to the load of details that sometimes threatened to overwhelm the chief executive.

The president's secretary, a slender, nondescript man who was highly efficient at his job, stepped into the room. "Excuse me, sir. I hate to disturb you, but I know you wanted to be informed when the specimens from the expedition led by Captain Lewis and Captain Clark arrived."

Jefferson stood, tall and erect, as excitement and anticipation gripped him. "They're here?"

"The first shipment, at any rate."

Jefferson grinned broadly, feeling a bit like a child about to be presented with a wished-for new toy. Then he remembered the dignity and decorum required by his office, and he said solemnly, "Very well. I'll be along to inspect them shortly. Thank you for informing me."

"Not at all, sir," the secretary murmured. He backed out of the office, closing the door behind him.

The president stepped out from behind his desk

and for a moment paced back and forth, not wanting to appear too eager. Then, deciding this was not a state occasion that demanded some sort of show, he threw open the office door and stalked out into the hall.

Servants were carrying in the crates, which had been brought to the President's House by wagon. The crates were being stacked along the wall, and a young man was prying the top off one of them with an iron bar.

"Excuse me, lad," Jefferson said, approaching the man and holding out his hand. "Could I do that?"

The workman frowned a bit in surprise, but one did not turn down a request from the president. He handed over the bar and said, "Sure. I mean, of course, sir."

Working quickly, using the muscles he had developed during a vigorous life as a planter in Virginia, Jefferson pried up the wooden lid of the crate. Inside, their roots buried in dirt wrapped in cloth, were several small plants the likes of which he had never seen before. Inside the crate a note in Lewis's familiar handwriting—complete with many misspellings, as usual—identified the plants as wild turnips from the vast plains in the center of the continent. His curiosity burning, Jefferson examined the plants for a moment, then grasped the iron bar and moved on to the next crate.

For the next few hours the president worked steadily, opening the large wooden boxes while the servants looked on with expressions carefully controlled not to show their amusement. Even though botany had been his hobby for years, Jefferson found a wealth of plants unknown to him. It was clear that the western half of the United States held many new discoveries.

He was studiously regarding a salmonberry plant when his secretary approached, a rather hesitant and confused look on his face. As Jefferson glanced up at the man, he immediately sensed that something was wrong.

"What is it?" the president asked, straightening. "Don't tell me I've forgotten an appointment with a group of senators or some such bothersome task."

"No, sir," the man said. "There's one more crate on the lawn, sir."

"Well, have the servants bring it in. Whatever it is, I wish to examine its contents."

"I'm, uh, not sure that would be a good idea, Mr. President."

"And why not?" Jefferson demanded, puzzled by the secretary's attitude.

"Well—it's growling."

Jefferson's broad forehead creased in surprise. "Growling?"

Clearly reluctant to say any more, the secretary bobbed his head.

"You mean that whatever is in the crate is—*growling*," Jefferson said.

"That's right, sir."

"All right. Let's go see what it is." Jefferson picked up the iron bar and strode toward the front entrance of the President's House.

The secretary and several other servants trailed behind the chief executive, emerging from the front door of the three-story Georgian mansion and walking down the four broad steps to the lawn in front of the residence. A crate somewhat larger than the others was sitting on the grass, near the wagon that had brought it.

As Jefferson approached the crate, he saw that several holes had been drilled into its top and sides to admit air. A rank odor was coming from the container. As the secretary had said, whatever was inside was growling, a deep, rumbling sound.

Clearly nervous about the situation, the secretary moved up beside Jefferson as the president inserted the tip of the bar under the lid of the crate. The secretary would have preferred to be elsewhere, Jefferson knew, but he regarded his place as with the president.

Exerting his strength, Jefferson leaned on the bar, and the nails holding down the lid began to give with a creaking sound. The growling grew louder. Jefferson glanced over at the secretary and saw the man licking dry lips. Then he grinned and finished prying the lid off.

"Well, well," boomed out the voice of the nation's leader. "What have we here?"

"Good Lord!" the secretary exclaimed. "What manner of creature are those?"

Jefferson looked down at the two black-furred animals pacing around and around in the crate. "They're bear cubs," he told the startled secretary. "Grizzly bear cubs, unless I miss my guess."

The secretary took a couple of quick steps backward as one of the cubs reared up and put its front paws on the side of the crate so that it could peer out the top. "I'll make arrangements to have them taken away and disposed of immediately, sir," he said shakily.

Jefferson threw back his head and laughed. "You most certainly will not. Order the gardeners to dig a pit in the lawn."

"You're going to have them killed and bury them here?"

"Not at all. The pit will be their new home."

"But—but what will people think?" The secretary sounded shocked to the core by the idea of keeping the bear cubs as pets.

"Well, I've never been one to worry overmuch about such things, now have I?" Jefferson asked in a slightly mocking tone. "Besides, those bears have every right to be here."

"Every right? I don't understand."

Jefferson's voice grew serious as he fixed the secretary with an intent look. "Since the Louisiana Purchase and the exploration of the West by Lewis and Clark, those bear cubs are as much Americans as you and I, my friend. Yes, indeed, just as much Americans as you and I."

Unlike the man for whom he had been named, Jefferson Holt never would have thought of a bear as an American. To the settlers around Marietta, bears were only an occasional nuisance. Most of the beasts had been killed or driven farther west by the advance of the pioneers, but every now and then hunters ran across the animals in the woods. Bears were one of the many things settlers kept an eye out for while working in the fields.

With the autumn harvest over, the land was ready to be plowed in preparation for the sowing of winter wheat. That was what Jeff Holt was doing in one of the fields on the Holt family farm, a quarter of a mile from the cabin. His younger brother Edward was helping him by clearing some of the rocks from the field.

As Jeff guided the plow behind one of the Holt mules, Edward filled his arms with rocks and complained, "Where do all these stones come from? We plowed this field just last spring!"

Jeff and Clay had developed a theory of their own about that when they were younger and had to perform the same task that Edward was doing now. They had decided that rocks in fields reproduced just as animals did. Jeff remembered how they had laughed uproariously about that behind their father's back.

He was not about to say anything of the sort to ten-year-old Edward, however. If such talk ever got back to their mother, Norah Holt would be liable to tan their hides, even if Jeff was a grown man.

Edward Holt was tall and sturdy for his years, and he tried to act more mature than he really was. With sandy-blond hair and gray eyes, he bore some resemblance to Jeff, and he idolized his older brother, although the two were not much alike in temperment. Jeff loved his brother dearly, but there were times when he thought Edward ought to act more his age

and not be so serious. All youngsters needed to have
at least a little mischief in them.

When he had dumped the load of rocks he was
carrying next to the trees at the edge of the field, Edward turned to his brother and called, "I'll be back in
a few minutes, Jeff!"

With a wave, Jeff acknowledged his brother's
statement. Edward vanished into the woods, and Jeff
knew he had gone off for some privacy to answer the
call of nature. Jeff kept plowing, the hard muscles of
his forearms standing out beneath his rolled-up
sleeves as he wrestled the blade of the plow back into
line. Despite the autumn coolness, a fine sheen of
sweat covered his brow. He didn't mind the hard
work; it was good to be doing his share to help the
family keep going. Soon, he thought, if he could ever
work up the courage to ask Melissa to marry him, he
would have to start thinking about his own place. His
father would probably make them a present of some
of the Holt family holdings, which were fairly extensive. Due to the hard work of Bartholomew, Norah,
and their children, the farm had grown and become
successful during the two decades since the family
had arrived in the Northwest Territory.

Of course, thoughts of marriage and a farm of his
own—a family of his own—were premature. He had
not even declared his love for Melissa yet, although he
hoped that she could sense how he felt about her. And
while he knew that she cared for him, he was not sure
that what she felt was the kind of deep love on which
a marriage should be based.

He was going to have to declare himself and ask
her for a commitment in return.

But that prospect made him more nervous, Jeff
ruefully admitted to himself, than he would have been
facing a band of marauding Indians. Not that he knew
what *that* was really like, either.

The sound of approaching hoofbeats pulled him
out of his reverie. He looked up as he grasped the
rawhide leaders and pulled back on them, bringing

the mule to a halt. Two men rode out of the woods on the opposite side of the field from where Edward had disappeared, and Jeff felt a shiver of apprehension when he recognized Zach Garwood and another of the Garwood brothers, Luther. Luther was younger than Zach, Pete, and Josie, but older than Aaron. He was dark and slender and probably the smallest of the brothers. Jeff knew him to be intelligent, maybe the smartest of the bunch, but he had always gone along with whatever Zach and Pete wanted to do. It was probably easier on him that way, Jeff thought.

As Zach and Luther rode toward him across the plowed field, Jeff steeled himself not to look over his shoulder to where he had last seen Edward. He had no idea what the Garwoods wanted, but they were likely up to mischief. Jeff hoped Edward would have the good sense to stay in the woods.

The brothers reined in, and Zach looked down at Jeff. "Hello, Holt. What are you doing?"

"If you ever did any work, you'd know, Zach," Jeff replied coolly. "This is called plowing. It's one of the jobs you do on a farm."

Luther grinned at Jeff's gibing comment. Zach, however, did not look particularly amused. "I know you're plowing. I was just wondering why."

"We'll be planting winter wheat soon, maybe some barley," Jeff explained. "As soon as some of the fall rains have come and the ground is ready, we'll be sowing the grain. Your pa doesn't let his fields lie fallow in the winter, does he?"

Zach frowned. "What my pa does or doesn't do is none of your damned business."

"You were the one who brought it all up," Jeff said with a shrug. "Can I do something for you, Zach? I'm busy."

Leaning forward in the saddle, Zach said, "I need a mule."

"Your pa's got mules."

"I don't want one of his mules." Zach's voice hardened. "I want yours."

"Then you'll have to speak to my father about buying him." Again Jeff wondered about Edward and prayed the boy was staying out of sight. The Garwoods were definitely up to something.

Zach shook his head. "Nope. I think I'll just take that mule. Get him for me, Luther."

Luther turned in his saddle to look over at his brother. "You sure about this, Zach?" he asked, a hesitant expression on his slender face.

"Dammit, of course I'm sure!" Zach snapped. "Now get that mule, like I told you."

"I'll have to cut him loose from the plow."

"Then do it!"

Jeff stood there stonily during the exchange. He knew Zach had no real interest in stealing the mule; that was just an excuse to goad Jeff into a fight. And unless he tried to resist, Zach would spread the story all over the area, altering it to make himself look like less of a thief and Jeff like more of a coward.

Luther reluctantly swung down from his horse. He cast a look toward Jeff that combined a trace of fear with a great deal of mockery. Luther did not really think Jeff would put up a fight, not in the face of two-to-one odds.

His courage growing when Jeff made no move to stop him, Luther slid his knife from the sheath on his belt and went to stand by the mule's head. He reached out, caught the harness by which the animal was hitched to the plow, and sawed through it, freeing the mule.

"Never mind," Zach told him suddenly. "I changed my mind. Wouldn't want a sorry, spavined creature like that. Get rid of him, Luther."

Luther drew back his knife.

Having kept an iron grip on his temper during the long moments of this exchange, Jeff had been hoping the Garwoods would tire of harassing him and go away. He knew that if he tried to drive them off, he would probably be letting himself in for a beating. But that wasn't his chief reason for not giving vent to his growing indignation. Only his concern for Edward's safety had enabled him to control himself.

Silently he cursed the carelessness that had led him to leave his flintlock leaning on a tree at the edge of the field. Then, as Luther thrust forward with the knife, Jeff felt his self-control slipping away, and embers of rage burst into flame.

The blade slashed the flank of the mule. It let out a loud *haaww!* of pain as it lurched forward. Luther shuffled back quickly, not wanting to be struck by the beast's flailing rear hooves. Then the mule broke into a gallop, heading across the field in an futile effort to escape the pain of the wound.

Zach and Luther burst into raucous laughter.

That was all Jeff could stand. He dropped the now-useless reins and threw himself forward, yelling, "Damn you!" as he launched a wild punch at Luther.

Luther saw him coming and tried to swing around, knife in hand, but he reacted too slowly. Jeff's fist slammed into his jaw, lifting Luther's feet off the ground as the impact of the blow sent him flying backward.

"I'll kill you for that, Holt!" Zach cried as he flung himself out of his saddle and tackled Jeff. Both of them sprawled to the earth next to the plow. Zach landed on top, his weight knocking the breath out of Jeff's body. Mercilessly Zach began pounding the smaller man with his fists.

Jeff knew he had to do something, and do it quickly. If he allowed Zach to keep him pinned, the brawny leader of the Garwood brothers would beat him senseless, if not worse. Zach might well make good on his threat.

Heaving himself up, Jeff tried to throw Zach off, but to no avail. He was still gasping for breath as Zach's blows drove into his belly and chest. Grimacing, Jeff cupped his hands and brought them looping around to slap sharply against Zach's ears. Clay had taught Jeff that move years earlier, but this was the first time he had been forced to use it.

Zach let out a howl of pain and stopped his pounding for a moment. Jeff took advantage of the opportunity by bringing his knee up sharply toward Zach's groin, but Zach recovered his wits just in time to twist slightly and take the blow on the thigh. It was enough to knock him halfway off Jeff, though, enabling Jeff to grab the front of Zach's shirt and shove him to the side. Desperately Jeff rolled free and came to his feet, staggering a little as he tried to catch his balance.

There was no reprieve. Jeff had been upright only an instant when Luther leapt on him from behind, slid an arm around his throat, and tightened it. Jeff gagged at the pressure on his Adam's apple and drove an elbow behind him, slamming it into Luther's belly. That loosened the younger Garwood's grip enough for Jeff to writhe out of his grasp. Jeff swung a backhanded punch that cracked into Luther's jaw, this time on the other side of his head.

So far there had been no sign of Edward, and Jeff was thankful for that as he turned to face Zach's next charge. The brothers would wear him down rather quickly, Jeff knew, but he planned to inflict some damage of his own before that occurred. He took a punch in the solar plexus from Zach and dealt out one that caught his opponent flush on the nose.

Zach yelled again, roaring like a maddened grizzly. He blocked a couple of Jeff's punches and stepped close enough to get his arms around the smaller man. Those arms closed in a fearsome grip, making Jeff feel as if he were about to be squeezed in two. Zach's maneuver had pinned his arms, so he could not strike back in the usual way. Instead, he lowered his head and butted Zach in the face, aiming for the nose— which still had to be hurting from the last blow he'd landed.

Zach gasped in pain, and for a second Jeff thought he might release him, allowing him to escape. But Zach continued to hold him off the ground in a bear hug. Then Luther joined in the battle again, raining punches on the back of Jeff's head and shoulders. Jeff flailed his feet out behind him, and blind luck guided one of the frantic kicks home: The heel of Jeff's boot thudded into Luther's groin, sending Luther staggering backward as he bent over, clutched at himself, and screamed.

That was the last bit of luck Jeff was blessed with, however. Zach tightened his arms even more, and Jeff thought he could almost hear bones cracking and splintering inside him. Pain shot through him, and a smoky haze began to obscure his vision. Then without warning Zach released him and gave him a hard shove. Jeff could not stop himself from falling. No sooner had he hit the ground than Zach was standing over him, kicking him, one bone-jarring impact after another, driving him farther and farther from consciousness until he was on the very edge of a vast, deep blackness. The next blow, he knew, would send him tumbling over the brink.

But before that happened, he heard Zach Garwood, panting for breath, declare harshly, "That's what all you Holts'll get sooner or later. The whole damn lot of you will pay for what your brother did to Josie. Remember that—and remember this!"

Then the final kick came, and Jeff felt himself falling into the darkness. He never knew when he landed, and he certainly did not know when Zach and Luther Garwood climbed onto their horses and rode away.

From where he was crouched behind the thick trunk of an oak tree at the edge of the woods, Edward Holt had watched in horror as his brother Jeff absorbed the savage beating from the Garwoods. More than anything he had ever desired, Edward had wanted to help Jeff, but there was nothing he could do. He was no match for either Zach or Luther by themselves, let alone together. If he had been able to get his hands on Jeff's flintlock . . .

But although he had hunted in the past, he had never shot at a human being. That would be different from taking a potshot at a squirrel or even a deer. He was sure he could never bring himself to point a rifle at another person and pull the trigger.

At that moment Edward hated himself for his helplessness and indecision. If he had run home when he'd first gone back to the edge of the woods and seen Zach and Luther talking to Jeff, he might have been able to fetch help in time. But he hadn't, and then it was too late. Running home at that point wouldn't have done Jeff any good. The Garwoods had had Jeff down, kicking him, and Edward had closed his eyes and put his hands over his ears as their brutal laughter threatened to drive him out of his mind.

Finally, after what had seemed like an eternity, Zach and Luther were climbing onto their horses and riding away, leaving Jeff sprawled bloody and motionless on the ground. Now Edward waited until they had disappeared into the woods on the other side of the field; even then he hesitated for a few moments. When he was sure the Garwoods were gone, he emerged from the trees and raced to Jeff's side.

Jeff was lying on his back, arms flung out. His face was bruised and swollen, and blood welled from several cuts on his forehead. Edward went to his knees beside his brother and said urgently, "Jeff! Can you hear me, Jeff?"

There was no response, and Edward's fear and guilt grew even stronger. Jeff was dead, and it was all his fault! Edward gave in to his emotions and began to cry, large tears sliding down his cheeks and falling to the plowed earth beside Jeff.

Suddenly, a low groan interrupted his sobs, and Edward stiffened in surprise. Jeff was not dead after all, he realized, and his heart leapt with hope. No longer could he afford to weep. He had to be strong now, to help Jeff.

Reluctant to touch his brother, Edward forced himself to lean forward and place a hand on Jeff's chest. He felt a heartbeat there, a strong pulse that made him even more optimistic. "Jeff!" he repeated. "Come on, Jeff, wake up!"

Jeff's eyelids flickered. Gradually, his eyes opened and tried to focus on the youngster leaning over him. Through swollen lips, he mumbled, "Ed-Edward?"

"You'll be all right, Jeff," Edward said fervently. "If you can stand up, I'll help you get home."

Jeff moved a hand and grasped Edward's arm, his grip weak and faltering. "N-no . . ." he said. "Can't move. You . . . you'd best go . . . get Pa."

Edward's head bobbed up and down. "All right, Jeff, that's what I'll do. You just keep still." His features twisted as he added, "I-I'm sorry I didn't help."

"You did . . . the right thing," Jeff told him. "I didn't want you . . . to get hurt."

Talking seemed to be exhausting what little strength Jeff had left, so Edward told him quickly, "Just stay quiet, Jeff. I'll be back in a few minutes with Pa." He caught his brother's hand and squeezed it in what he hoped was a reassuring gesture, then stood up and sprinted as hard as he could toward the cabin, a quarter of a mile away, the wind in his face drying the few remaining tears that welled from his eyes.

"Bartholomew Holt, hold still!" Norah Holt said, her voice dissolving into laughter as she removed the scissors from the vicinity of his head. She was a petite and attractive woman, approaching middle age, and her face seemed to radiate happiness. The hem of her long skirt dusted tufts of hair along the broad floorboards, mingling Bartholomew's gray hair with that which she had just trimmed from the others in the family.

"I'll be still if you'll refrain from nicking my ears, woman," Bartholomew answered. His eyes scanned the room, stopping far to one side, where two children stood, the boy trying to smother his giggles in his hands. "You young'uns best keep away from your mama, so she doesn't slice my ears off altogether."

"Oh, you," Norah said, giving her husband's shoulder a shove.

Laughter erupted from the two youngest members of the Holt clan, seven-year-old Susan and five-year-old Jonathan, fading away a moment later as a noise from outside caught their attention. They frowned in silence. Then Jonathan ran over to open the door. Before he could tell his parents that his older brother Edward was coming, they all could hear his breathless screams.

"Oh, God," Norah cried as she followed her husband out the door. Bartholomew had jumped up immediately and after standing motionless on the porch for a few seconds, ran out to meet Edward as he raced into the yard.

Bartholomew caught his son's shoulders and demanded, "What is it, lad? What's wrong?"

"It—it's Jeff," Edward panted. "He's hurt—hurt bad, Pa!"

"An accident? Plowing?"

Edward shook his head, swallowed hard, then said, "Zach and Luther Garwood—they beat him and stabbed the mule."

Norah caught at her husband's arm. "Find out later what happened, Bartholomew! Go get Jeff!"

"We'll need the wagon," Bartholomew said, making decisions and putting them into operation with the usual crisp efficiency he displayed in a crisis. "Give me a hand hitching up the team, Edward."

Ignoring the pulse hammering in his head and the ball of sickness in his stomach, Edward did as his father commanded, helping him lead the horses from the barn and hitching them to the wagon the family used to take produce into Marietta on market days. After a few minutes, while Norah tried to calm the fears of the younger children, Bartholomew and Edward climbed onto the wagon and headed to where Jeff lay.

As he drove, Bartholomew asked Edward what had happened, and the boy gave a sketchy account of the fight between Jeff and the Garwood brothers. Bartholomew's mouth was set in a thin, angry line as he listened. His thoughts went back to the scene he had witnessed a few weeks earlier, when he had saved the young Lenape from Zach and Pete Garwood. This time Luther had been involved in the devilment rather than Pete, but Zach was there again, no doubt behind both events. All of the Garwoods bore a grudge against the Holts, but Zach seemed to be carrying the strongest hate.

Just before the wagon reached its destination, Edward suddenly blurted out, "I'm sorry, Pa! It's my fault Jeff got hurt. I should have helped him, but I didn't. I let him down."

"Nonsense," Bartholomew said without hesitation. He looked down at the boy. "Getting yourself slapped around by the Garwoods wouldn't have changed anything, and if you hadn't stayed out of sight, there wouldn't have been anyone to fetch help. Besides, from what you told me, Jeff gave a pretty good account of himself. He might not have been able to do that if he'd had to be worrying about you."

The words made sense, but Bartholomew could tell that Edward was not completely convinced. That would come with time, especially once Jeff had recovered and was able to tell Edward the same thing.

Bartholomew offered up a silent prayer that Jeff *would* recover.

A minute later he hauled back on the reins and brought the team to a stop near Jeff. Bartholomew's heart pounded as he hopped down from the wagon and hurried to his son's side. He felt a little relieved when he saw that Jeff was conscious and seemed to be breathing normally.

"Are you all right, son?" Bartholomew asked as he dropped to one knee beside Jeff. Bartholomew scowled as he realized what a ridiculous question that was. Of course Jeff was not all right; any fool could see that.

Jeff managed to summon up a slight smile. "I'm
. . . a mite under . . . the weather."

"Anything broken?"

"Don't . . . think so. Maybe a cracked rib. Hurts
when I try to . . . to breathe deep."

"Well, just lie still and don't worry. I'll take you
home, and your mother will tend to you. She'll have
you back on your feet in no time." Bartholomew hesitated a moment, then said, "This'll hurt, Jeff, but I've
got to pick you up and put you in the wagon."

"I know. Go ahead, Pa."

Bartholomew turned his head and called Edward
over. "Help me raise his shoulders, lad," he instructed. Edward knelt and gently took hold of Jeff's
shoulders, lifting them so that Bartholomew could slip
an arm around them. Bartholomew's other arm went
behind Jeff's knees, and then he straightened with a
grunt of effort echoed by a gasp of pain from Jeff.
Bartholomew's muscles had been strengthened by decades of hard work, but Jeff was dead weight at the
moment. The older man staggered a little as he carried
his son to the wagon and placed him carefully in the
back.

Edward fetched Jeff's rifle and leapt into the bed
beside Jeff. "I'll ride back here with him, Pa."

"That's fine." Bartholomew clambered up onto
the seat, grasped the reins, and quickly got the vehicle
turned around and headed back toward the cabin.

Norah had sent the younger children behind the
cabin to play while she waited in front, but Susan and
Jonathan were peeking around the corner when Bartholomew drove up. Seeing the bloody, battered form
of her son, Norah cried out in horror, but she allowed
herself only that one moment of weakness. Drawing
on the strength of will that had allowed her to survive
many years on the frontier, she said, "Bring him into
the house."

As gently and carefully as he had placed Jeff into
the wagon, Bartholomew lifted him out of it and carried him through the open door of the cabin. Norah

hurried ahead of them, saying, "Put him over here on our bed."

The bed she shared with Bartholomew was the largest one in the cabin, and it also had the most comfortable mattress. Bartholomew laid their son on the thick comforter. Norah brought a cloth and a bowl of water from the long counter on the other side of the room and began to clean the dried blood from Jeff's injuries. He moaned a little, then said thickly, "I'll be all right, Ma. Just need to . . . rest awhile."

"You'll lie there and be still and let your mother tend to you, young man," Norah said sternly. "Now be quiet."

Jeff managed a feeble grin. There was no arguing with Norah Holt when she took charge of a situation.

Bartholomew turned and found Edward standing in the doorway of the cabin. "Is he going to be all right?" the ten-year-old asked.

"I'm sure he will be." Bartholomew smiled. "Your mother wouldn't allow anything else, now, would she?" He put his hand on Edward's shoulder and led him outside. They would stay close by, in case Norah needed any help, but for the time being, Bartholomew knew it would be better to stay out of her way.

"Pa?" Edward looked up at him. "What are you going to do?"

"About what?" Bartholomew asked, although he knew all too well what Edward meant.

"About the Garwoods. They hurt Jeff. We can't let them get away with that, Pa."

Bartholomew's fingers tightened unconsciously on Edward's shoulder. "You let me worry about the Garwoods, boy. I don't want you getting any notions about having to go pay them back for what they did. That's what gets feuds started in the first place, and there's already enough bad blood 'tween them and us."

Edward stared up at him, an expression of disbelief on his face. "You mean you're not going to do anything?"

"I didn't say that," Bartholomew replied, trying not to lose his temper with the youngster. Edward was unusually mature most of the time, but he didn't yet understand all the complexities of the situation that existed between the Holts and the Garwoods. Naturally, though, he was upset by what he had witnessed, and he deserved some sort of an explanation. "I'll be paying a visit to the proper authorities," Bartholomew went on, "and telling them what happened. That's what civilized folks do when there's trouble. Ohio isn't the wild frontier that it was when your mother and I first came here, son. It's not the Northwest Territory anymore. We've got laws and men whose job it is to enforce them."

"Seems like law is too good for the likes of the Garwoods," Edward said.

Bartholomew remembered how he had been forced to take things into his own hands in the past. Perhaps the boy was right. But only after every other means had been tried to settle the problem would he exact his own justice this time, Bartholomew thought.

He squeezed Edward's shoulder again and said, "Why don't you go keep an eye on your little brother and sister for us, son? Make sure those two hellions don't get into any mischief. That's the best way you can help right now."

Edward did not look convinced, but he did as his father said and went behind the cabin to watch Susan and Jonathan.

When Norah came out a little later, she found her husband leaning against the wall, a brooding expression on his weathered face as he smoked his pipe. Instantly he straightened and looked at her intently. "How's Jeff?" he asked.

"He's sleeping now. He'll be all right, Bartholomew. He's going to be so sore and bruised he won't be able to move around much for a few days, and he may even have a cracked rib or two, as he told you, but everything will heal with plenty of rest and good food."

"You're the one to give him that," Bartholomew said with a relieved smile. His expression grew grim again as he lowered his voice and said, "Somebody's got to do something about those damned Garwoods."

"You'll be going to see the constable, I expect?"

"Aye, as soon as I've looked at the poor mule, but I doubt Jasper Sutcliffe is likely to do anything about the beating. He's never shown any inclination to cross the Garwoods before."

"They never hurt anyone this badly before," Norah pointed out.

Bartholomew knocked the dottle from his pipe and said, "Now that you've told me Jeff will be all right, do you know what the worst thing is about this whole mess?"

Norah shook her head.

"I can't totally blame Zach and Luther Garwood, or any of the Garwoods for that matter." The pipe in Bartholomew's hands trembled a bit from the depth of the emotion he was feeling. "I'm just as angry at Clay as I am at them."

"Clay!" Norah exclaimed. "Oh, Bartholomew, you know the Garwoods held a grudge against us long before any of the trouble between Clay and Josie came about. You can't—"

"I most certainly can," he interrupted. "He's the one who brought this particular evil down on our heads." His voice grew angrier as he went on. "The rest of the family is paying now for what he did, while he's off gallivanting somewhere in the wilderness."

"If he's even still alive," Norah said quietly, her voice little more than a whisper.

"Aye." Bartholomew turned his head to look westward, where their oldest son had vanished more than two years earlier. His hushed tone echoed Norah's as he repeated, "If he's even still alive . . ."

CHAPTER SIX

Jasper Sutcliffe, the constable for Marietta and the surrounding area, had an office in town. Actually, the constable's office was combined with the stable's office, which Sutcliffe operated, and although he generally took the buying and selling of horses more seriously than he did his law enforcement duties, he continued, time after time, to be elected to the position of constable. Some said this success was due to the many favors owed him by the more influential settlers, and there was probably some truth to that theory. Sutcliffe would go out of his way to help a prominent citizen, unless it required too much of an effort.

The day after Jeff's beating at the hands of Zach and Luther Garwood, Bartholomew returned home after paying a visit to Sutcliffe's office. His face was brick red from anger.

"That grinning jackanapes isn't going to do a damned thing about the Garwoods," he said as he hung his hat on the hook just inside the door. "Told me he couldn't take action just on my say-so, that he'd have to hear the story direct from Jeff."

"I don't mind telling him what happened," Jeff said from the bed, where he was propped up on several pillows. Norah was perched on the edge of the bed beside him. "Is he coming out here?"

"If he can find the time, he says," Bartholomew replied, still angry. "You know what that means. He'll never show up."

"Well, then, I'll have to go to him," Jeff said.

His mother put a hand on his shoulder as he started to lift himself into more of an upright position. "You'll do no such thing," she told him sternly. "You won't be in any shape to travel for several more days, Jefferson, and even then you shouldn't go rushing around the countryside."

"I'm not going to rush anywhere. I'm just going to town to see the constable and lodge a complaint against Zach and Luther."

"It has to be done, Norah," Bartholomew said. "Otherwise, the Garwoods will think they've gotten away with hurting our son."

"All right. But only when I say Jeff is up to it." Norah's tone made it clear that she would tolerate no argument on the subject.

Wisely, Jeff and Bartholomew went along with her. Jeff eased himself back on the pillows, glad for the excuse not to make the trip to town. In fact, the idea of sitting in a jolting saddle or wagon for several miles was almost more than he could take; actually doing it would have been an ordeal beyond imagining.

His entire body was a mass of aches and pains, mostly in his midsection, although his head was also throbbing. The slightest movement increased his discomfort. Norah had placed poultices on his bruises and wrapped strips of fabric tightly around his rib cage to keep him from moving too much, and she fed him broth, tea, and freshly baked bread. He seemed to be drawing some strength from the food, but he knew he would not soon be back to normal.

Edward spent a great deal of time in the cabin, sitting near the bed and talking to Jeff. He reassured him that the injured mule would soon be fine. Although the boy never mentioned it, Bartholomew had told Jeff about Edward's guilt. As far as Jeff was concerned, Edward hadn't done anything to feel guilty about. He had shown uncommon good sense by staying out of the fight, but when Jeff tried to tell him so, Edward just dropped his head and stared silently at the floor.

His brother's torment was just one more mark against the Garwoods, Jeff reasoned. They had gone too far with their bullying this time, and like all bullies their methods were going to backfire sooner or later. Jeff was sure that once Sutcliffe had heard his story, he would have to take action against Zach and Luther.

And if he did not, Jeff thought, perhaps it would be time for the Holts to start standing up for themselves again.

"Are you sure you want to do this by yourself, son?" Bartholomew asked anxiously. Norah stood beside him, her face mirroring the concern in her husband's voice.

"I'm sure," Jeff said as he reached up to grasp the horn of the saddle on the back of his favorite mare. "Don't worry. I'm strong enough to ride to town and back. It's only a few miles."

A week had passed since the violent encounter with Zach and Luther Garwood. The swelling had gone down from Jeff's face, and he could now move around without feeling shooting pains in his chest. Some bruises, turned sickly shades of purple and yellow, still remained, but he felt strong enough to pay a visit to Jasper Sutcliffe, and he did not want to delay it any longer.

As he swung up into the saddle, Jeff felt a slight dizziness, but he did not let on. His mother and father, his brothers and sister, had all worried enough about him during the past week. He wanted to show them that he was all right again, that they could stop being concerned about him. The best way to do that, he had decided, was to handle the visit to the constable by himself. There was indeed a good reason, he reflected, why the Holts were known for their stubbornness.

"All right." Bartholomew rested his hand on the rump of Jeff's mount. "Just be careful, and if you're not back after a bit, I'll ride out and make sure nothing's happened."

"Not too soon, I hope," Jeff bristled. "After I see Sutcliffe, I might stop at the tavern for a mug of ale." He glanced at his mother's disapproving frown. "Or I might not. I'm just saying not to come running after me like I'm a little boy, Pa."

"Aye, you're a grown man." Bartholomew handed up Jeff's loaded .45 caliber flintlock, a Kentucky rifle like his own. "But you'll always be my son, too, and don't you forget it. Now go on, if that's what you're determined to do."

Jeff gathered the reins and turned the horse's head, pointing it down the trail toward Marietta. He didn't look back as he urged it into an easy trot, but he knew his parents were watching, and Edward, Susan, and Jonathan were probably sneaking a look around the corner of the cabin, too, even though Norah had sent them to play.

The long rifle rested on the pommel of the saddle in front of him, held there by the grip of one hand. The Garwoods had served notice that the bad feeling between them and the Holts had turned more serious, perhaps deadly. Jeff was not going to take a chance of riding unarmed into an ambush.

But something was very wrong, he thought, when a man had to fear not only for his life but for his family's because of something that had not been his doing.

More than once he had heard his father express resentment for the trouble Clay had caused. Out of loyalty to his brother, Jeff had always defended Clay. Besides, he had never really believed Josie Garwood's accusations. Not that it would have been impossible for Clay to bed her; Josie was attractive enough and had been even more so a few years earlier, when she still had a certain innocence about her. Jeff knew, however, that Clay was too honorable to have deserted her if he had really fathered her child.

Or at least Jeff *hoped* that Clay was too honorable to do such a thing. Lately he had begun to wonder— and that only made him feel more disloyal.

Those gloomy thoughts were going through his head as he rode toward Marietta, studying the woods on either side of the road in front of him. So far there had been no sign of trouble. Zach and the other Garwoods had no way of knowing he was riding to town, and he didn't believe they could afford to neglect the chores on their farm to keep a constant watch on the road.

Jeff saw only a few people on the way to Marietta. He lifted a hand in greeting to those working in the fields, and he spoke to those he met on the road. The greetings he received in return ranged from warm and friendly to cool and distant—typical of the way the Holts were regarded in the area. Quite a few people— too many, in Jeff's estimation—had given credence to what Josie Garwood had to say.

When he reached the stable where Jasper Sutcliffe maintained his office, he reined in, dismounted, and tied his horse to the rail outside. He heard voices coming from inside the big, barnlike structure. Cradling the long rifle in the crook of his left arm, he stepped into the entrance and looked around for Sutcliffe.

The constable was standing ten feet away, talking to a couple of men whom Jeff recognized as loafers who could often be found talking and smoking their pipes in town rather than working the fields on their farms. The conversation between Sutcliffe and the two men came to an abrupt halt as they realized that someone else was standing there.

"Hello, Holt," he said. "Something I can do for you?"

"I want to lodge a complaint with you, Mr. Sutcliffe," Jeff said.

"Oh? You talking to me as the owner of this stable or as the constable?"

He knew the answer to that as well as any of them, and the comment drew chuckles from the two onlookers. Jeff told himself to stay calm. "As the constable, Mr. Sutcliffe. I want to report that I was attacked and beaten by Zach and Luther Garwood."

Sutcliffe rubbed his jaw. He was a stocky man, a little below medium height, with thick, dark hair and small eyes. He wore a linsey-woolsey shirt, a leather vest, whipcord breeches, and high-topped boots. "Your pa came by and mentioned something 'bout that," he said. "I've been aiming to get out your way and ask you 'bout it. Just haven't gotten 'round to it yet. But I can't take action without a complaint and direct testimony from the injured party, you know."

"Well, you've got your complaint and your direct testimony now, Mr. Sutcliffe," Jeff said. "I just told you what happened."

"Yes, you did." Sutcliffe paused, then said, "Trouble is, Zach and Luther Garwood told me almost a week ago that you jumped them."

Jeff's left hand tightened on the stock of his rifle, and his right clenched into a fist. "They're lying."

Sutcliffe shrugged. "They were pretty bruised and beat up. Luther was still hobbling around from being kicked in the, ah—family jewels." The other two men chuckled again, and Sutcliffe went on. "Zach said they was cutting across one of your fields when you came at them, pulled them off their horses, and started pounding on them."

Jeff felt his impatience and frustration starting to

get the better of him. "That's a damned lie, I tell you!" he exclaimed. "They were in our field, all right, but that's the only part of their story that's true."

For a moment Sutcliffe worried at one of his teeth with his tongue. Then he spat on the ground and said casually, "I'm afraid it's your word against theirs, Holt. And that's two to one."

"My brother Edward was there," Jeff said tightly. "He can tell you what happened."

"The boy's what . . . ten years old?" Sutcliffe shook his head. "I'm afraid I couldn't put much stock in anything he'd say. It's too easy to influence a youngster like that, get him to say whatever you want him to say."

"You mean you're not going to do anything about the Garwoods?" It was difficult for Jeff to believe that the constable could pass this matter off so lightly, but that was obviously Sutcliffe's intention.

"Look at it this way, Holt. I didn't come out to your pa's farm and arrest you on the Garwoods' say-so. I'm not going to arrest them on yours, either." Sutcliffe's voice grew harsher as he continued, "Besides, any trouble between the Holts and the Garwoods is a personal matter, and the law don't have any place in it. So leave me out of it." He gave a coarse laugh. "Your brother caused the bad blood. He's the one ought to come back and put a stop to it."

Jeff felt hollow inside. His father had warned him not to rely on Sutcliffe's doing anything to see that Zach and Luther answered for what they had done. Now Jeff could see that Bartholomew had been right. Ohio might not be the wild Northwest Territory anymore, but that did not mean it was completely civilized.

"What about trespassing?" Jeff asked suddenly, taking a new tack. "Zach and Luther admitted they were on Holt land. Why don't you arrest them for trespassing?"

"Nobody 'round here begrudges somebody cutting across their place," Sutcliffe responded with a sneer. "You don't have any crops in yet. It's just now time to start planting the winter wheat."

"You're afraid of the Garwoods, aren't you?" The angry words left Jeff's mouth before he could stop them.

Sutcliffe's already florid face grew even redder as he flushed with rage. "Here, now, you got no call to talk like that, boy! You'd best remember that I'm the law around here, and I deserve a little respect."

"Damned little, if you ask me," Jeff shot back.

The two loafers were looking on with greater interest now, curious to see how Sutcliffe would react to this affront to his authority. The constable glanced at them, and Jeff knew what Sutcliffe was thinking: He could not back down now, because if he did, the story would be all over Marietta by the end of the day.

Sutcliffe stepped forward, his fists clenched. Jeff was unsure what he would do if the man took a swing at him. He had been raised to respect authority, but not when it was being abused. Still, if he struck Sutcliffe, he could rightly expect to wind up in Marietta's new jail, a square, sturdy building constructed of thick timbers.

The tension was abruptly defused, however, by the arrival of Josie Garwood. "Jasper, I—" But the sight of Jeff Holt made her stop short.

As for Jeff, all he could do was stare as he tried to make sense of the questions brought to mind by Josie's presence. Was there more to the constable's reluctance to arrest the Garwood brothers than his dislike for the Holts? Was Sutcliffe one of the men in Marietta who sampled Josie's wares?

"I didn't know you were busy," Josie finally said.

"I don't intend to be for long. Just wait outside." Sutcliffe looked at Jeff. "You don't know when you're well-off, Holt. I ought to put you behind bars for what you did to Josie's brothers, but I'm not going to. Not if you get out of here right now and don't bother me with your petty complaints."

Nothing would be gained from pushing this fur-

ther, Jeff realized. The trip into town had been wasted.
With a bitter taste in his mouth, he drew a deep
breath. "All right," he said. "If you want us to take
care of this ourselves, that's just what we'll do." With
that, he turned on his heel and stalked out of the stable.

Sutcliffe followed him to the door. "You mind
your manners, boy," he called out as Jeff swung up
onto his mare. "You break the law, and you'll wind up
in jail, mark my words."

Jeff gave him one more scornful look, then turned
the horse and rode away, heading down Marietta's
main street.

So sick with disappointment and frustration was
he that he barely noticed the residual aches from the
beating. He was confused, unsure of what to do next.
The Holts had always been law-abiding folks, or so his
father had told him. If Jeff took his gun and went after
the Garwoods, not only would he be risking jail, but
he would also be doing something he didn't even
want to contemplate: sinking to the same level as
Zach.

He reined in as he came to a tavern owned by an
Irishman named Kevin Meaghan. Jeff had told his father he might stop for a drink, and right now that
sounded like a pretty good idea. After tying his horse
to the rail, he went into the shadowy main room of the
tavern.

Meaghan's place was not the fanciest drinking establishment in Marietta. Far from it, in fact. Built of
unpeeled logs, it had a low ceiling and a floor of
pounded dirt. The bar was a long split log set on several empty whiskey barrels. A few rough-hewn tables
and benches were scattered about, but most of the customers just stood at the bar to down their corn liquor.
Kevin Meaghan was known for making a particularly
potent brew; too much of his whiskey, it was said,
would lift the top off a man's skull.

Jeff did not intend to sample the corn liquor today; his head was not ready for that. Instead, he asked

the burly, red-bearded man behind the bar for a mug of ale. Meaghan drew it for him from a cask, and Jeff slid a coin across the log in payment. Carrying the mug, he headed for a table in the corner.

He slid behind the table and sank down on the bench next to the wall. As he sipped the dark, strong ale, he hoped the other customers in the tavern would see that he was in no mood for company and have the good sense to leave him alone.

Staring down at the table, he wondered why he could not just do like everyone else—condemn his brother Clay and have done with it. When they were younger, he and Clay had always gotten along well, Jeff having had the usual admiration of a younger brother for an older one. In Clay's case, Jeff had been convinced, that admiration was justified. Now his emotions were mixed. He wanted to continue to believe in Clay, to believe that Clay had been telling the truth when he had denied responsibility for Josie Garwood's pregnancy. But Jeff was no longer sure what to think.

He remembered the stunned look on Clay's face when Josie had come up to him in town and confronted him. Jeff had been standing right there, and he would have sworn that Clay's astonishment was that of a man who had no idea what his accuser was talking about. Perhaps Clay had just been surprised that bad luck had caught up to him. . . .

Jeff still recalled the pathetic tremble in Josie's voice as she had asked, "But you'll marry me, won't you, Clay?"

Clay had just looked at her for a moment, his face stony. "This is none of my doing," he had told her, "and I won't marry you, Josie, now or ever."

Josie had stared at him for what seemed to Jeff like an eternity, her eyes shining with tears. Then she had turned and hurried away, her shoulders slumped with defeat. Clay had just looked at Jeff, shrugged his shoulders, and assured his younger brother that Josie did not know what she was talking about.

Less than two weeks later Clay Holt had left Marietta, heading west.

Now, as the memories played out so vividly in Jeff's mind, Clay's actions did not seem like those of an innocent man. No matter what he had wanted to believe at the time, Jeff had to admit the possibility that Josie had been telling the truth.

But that was no reason for her brothers to make life miserable for all the other Holts. And why had they waited until now, nearly three years after Clay had left, to resort to violence against his family?

Lost in his thoughts, staring into his mug of ale, Jeff had not seen the four roughly dressed men enter the tavern. He didn't notice their presence until they loomed between him and the light coming through the door. A mixture of fear and anger shot through him as he glanced up and recognized the Garwood brothers.

Zach stood a little in front of the others, flanked by Pete on his left and Luther on his right. Standing just behind Luther was the youngest of the Garwoods, Aaron, who at nineteen tended to follow his brothers like a puppy, always eager to impress. He had the same slender build as Luther, but he lacked Luther's intelligence. His skin was fair, like Pete's; his hair was brown, his eyes gray. In earlier years, Aaron had been the only Garwood Jeff instinctively liked, but that had vanished with the enmity that had sprung up between the two families.

Zach spoke first. "Hear tell you've been to the constable."

"Yes, but don't worry," Jeff replied, his jaw tight. "He's not going to throw you in jail, where you belong."

"You're the one who ought to be worrying, Holt," Pete said, "attacking us the way you did."

"That's a damned lie, and you know it."

Zach shrugged and gave Jeff a smug grin. "Seemed to me like Jasper Sutcliffe believed it."

Jeff's fingers tightened around the mug; he

longed to smash it in Zach's face. "You've made your point, Garwood. The law isn't going to help the Holts. Now can't you leave a man alone and let him have a mug of ale in peace?"

The sneer spread across Zach's face. "A man, yes. But you're not a man. You're a Holt. And Holts crawl on their bellies, so you must be a worm."

This was not the first time Jeff had heard such talk. It never failed to anger him, but he controlled his fury and looked down at the table again, hoping that if he ignored the Garwoods, they would go away.

They were not going to be discouraged so easily, however. Their sole purpose in coming to the tavern had been to goad him into a fight, so they could hand him another beating. Of that he was well aware. He was also aware that in his weakened condition, he would not be able to put up much of a struggle. He continued to stare at the table, saying nothing.

Suddenly Pete swore and stepped forward, grasping the side of the table opposite Jeff. Muscles bunched in Pete's broad shoulders as he heaved upward.

Jeff leaned back sharply as the table came up at his face. "Look out, you fool! You'll turn it over!"

But that, of course, was exactly what Pete intended. Jeff threw himself backward as the table rose and came crashing toward him. Jerking his legs out of the way, he rolled off the bench and landed on the tavern's dirt floor, flinging up an arm in a futile attempt to ward off the heavy table, which could easily crush him.

His proximity to the log wall was all that saved him. As the table overturned, it struck the logs and wedged itself between two of them, forming an angle with Jeff underneath it. He scrambled out before the table could slip and collapse on him, emerging just in time to catch a punch on the jaw from Zach, who had been waiting for him. The blow drove Jeff against the rear wall of the tavern.

His head was ringing, and he vaguely heard

Kevin Meaghan shouting at the Garwoods, telling them to take their trouble outside if they had to fight. Zach and his brothers ignored the tavern keeper and closed in around Jeff. All four of them had their fists cocked, ready to pummel him into unconsciousness— or worse.

A sudden blast of exploding black powder filled the room, and not even the Garwoods were able to ignore that, especially when a ball tore through Zach's hat, plucking it from his head. The ball whined past to thud into the wall.

"If you've got a fight with anybody, it's with me, Garwood," Clay Holt announced from the doorway of the tavern.

Zach and the others whirled around. Jeff steadied himself against the wall, then leaned to the side to peer, thunderstruck, around his opponents.

All of them saw a tall, dangerous-looking dark-haired man, armed not only with the .54 caliber Harper's Ferry rifle he had just fired but also with a brace of North and Cheney flintlock pistols, which were tucked in the broad belt around his waist. An Indian tomahawk hung from the belt as well, a long-bladed hunting knife sheathed beside it. Clay was wearing buckskins and a coonskin cap, and two powder horns were hanging from a strap slung over his shoulder. With his sunburned skin and wilderness garb, he probably looked more Indian than white in the eyes of so-called civilized men. He certainly looked savage as he glared at the Garwoods with murderous fury.

"Clay!" Jeff exclaimed, and at the same moment Zach yelled, "You bastard!" Zach moved first, ignoring Jeff as he lunged toward Clay, cursing and swinging a roundhouse blow.

Easily avoiding the wild punch, Clay stepped nimbly to the side and drove the butt of his rifle into Zach's side as Zach, off-balance, stumbled past him. But that move gave Pete enough time to reach Clay, and the biggest Garwood slammed a hamlike fist into

Clay's chest. The blow staggered Clay, and Pete followed up quickly, moving with surprising speed for a man of his size.

Jeff started forward to help his brother. He was shocked at Clay's unexpected reappearance, but there would be time to ask questions later. What mattered now was making sure that Pete Garwood did not beat him to death.

Before Jeff could reach Clay's side, however, strong hands grabbed him and hauled him to a stop. Luther Garwood jerked him around, and Jeff saw Luther's fist coming toward his face. Jeff let himself sag in the grip of Luther's other hand, moving his head to the side just enough to let the blow pass harmlessly. Stepping closer to Luther, Jeff drove a fist into his stomach, and breath laden with whiskey fumes spewed out into Jeff's face. Jeff shoved Luther aside. He saw Pete still throwing a flurry of punches at Clay.

"Come back here, dammit!" That cry came from Aaron Garwood, who jumped on Jeff's back and wrapped his arms around him. Jeff felt himself falling. He tripped over a bench beside another table and went down heavily, Aaron tumbling over with him, clawing at Jeff's face.

Jeff was able to get his elbow up and snap it into Aaron's throat. The younger man gagged and turned pale, and his grip on Jeff loosened. Jeff rolled away and got to his feet, wincing at the pain shooting through his side. He knew that the ribs he had cracked in the previous fight might well cause even more serious damage by puncturing a lung, yet he could not let Clay face the Garwoods alone.

As Aaron was trying to get to his feet, Jeff brought a foot up and kicked him in the stomach, feeling a little guilty about doing it even as the blow landed. With two-to-one odds, however, fighting fair had to be the least of his concerns. Survival was all he had time to worry about.

Even as Aaron rolled away, clutching at his stomach and mewling in pain, Luther joined the fight again. He brought his fists down on the back of Jeff's neck, staggering him. Jeff stumbled forward and collided with someone, his fingers catching the sleeve of a buckskin jacket in an effort to stay upright. As he lifted his head he found himself staring into the eyes of his brother at a distance of less than six inches.

A trickle of blood was running from one corner of Clay's mouth, and his left eye was starting to swell shut. But he simply said, "Howdy, Jeff. It's good to be home."

Jeff did not have time to reply. Movement over Clay's shoulder caught his eye, and when he glanced in that direction, he saw Pete Garwood holding a keg of whiskey above his head as he advanced, ready to smash it down on Clay's head. "Look out!" Jeff yelled as he pushed Clay aside and dove the other way himself.

Pete stumbled over them and fell, landing on the keg, which shattered, spreading a pool of whiskey around the fallen Pete. The pungent smell of the spilled liquor cut through the fog threatening to engulf Jeff's brain. More alert now, he ducked out of the way as Zach Garwood swung a punch at his head.

The tavern's other patrons had headed for the door when the fight broke out, and now the Holt brothers and the Garwoods were the only ones in the place except for the owner. Meaghan stood behind the bar, still shouting at the combatants, who continued to ignore him.

Jeff found himself back to back with Clay, who was holding a broken timber from one of the benches. Jeff had not noticed when the bench had been broken, having had his own hands full, but Clay was whipping the length of wood back and forth in a deadly motion. The Garwoods, not wanting to challenge him, all charged at Jeff instead—all except Aaron, who was still out of the fight.

Jeff blocked a couple of blows, but too many came for him to ward them all off. Fists cracked against his jaw, and he started to go down again until Clay caught him under the arm with a hand. With the makeshift club in his other hand, Clay lashed out at the Garwoods. The wood smashed against Zach's right shoulder, making him fall back. Clay next jabbed the cudgel at Pete's solar plexus, but the big man blocked the thrust, his hand closing over the club in an attempt to wrest it away.

Clay brought up a foot shod in a calf-high moccasin. When it landed in Pete's groin, the big man screeched, releasing the club. Clay whipped it across his face, laying open a wicked gash in Pete's left cheek. Pete backed off, shaking his head and bellowing. Drops of blood sprayed from the cut on his face.

Features pale with pain, Zach stood back, too, holding his injured shoulder. His right arm hung limp and useless at his side. Pete was out of the fight for the moment, and so was Aaron. That left Luther, and when Clay lifted the club and turned toward him, saying, "Come on, get your share, too," Luther flinched away from him and shook his head.

"Zach!" Luther cried. "Dammit, Zach, what do we do now?"

"Bastard near broke my shoulder." Zach was trembling with a mixture of suffering and rage as he looked at Clay. "Get him!"

Still Luther hesitated, and Clay smiled grimly as he put an end to the discussion. He dropped the club and drew both pistols from his belt, cocking and leveling them at the Garwoods, who were huddled together on the other side of the room.

"This fight is over," Clay declared. "Now get the hell out of here, all four of you, and don't let me catch you bothering my brother or any of my family again. Because I'll kill you if you do. You understand me, Zach?"

For a moment Zach made no reply, but then his mouth twisted bitterly. "I understand, Holt. But this ain't over yet. You should've stayed in the mountains, you bastard. You'll be sorry you came back here."

"Maybe I already am." Clay gestured toward the doorway with the pistols. "Get moving."

Kevin Meaghan had crouched down behind the bar when Clay drew his pistols. Lifting himself only far enough to peek over the barrel behind which he had concealed himself, he called out, "Wait a minute! What about the damage to my place? You fellas busted up my tables and benches!"

"What about it, Zach?" Clay asked. "Since you and your brothers started this little ruckus, seems like you ought to pay for it."

"This is robbery, goddamned robbery," Zach growled. But he went on, "Luther, pay Meaghan for the damage."

"Never mind," Clay commanded. "I enjoyed that so much, I'll take care of the charges myself. Just get out." His upper lip curled in contempt. "I don't think I can take the smell anymore."

The Garwoods slunk out of the tavern. Zach walked by himself, his back straight despite the pain etched on his face. Pete had to be assisted by Luther and Aaron, who was still hunched over and gasping for breath himself.

As they left, Jeff felt light-headed, and the room was spinning. He was aware that Clay was turning toward him, but he was unable to reply when Clay said, "Well, that was a mighty unfriendly welcome—"

He broke off, seeing how weak Jeff was. Clay hastily tucked away one of his pistols so that he could grasp his brother's arm. "Come on," he said to Jeff. "Let's get you sitting down."

Clay helped Jeff to one of the benches. The tavern's customers, who had left when the brawl broke out, filtered back in. Clay put away his other gun, retrieved the rifle he had dropped near the doorway, and then sat down next to Jeff. "Are you all right, Jeff?" he asked anxiously. "Did those skunks hurt you worse than I thought?"

Jeff rested his palms on the table and took deep breaths, and gradually his head cleared a little. The ache deep in his side was still there, however. "That wasn't my first run-in with the Garwoods lately, Clay. Zach and Luther beat me pretty bad about a week ago."

"Damn!" Clay exclaimed between gritted teeth. "Have they been after you ever since I left?"

Jeff shook his head. "No, not really. Zach has never been one to let an insult go unsaid, but he's only recently taken to violence. Pa heard yesterday that the Garwood property is in danger of being taken for unpaid taxes, so I guess that could be the reason Zach's going over the edge."

"I knew I should have shot the sons of bitches!"

"I'll be all right," Jeff told him. "I'm getting my breath back now. I just wish I'd quit running into them when they're looking for trouble."

"As soon as you feel up to it, I'll help you get home. You reckon Ma and Pa will be surprised to see me?"

"About as surprised as I was," Jeff replied, not adding that their parents might not be completely happy Clay had returned. Oh, they would be glad to see their oldest son, right enough; but Clay's presence might aggravate the already bad situation with the Garwoods.

After a moment of silence, Clay said, "Well, you could say you're glad to see me. It's been a hell of a long time, after all."

Jeff smiled wearily and held out his hand. "It's good to have you home, Clay."

The brothers clasped hands, and at that moment Jasper Sutcliffe came into the tavern. The constable pushed back the beaver hat on his head and watched Meaghan cleaning up the debris from the broken benches. "I was told there was some trouble over here. Now I see the proof of it." Sutcliffe glowered at Clay. "I'm a mite surprised you ever came back to these parts, Holt, but I'm not surprised that you've already caused some new trouble."

Clay shook his head. "It's old trouble, Constable,

and I didn't cause it. I just got here in time to stop Zach Garwood and his brothers from attacking my brother—for the second time in a week."

"Yes, I heard about that," Sutcliffe said. "The Garwoods tell a different story. No doubt if I asked them what happened here, their account would be different from yours."

"No doubt," Clay agreed dryly.

The constable looked over at the tavern keeper. "Have you been paid for damages, Kevin?"

"Not yet," Meaghan said sullenly. "Clay Holt agreed to take care of it, though."

"And so I will," Clay declared. "Will a couple of eagles be enough?"

Meaghan scratched his freckled, balding scalp. "I reckon so," he said after a moment.

Clay took a pair of ten-dollar gold pieces from a small buckskin pouch slung over his shoulder next to one of the powder horns. He flipped each of the coins in turn to Meaghan, who plucked them deftly out of the air, then slipped them into his pocket.

"You satisfied now, Constable?" Clay asked. "My brother's not feeling very well, and I'd like to take him home."

"All right," Sutcliffe said grudgingly. "I don't want you making a habit of brawling here in Marietta, though, Holt. If that's what you plan on doing, you might as well head back west right now."

"I didn't come looking for trouble. I just want to visit my family."

"Pay your visit, then, and get out of these parts as soon as you can. If there's another disturbance, I'll come looking for you."

Clay did not respond to the threat. He sat at the table next to Jeff, stonily regarding the constable. After a moment, Sutcliffe cleared his throat, turned, and stalked out of the place.

Jeff's head was clearer now, and he said, "I think I'm up to traveling now. My horse is outside."

"So's mine," Clay said. He stood up, grasping

Jeff's arm to assist him to his feet. "Let's go see the rest of the family."

As they left the tavern, Jeff was grateful for Clay's grip on his arm, just as he had been glad Clay showed up when he had. After untying the horses, Clay helped Jeff onto his mount, then swung up on his own.

"Remember the way home from here?" Jeff asked.

"I haven't been gone *that* long," Clay replied. "If you were feeling a mite stronger, I'd challenge you to a race."

Jeff said, "Another day."

"I'll hold you to that. Now, come along."

As he fell in beside Clay on the road leading out of Marietta, Jeff glanced over at his older brother and studied him quickly. Clay had not really changed much; he had always favored buckskins, so his outfit was similar to what he had worn growing up. He was more heavily armed now, of course, and he had not sported a coonskin cap when he left Ohio. The main difference, Jeff decided, was in the lean, hard angles of Clay's face, visible even under his beard. Wherever he had been for the past few years, time had toughened him. Most men would think twice now before crossing Clay Holt.

The trouble was, Zach Garwood was not like most men. Zach would never forget a grudge or forgive an injury, real or imagined, and now that his family was in danger of losing the farm, Zach's penchant for vengeance was growing more and more out of control.

As much as he had missed Clay, Jeff thought, it might have been best if the oldest Holt son had never come home.

PART II

After smoking for some time, Captain Clark gave a small medal to the Chayenne [sic] chief, and explained at the same time the meaning of it. He seemed alarmed at this present, and sent for a robe and a quantity of buffalo-meat, which he gave to Captain Clark, and requested him to take back the medal; for he knew that all white people were "medicine," and was afraid of the medal, or of anything else which the white people gave to the Indians. Captain Clark then repeated his intention in giving the medal, which was the medicine his great father had directed him to deliver to all chiefs who listened to his word and followed his counsels; and that as he [the chief] had done so, the medal was given as a proof that we believed him sincere. He now appeared satisfied and received the medal, in return for which he gave double the quantity of buffalo-meat he had offered before. He seemed now quite reconciled to the whites, and requested that some traders might be sent among the Chayennes [sic], who lived, he said, in a country full of beaver, but did not understand well how to catch them, and were discouraged from it by having no sale for them when caught. Captain Clark promised that they should be soon supplied with goods and taught the best mode of catching beaver.

—from "The History of the Lewis and Clark Expedition"

CHAPTER SEVEN

As Clay Holt had told his brother, he had not been away from home for so long that he had forgotten the way. He also recalled the landmarks along the road, confirming with Jeff the names of the families who lived in the farmhouses they passed. In a few cases the names were different—people had died or moved. And some of the stands of trees that Clay remembered were gone, too, cleared away to make more fields for crops. But by and large, Ohio had not really changed much.

Indeed, Clay felt as if he had come home at last, after his long sojourn in the wilderness. The only trouble was that the hatred the Garwoods felt for him and his family had not changed either.

After the Holt brothers had ridden for a while, Jeff commented, ''You really look like you came out of the wilderness, Clay.''

''What makes me look different from other folks around here? Lots of people wear buckskins.''

''Yes, but they don't go around armed for battle.''

Patting the stock of his rifle, Clay said, ''This flintlock went over the Rockies and back with me. It was made for the expedition at the government armory and arsenal in Harper's Ferry, Virginia. You won't find a truer gun."

Jeff admired the rifle. "It's a beauty."

"I thought you'd like it." Clay turned in the saddle and reached for another rifle tied behind his bedroll. "This one's for you. It's not quite the same as mine. They're both model 1803s, fifty-four calibers, but mine is full-stocked and has sling swivels. The ones the armory made after equipping the expedition don't. Other than that they're alike."

Jeff took the rifle from his brother and examined the flintlock mechanism. Then he sighted an imaginary target in the distance, cocked the rifle, and pulled the trigger on the empty weapon. "I surely do thank you, Clay." He looked over at his brother. "I surely do."

Jeff pointed at the pistols tucked under Clay's belt. "Did you carry those on the expedition, too?"

"Yes. It's a rough land out there, Jeff. A man usually needs all the advantages he can get. Remember that if you ever go west."

Jeff shook his head. "That's not very likely."

"A man never knows," Clay said, and then they rode on in silence.

When they came in sight of the Holt cabin, Clay felt a peculiar tightness across his chest, and his pulse pounded a bit faster. He would not have thought that just seeing the old homeplace would affect him like that, but there was no denying what he felt.

Susan and Jonathan were playing in front of the cabin, while off to the side Edward was splitting wood for kindling. Norah was next to the front door, working at the churn, and Bartholomew had just emerged from the barn out back and was dusting off his hands after forking some hay from the loft into the stalls for the milk cows. The first one to notice the two approaching riders was Jonathan, who looked up and announced, "There's Jeff coming back! Who's that with him?" His young voice carried clearly in the still air.

"That's Clay!" Susan squealed. She started toward them at a run, her long blond hair bouncing on her shoulders, and Edward followed her, dropping his ax and calling Clay's name. Both of them remembered their oldest brother, although Susan's memories of him were rather faint. Jonathan had been only a toddler when Clay left.

Norah stood up and called Bartholomew, and when he was at her side, she put an arm around his waist and hugged him. From that distance Clay could not read the expressions on either of their faces, but he knew they were watching him intently.

Something, perhaps their stiff stance, told him they were not completely glad to see him.

Susan threw herself at him after he had drawn rein in front of the cabin and dismounted. Jonathan hung back a little; he did not really remember Clay, and the appearance of this tall, buckskin-clad stranger was a little forbidding. As for Edward, he was as excited as Susan, but his determination to act mature made him hesitate, too.

Clay put his arms around Susan and lifted her in a hug. "Hello," he said. "Who might you be?"

She looked at him in horror, her brown eyes wide. "Clay! Don't you remember me? I'm your sister!"

"Nope." He shook his head. "My sister's a little girl, not a young lady like you. Her name's Susan. You know her?"

"I'm Susan!"

"Can't be." Clay pretended to study her with great intensity. "Well, now that you mention it, I reckon I see a little resemblance. . . . By golly, I think you *are* Susan!" With that, he hugged her tightly and patted her back.

After he had placed her on her feet again, he looked over at Jonathan, who was watching Clay shyly but with great interest. "And who's this? Can't be little Jonathan!"

"I *am* Jonathan," the boy said firmly. "Who're you?"

"Your brother Clay."

"I don't remember you."

"Well, I remember you, sprout," Clay said gently as he stepped over to Jonathan and knelt in front of the lad. He ruffled Jonathan's brown hair and then held out his big palm. "Why, I recollect when you weren't much bigger'n my hand. You've grown a mite since then."

"You're really my brother?" Jonathan asked. Clay nodded solemnly. The boy threw his arms around Clay's neck.

Clay returned the hug, then stepped over to greet Edward. Sensing that the ten-year-old wanted to be regarded as a grown-up, Clay extended his hand and said, "Hello, Edward. Good to see you again."

Edward shook Clay's hand, Clay's fingers all but swallowing his. Then his resolve broke and, throwing his arms around Clay's waist, he said, "I'm glad you're home."

"I'm glad to be here," Clay replied, completely sincere.

Turning at last to his parents, he saw that Jeff had dismounted and was speaking to them in a low voice. Clay had a pretty good idea what his brother was telling them about—the fight with the Garwoods in Meaghan's tavern.

Clay could tell from the stern expressions on his parents' faces that they intended to take a hard line with him. Norah's resolve proved as fleeting as Edward's, however, and as Clay smiled at her and said "Hello, Ma," her eyes began to shine with tears.

She stepped forward and clasped both his hands. "You—you look good, Clay," she said, her voice trembling a little but still under control. "How are you?"

"I'm fine, Ma," he replied. "Never better."

That was stretching the truth a mite—he had some aches and pains from the brawl in the tavern, and he could already feel civilization starting to close in on him like the bars of a cage—but he supposed a little lie was allowable under the circumstances. He held his mother's hands for a moment, then turned to his father. "How're you doing, Pa?"

"Tolerable." Bartholomew slapped his oldest son on the shoulder. "You look like the mountains were good to you, lad."

Clay said, "How'd you know I went to the mountains? There're other places in the West."

"When you were little, you always talked about seeing what was on the other side of the mountains," Bartholomew told him. "I just figured you wound up there."

"You figured right, Pa. I've been to the Pacific Ocean with Lewis and Clark."

The whole family had gathered around him, and with this news they all gaped in surprise. The Lewis and Clark expedition had been the talk of the territory, ever since word had come several weeks back concerning the safe arrival of the party in St. Louis. Even those settlers who had no wanderlust and were perfectly content to remain right where they were, found their curiosity inflamed by the discoveries made by Lewis and Clark. With the Louisiana Purchase the country had doubled in size, but most citizens had not felt those vast new lands were really theirs until Americans had begun their explorations. Now it was only a matter of time, most folks agreed, until all the new territory was opened up for settlement.

"You're going to have to tell us all about it, son," Bartholomew said.

"But after we've had some supper," Norah added quickly. "You've come a long way. You must be hungry."

"I could eat," Clay admitted. "Boudins are mighty good, but if I remember right, they can't hold a patch to your cooking, Ma."

"Boudins?" Edward echoed. "What are boudins?"

Clay grinned. "Buffalo guts. You cook them over a campfire. They make fine eating."

Edward looked a bit queasy. "I'll take your word for it, Clay," he said, and that drew a laugh from the others.

They went inside together, and for the first time in almost three years, the Holt family was complete.

Even if Norah Holt had not been a good cook—and she was—Clay would have enjoyed the meal prepared by his mother. Roasted ears of corn, turnip greens, squash, and squirrel stew; fresh johnnycake, still warm from the oven with molasses poured over it; cups of milk that had been cooling in the root cellar all day—it was a feast compared to some of the meals he had been forced to make do with since leaving home. Clay ate heartily, putting away as much by himself as his sister and brothers combined.

"Doesn't look like your trip hurt your appetite any," Bartholomew commented dryly as Clay reached for yet another piece of johnnycake.

"Can't get chuck like this in the mountains," Clay replied around a mouthful of food.

"My, how you talk now!" Norah said. "You've turned into a backwoodsman, Clay."

He shrugged. "It's not a bad life."

"Are you going back to it?" Jeff asked. He had been fairly silent during the meal.

Clay hesitated, aware that the younger children were looking intently at him. They were glad to have him back, and they would be disappointed if he said he did not intend to stay long. "Don't know," he said finally. "Have to wait and see."

"I hope you stay, at least for a while," Edward said, and Susan and Jonathan agreed enthusiastically. As he watched and listened to them, Clay only now realized how much he had missed them.

After the meal Bartholomew got a small blaze going in the fireplace to ward off the autumn chill. He and Norah sat in their usual rocking chairs, while the rest of the family found places on the floor. Clay sank down cross-legged in front of the fire and spent the next hour telling them about his adventures with Lewis and Clark. For the sake of the younger children, he glossed over or left out some of the more unsuitable details—such as the overly friendly, even amorous welcome the explorers had gotten from some of the Indian women they encountered—concentrating instead on describing the great plains, the majestic mountains, the streams, the trees, and the Pacific itself. The word picture he painted of their first glimpse of the mighty ocean, rolling out of a mist in thunderous waves that crashed on rocky shores, held all of them enthralled.

Finally, when Clay was finished, Bartholomew rocked in his chair, puffed on his pipe, and said, "You've beheld a lot of things these old eyes will never see for themselves, son. But listening to you, I feel I've been there and heard those waves and felt the mist on my face." He swallowed hard. "Thank you, Clay."

"You're welcome, Pa," Clay said quietly. Norah leaned over, rested a hand on his shoulder, and squeezed. Clay looked over at Jeff, and Jeff smiled.

The young ones began to bubble over with questions again, and Clay spent another hour answering the ones he could. At last Norah put a stop to it, telling Edward, Susan, and Jonathan to say good night and head up to the loft. They were reluctant to go, of course; they would have been willing to stay up all night if Clay had continued spinning yarns, but Norah was firm. Susan and Jonathan hugged Clay's neck, and Edward shook hands with him again, and they scrambled up the ladder pegs that led to the loft. For a short time there was some rustling around from up there as the three youngsters settled down on their straw mattresses, but gradually they grew quiet.

"I reckon they're asleep and we can talk plain," Bartholomew said after a few more minutes. "Clay, as glad as I am to see you again, boy, your coming back here is liable to cause some real problems."

"I know," Clay said. "I suppose Jeff told you about what happened at the tavern this afternoon."

"Yes, he did. It's a stroke of luck neither of you was hurt worse than you were."

Clay said, "The Garwoods got the worst of it."

Bartholomew leaned forward, a frown on his lean face. "That's not the point, son, and you know it. Just because you managed to whip the Garwoods this time doesn't mean you will the next time. And it doesn't mean that Zach won't do some fool thing like try to ambush you or Jefferson one fine day, either." He sat back, stuck the pipe in his mouth, and puffed furiously on it in his agitation. Norah reached over and patted his knee, but the gesture did not seem to calm him much.

"I know you're just worried about the family, Pa, and I can't blame you for that," Clay said. "Didn't want the kids to know about it yet, but I'm not planning to stay very long. I just wanted to see all of you again and let you know I was still alive. I'll be heading back in a few days."

"So soon?" Norah bit her lip for a second, then went on, "I'm as worried about all this trouble as your father is, Clay. You don't know how bad things have gotten—"

"He ought to have a pretty good idea," Jeff interrupted. He turned to Clay and said, "Zach Garwood's got it in for all us Holts now, and the others let him pretty much lead the way. None of them have the gumption to go against him. I reckon he'd like to see all of us dead."

Clay looked at his brother for a long, awkward moment, then broke the silence by saying, "Because of me, you mean."

"Because of that business with you and Josie Garwood. You know that's what started it."

"Dammit!" Clay suddenly exploded. He flashed a glance of contrition at his mother and muttered,

"Sorry, Ma. It's just that there wasn't any business with me and Josie Garwood. Never has been, never will be. It was all in that gal's head."

"I believed that for a long time, Clay," Jeff said. "I still want to."

"But you don't, is that it?" Clay challenged him. He was angry now, and he had to make an effort to keep his voice down. He did not want to wake up the children and have them overhear any of this.

Before Jeff could answer, Bartholomew said, "Listen, Clay. You're our son and Jeff's brother. Naturally we want to believe you. But you've got to admit, it looked mighty bad the way you ran off right after Josie said you were . . . that you had—"

"We all know what Josie said," Clay replied heavily. "But it was lies, every bit of it. Maybe she deluded herself into believing what she was saying, I don't know. But I do know I'm not that baby's pa! Shoot, I don't even know if it's a boy or a girl."

"A little boy," Norah said softly. "With dark eyes and dark hair. He's really a very sturdy child."

"But not mine." Clay got to his feet, uncoiling from his cross-legged position with the grace he had learned from watching dozens of Indians do the same thing. "If my being here is going to cause that much trouble, maybe I should just leave tonight."

Norah reached out and caught his hand. "No!" she said fervently. "You can't go yet, not when you just got here."

Clay looked over at Bartholomew. "Pa? What do you think?"

Bartholomew's brow was creased with concern, but he said slowly, "I don't want you to go either, son. For too long a time we didn't even know if you were dead or alive. I won't tell you not to go back west. I know we couldn't hold you now, not when you've been there already and seen the things you've seen. But we'd like for you to stay here for a while first."

That left Jeff, the one who had suffered the most in recent weeks because of the grudge held by the

Garwoods. Clay met his brother's eyes. "What about you, Jeff?"

"You ought to know better than that, Clay. I'm not afraid of the Garwoods, and I didn't think you were, either."

Clay held out a hand. Jeff took it, and Clay helped him to his feet. "All right," he said, clasping Jeff's forearm in the manner of Indians making a pact. "I'll stay for a spell. And if the Garwoods give us trouble, we'll give it right back to them."

Jeff nodded in agreement. Bartholomew and Norah, however, still looked worried, and Clay didn't miss their expressions of deep concern.

Later, Clay and Jeff climbed into the loft to sleep with the children, and Clay felt another surge of nostalgia as he stretched out on a thin mattress and pulled a quilt over him. Moonlight shone through the oiled paper in the single small window, and he could hear the wind blowing gently, along with the occasional hoot of an owl and the rustling of small animals in the brush. He had spent most of the nights of his childhood in the loft, warm and secure in the knowledge that his parents were down below to take care of any problems that might arise.

Then he had grown up and realized that some problems were beyond even the capabilities of parents to solve. A man had to take care of his own troubles, although they might not always be his fault.

The friction between the Holts and the Garwoods had always been there, but it hadn't been a problem until Josie had spread her lies. Maybe now it was time she finally told the truth and ended it. As he lay there listening to Jeff's deep, regular breathing and struggling with the problem of the Garwoods, Clay's determination grew.

Before he left Ohio, he would pay a visit to Josie Garwood and convince her that she could put a stop to all the trouble before it turned even more deadly. She had to listen to reason. If she didn't, Clay thought grimly, there was no telling just how bad the situation might end up.

At breakfast the next morning, over bacon and more johnnycake, Bartholomew said, "As long as you're here, Clay, I could use a hand getting that big stump out of the north field."

"Is that still there?" Clay asked. "I figured you'd have had it pulled up by now."

Jeff reached for more bacon and said, "We've just begun work on it again. We have almost all the roots chopped through. It's been slow going, though, since I've been laid up." He hated to admit that, just as he had hated the long days of recuperating from his injuries while his father and Edward kept the farm going. They had been forced to finish the plowing and the sowing of the winter wheat by themselves. Not that the work was too much for Bartholomew and Edward; Jeff just didn't like being unable to do his share.

"Sure, I'd be glad to help," Clay said. "I've got my 'hawk, so we won't have to take turns with the ax."

"I'll come along, too," Jeff declared.

Norah turned a concerned look toward him. "Are you sure that's a good idea? After that trouble yesterday, when you were barely healed up from the last time—"

"I'll be all right, Ma," Jeff told her, and he meant it. He had some painful bruises, but his ribs had stopped hurting and he felt limber enough that morning. "No reason for me not to lend a hand."

"Well, if you're sure . . ." she said dubiously.

"I'll keep an eye on him and make certain he doesn't do too much," Bartholomew told his wife.

Jeff felt a tingle of resentment. They were talking about him as if he were some sort of child who had to be looked after. Clay had been home less than twenty-four hours, and already Jeff was the little brother again. He swallowed that feeling and concentrated on his food.

When the meal was over, everyone went outside, and Bartholomew got his ax from the barn. The men headed for the north field, while Norah and the children did chores around the cabin. Jeff took his new Harper's Ferry rifle with him in case of trouble. The Garwoods were not the only threat to be considered. Wild animals were not as common in the area as they had once been, but the settlers still had to keep an eye out for occasional bears, bobcats, and the like.

The stump was all that was left of a massive oak tree. It had been sitting in the middle of the field for years, frustrating Bartholomew's efforts to remove it. Not even mules had been able to pull it up, so eventually Bartholomew had decided to dig down around it, cutting its extensive network of roots, some of which were almost as thick as young trees themselves. The process was long and laborious.

Only a few clouds dotted the sky that morning, and the sun was surprisingly warm as Bartholomew and Clay climbed down into the trench that had been dug around the stump. They began to work, Bartholomew chopping at the roots on one side with his ax, Clay using his tomahawk on the other. It was not long before the faces of both men were beaded with sweat. Clay had to bend over to use the short-handled tomahawk, and its edge was not as keen as that of the ax, so he had the more difficult job. Jeff watched him for a while, then finally said, "Here, let me spell you at that."

Clay shook his head. "I'm all right. This is easier than paddling a canoe from dawn to dark."

"You know, I'm perfectly capable of using that 'hawk, if that's what you're worried about."

Clay glanced up at him. "I didn't say I was worried. I just don't need any help right now."

"No, you never did, did you?" The sharp words were out of Jeff's mouth before he could stop them. He turned and stalked a few feet away, aware that Clay was watching him. His back turned to the stump, Jeff stood there, watching the woods at the edge of the field, listening to the steady, rhythmic *ka-chunk*! of his father's ax.

After a few moments Clay came up beside Jeff and held out the tomahawk. "Here," he said. "I reckon you're right. I could use a break."

Jeff did not say anything. He knew that Clay was only trying to make peace and that he himself was acting like a spoiled brat. But he took the tomahawk and went back to the stump. He jumped into the trench and leaned over to hack at the thick, twining roots.

Bartholomew paused to wipe sweat from his forehead and out of his eyes. "Indian summer," he said. "I've never seen it fail. Just when you think winter's coming in, the days get hot again."

Jeff hacked away at the tough, tangled roots, working at a fast pace. The air grew warmer as the sun rose higher, and soon the sweat running into his eyes blurred his vision, but stubbornly he continued. He knew he was pushing himself too hard, but he kept at it anyway, until Clay practically had to rip the tomahawk from his hands. A wave of dizziness passed through Jeff as he climbed out of the trench and sat on the ground. His head quickly got back to normal, and although he was breathing hard and was drenched with perspiration, he felt pretty good. *Nothing wrong with the weariness of good, honest labor*, he thought.

Bartholomew had intended to spend only the morning working on the stump, but when they returned to the cabin for the noon meal, he suggested they return to the field after they had eaten. "We're close, boys. I can sense it," he said. "We're going to have that stump out of there by nightfall."

"I hope so, but I wouldn't count on it," Clay said. "It's more stubborn than a grizzly bear."

"So am I," Bartholomew said.

Edward, Susan, and Jonathan took advantage of the opportunity to ask Clay more questions about his adventures, and between bites of food he supplied them with stories. Clay usually played down his own part in the yarns, Jeff noticed, but he would have been willing to wager that Clay had been right in the middle of any trouble the Lewis and Clark expedition encountered. That was just Clay's way. Jeff felt a twinge of remorse for his childish outburst earlier at his brother.

After they were finished eating, the men headed for the north field again, Bartholomew carrying the ax, Clay his 'hawk, and Jeff the flintlock rifle. They set to work as soon as they arrived, and by the middle of the afternoon, Bartholomew's optimism was rewarded. All the roots were cut through except the huge taproot directly under the stump.

"Go back to the cabin and fetch a team of mules," Bartholomew commanded Jeff as he sat resting on the edge of the trench. "We'll pull this thing over to where we can get at that main root better."

Leaving the rifle with them, Jeff hurried back to the cabin and soon returned with a pair of harnessed mules and plenty of rope. Bartholomew and Clay quickly wound the rope around the stump, Clay lying on the floor of the trench to pass the rope under the stump as well, and when it was secure, Bartholomew took the other end to the mules to hook to the harnesses.

After picking up the ax his father had left lying on the ground, Jeff slid into the trench and stood beside Clay. "You handle the mules, Pa," he called to Bartholomew. "Clay and I can take care of this root."

Clay looked over at him. "I figured you'd handle the mules," he said.

"Well, you figured wrong." Jeff was tired, bone tired, but he wanted to be in on the completion of this chore.

Bartholomew hauled on the mules' harnesses, shouting at the animals and pulling until he got them moving. The rope around the stump grew taut. With a groan the stump began to move, a fraction of an inch at a time at first and then farther. After several minutes of straining, the mules jerked forward as the bulk of the stump lifted up and pulled to the side, exposing more of the taproot.

"Hold 'em, Pa!" Clay shouted, and he bent to work, chopping at the taproot with the tomahawk.

"That'll take too long," Jeff told him. He lifted the ax. "Stand back!" He waited until Clay stepped out of the way, then brought the ax down in a sweeping motion, all the strength of his back and shoulders behind it. The blade bit deeply into the thick root.

Jeff chopped at the root several more times, making a little more progress with each blow. Then, between strikes, Clay reached out and grasped the ax handle. "I'll take it now," he said, his voice quiet but firm. Jeff thought about arguing, but then he relented. Clay had a right to do his part, Jeff thought. Clay had been fighting the stump all day, too.

Smoothly, as if he were merely chopping wood for a fire, Clay raised the ax and let it fall again and again. As he watched the blade cleaving the stubborn fibers of the root, Jeff realized just how strong Clay really was. He could probably use the ax like that all day without getting too tired.

Then the remaining strands of the root began to tear. "She's letting go!" Jeff called to his brother. "Watch out, Clay!"

Giving the root one final swipe with the ax, Clay stepped back quickly against the trench, joining Jeff. With a ripping sound, the taproot parted, and the mules abruptly staggered forward as the resistance on the taut rope was released. In a matter of seconds they had hauled the massive stump clear of the big hole around it.

Jeff gave a shout of triumph, and Clay joined in, pounding his brother on the back—but carefully, so as not to reinjure Jeff's ribs. Bartholomew halted the mules, then stepped over to his sons and helped them out of the trench. "Well, I told you we'd do it," he said, gesturing toward the low-hanging sun. "And before nightfall, too."

"You sure did, Pa." Clay stepped over to the stump and slapped its rough, bark-coated flank. "This old stump was no match for three Holts."

A warm feeling went through Jeff. He was proud to have taken part in this task with his father and brother. For a moment the jumbled emotions he felt for Clay had been forgotten. He could tell that their father felt the same way.

Arms around each other's shoulders, Clay and Jeff went back to the cabin, Bartholomew following along with the mules. Norah and the children hurried out of the cabin in response to their hails as they approached, and the rest of the family joined in the celebration when they heard that the stubborn stump had finally been defeated. Norah set to work preparing supper while the men washed up. The meal was every bit as good as the previous evening's.

She had made apple cobbler for a special treat, and over a plate of it, Clay said, "You make it awful hard to think about leaving again, Ma."

"Well, I don't suppose you have to," she said.

Jeff glanced at the younger ones. Their faces had taken on a sudden look of worry.

"I didn't know you were going to leave, Clay," Susan said. "I thought you planned to stay here with us."

"I am staying, for right now," Clay said quickly. "Don't know what I'll do in the future, darling. Some of the men I went west with—well, they're going back to trap beaver. I've given some thought to joining them."

Jonathan said, "I want you to stay!"

"We'll see, little brother," Clay promised, then changed the subject, and the children seemed to forget about their momentary concern.

Jeff knew better, though. He knew that his father had been right the night before when he'd said that Clay could stay on the farm no more than temporarily. Once a man like Clay had been adventuring, he would have to go back to it sooner or later. The family would just have to enjoy his company while he was home—and hope that his presence did not prod the Garwoods into causing more trouble.

In the meantime he had an appointment to keep. He would have enjoyed sitting around the hearth and listening to more of Clay's tales, but several nights earlier he had promised Melissa that he would visit her again before too much time went by. And that night, it seemed as if months had gone by since then, instead of days.

He pushed his chair back from the table and stood, saying, "I hope it's all right that I go out for a while this evening."

Norah frowned. "Don't you need to rest after all that work today, Jeff?"

"I'm fine, Ma, just a little tired."

Bartholomew looked shrewdly at his second son. "Going over to see the Merrivale girl?"

Jeff blushed a little, but before he could answer, Clay said, "Melissa Merrivale? That scrawny little thing? You're courting her, Jeff?"

"It's none of your business, Clay Holt," Jeff replied. "And neither is whether or not Melissa is . . . well, scrawny!"

Clay threw back his head and laughed. "I'd wager she's not anymore, the way you're acting. Sorry, Jeff. Didn't mean to pry."

"You go ahead if you feel like it, Jeff," Bartholomew said. "But take your rifle, and keep a sharp lookout."

"I always do these days, Pa." Jeff stepped around the table to where Susan and Jonathan were sitting and gave them each a hug, since they would likely be asleep by the time he returned. Then he said good night to Edward, took his new rifle from the pegs on the wall where he had hung it earlier after returning from the north field, and stepped outside. Clay followed him, then paused in front of the door in the gathering shadows of dusk. He began packing tobacco into his pipe for one of his infrequent smokes.

Jeff looked over his shoulder at him. "You're not planning on trailing along after me, are you?"

"It's usually the other way around, isn't it, the younger brother tagging along with the older one?"

Jeff flushed. "You don't have to remind me that you've got a few years on me, Clay. Just remember that I'm a grown man now, too."

"Sure," Clay said with a shrug. "Didn't mean any offense."

"Well, maybe I'm a little touchy about some things," Jeff admitted.

"Seems to me you're touchy about a lot of things." Clay's voice was quiet, pitched low enough that it would not be heard in the cabin.

Jeff controlled his temper, but his fingers tightened on the stock of his rifle. "Clay, I've already told you I'm glad you came home, even if it *is* liable to mean more trouble with the Garwoods. But you can't come in here and start bossing me around again like we're still youngsters. Those days are over."

"Aye, they certainly are. All I wanted to do was bid you good night, Jeff."

"Oh." Now he felt foolish. "Good night, then." He turned and strode out of the small yard in front of the cabin.

The heat of the Indian summer day dissipated quickly after sunset, leaving the air pleasantly cool by the time Jeff reached the Merrivale house. Already the stars stood out brilliantly against the darkening sky above, and a large, golden moon was rising to the east. Budger, the Merrivales' dog, greeted him as usual with clamorous barking, thus alerting the family that someone was approaching. Jeff was not surprised when the front door opened before he could reach it. Budger's barking would have roused the dead.

The tall, broad-shouldered figure of Charles Merrivale, was silhouetted plainly against the lamplight behind him, filling the doorway. Jeff paused when he saw that Merrivale was carrying a smoothbore shot-gun.

"Oh, it's you, Holt." Merrivale lowered the double barrels of the fowling piece. "Thought it might have been a savage sneaking around."

Jeff knew it would be a waste of time to point out to Merrivale that there hadn't been any Indian trouble in the area for over ten years. The local Lenape were quite peaceful, according to his father. Instead, Jeff said, "Good evening, Mr. Merrivale. You're well, I trust?"

"You don't give a damn how I am, boy, and you know it." Behind him, Merrivale's wife overheard his comment and let out a shocked gasp, and he commented over his shoulder, "I'm just speaking the truth, Hermione."

The last thing Jeff wanted was to get into an argument with the father of the woman he loved. He said quickly, "I've come to see Melissa, Mr. Merrivale. Is she here?"

"I know good and well why you're here, Holt." Jeff was close enough now to see that Merrivale was scowling. "Melissa is indisposed. She doesn't feel like seeing you."

Jeff felt a touch of alarm. "You mean she's sick?"

"I mean what I said!" Merrivale answered harshly. "She's indisposed, and she can't see you. That's all you need to know."

Now anger mixed with Jeff's concern about Melissa. Merrivale's high-handed attitude was rubbing him the wrong way. "Was that Melissa's idea—or was it yours, sir?" Despite the honorific, his voice made it clear that he had little respect for the older man.

"None of your damned business," Merrivale snapped, and he raised the shotgun again. "Now I'll thank you to get off my place, young man. Otherwise, I'll have to pepper your hide with bird shot!"

Jeff tensed, and for a second he thought about raising his own rifle so Merrivale could see how *he* liked being threatened. It would hardly win Jeff favor in Melissa's eyes, though, to get into a gun battle with her father. He saw a flash of lamplight on red hair as Hermione Merrivale tugged at her husband's sleeve in an effort to make him lower the gun, but Merrivale simply shrugged out of her grip and took a step out the door toward Jeff.

"I'll go, sir," he said quickly, hating the idea that Merrivale probably thought he was backing down because of cowardice. Actually, he was not afraid of the ponderous fowling piece. If it was loaded with bird shot, as Merrivale had said, the charge would do little but sting at that range. Jeff's new flintlock was much more deadly.

Jeff turned and started to walk away, but Merrivale called out, "I hear your brother finally came back. Do you know if he intends to face up to his responsibility at last?"

"I didn't ask him," Jeff replied without turning around to face Merrivale. "Clay's plans are his own business."

This time, Merrivale did not stop Jeff as he stalked away. He was filled with fury. Merrivale had no right to prevent him from seeing Melissa, he told himself. And yet he knew that in the eyes of the law, Merrivale had every right to do just that. If Jeff had opposed him by force, the ire of Constable Sutcliffe would have come down on his head. Sutcliffe was already looking for an excuse to clap at least one Holt into irons and throw him into jail.

As Jeff strode along the trail, the lights of the Merrivale cabin disappearing behind him, he wondered where Melissa had been during the exchange with her father. Had she been right inside, where she could hear every word? Or had Merrivale sent her to her room before he opened the door? She would have hated Jeff for fighting with her father; would she hate him as well for knuckling under?

Those thoughts were going through his head when he heard a sudden rustling in the brush beside the road. Stopping in his tracks, he faced the noise and brought up the rifle. It might be the Garwoods there in the deep shadows, or some sort of wild animal, or perhaps even highwaymen. Whoever it was, they would find Jefferson Holt ready for trouble—and in the mood for it, too.

"Come out of there!" he called firmly. "Show yourself or I'll shoot."

His breath caught in his throat, and his eyes widened as a vision of beauty stepped from the bushes into the moonlight washing down over the road. Melissa's long, dark ringlets shone in the silvery light, and her pale, delicate features looked even more striking.

"Would you really shoot me, Jeff?" she asked mischievously. "Or would you just try to scare me?"

He realized he was still holding the flintlock level with her and lowered it abruptly. "I'm sorry, Melissa. I didn't know it was you."

She moved closer to him. "I had to follow you after I heard the awful things my father said." Her voice became solemn. "I'm sorry, Jeff. He has no right to treat you that way."

"No harm done." He was not going to tell her what he really thought of her father.

"Yes, there was harm done," she insisted. She was moving ever closer to him. She reached out to him, and he saw that her arms, bare in the short-sleeved dress she wore, were covered with goosebumps from the growing chill in the night air. She had ventured out into the woods, in the darkness, just to come after him and apologize for her father's treatment of him. Jeff felt himself growing warm. She would not have done such a thing if she did not genuinely care for him.

"Melissa . . ." he began.

She stopped him by moving into his arms, lifting her face to his and kissing him.

Jeff still held the rifle in one hand. He forgot everything his father and Clay had taught him about firearms in that moment and dropped the gun, using both arms to embrace Melissa and draw her tightly against him. This was a very improper kiss, he knew, nothing at all like the shy little pecks that should pass between two courting young people. This kiss was hard and passionate, searing in its heat. Jeff felt the warmth and softness of her flesh beneath his hands, and he knew that what was between them had suddenly gone beyond simple courting.

They were kissing now like lovers.

Cold reality had to intrude, however, and when the kiss finally ended, Jeff whispered, "You're going to get in trouble with your father, slipping out like this to meet me. He said you were indisposed—"

"A lie," Melissa said forcefully. "He just didn't want me to see you. He heard about your brother coming home and that brawl the two of you had with the Garwood boys in one of the taverns. He said such behavior was shameful and that I wasn't to associate with you anymore. He waited last night to see if you were coming to visit me, and he waited again tonight."

"I couldn't stay away any longer," Jeff said.

"I'm glad you came." She buried her face against his chest for a moment, snuggling in the comfortable embrace of his arms. "Don't worry about my father. He thinks I've retired for the evening, and my mother will keep him distracted. At least she approves of you." Melissa suddenly giggled. "So do I."

Unable to resist the temptation of her lips, Jeff kissed her again, long minutes slipping by unheeded as they held each other. Eventually, as she rested her head against his shoulder and he stroked her hair, he spoke again, though the words that came out were a surprise to him.

"Melissa, will you—will you do me the honor of becoming my wife?"

She gasped and looked up at him, as taken aback as he was. "Do you mean it, Jeff?"

"Of course I do," he said. He knew now that she loved him, just as he loved her, and the passion and trust she had demonstrated that night had prompted the question that had been much on his mind in recent weeks. Suddenly a great fear shot through him, a fear that she would say no.

"Yes," she said, her voice trembling slightly. "Yes, Jefferson Holt, I would be proud and happy to marry you."

Jeff wanted to whoop out loud as joy flooded through him. Instead, he kissed her again, and as he did, a thought sprang up unbidden in his mind: *This is going to lead to even more trouble with her father*.

But that was a worry for another day. At that particular moment, all he wanted to do was kiss the woman he loved, the woman he was going to marry. And any thoughts of the irascible Charles Merrivale, or of Zach Garwood and his troublemaking brothers, or of any other problems that had plagued the Holt family in the past . . . those thoughts were far, far away.

CHAPTER EIGHT

C lay had thought about following his brother the
night before, just to make sure that Jeff was all
right. Jeff had been through a great deal in recent days, and if the Garwoods had picked that night
to jump him again, he probably wouldn't have been
able to put up much of a fight. Clay was confident he
could have trailed Jeff to the Merrivale farm and back
again without his younger brother's ever knowing,
since the years in the wilderness had taught him how
to move quickly and quietly through the woods. In the
end, though, Clay had decided to leave Jeff to his own
devices; he had confidence enough in Jeff's ability to
take care of himself.

When Jeff slipped back into the cabin long after
everyone else in the family was asleep, Clay's confidence was rewarded. He had expected the hard day's
work to make sleep come easily, but instead he was
still awake, rolled in a quilt, listening to the gentle

160

breathing of his brothers and his sister, when below him he heard the faint creaking of the door's leather hinges. A moment later Jeff came climbing up the pegs to the loft, stepped carefully over the sleeping forms, found his own mattress, and stretched out. For a moment Clay thought about saying something to him, but he decided against it. Talking might wake up the others, and they all needed their sleep.

As if he had been waiting for Jeff to return safely, Clay found himself dropping off quickly. He slept soundly the rest of the night.

Over breakfast the next morning Clay dipped a biscuit in a pool of molasses on his plate and bit off a chunk as his father asked, "What do you plan to do today, son?"

After a moment Clay replied, "Thought I might go over to Marietta and take a look around. I didn't see much of the town the other day when I came in. Looked like it had changed some, though."

"Aye, it's grown." Bartholomew did not say anything about how Clay's previous visit to Marietta had been cut short by the fight in Meaghan's tavern, but Clay could tell he was thinking about it.

"Hope you didn't need me to do anything around here," Clay went on quickly. "I could wait to go to town." Even as he spoke, he was hoping his father would not take him up on the offer. The trip into Marietta was just an excuse to get off the Holt family farm. What he really wanted to do was find Josie Garwood. He did not want to put off the confrontation any longer.

Even if he could persuade Josie to recant her story about his being the father of her child, he suddenly wondered, would anyone believe her at this late date? Folks in the area, Josie's brothers included, had had nearly three years to think the worst of him. Those opinions were not likely to change overnight.

All he could do was try, though, and that was what he intended to do.

Clay was afraid that Jeff might volunteer to go to

Marietta with him, but instead he seemed wrapped up in thoughts of his own, thoughts concerning Melissa Merrivale, Clay would have wagered, and he grinned a little as he looked down at his plate. He hoped Jeff would find happiness with Melissa.

Everyone spread out to do chores after breakfast. Clay took his flintlock, went to the barn, and saddled his horse, and when he led it out, he found Jeff waiting for him. Jeff looked straight at him and said, "You're up to something, Clay. Might as well tell me what it is."

"Up to something?" Clay echoed. "I don't know what you're talking about, little brother. Like I said inside, I'm just going to take a look around Marietta."

"What if you run into the Garwoods?"

Clay shrugged. "I don't want any trouble. I won't bother them if they don't bother me."

"That's not very likely," Jeff said, giving a snort of disbelief.

Once again Clay's shoulders rose and lowered in a shrug. "All I can tell you is that I'm not looking for Zach and his brothers, and that's the truth."

"All right," Jeff said reluctantly. "But watch yourself while you're gone."

"Sure." Clay swung up into the saddle and heeled the horse into a trot, heading it away from the farm. Even without turning around, he knew that Jeff was watching him depart.

It was a couple of miles to Marietta, but before the road reached the town, a small lane branched off to the east. That trail led past the Garwood farm, which was smaller and scrubbier than the Holt family holdings. Old Alfred Garwood had never possessed the touch necessary to be successful at working the land, as Bartholomew Holt had, and Garwood's sons had not been much help either. The family had made a living and fed themselves from their crops, but the farm had never grown and prospered as had many others in the area.

Clay intended to take that lane when he came to

it, but as he approached the fork in the road he saw a pair of figures walking well ahead of him toward Marietta. They were a woman and a little boy, and Clay recognized the woman's thick, luxuriant dark hair. As he overtook them she heard the sound of hoofbeats and turned to face him. He saw her hand tighten on the little boy's shoulder.

Clay reined to a stop. "Hello, Josie," he said.

"Clay." Her voice was husky and level. "I heard you were back. I saw the evidence, too. Zach can't hardly use his right arm because of you."

Clay grimaced. This discussion was not starting off the way he had hoped it would. "Your brothers started the trouble, Josie. I was just defending Jeff and myself."

"Oh, I know that. I know not to believe most of the things Zach says, so I was pretty sure you and Jefferson didn't jump Zach and the boys for no reason. Why did you come back, anyway? I thought I'd never see you again."

"Wanted to visit the family. I've been gone a long time."

She smiled slightly. "I know."

Clay studied her for a moment. She was still attractive, but the past few years had not been overly kind to her. Even though she still possessed her beauty, time had coarsened it somewhat. She could not be any more than, what, nineteen or twenty years old? Yet she looked several years older.

Josie pushed back a lock of her black hair, then smiled down at the boy standing beside her. "I don't think you've met my son," she said to Clay. "This is Matthew."

Clay leaned forward in the saddle and spoke to the toddler. "Hello, Matthew."

The boy did not say anything in return. Instead, he turned and sidled partially behind Josie, then buried his face in her skirts. Josie laughed a little. "He's shy sometimes," she explained. To Matthew, she said,

"You don't have to be scared of Clay, honey. Especially not Clay."

The tall, buckskin-clad man on horseback stiffened a bit. He knew what she was getting at, and he felt a touch of fresh anger. There was no telling what sort of stories she had been feeding the boy. Even though Matthew was still quite young, she could have been filling his head with all kinds of lies.

"Look, Josie," Clay said, his growing impatience making his voice sharper than he had intended. "I want to know why you're still sticking to that story you told when you know perfectly well it's not true."

"Story?" Josie repeated innocently, although Clay could see a malicious gleam in her eyes. "What story would that be, Clay?"

If she wanted it put in plain language, he thought, then so be it. He swung down from the horse so that he could face her. "I'm talking about the out-and-out lie that I'm the father of that boy."

"Are you saying you're not?" she asked, tossing her head defiantly.

"You know I'm not," he said flatly. "You know we never laid together, even though you wanted to, that night of the dance."

Her hand came up to slap him, but he grasped her wrist before the blow could land. She pushed against his grip but could not overcome his strength. Her hand remained trapped in midair. She had let go of Matthew, and the boy backed away a couple of steps, unsure of what was going on but certain it was bad.

"You bastard!" Josie hissed at Clay. She balled her other hand into a fist and struck at his face.

He blocked the punch and jerked her forward, pulling her against him so that she no longer had a good angle from which to strike at him. "Stop it, Josie!" he grated.

"Damn you, why did you come back? *Why?*" Suddenly a moan came from her throat, and she slumped against him. Her head tilted back. She was tall for a woman, and it was easy for her to lift her face to his. Before Clay knew what was happening, her mouth was pressed hotly against his. Her lips parted, and he could feel the heat and passion that had abruptly gripped her.

He still had hold of her wrist. His other arm looped around her and drew her even more tightly against him. Her body seemed to mold to his, and the warmth of her soft flesh enflamed his senses. Knowing that he was making a bad mistake but unable to stop himself, he returned her kiss. Josie had always been able to make him downright crazy with desire for her.

And some things, he now discovered to his horror, never changed. As they stood there in the road, his mind went spiraling back, back to a time almost three years earlier. . . .

Barn raisings drew folks from miles around, and this one was no exception. Families from all over the Marietta area had come to help Otis Thornton put up a barn, and they had stayed afterward for a celebration that was lasting far into the night. Several men had brought their fiddles, providing music for the couples whirling around the open area in the center of the new barn. Some of those who preferred not to dance were standing around watching, clapping their hands in time to the music. The rest of the group tended to split up, the men heading for one side of the barn to talk about crops and the weather—and pass around a jug of corn squeezin's on the sly—while the women went to the other side of the cavernous structure to keep an eye on the children and talk.

All Clay was interested in was the pretty girl he was whirling around in his arms.

Josie Garwood laughed, and it sounded like music to Clay. Josie was as attractive as all get-out, in Clay's opinion, and he had been a little surprised when she had agreed to go to the barn dance with him. Of course, like most of the young men in the area, he had heard rumors about how, well, *friendly*

Josie could be on occasion. Clay didn't know whether there was any truth to the stories or not. He did know that he did not have much use for her brothers, especially Zach, and that old Alfred Garwood had never been very friendly to the Holt family. Garwood's hostility stemmed from his contention that Bartholomew Holt's land was much better for farming than his, as in fact it was. Garwood thought that was unfair; he was a veteran of the war against the redcoats, just like Bartholomew, and he had been granted the same number of acres. He seemed to think, though, that Bartholomew had somehow conspired to lay claim to some of the best land in the area.

That was ridiculous, of course, Clay thought. The claims had been awarded by lot, and it was only chance that had given Bartholomew Holt such fertile land, while Alfred Garwood had gotten a farm with poorer soil and not as much water. The Garwood place might suffer a little in comparison with the Holts', but all the land in that part of the Northwest Territory was fertile. Garwood could have made a better success of his farm, in Clay's opinion, if he had only tried a little harder.

At any rate, Clay had been a bit surprised that Garwood had allowed his only daughter to accompany one of the Holts to Thornton's barn dance. During the course of the evening, however, he had gotten to know Josie well enough to realize that she did not particularly care what her father might want. She had a mind of her own, she had told him, and she did as she pleased.

Clay was glad she had pleased to go with him.

The music came to an end, and the dancers stopped where they were on the dirt floor, which had already packed down from the constant tramp of boots and shoes. Old Mr. Curtis, one of the fiddlers, called out, "We'll play some more later, folks. Fiddling's thirsty work, so the boys and me figger to get us a nice long drink of branch water. We'll be back, though."

In a low voice, Clay said to Josie, "I'd wager that branch water will have a little something mixed in with it."

"I think you're right." She was a little breathless from dancing, and her cheeks glowed pink. Clay thought the flush made her even more attractive.

"What would you like to do now?" he asked.

"It's a pretty night," Josie replied. "Why don't we step outside for some air, maybe even take a walk?"

"All right. That sounds mighty fine to me." Clay linked his arm with hers and escorted her toward the big double doors that stood open at the barn's front entrance. Other couples were strolling in and out, taking advantage of the opportunity to cool off. As Clay and Josie walked toward the doors, he suddenly became aware of the pressure of eyes on him. He turned his head and saw Zach Garwood, standing with his brother Pete, watching them. As Clay and Josie went by, Clay could feel the hostility directed toward him and knew that the Garwood boys shared their father's attitude. None of them liked the Holts.

It had not always been that way. Once, in the days when the area was first being settled, Clay Holt and Zach Garwood had been the best of friends. They had roamed the wooded hillsides together, hunting and fishing, engaging in the kind of rough-and-tumble camaraderie that boys shared if they were lucky.

Somewhere along the path of time, though, all that had changed. Clay had plenty of rough edges about him, but Zach had a cruel streak, which became more and more evident as he grew older. While Clay enjoyed a good fight, regardless of the outcome, Zach seemed to draw pleasure from hurting his opponents. Clay did not like to think such things about someone who had been his friend, but there had been no denying it after a while. He had seen too many of Zach's bruised and bloodied victims.

Also, as Zach and his brothers grew older, they came to accept the things their father had drummed into their heads: The Holts had stolen land that should have been his; the Holts were liars and thieves; the Holts were the enemies of the Garwood clan and always would be. Eventually, Clay had started avoiding Zach because the other boy was constantly trying to pick a fight. That had been the end of their friendship.

Now, as he walked out of the barn with Josie, Clay thought he saw pure hatred in the eyes of Zach and Pete. Luther, the next to the youngest Garwood, was nearby, but he wasn't paying attention to his sister and Clay. Aaron, the baby of the family, was engaged in some horseplay with a group of other boys.

Clay met Zach's eyes levelly but did not slow down or say anything. With Josie beside him, he walked out of the barn into the pleasant spring night.

Josie turned to the left, toward a thick stand of trees some fifty yards from the barn. She looked up, toward the moon and the stars that glittered thickly in the night sky, and said, "I love walking in the moonlight, don't you?"

"Well, I suppose so." Clay had never really given the matter much thought. "It's all right if the moon's full enough for you to see where you're going."

Josie laughed, a throaty sound that did something to Clay's spine. "You really know how to talk to a girl, don't you, Clay?" There was more than a hint of mockery in her voice. He started to take offense, but then she laughed again, more warmly this time, and pressed her fingers against his arm. "I'm sorry. You're a sweet young man, and I shouldn't tease you."

"Not that young," Clay said. "I'm older than you are."

She shook her head. "I was born older than you, Clay Holt, no matter what the calendar may say."

He understood. She was naturally flirtatious, and she was comfortable in situations such as these. He was just the opposite. During the barn raising, he had done his share, and more, of the work, and it had been no great challenge. Thinking of something to say to this lovely young woman, however, now that they were away from the crowd inside the barn . . . that was much more difficult.

"How far did you want to go?" he asked.

"Excuse me?"

"I mean, how far did you want to walk? We're nearly to the trees."

"I don't mind strolling through the woods. It might be fun."

Clay heard the music start again inside the barn, bows scraping against fiddle strings. He paused and suggested, "Maybe we ought to go back, now that we've gotten some air."

"Please, not yet," Josie said quickly. They had reached the edge of the woods, and without pausing, she walked on into the deep shadows beneath the trees. Clay had no choice but to let go of her arm or go with her.

He went with her. It was not a difficult decision.

Josie didn't stop until the darkness had completely engulfed them. Then she halted and turned to face him, her features a pale blur in the shadows. As she leaned toward him, Clay could make them out better.

"Do you like me, Clay?" she asked suddenly in a voice that was little more than a whisper.

"Do—I like you?" The question had taken him totally by surprise. He groped for the words to answer her. "Well, of course I like you. I asked you to come to the barn dance with me, didn't I?"

"I wasn't sure if you asked me because you wanted to, or if you just wanted to annoy my brothers."

Clay said emphatically, "I promise you, Josie, I wasn't even thinking about your brothers."

"I know you and Zach don't get along very well anymore, and I just thought—"

"No," Clay insisted. "That didn't have a thing to do with it."

Josie's lips curved softly in a smile. "You've probably heard stories about me," she said, her voice trailing off tantalizingly. She was closer than ever to him now.

"Nope," Clay lied.

"I don't care if you have. Most of them aren't true, anyway."

Most of them? Clay's heart began to pound in his chest. Why was she saying these things to him? What was she getting at? Just what was Josie Garwood after?

In the next moment he found out.

She lifted herself on her toes and put her arms around his neck, then pulled his face down to hers. She pressed her lips against his in complete abandon.

Clay's muscles tensed, and his eyes opened wide in surprise. But his arms went around her and pulled her to him, and she began to writhe in his embrace.

When she finally broke the kiss, Clay could hardly get his breath. "Josie . . ." he whispered, and that was all the respite he got. She was kissing him again, kissing him with a hunger and a passion unlike anything he had ever encountered.

He was wearing a linsey-woolsey shirt, and he could feel the insistent prod of her nipples against his chest through the thin homespun gown she was wearing. Her breasts were pressed hard into him, and her soft belly moved insistently—maddeningly!—against his groin. She moaned, deep in her throat, and Clay knew without any doubt what she wanted.

His pulse was hammering crazily in his head. There was no way they could be seen in the shadows, he thought, even though the barn was close enough for them to hear the music, the talking and laughter of other people at the dance. His own family was there, as well as hers, and Clay felt a sudden flash of guilt.

But the things she was doing to him were making him forget every other consideration. The tide of desire rising in him was strong enough to wash away everything else. He could do nothing but let it carry him along.

Josie sank to her knees, and Clay went down with

her. There was little undergrowth, and the ground between the trees was covered with a thin carpet of grass. They might be a little uncomfortable, Clay thought fleetingly, but he was beyond worrying about that.

Josie clutched at his body, bringing him with her as she slowly leaned back and lay down. He began to fumble with her long skirts, but then he hesitated one last time. "Are you sure about this, Josie?"

"I'm sure," she told him, her voice husky and strained with wanting. "I've been looking at you for a long time, Clay, thinking about what it would be like with you. I decided I couldn't wait until after we're married."

His hand was sliding up the smooth skin of her thigh, but the caress came to an abrupt halt at her words. "Married?" he repeated.

"Of course." She reached for his belt, moving quickly now, and he suddenly realized that she was trying to distract him. She had made a mistake, and she knew it.

He caught her hand and stopped her. "I don't remember asking you to marry me, Josie." He peered down intently at her, wishing there was more light so he could read her expression better.

"But—but you're lying with me, Clay. We'll have to get married."

"I can't do that."

"But why on earth not?"

How could he explain it to her? He liked Marietta, liked the farm, and he loved his family, but lately there had been a restlessness in him, a vague unease that told him he was supposed to be somewhere else. He had listened to the older men who gathered in Steakley's store on Saturday afternoons and talked about the exploration of the West. A lot of country was waiting out there. Plenty of room for a man to roam around in. Clay already knew the countryside around Marietta like the back of his hand. He was ready to see something new.

He could not do that if he was tied down by a wife.

"I just can't," he said to her. "Lord knows, I want you right now, if you don't mind my speaking plain. You're a beautiful woman, Josie. But I can't marry you."

For a long moment she did not say anything. Finally, in a voice taut and cold with anger, she told him, "Then get the hell off of me."

Clay rolled to the side, winding up on his back, propped on his elbows. He watched as Josie got to her feet with a flounce of her skirts. For a second he thought she was going to kick him, and he scrambled up. He could tell by the way she was standing that she was mad enough to spit.

"I don't believe this," she said, more to herself than to him. "You don't know what you're passing up, Mr. Clay Holt."

He was pretty annoyed himself, and that was why he said without thinking, "Maybe not, but I've heard enough tales that I can make a pretty good guess."

"Oh!" Josie exclaimed in a mixture of fury and surprise. "You bastard!"

Clay had never heard such language from a female before, and his shock left him flat-footed enough that she was able to whip her hand around and crack the palm across his face in a resounding slap. The blow stung like hell, and he quickly caught her arms before she could strike again.

She was panting in rage, cursing him with a fluency that would have done a riverboatman proud. Clay kept a tight grip on her upper arms and shook her, none too gently. "Stop it, Josie!" he said. "Settle down, gal! I didn't mean anything."

"The hell you didn't! You think I'm a whore, just like everybody else around here! Well, I'm not, you understand? I'm not!"

"Dammit, calm down. I'm sorry, Josie. Now, if you keep hollering like that, everybody from the dance is going to come over here to see what's going on, and then folks really will think bad things about you."

"But not about you." She had lowered her voice, but the words were harsh and strained. "They'd call me a slut, but nobody would think twice about Clay Holt lying with me. You wouldn't be the one they told stories about."

He shook his head. "Maybe it's not fair," he admitted. "But it's not my fault folks think like they do. Come on, Josie. We're going back to the dance, and we're going to act like everything's all right."

"To hell with the dance and to hell with you," she spat. "If you're too good for me, I'll find somebody who isn't. I'll find somebody who wants me. Just get away from me and leave me alone."

"Josie—"

"Get away!"

He released her arms and stepped back quickly, lifting his hands so that his palms were turned toward her in a gesture of peace. "Hold on. If you want me to leave, I will. No need to cause any more ruckus."

She was half sobbing as she said, "Just get the hell away from me."

Clay hated to leave her by herself in the woods, but the barn and the crowd of people were nearby. Nothing would happen to her, he told himself. She would stand in the shadows for a while until she had calmed down, and then she would return to the dance and be as vivacious as ever. He turned and strode away, making his way through the trees and walking quickly to the barn, hoping no one would notice that he was coming back alone.

Behind him the woods waited, still and dark.

The next time he had seen Josie Garwood—the only time he had seen her until today—she had told him that she was pregnant and he was responsible. Both of them knew it was a bald-faced lie, of course, but the knowledge did not stop Josie from sticking to the falsehood and spreading it all over Marietta. He had sensed a desperation in her that day, seen a pleading in her eyes that said he could make everything all right if only he would marry her.

He had not been able to do that. He did not want to hurt anybody, but his restlessness was too strong. It was impossible for him to stay in Marietta, doubly so once the rumors had started. Less than two weeks later he had packed his gear, said good-bye to his startled family, and set out for the West, arriving in St. Louis to hear about a couple of army captains named Lewis and Clark who were recruiting men for a journey of exploration across the Rockies. . . .

And now the long road that was life had brought him back home. Josie Garwood was in his arms once again, and the memories flashed through his mind in an instant. He stiffened as it all came back to him. Feeling a surge of panic unlike anything he had experienced during the long, perilous trip to the Pacific and back, he pulled his mouth away from hers and thrust her from him.

"No," he rasped.

She caught at his arms. "Clay—"

"Not this time," he broke in. "You're not going to get me so worked up that I don't know what's going on. You lied about me, Josie. You turned folks against me until even my own family isn't sure what to believe anymore." He looked down at the boy, who stood several feet away, obviously confused and a little scared. "I reckon you found somebody else that night, just like you said you would, and he wouldn't marry you, either."

"Clay." That old desperation was in her voice. "You were always different, Clay. I liked you. I knew there was some good in you. And you can still make things right. You can marry me now and give Matthew a father. If you do, I'll see to it that my brothers don't ever bother you or your family again."

That put it plainly enough, he thought. After all this time, she was still trying to force him into a marriage he did not want. His jaw clenched tightly in anger. He had never liked anyone prodding him.

And yet . . . a small part of him was attracted to the notion. He had seen how Zach and the other Garwoods were making life miserable for his family, and here was a way to stop that once and for all.

Would Josie be able to stop Zach, though? Clay asked himself. Or had things already gone too far? There was no way of knowing for sure if she could keep her promise.

"I can't do it, Josie," he said heavily. "Maybe a part of me wants to, but I can't. I reckon I made a mistake running off when I did—I should have stayed and made you tell the truth then. But I'm not going to give in to threats."

"But Zach—"

"Zach and your other brothers had best leave the Holts alone," Clay said. "Because if they don't, sooner or later somebody's going to get killed." He took a deep breath. "Tell Zach, Josie. Tell him I'm not Matthew's father. If anything will put an end to the trouble, that will."

She looked at him for a long moment, and Clay could see tears shining in her eyes. Slowly, she shook her head. "It wouldn't do any good."

"You don't know that."

"I know Zach. And I know it wouldn't help."

"Then there's nothing I can do for you." Feeling hollow and defeated, he turned toward his horse. He had been hoping that Josie would be reasonable about this, but deep down he had known how unlikely that was.

She did not say anything as he mounted up and turned the horse toward Marietta. Only as he heeled the horse into a trot did she call out to him.

He did not look back, and he did not slow down.

Josie Garwood stood and watched the man ride away. She was riveted to the spot by her anger and her hatred—and by memories of her own.

She had not really planned to seduce Clay Holt on the night of Thornton's barn dance. When he asked her to go with him, she had accepted more to get back at her brother than anything else. She had heard Zach railing about all the Holts and Clay in particular many times, and she knew how annoyed he would be if she accompanied Clay to the celebration.

But something was different about Clay, and once she had spent some time with him, she could not deny it. He was decent, and he was kind.

And she was not used to either one of those things from the men in her life.

As she stood trembling in the woods after he had spurned her, wondering what in the world she was going to do next, a sudden rustling behind her made her spin around. A figure loomed out of the darkness.

"Take it easy, Josie," the man said. "It's only me."

"You scared me, Zachariah," she gasped, her hand flattened over her heart. "I didn't know you were out here."

"I thought as much," Zach said as he stepped closer to her, "the way you were throwing yourself at Holt."

"That's none of your business, Zach," Josie said, edging away from him. She knew how unpredictable he could be. There was no telling how Zach would react to something that bothered him—but it was generally unpleasant.

He laughed harshly. "My sweet little sister acts like a slut and a trollop, and you say it's none of my business? The hell it's not!" He sprang toward her.

Josie had sensed what he was about to do at the last instant, and she tried frantically to dodge him. He was too fast for her, though, and caught one of her arms, jerking her toward him. He grabbed her other wrist as she struck at him.

"Dammit, Zach, let go of me!" she cried as she struggled futilely in his strong grasp. "You've got no right—"

"You're my sister," he grated. "I got every right in the world."

And then his mouth came down on hers, hard and cruel, in a kiss that was as much brutality as passion.

Josie kept resisting, but as always, he was too strong for her. In a matter of moments, he had her pinned on the ground, her skirts pushed up and a knee thrust painfully between her thighs. "Go ahead and fight," he told her and gave a harsh laugh. "I don't mind. But if you scream, I'll kill you."

She knew he meant it. Out of breath and hurting from his weight on top of her, Josie went limp. Fighting him would not do any good; it never had before. She lay there, enduring in silence the pawing of his rough, callused hands. She gritted her teeth at the pain of his joining her—but she said nothing.

Zach laughed once more as he began to move against her. "If you're good enough for a Holt, by God you're good enough for your own brother," he rasped. She turned her head aside from his whiskey-reeking breath and prayed that the ordeal would soon be over. It usually did not take long. Zach went on, "I know you, you slut. Holt wouldn't do it, but there's been plenty of others, haven't there?" When she did not answer, he tightened his grip on her shoulders. "Haven't there!"

"Yes," Josie said, her voice sounding strange and far away to her ears. "Plenty of others."

That was all it took. Zach stiffened, gasped, and a moment later slumped against her, spent of his lust and hate.

But it was a lie, Josie thought. There had not been any others. The stories about her were all untrue. There had never been anyone except Zach, never since that night when she was fourteen. . . .

Which meant that only one person could be responsible for the new life she suspected was growing within her.

Zach pushed himself off her, leaving her

sprawled on the ground as he stood up and adjusted his breeches. When he was done, he pointed a finger at her and said, "You tell anybody about this, and I'll kill you. But you already know that, don't you?"

"I know," she whispered, unable to give voice to her words because of the lump in her throat. "I won't tell."

"Damn right you won't," he said with a sniff of disgust. Then he turned and stalked off into the shadows.

Of course she would not tell, but not because she was afraid of him. She would never be able to stand the shame of admitting what had happened, what had been going on for years now. But soon, if what she suspected was true, soon she would have to do something.

That had been in the back of her mind when she brought Clay Holt to the woods, she realized. As she slowly got to her feet and straightened her skirts, she knew that was why she had given in to impulse and mentioned marriage to him. If he had agreed, her problems would have been solved. Zach would have had to leave her alone if she was married, and Clay never would have known that the child was not his. But she had been too anxious and had brought up the subject too soon. If only she had waited, she thought despairingly. If . . .

Abruptly she shook her head. That kind of thinking would not do her any good. She had to come up with some other solution, and she knew it had to involve Clay Holt.

But the plan she had tried didn't work, and Clay went west to the mountains instead of marrying her. Just as Josie had suspected, she was indeed pregnant, and as the child grew within her, so did the bitterness she felt, not only for her brother but for Clay as well. Perhaps it did not make sense to blame him; in some lonely, isolated moments, Josie recognized that. But he could have saved her, could have made everything right for her, and he had refused. He had turned his back on her.

It was only fair that he and his family suffer, too, just as she was suffering. Eventually Josie had come to believe that. She stuck by the story she had told, and no one could contradict her once Clay left. Zach was not about to tell the truth. Instead, he had used the circumstances to justify his growing hatred of the Holt family.

Time had passed, and Matthew had been born. Josie had been able to ignore most of the things that had been said behind her back as her belly swelled. She paid little attention to the cruel comments of the settlers about poor Josie, full of child and no husband. But after the baby came, there were things she needed, things that Matthew needed. The Garwood farm was steadily growing less productive, and it was difficult for the family to provide for her and the child.

Zach had always accused her of sleeping with other men, and that rumor had spread. Most folks probably figured she didn't know who the father of her baby was. If she was going to be tarred with that brush, she finally decided, she might as well deserve it; if everyone already thought she was a trollop, she might as well become one.

It had not been difficult, and she hadn't even found it that objectionable. The men were all faceless, and she was able to shut her mind to them, almost as if they were not really there. Matthew was healthy and happy and growing, and she had a life. Not much of one, perhaps, but it was hers, and she was coping with it.

And then, from out of the blue, Clay Holt had shown up again, and all the bitter hurts had come flooding back. . . .

"Mama."

The small voice and the pudgy little hand tugging insistently at her skirts brought Josie back to the present with a jolt. Clay was no longer in sight; he had disappeared down the road to Marietta. Josie took a deep breath and looked down at her son. She forced a smile and asked, "What is it, Matthew?"

"Go, Mama. Go town."

She bent to pick him up. "Yes, darling, we're going to town. I'll get you some molasses candy at the store. Would you like that?"

Matthew squirmed and nodded.

Josie held him tightly. The candy would not be hard to get. All she needed to do was let old Steakley fondle her for a few minutes, and she could have practically anything she wanted in his store.

She squared her shoulders and started down the road, carrying her son.

CHAPTER NINE

To the surprise of both Jeff and Clay, no more trouble cropped up during the next few days. No ambushes by the Garwoods, no "accidental" meetings in town that rapidly turned into fights, no sign of Zach and his brothers at all, in fact. It was as if the Garwoods were avoiding them.

Jeff did not spend a great deal of time pondering the situation. Instead, his head was full of thoughts of Melissa. Even now he could hardly believe that she had agreed to marry him. So far, they had not said anything about their engagement to anyone, not even Melissa's mother. Jeff trusted Hermione, and Melissa assured him that she would approve of the match. But her father was a different story, and they had decided to keep their plans secret until they could figure out a way to break the news to him.

Charles Merrivale would not react well when he found out; Jeff was sure of that. He might even take his old blunderbuss and come after Jeff. But it didn't really matter what Merrivale did, not in the long run.

Melissa was going to be his wife, Jeff thought, and that was all that counted.

Clay's thoughts were occupied with things other than the Garwoods, too. He had intended to be gone from Ohio after only a few days, but somehow his visit had stretched into more than a week. He knew the younger children did not want him to go, and he suspected that his parents and Jeff wanted him to stay, too, despite the friction when he had first returned. Besides, it was good to work on the farm, to stretch muscles that had not been used much during the expedition with Lewis and Clark. He was remembering some of the rewards of laboring on the land. A farmer stayed tired most of the time, but he had the pride of accomplishment, of starting with little or nothing and turning it into something worthwhile.

But still, as Clay stood at the open door of the cabin, smelling the wet morning air and looking west, something seemed to be calling to him. He wondered how Colter, Hancock, and Dickson had done on their fur-trapping trip.

Thick gray clouds hung low to the ground. Saturday had dawned gloomy, a fine mist in the air, and the wind carried a chill that had not been present since spring. Indian summer was over, and winter would indeed be coming soon.

Stepping up behind Clay, Bartholomew Holt looked out at the weather, then said to his family, "It's not a very good day for it, but we need supplies. What do you say we all go into town this afternoon?"

Susan and Jonathan shouted their agreement, and Edward stood by with a quiet smile. Now that the weather had turned worse and there would be less work to do on the farms, the schoolmaster in Marietta would begin holding classes. They would last until spring, when the youngsters would be needed in the fields again. Edward had already been to school a couple of times, and this year Susan would begin her book learning. Little Jonathan still had some time left before he would have to make the walk to town, to the big, whitewashed school building on the hill.

"I suppose you're right, Bartholomew," Norah said as she looked through the open doorway at the drizzle. "Perhaps the rain will let up before we're ready to go, though."

Clay and Jeff exchanged a glance. Marietta was always more crowded on Saturday afternoons, and both men knew they stood a better chance of encountering the Garwoods. But it didn't make sense to put off getting needed supplies just because they might run into Zach and his brothers. Jeff was fairly confident the Garwoods would not try to start a fight while a lot of the other settlers were around.

The matter settled, the family went on about the morning's chores, then ate their noon meal. By the time they were ready to go, the drizzle had stopped, but the air was still heavy with moisture. As Clay helped his father hitch the team to the wagon, he was glad he had the thick, buffalo-hide cape he had been given in one of the Shoshone villages during the expedition.

After everyone had climbed into the wagon, Norah tucked an old bearskin robe around the younger children to keep them warm. She and Bartholomew rode on the seat, while Clay and Jeff sat in the back with the youngsters. Susan suggested they sing songs to help keep warm, and soon voices were lifted enthusiastically as the horses pulled the vehicle down the road toward Marietta.

It did not take long to reach town. Bartholomew brought the wagon to a stop, parking it with four others in front of Steakley's store. Several men stood under the awning on the long porch, talking, whittling, and chewing tobacco or smoking pipes. Saturday afternoon at the store was as much a community get-together as a church social or a barn raising, but attendance was more fluid, with families coming and going all through the long afternoon and into the evening. Women and children filled the aisles of the establishment, while the men generally congregated on the porch. As the Holts got down from their wagon, Norah herded Edward, Susan, and Jonathan into the building, leaving her husband and her two older sons to follow at their own pace.

Bartholomew stepped onto the porch, pulled out his pipe, and began to fill it as he drifted over to one of the groups of men. He picked a long splinter off the log railing that ran along the edge of the porch. Several oil lanterns were hung along the front of the building, and Bartholomew set the splinter aflame in the closest one, then used it to light his pipe.

As Jeff and Clay moved up alongside him, Bartholomew said to the other men, "You know my sons."

The men were accustomed to seeing Jeff with the rest of the family, but it had been a long time since Clay had been with them. They all had heard the story spread by Josie Garwood, of course, but none of them said anything about it. They were plainspoken folks, but they also possessed some measure of discretion.

"How's everything, Bartholomew?" one of the men asked, and that drew Bartholomew into the ongoing discussion of crops and weather. He told about the uprooting of the stump in the north field, the stump that had been plaguing him for years, and both Clay and Jeff could hear the pride in his voice when he spoke of the part his sons had played in the task. From there the conversation drifted to politics; Steakley had just gotten a copy of a Pittsburgh newspaper that was only a few weeks old, and already it had become tattered from being passed around so much.

The crowd was just about evenly split in their opinions of Thomas Jefferson and the job he was doing as president. Clay listened with interest but did not speak up; he felt he had a personal stake in Jefferson's presidency. If the president had not sponsored the journey of exploration into the newly acquired Louisiana Territory, Clay would not have had the chance to be one of the first white men to cross the Rockies and see the Pacific. He would always be indebted to Jefferson for the part the president had played in making that possible.

Jeff's interest in the discussion was only half-hearted. He was paying more attention to the main street that ran in front of the store, watching for a wagon carrying Melissa and her parents. Of course, it was possible the Merrivales had already made their weekly trip to town, but Jeff was hoping that was not the case. He was eager to see Melissa again. During the past few days he had waited in the woods near the Merrivale cabin every evening, but Melissa had been able to slip out and meet him only once in that time. He missed her desperately. Of course, he thought, he missed her desperately when they had been apart only a few hours. Soon they would have to work out the details of their marriage—the sooner the better as far as Jeff was concerned.

The double doors leading into the store opened, and Norah Holt appeared. "Bartholomew, I want you to help me pick out some cloth for a new pair of curtains," she said.

He grimaced. "Now, Norah, you know I'm no good at things like that."

"You live there, too, and you ought to have a say in such matters," she insisted. "Come along."

Bartholomew grinned sheepishly at the other men and said to Clay and Jeff, "You heard your mother, lads. And if I'm going in, the two of you are, too. Come on."

Clay and Jeff followed him into the store. Bartholomew might complain good-naturedly in a situation like this, but they both knew he did not really mind.

They found Norah and the children at the back of the right-hand aisle, where several bolts of cloth were stacked on the wooden shelves. While Bartholomew pretended an interest in the decision that Norah was offering him, Clay and Jeff drifted over to the long counter at the rear of the store. Part of the counter was taken up with glass-enclosed display shelves, and a selection of hunting knives was arrayed on one. Clay and Jeff were studying them when the proprietor approached them from the other side of the counter.

"Interest either of you boys in a knife?" Steakley asked, leaning on the countertop. "Got the finest blades in Marietta."

Clay slipped his hunting knife from its sheath and held it up so that the light from a nearby candle shone on its long, heavy, slightly curved blade. "Think I'll stick with what I've got," he said. "It hasn't let me down yet."

Steakley drew back a little from him. Clay was an impressive sight in his buckskins, buffalo-hide cape, and coonskin cap. "That's fine, Clay," the storekeeper said quickly. "Don't reckon I'd trade that in, either."

"I might need a new hunting knife sometime, Mr. Steakley," Jeff said.

"Going beaver trapping with your brother?" Steakley asked.

"Who said anything about beaver trapping?" Clay asked sharply.

Steakley looked uneasy again. "Well, nobody, really. Folks just sort of figured that you'd go back west. There's been talk that the fur trade's really going to open up now in the mountains, ever since that expedition you went on with Lewis and Clark. But I didn't mean no offense—"

"None taken," Clay broke in. "Didn't mean to sound like I did. I was just a little surprised."

Jeff laughed. "Anyway, I'm not going trapping. I've got plenty to keep me busy right here in Ohio." He was thinking about Melissa, of course, and the thought sent a warm glow through him.

That feeling was shattered a moment later when a harsh voice boomed out from the front of the store, "Looks like you let just about anything in here these days, Steakley. You must not care who you do business with."

Clay and Jeff swung around, both of them recognizing Zach Garwood's voice. Zach had just entered the store and was sauntering down the main aisle, followed by Pete, Luther, and Aaron. A moment later Alfred Garwood came in with his daughter, Josie, who was holding little Matthew's hand, pulling him along. The toddler appeared to be in a surly mood.

"Pa," Jeff said in a low but intense voice. He looked over and saw Bartholomew emerge from the other aisle, shepherding the rest of the family with him.

"I heard, son," Bartholomew said. "It's nothing to worry about. Just ignore them."

That was easier said than done, Jeff thought. Zach swaggered all the way down the aisle and then leaned on the counter, only a few feet away from the Holts.

"I said you ain't particular, Steakley, about who you have in your store," Zach said mockingly. "You even deal with Holts."

"I deal with anybody who's honest and willing to pay, Zach," the storekeeper replied in a rare display of gumption. "That's the only way to stay in business. Reckon you wouldn't know about that, however."

Eyes cold and angry, Zach looked at him. "And I sure as hell don't need any lessons from you, old man."

"Sorry," Steakley muttered, backing off.

Zach turned toward the Holts as his brothers came forward. Following his example, they leaned on the counter, too. He asked, "What're you doing here?"

"Buying supplies, Zachariah," Bartholomew answered. "I imagine the same thing brought you to town today."

"That's right. But I don't much like having to buy things from the same store where you are."

Bartholomew sent a warning look to Clay and Jeff, who had tensed at Zach's insolent tone. Then he said, "I reckon you can go somewhere else. There's other trading posts around here."

Zach shook his head. "I like it here. Why don't you and your bunch get the hell out, old man?"

Clay waited impatiently, wondering how much his father was going to take. Zach Garwood needed to be taught a lesson in manners. Jeff, on the other hand, hoped that Bartholomew showed restraint and refused to let Zach anger him. With Norah and the children here, this was no place for a fight. They were already outnumbered, and some of the layabouts on the front porch were known to be cronies of the Garwoods. If a brawl started, they would probably pitch in and make the odds even worse. The Holts could not count on any help from Steakley or the other men; the prevailing attitude seemed to be that they had gotten themselves into this mess—or rather that Clay had—and they would have to deal with it themselves. And if there was a fight, Constable Sutcliffe would undoubtedly show up after it was over, blaming the Holts for the trouble.

Bartholomew took a deep breath, obviously trying to control his temper. He turned away from Zach as Alfred Garwood and Josie ambled up. Josie had given up on getting Matthew to cooperate with her and had let go of the child, allowing him to wander up and down the aisles of the store. The other women who had been shopping were now steering their children toward the front of the building, away from trouble.

"Hello, Alfred," Bartholomew said pleasantly to Garwood. "How are you today?"

"Rheumatism's actin' up," Garwood replied sourly. "It's this damned weather. Makes my joints stiffen up."

"Sorry to hear that," Bartholomew said. "You'd best speak to your boy here and tell him he ought to be more polite to his elders."

"Zach's a grown man. He does as he pleases." With that, Garwood turned and headed for the pickle barrel in the corner, making it plain that he was not going to interfere in his son's harassment of the Holts. Neither was Josie, who was standing by with an interested yet enigmatic look on her face, waiting to see what was going to happen.

"What should we do, Zach?" Pete asked with a broad, wet-lipped grin. "You want me to shoo 'em out of here?"

"Like they were a flock of dirty chickens?" Zach asked. "That's a good idea, Pete." He straightened. "Maybe we'll all do some shooing."

Jeff felt a surge of despair. The Garwoods were not going to be turned aside. He glanced over at Clay and saw a faint smile playing on his older brother's lips. Clay was looking forward to the fight, Jeff realized.

Footsteps from the front of the store and a woman's sudden gasp of surprise made Jeff look in that direction, and he stiffened as he saw who had just entered. Charles Merrivale stood there, his wife beside him. The tension between Garwoods and Holts was obvious.

And just to Merrivale's left was Melissa, her eyes wide with fear.

The fear that set Melissa Merrivale's heart to pounding was for Jeff, not for herself. She assessed the situation at a glance, and there was no mistaking what was about to happen. The belligerent stances of the Garwood brothers, coupled with the tense attitudes of the Holts, could mean only one thing. Trouble was about to break out.

Jeff had fallen afoul of the Garwoods several times in recent weeks, and each time he had been hurt. That was because his nature was basically a gentle one, Melissa knew. Jeff would fight when he was forced to, but he lacked the ruthlessness, the urge to hurt or even kill his enemy, that Zach and the other Garwoods possessed. Zach was the worst of the bunch, Melissa thought, and at that moment he was standing with his jaw thrust out arrogantly, his arms held loosely at his sides, his hands clenched into fists. He was ready to start throwing punches at any second.

If a fight started, Jeff would be hurt, perhaps even badly hurt, Melissa realized. She had to stop this right now, before things got out of hand. But how?

The answer popped into her mind. It would require drastic action, but she knew instinctively it was the only thing she could do.

"Jeff!" she said loudly, drawing the attention of the other people in the store and the ones just outside on the porch. She grasped her father's arm and started forward, propelling him with her. Charles Merrivale's shock at her action was such that he did not resist at first and let his daughter steer him down the aisle toward the rear of the store.

"I'm glad you're here, Jeff," Melissa went on, still speaking loudly. Out of the corner of her eye, she saw the Garwoods glowering at her, but she ignored them and forged ahead. "This is perfect. Your family is here, and my family is here, so we can make that announcement we wanted to make."

Jeff had been staring at her with a mixture of concern and puzzlement, but now his expression suddenly changed as he realized what she was talking about. "Melissa!" he exclaimed. "You can't—"

"Why not, darling?" she asked as she came up beside him. With her right hand still holding her father's arm, she linked her left arm with Jeff's right.

Charles Merrivale echoed, "Darling?" His already florid face turned an even deeper shade of red. "What the devil is going on here?"

"It's simple, Father," Melissa said, giving Jeff a meaningful glance. "Jefferson Holt has asked me to be his wife, and I've accepted. We're going to be married."

"Married!" Merrivale exploded as his wife let out a cry of surprise. The Holts were equally shocked, all except Clay, who gave Jeff a knowing smile.

"When did this happen, son?" Bartholomew asked, his expression solemn.

"Not long ago," Jeff replied. "We didn't want to tell anyone until we'd made our plans—"

"Jefferson Holt." Merrivale's voice was quietly quivering with rage. "I ought to thrash you! Asking for my daughter's hand in marriage without securing my blessing first. I'll not have it, do you hear me?"

Still smiling, Melissa said in a low voice, "You don't have anything to say about it, Papa. It's already done."

Hermione moved in quickly from the other side, saying, "I think this is wonderful, Charles. I'm sure Melissa and Jeff will be very happy together." She turned to Jeff and put her arms around him to hug him. "Welcome to our family, Jefferson."

Norah, beaming with happiness and relief, stepped over to Melissa. "Jeff couldn't have chosen a more wonderful bride." She hugged the young woman.

At the same time Clay slapped Jeff on the back, then pumped his hand in congratulations. Bartholomew joined in the handshaking and took his turn hugging Melissa, while Edward, Susan, and Jonathan flocked toward the happy couple. Jeff slid an arm around Melissa's shoulders and held her tight.

"Have all you people gone mad?" demanded Charles Merrivale. "I said there wasn't going to be a wedding!"

"You said no such thing," Hermione told him in a tart voice. "You're simply having a bit of trouble adjusting to the news, but when you do—and that will be soon—you'll be as happy for the children as I am, Charles." Her tone made it clear that she would tolerate no argument.

It was exceedingly rare for Hermione Merrivale to stand up to her husband, and he stared at her in wide-eyed surprise. Then, unwilling to contradict his wife and his daughter in public, he took a deep breath and reluctantly held out his hand to Jeff. With a teeth-baring grimace, he said in barely civil tones, "Welcome to the family, young man."

Melissa tried not to sigh too heavily in relief as Jeff shook her father's hand. She cast a glance over at the Garwoods. Pete, Luther, and Aaron seemed rather confused as they stood by and watched the fuss over the young couple. Zach's dark eyes smoldered with rage as he looked on. He knew perfectly well what Melissa had done and why. More people were crowding into the store now to congratulate Jeff and Melissa, and the air of tension and hostility that had pervaded the place only moments earlier had utterly evaporated. There would be no fighting in there today; Melissa's surprising announcement had seen to that.

She heard a low, throaty laugh and looked around to discover that it was coming from Josie Garwood. It appeared that Josie appreciated the irony of the situation. Her father had come up beside her during the commotion, and as she grasped his arm, she said, "Come on, Pa. Let's get what we came for and get out of here."

Alfred Garwood said, "Sure. Come along, Zachariah, and bring your brothers!" He headed for the far corner of the store.

Melissa felt Jeff's arm tighten around her shoulders, and she looked up at him. He had recovered from his own surprise and was smiling happily now. She could see, too, that he shared her relief. Jeff had not wanted a fight any more than she had. He said quietly, "We didn't get a chance to do any planning."

"Don't worry about that," she told him. "My mother and her friends will take care of everything, I'm sure. They love to take charge of things like weddings."

Jeff chuckled. "I'd say your mother isn't the only one who likes to take charge."

Melissa glanced at the Garwoods, who had withdrawn to another part of the store, and said, "I just did what I thought needed to be done."

And she would do it again, she thought. She loved Jeff Holt so much that she would do anything to protect him, even if it meant defying her father, as she had done today.

Mrs. Jefferson Holt. It had a very nice sound, Melissa decided, a very nice sound indeed.

It was amazing how quickly time could pass, Jeff discovered over the next few weeks. Things were happening so quickly that he could hardly keep up with them. First, he and Melissa had set their wedding date for early November. The worst of the winter storms would not have arrived yet, in all likelihood, and that would give him time to make sure they had a place to live. On the same day their engagement had been announced, Bartholomew made a gift of land to his second son, the north field. Land could be cleared nearby for a cabin, and with Clay's help, it would be ready for Jeff and Melissa to move into on their wedding day.

Jeff worried some about how Clay would take all of this, but he soon found that there was no need for concern.

"Hell," Clay told him privately that night as they stood in the doorway of the cabin, after everyone else had retired, "I don't want that land. You know as well as I do that I won't be staying here. I'm heading west again."

"Not until after the wedding, I hope."

"Nope, not until after the wedding. I thought I'd be gone before now, but things seem to keep holding me back. I'm sure not going to miss my little brother's wedding. And we've got a cabin to put up between now and then, too."

Jeff put his hand on Clay's shoulder. "I really appreciate everything, Clay. I don't know how to thank you."

"No need," Clay replied, shaking his head. "You'd do the same if things were turned around, wouldn't you?"

"You know I would."

"Then there's no need to say any more."

Sometimes it felt mighty good to have a big brother, Jeff thought.

It rained for a couple of days after that, but as

soon as the weather was decent again, Jeff and Clay began working on the cabin, devoting themselves to that task while Bartholomew and Edward handled the other chores on the farm. Clearing the area for the cabin came first. The trees they felled would be used as logs for building. Day in and day out, the woods rang with the sound of axes as Jeff and Clay worked. Jeff's injuries had healed for the most part, and he felt himself growing stronger as the days passed.

The cabin would be small, one room with a loft. It could be added on to later as their family grew. That thought gave Jeff a warm feeling as he worked. He and Melissa wanted a large family. She had been an only child, but Bartholomew and Norah Holt had had eight children, although only five of them survived infancy. As the family helped settle what had been a wilderness only a few decades earlier, Bartholomew and Norah had suffered other troubles and tragedies, but they had persevered, helping each other and drawing on each other's strength. Jeff just hoped that he and Melissa would do as good a job with their own family.

He saw her nearly every day now. She ate dinner with his family at least once a week, and Hermione insisted that Jeff take as many of his meals with them as he wanted. Evidently Charles Merrivale had reconciled himself to the idea of the impending wedding, albeit reluctantly. He had little to say to Jeff, and his few comments were usually spoken in a sullen growl. But at least Merrivale had not taken a shotgun to him, and Jeff was thankful for that.

The wedding, it was decided, would be held in the big main room of the Merrivale house, and afterward everyone would adjourn to the Holt farm for a dance in celebration of the newlyweds. If the weather permitted, the party would be held outside. Otherwise, it would be moved into the spacious barn. As the auspicious date approached, Bartholomew and Edward moved the livestock to a back field and cleaned out the barn, just in case.

Jeff and Clay had the walls of the new cabin up, and on a Saturday, one week to the day before the wedding, several men from the surrounding farms arrived to help them raise the roof. There was no dance this time when the long day's labor was done, but Bartholomew brought a jug to pass around as toasts were drunk to Jeff and his bride. For the first time in quite a while—since the confrontation between Clay and Josie Garwood nearly three years earlier, in fact— Jeff felt as if the Holts were truly part of the community again. That was one more thing for which he was grateful to Melissa.

There had been no more trouble with the Garwoods since Melissa had averted the near clash in Steakley's trading post by announcing the engagement. Jeff brought up that subject as he and Clay worked together during the last few days before the wedding, building the furniture that Jeff and Melissa would need to start their new life together.

"Maybe the Garwoods have given up on that grudge," Jeff suggested as he planed a slab of wood for a tabletop. "Maybe they finally figured out how foolish the whole thing was."

"I wouldn't bet on it," Clay grunted. He was hewing legs for the table out of the trunks of several saplings. "They're not the kind to give up on anything, especially Zach. He'll hang on to his hate forever—or at least until somebody kills him. And that's bound to happen sooner or later, the way Zach goes looking for trouble. The sooner the better, you ask me."

Jeff thought Clay spoke of killing too casually.

"You keep your eyes open," Clay went on. "Zach and his brothers are just biding their time."

"Have you talked to Josie since you've been back?" Jeff asked.

Clay's features hardened into an unreadable mask. "Ran into her one day on the way into town," he said curtly.

"The two of you didn't come to any kind of—understanding?"

"Nothing to come to an understanding about." Clay did not look up from his work. "She's still lying, and I still won't have any part of it."

After a minute had passed, Jeff said, "You see the boy?"

"I saw him." Clay's tone indicated plainly that he did not want this discussion to continue, so Jeff changed the subject.

It stayed in his thoughts, though, and for the first time in quite a while, he realized he believed Clay again. Despite his hardened exterior, Clay was good with children; when he was around youngsters was about the only time he let his gentle side come out. Jeff knew his brother well enough to be sure that if Clay had indeed fathered little Matthew Garwood, he would not have been able to turn his back on him.

It was good to be able to have faith in Clay again. In fact, Jeff mused, plenty of good things had been happening lately, to go along with the bad ones.

Almost before Jeff knew it, the day of the wedding dawned. The weather was unusually warm for November, and fluffy white clouds floated in the deep blue sky overhead. It was a gorgeous day, and Jeff knew the party following the ceremony would probably last long into the night. He and Melissa would slip away before it was over. They would have some celebrating of their own to do, in private.

Jeff spent the day making sure that everything was ready at the new cabin. Melissa had already brought some of her things over and helped fix the place up the way she wanted. In addition to the table and benches, the churn and the spinning wheel, the cabinet for kettles and pots and other cooking utensils, there was a brand-new bed, attached to one wall. Several quilts covered the thick mattress stuffed with straw, the top one, Melissa's favorite, made by Hermione Merrivale. On the other side of the room the peg ladder led up to the loft, and at the rear was the fireplace with a heavy oaken beam for a mantel. The walls were securely chinked with mud; Edward, Susan, and Jonathan had come over to help with that part of the construction. On either side of the door was a small window, covered with greased paper. It was a snug little cabin, and Jeff was quite pleased with it. Melissa seemed to be, too.

Still, as Jeff puttered around the cabin, he felt his nervousness increasing. In a few hours he would be getting married, and although he wanted Melissa to be his wife more than anything else in the world, there was no denying that his life would be changed forever by the events of that day. Growing up, he had assumed that Clay would marry first, since he was several years older. Now he was not sure that Clay would ever marry. In a few days he would again head into the vast western wilderness, and it was entirely possible that his family would never see him again.

That was a sobering thought, and it only increased Jeff's sense of unease. He tried to put his mind on more cheerful subjects, but it was difficult.

"The way you're frowning, Jeff, a man would think you weren't happy about getting married."

Jeff looked up and saw Clay lounging in the doorway, one shoulder against the jamb. Jeff knew he must have really been distracted not to have heard his brother approaching.

"I was just thinking."

"Might be that's not the smartest thing to do on your wedding day," Clay commented dryly.

"Do you think I'm doing the right thing? By marrying Melissa, I mean."

Clay hesitated, then stepped into the cabin. "I reckon most men have asked themselves that question on their wedding days, all the way back to ol' Moses and those other fellows in the Bible. Let me ask you a question: Do you love Melissa?"

Jeff did not have to think about it. "I surely do."

"Then you're doing the right thing. She's a mighty fine girl, Jeff, grew up smart and brave, and those are things you don't always find in people. Treat her right."

"I intend to," Jeff promised.

Clay stepped up to him and slapped him on the shoulder—something that had been happening to Jeff a great deal lately as people congratulated him. "Well," Clay said, a broad grin spreading across his face, "let's go get you married."

CHAPTER TEN

The wedding ceremony was performed by the local minister, the Reverend Josiah Crosley, a round-faced young man with an infectious smile. The Merrivales' cabin was packed with guests as Jeff and Melissa stood hand in hand in front of the massive fireplace. Clay, looking uncomfortable in a suit, stiff collar, and cravat, stood next to Jeff as his best man. He had to make an effort to look solemn while he watched Jeff pale as the ceremony progressed. The boy was liable to faint dead away if the preacher did not get things moving a little faster, Clay thought.

Melissa wore a long gown made of white silk, and as far as Jeff was concerned, she had never looked lovelier. Her father had sent back East for the material to make the dress. Charles Merrivale might not have approved of the marriage, but Jeff had to admit he had not spared any expense to make the wedding itself a memorable event for his daughter. The room was decorated with wildflowers, and Merrivale and his wife were both wearing their Sunday best. Hermione was especially attractive in a green silk gown. As for the Holts, they did not have the finery the Merrivales possessed, but Norah had made sure their clothes were spotless. Jeff, Clay, and Bartholomew wore their best cutaway coats, and their cravats were expertly tied. The younger children were well scrubbed; even little Jonathan had stayed clean so far.

The wedding guests stood quietly as Reverend Crosley continued with the ceremony. Jeff tried to pay attention to the words the preacher was saying, but it wasn't easy. His mind was full of thoughts of the future, ranging from that night—he was thinking a great deal about that night—to the years that would roll past while he and Melissa made their life together. Marriage was a fine thing, he told himself.

But if it was so all-fired wonderful, why did his knees feel as if they weren't going to hold him up much longer? Why were there tiny beads of sweat on his forehead? Why did his mouth feel so dry he could have planted corn in it? Clay had said it was normal for a fellow to feel this way when he was getting married, but suddenly nothing about it seemed normal to Jefferson Holt. What if he was making a terrible mistake?

Jeff realized abruptly that the preacher was looking at him, waiting for something. Josiah Crosley repeated softly, "Do you take this woman as your lawful wedded wife, Jefferson?"

Turning to look into Melissa's eyes, all of Jeff's uncertainties vanished. A Holt knew when something was right, and he was not about to let it get away from him just because of a few foolish doubts. Jeff said in a firm voice, "I do."

Crosley said, "And do you, Melissa, take this man Jefferson . . ."

There was a roaring in Jeff's ears, and he figured out after a moment that it was his own blood pulsing in his head. He saw Melissa's lips move, her warm, soft lips forming the words *I do*, and then the preacher said something else and Melissa turned to Jeff. He put his arms around her and kissed her. It seemed like the thing to do.

Well, he thought a minute later, *this marriage business wasn't so bad after all.* Melissa squeezed his hands, and together they turned to face the crowd of well-wishers.

After that, there was a lot of handshaking and hugging and congratulating. Even Charles Merrivale looked almost happy as he hugged his daughter and then shook Jeff's hand. Perhaps his father-in-law really would come around in time and accept him, Jeff thought.

While the newly married couple was surrounded by guests, Clay Holt studied the crowd. The Garwoods had not shown up for the wedding. That was no real surprise, but he would not have put it past Zach and his brothers to try to disrupt the ceremony and spoil the day.

Bartholomew stepped up onto a bench and held up his hands, calling for quiet. When he had the attention of everyone in the room, he said in a loud voice, "All of you are invited back to the farm with us for a celebration in honor of the bride and groom. There'll be music for dancing, and some of the ladies have cooked up a real feast for us. You're all welcome, so come along and kick up your heels! We've got us a wedding to celebrate!"

Applause and enthusiastic shouts greeted the announcement. The crowd thinned out as guests left the Merrivale house to head for the Holt farm. Jeff and Melissa were escorted out to a phaeton decorated with brightly colored bunting and drawn by a team of fine black horses. The carriage belonged to Charles Merrivale, but for that day the wedding couple would be using it.

As Melissa settled beside him on the seat, Jeff picked up the reins. He flicked them and got the horses moving. Melissa held his arm and leaned warmly against him. Children ran alongside the phaeton as it rolled down the road toward the Holt farm, the wedding guests following after it, some in carriages and wagons, some on horseback, and others on foot.

Clay had brought his horse, and he mounted now, then pointed the animal through the woods to a shortcut that would get him to the farm before Jeff and Melissa. As he rode, he took off the cravat and opened his collar, glad to have the confounded thing off his neck. He smiled as he tucked the cravat into his saddlebag, but then, as his fingers brushed the butt of the pistol he had put there earlier, his expression grew more serious. He took the pistol out, primed and loaded it, and slipped it underneath his belt.

Clay had not told anyone of his plans. On the off chance that the Garwoods might have gone to the Holt place to ready some kind of trap, he had decided to get there first and check everything to be sure the farm was safe before Jeff and Melissa arrived. A cautious man generally stayed alive longer than one who was careless.

Clay saw nothing suspicious—no strange horses, at least—when he came in sight of the farm. Several tables had been brought over from neighboring farms earlier in the day, and now they were lined up in the large open area to one side of the cabin. They would be loaded with platters of food that had been prepared by the ladies of the Marietta area.

Drawing the pistol and gripping it tightly, Clay rode past the cabin and into the barn. Still nothing unusual. He reined in. He had halfway expected the Garwoods to try something. It was not like them to pass up such a ready-made opportunity to wreak havoc on the Holt family. But if that was indeed the case, Clay was going to accept the good fortune with gratitude.

He unsaddled his horse, put the animal in one of the stalls, then went back outside. As he looked down the road, he could see the wedding procession approaching, led by the phaeton carrying Jeff and Melissa. Clay put the pistol away, tucking it behind his belt in the small of his back so that the tails of his coat concealed it. He pushed his hat to the back of his head as he waited for everyone else to arrive.

Soon the Holt farm was quite busy. A steady stream of ladies went into the cabin and then came back out again, each bearing another platter of food on her return. There was fried chicken, roasted wild duck, ham, and venison steaks; bowls of potatoes, beans, squash, and cabbage; biscuits, johnnycake, corn pone, and fritters; deep-dish apple pie and cake; and plenty of molasses and honey. Another table held jugs of fresh milk, along with a pot of coffee and one of tea. Most of the settlers could not afford such extravagances as coffee and tea, but Charles Merrivale had furnished this luxury to make the day special.

The elderly men who provided music for most of the barn dances brought out their fiddles and began tuning them, although the serious dancing would not get under way until after sundown. In the meantime, the guests would occupy themselves eating and visiting with the bride and groom. Chairs were brought out of the house for Jeff and Melissa, and they were seated in front of the cabin in a place of honor. Guests filed past them, shaking hands and offering congratulations.

Jeff's face soon began to ache from the constant smiling and talking. He was not accustomed to having such a fuss made over him. Of course, most of it was actually directed at Melissa, he realized. The bride was really the center of attention at a wedding celebration. In this case, when the bride was not only radiantly beautiful but also the daughter of a well-to-do, influential man, people were naturally going to want to speak to her and offer their best wishes. Still, Jeff had to admit he was enjoying himself.

He looked for Clay amid the crowd and finally spotted him leaning against the corner of the house, munching on a piece of johnnycake. Jeff knew his brother was keeping watch for any trouble, and he felt grateful for that. Later in the evening, when the dancing started, some of the men would probably pass around jugs of corn liquor they had brought in their wagons. It was possible that some of them would have too much to drink, but Jeff did not anticipate anything that Clay could not handle.

Heaping plates of food were brought to the young couple; it proved tricky to balance them on their knees while they ate and continued to visit with the guests, but Jeff and Melissa managed as best they could. All in all, Jeff thought, things were proceeding as smoothly as anyone could have wished. Now that the ceremony itself was over, his nervousness had vanished, and he was having the time of his life. It would only get better a little later when he would have the opportunity to dance with his wife for the first time.

His wife. . . . Lord, he liked the sound of that!

The sun slid down to the horizon and dipped beneath the trees. As the shadows of dusk began to gather, lanterns were lit, along with a stack of wood that had been piled in front of the barn for a bonfire. The fiddlers sawed on their instruments while another man clapped out the time and stamped his foot, and many of the guests gathered to dance. Before anyone else started, though, Jeff and Melissa were escorted to the center of the big circle that had been formed. ''The wedding couple gets the first dance,'' the caller shouted, and cheers went up from the crowd.

Jeff took Melissa in his arms and launched into a reel. They moved wonderfully well together, he thought, and he was sorely tempted to kiss that smiling face only inches from his. In fact, that was exactly what he did, brushing his lips across hers, and both of them stumbled a bit in their steps before recovering their composure. That drew laughter and more cheers and applause from the guests.

This was what it was like to feel giddy with happiness, Jeff supposed. After all the grim, unpleasant events of the past few months, today was exactly the tonic he had needed. They had all needed this, Jeff thought. Maybe the wedding would mark the beginning of a time of peace in Marietta.

Other couples started dancing, including Charles and Hermione Merrivale. Melissa's father did not look particularly enthusiastic, but Hermione would not be denied. Soon the area between the cabin and the barn was full of swirling figures. Most people on the frontier danced and danced well; it was one of the few forms of recreation in a generally hard life.

After a few songs had been played, Jasper Sutcliffe left the dance floor and headed for the Merrivales. With a show of smiles and handclasps, he took leave of them and walked to where Jeff and Melissa were resting. He was going home, he explained, because he was developing a headache and thought he would be better off there. Melissa was entirely sympathetic and expressed concern for his health, but Jeff was skeptical of the constable's excuse. Ever since he had seen Josie Garwood at Sutcliffe's office that day, Jeff had believed beyond a doubt that the constable was one of her lovers. He had noted her absence that evening, and he suspected that Sutcliffe had arranged to meet her while everyone else was celebrating.

As night fell, the flames leaping from the bonfire seemed to grow brighter, casting their glow over the party. The music was loud and raucous, and everyone seemed to be laughing now. The celebration would go on far into the night.

Jeff and Melissa would be gone long before then. They would slip off to their own cabin without anyone noticing they had left—if they were lucky. If they were not that fortunate, it was possible some of the guests, mostly young men with whom Jeff had grown up, would follow them and drunkenly serenade them outside the cabin. That would be distracting at best. There had been instances when brides had been taken from their husbands on their wedding nights in mock kidnappings, but Jeff didn't think they would have to worry about that.

They would not be leaving the party until later,

though. For now they would enjoy the music, the dancing, and more of the food.

Clay moved among the crowd, occasionally dancing with one of the young ladies in attendance. He spotted jugs being passed around among the male guests. He enjoyed a drink of good corn whiskey as much as the next man, but it did sometimes lead to trouble at gatherings such as this. Still, he knew better than to try to put a stop to it. He would deal with any scuffles as they occurred.

He was on his way back to the cabin when he saw several men standing at the tables, filling plates with food. Even with their backs to him, he recognized them immediately. He stopped dead in his tracks. A moment later, when Zach Garwood turned around, a plateful of food in his hand, he greeted Clay. Behind him his brothers continued piling ham, chicken, and johnnycake on their plates.

Clay recovered from his surprise and looked around to see if Josie had come with them, but he saw no sign of her. He walked over to Zach. He was acutely aware of the pistol snugged behind his back and wondered if he should reach for it. Zach did not appear very threatening at the moment, however, not unless he intended to attack Clay with a plateful of home-cooked food.

"Hello, Holt," Zach said pleasantly enough. He was wearing clean clothes and was freshly shaven; Clay could smell the bay rum on him.

"Zach," Clay said curtly. "What are you doing here?"

"Why, the boys and I thought we'd take in the celebration and offer our congratulations to the happy couple," Zach answered in an easy, casual voice. "That's what wedding parties are for, aren't they? And we figured the whole community was invited, since that's the way it's usually done. Ain't that right?"

Clay's jaw tightened. Zach had a point, as much as Clay hated to admit it. No formal invitations had been issued for either the wedding or the party. Instead, word had been spread throughout the town and the farms of the surrounding countryside, and anyone who wanted to attend was free to show up. A wedding was nearly always a community event.

Pete, Luther, and Aaron Garwood had finished getting their food, and now they joined Zach, the three of them hanging back slightly in a watchful attitude, waiting to see what would happen next. That attitude was shared by the other guests who had noticed the Garwoods. The fiddlers kept playing, but the sounds of talk and laughter gradually died away as more and more of the guests became aware of a possible confrontation between Clay and the Garwoods.

Clay was saved from having to make a decision. A hand grasped his elbow, and he looked over to see his father. Bartholomew was smiling, but he regarded the Garwoods cautiously. "Welcome to you and your brothers, Zach. Glad you could come."

"Thanks, Mr. Holt." Zach hefted the plate of food in his hands. "Quite a spread you've got here. The boys and I thought we'd come by and say howdy."

"Enjoy yourselves," Bartholomew told him. "There's plenty to eat, and the music's just fine for dancing."

"Sounds good. Right, boys?" Zach asked his brothers over his shoulder. There was a chorus of agreement from Pete, Luther, and Aaron.

Bartholomew exerted a little pressure on Clay's arm. "Come along, son. Let's allow our guests to join in the celebration."

"Sure," Clay grunted. He let his father steer him away from Zach and the others, but he glanced back once. His eyes met Zach's, and he saw nothing there except hatred.

"This is your brother's wedding day, Clay," Bartholomew said in a low voice. "Don't ruin it by making a scene."

"I wasn't planning to, Pa," Clay said coolly. "I hadn't decided what to do when you came up."

"No, but I could tell what you were thinking." Bartholomew's tone was stern. "I don't want a brawl here, boy. Not tonight."

Clay said, "I won't start any trouble. But I won't back away from it, either."

"Fair enough. Now, why don't you go get a drink? Old Erasmus Newton's passing around a jug of mighty fine corn squeezin's."

"I'll give it a try."

Clay wandered over to a group of men and took the jug that was offered to him by a burly, gray-bearded settler. A quick pull on the jug sent liquid fire splashing down Clay's throat, and when it reached his stomach, it erupted in a bonfire to rival the one that was already lighting up the night. He gasped for a moment, eyes watering, then handed the jug back to its owner and said hoarsely, "That's prime, Mr. Newton, really prime." The settler gave him a gap-toothed grin and winked.

For a few minutes Clay seemed to be listening to the yarns being swapped by the men, but he was really watching the Garwoods. They had settled down on a bench to eat, and as they did, they paused from time to time to clap along with the music. They *seemed* peaceable tonight, but appearances could be deceiving, Clay knew, and he was sure that Zach was up to something. Clay had a hunch that before the night was over, he would find out what it was. He just hoped the discovery would not prove too unpleasant.

After a short while Clay sought out Jeff and Melissa. They had been dancing again, and Clay found them emerging from the crowd after a song had ended. He hugged Melissa and kissed her on the cheek, then said to her, "What do you think of the party so far?"

"I think it's all been lovely," Melissa said. "A girl couldn't have wanted a better wedding day than this."

"Glad to hear it." He said to Jeff, "I reckon you

noticed some new guests who came up a little while ago."

"The Garwoods? I saw them," Jeff replied. "They don't seem to be making any trouble so far."

"Perhaps they've called a truce," Melissa suggested. "That would be wonderful."

"Yep, it would," Clay said to his new sister-in-law. "But I sure wouldn't count on it."

"I'll be satisfied if they just behave themselves tonight," Jeff said.

"I'll see that they do." Clay moved on while Jeff and Melissa went to sit down and catch their breath.

With all the liquor being circulated at the party, it was inevitable that some men would get drunk, and it was equally likely that there would be trouble, even if it was just someone's getting sick. The celebration had been in full swing long enough now that Clay was not at all surprised when he spied a couple of men shoving each other in anger. Quickly he walked up to them as a crowd began to form. Grasping a shoulder of each man, he said sharply, "Hold on, boys. There's no fighting here, not tonight."

"He ran right into me," one of the men complained. "Clumsy as a damned ox."

"Clumsy?" the other man repeated angrily. "Hell, you ran into *me*!"

Before they could trade any more accusations, Clay said, "It doesn't look like either one of you is hurt, so there's no harm done. Why don't the two of you go on about your business?"

"Ain't gonna," growled one of the men.

"Then you'll have to fight me first, if you're so all-fired set on starting a ruckus," Clay said quietly.

The two men looked at him. Even in Sunday-go-to-meeting clothes, Clay Holt cut an impressive figure, and despite the corn liquor they had consumed, both men remembered that he had been across the Rockies and back with Lewis and Clark. Neither of them wanted to fight a man like that.

They muttered apologies and drifted apart, their quarrel forgotten.

That was only the first of several squabbles that Clay broke up before they developed into full-blown fights. The most difficult task he faced was persuading Erasmus Newton, who had partaken of too much of his own brew, that not every woman at the party was waiting anxiously to dance with him, especially since he had a reputation for trampling on his partner's feet in his enthusiasm. As Clay hung on to Newton's arm and all but dragged the man away from the circle of dancers, he said, "Come on, Erasmus. You need some of that coffee Mr. Merrivale brought."

"Don't want coffee," the bearded settler rumbled. "Got my own corn squeezin's to drink—if I c'n 'member where I put that damned jug."

Clay finally managed to steer Newton over to one of the tables and got him to sit down on a bench. He poured coffee into a pewter mug, shoved it in front of Newton, and patted the man's broad back. "Just drink that, Erasmus, and you'll feel better in a little while."

"Feel just fine right now—" Newton insisted, but then he slumped forward over the table and emitted a snore so loud that his big frame quivered.

Clay smiled and shook his head. Later, when Erasmus woke up, he would swear never to touch the demon's grog again—a vow that would not last long.

As Clay strolled back toward the fiddlers, he passed the corner of the Holt barn, and a flicker of movement caught his attention. The woods grew close to the rear of the barn, casting thick shadows there, and Clay peered intently in that direction. Even if somebody was behind the barn, he told himself, it wasn't necessarily trouble in the making. One of the guests could have slipped back there to relieve himself.

But it could also be one of the Garwoods skulking around, Clay thought, and if that was the case, the man was definitely up to no good.

Suddenly his keen eyes focused on a shape moving slowly from the barn toward the trees. Whoever was there was acting suspiciously. Clay hurried along the side of the large barn, reaching under the tails of his coat for his flintlock pistol as he called out, "Stop right there, mister!"

Instead of stopping, the man broke into a run, dashing for the cover of the trees. Clay could see the figure well enough now to be sure that it was male, but that was all he could tell. It was much too dark to recognize features or even clothes. Clay grimaced as he came to a stop and raised the pistol, his thumb reaching to cock the flintlock. At this range, in the dark, he thought, it was a chancy shot.

He hesitated. He didn't know who the man was or what he had been doing. Did he really want to try to shoot him? Slowly, Clay lowered the gun.

The figure disappeared into the trees. Clay trotted toward the rear of the barn, keeping an eye on the spot where the lurker had vanished, just in case the man came back and tried to ambush him. At the back corner of the barn, Clay peered carefully around it, the flintlock held ready for instant use. He didn't see anything except a strange red and yellow glow, low to the ground near the rear wall.

With fear sweeping through him like a cold wind, Clay realized what he was seeing. It was the sputtering and sparking of a trail of gunpowder that had been laid along the ground—a trail that led right up to the wall of the barn!

Clay threw himself back around the corner of the barn just before the world blew up in his face.

The roar shattered the night, completely drowning out the music of the fiddlers and the laughter of the crowd. Clay's ears rang from the explosion, but he was not deafened. He could hear the screams of the women, and a man giving one of the frontier's most dreaded cries.

"Fire!"

Clay stumbled back to the rear corner of the barn, looked around it, and saw a gaping hole in the wall of

the log structure. The straw that was stored in the barn
had begun to blaze. Cursing, he whirled and ran toward the front of the barn. His horse was in there, and
he had to get the animal out.

Men raced to the well beside the cabin, grabbed
the bucket that hung there, and lowered it, but Clay
knew it was not going to be nearly enough to fight the
blaze. They needed a dozen buckets, maybe more.

He darted through the open double doors at the
front of the barn, the pistol still in his hand, before
anyone realized what he was doing. When he reached
the stall where his horse was, he jammed the weapon
underneath his belt and opened the gate across the
stall. The explosion and the smoke from the fire had
scared the horse, and it danced around skittishly as
Clay tried to get it under control. Finally, he tangled
his fingers in its mane and flung himself on its back,
mounting as he had seen Indians do. He jerked the
horse's head around and dug his heels into its flanks,
sending it leaping out of the stall.

With a thunder of hooves he rode out of the barn,
sending frightened bystanders scattering. He hauled
back on the horse's mane, bringing the panic-stricken
animal to a halt long enough for him to slide off. The
horse raced off into the night, and Clay let him go. He
had more pressing matters to attend to.

Some guests must have had buckets in their wagons, for a line had formed, and the men were passing
several buckets back and forth between the well and
the burning barn. Jeff, Bartholomew, and Charles Merrivale were working side by side at the moment, Jeff in
the forefront so he could take each bucket handed to
him, dash into the barn, and fling the water on the fire.

Clay rushed over and joined in, filling a gap in
the line. He was glad they had emptied the barn of
other animals in preparation for the celebration.

The other guests had drawn well back, the
women keeping the children away from the blaze. For
long minutes that seemed more like hours, the settlers
fought to bring the fire under control, and finally the

flames died down. The roof of the barn had not ig-
nited, for which everyone was grateful. When the
flames were extinguished, the barn was still standing,
although heavily damaged.

Their faces grimy with smoke, Bartholomew and
his two oldest sons surveyed the destruction. He
frowned at the hole that had been blasted in the rear
wall. "What the devil happened back here?"

"Somebody set a keg of powder against the wall
and then poured out a trail of powder leading to it,"
Clay said. "I stumbled on it just before it went off, but
I didn't have a chance to put it out."

"Who would do such a thing?" Jeff asked, his
voice husky and strained from the smoke he had swallowed.

"Do you really have to ask that?" Clay said.
"There's only one bunch that would be low enough
and vicious enough." He turned and stalked off, his
eyes searching the faces of the guests. He was not surprised when he spotted Zach, Pete, Luther, and Aaron
Garwood standing at the edge of the crowd.

Other men backed away as Clay strode up to the
Garwoods. Zach said, "Bad luck, Holt. Wonder what
caused your barn to catch fire like that?"

"You know damn well what caused it," Clay accused hotly. "You or one of your brothers set off a keg
of powder back there! You could have killed somebody, you bastard!"

Zach stiffened. "You got no call to blame us," he
shot back. "We didn't have anything to do with your
damn barn, right, boys?" The others echoed his decla-
ration.

"You're a goddamn liar, Zach," Clay said, taking
a step toward the Garwoods. "And this time you're
going to pay for what you've done."

Seeing that Clay was not going to back down,
Zach struck the first blow instead. Leaping forward,
he threw a punch at Clay. Clay ducked to the side,
moving quickly enough so that Zach's punch barely
touched the side of his head. For an instant, Clay

thought about reaching for his pistol, but he knew he wanted more satisfaction than using a gun could bring him.

He wanted to beat Zach Garwood with his own hands.

Clay hooked a blow into Zach's stomach, but before he could land another punch, Pete howled in anger and charged. He slammed a fist against Clay's jaw. Clay staggered back, red lights seeming to burst behind his eyes. He shook his head, trying to clear it. He knew Pete would not give him much of a chance to recover.

As Pete lunged forward, Jeff flashed by Clay and met him with a fast combination of straight punches that rocked the bigger man. Jeff ducked under a looping blow from Pete and continued to pepper him with jabs.

Clay went after Zach again. The two men were roughly the same size, and they stood toe-to-toe for a long moment, trading punches. Then one of Clay's blows landed particularly clean, staggering Zach. Clay turned halfway to the side and launched a kick that caught Zach in the stomach and threw him backward, almost lifting him off his feet.

In the meantime, Bartholomew Holt, finally roused to anger, was struggling with Luther Garwood. Norah and the children, along with Melissa, were watching in horror. The rest of the crowd had formed a large circle around the brutal melee, not taking sides actively, although quite a few of the men were calling out encouragement to one family or the other. The cries blended with the harsh breathing of the combatants and the thud of fist against flesh.

Zach sank to his knees, clutching his stomach where Clay had kicked him. Clay started toward him, eager to press his advantage, but Aaron Garwood blocked his way. The young man was pale and wide-eyed with fear, but his fists were clenched with determination.

"Get out of the way, boy!" Clay rasped at him. "I don't want to hurt you—"

"Come on, Holt!" Aaron interrupted. "Come on, you bastard!" Bravado warred with the slight tremble in his voice.

With a shrug of resignation Clay started forward, determined that nothing keep him from Zach. He feinted to his left and, when Aaron went that way, too, veered in the other direction, clubbing a fist against the side of the young man's head. Aaron almost went down, but he was stubborn. He twisted around and grappled with Clay, trying to get an arm around his opponent's neck.

Zach was almost on his feet again, and Clay knew he had no time to waste with Aaron. He reached up, caught Aaron's arm at the elbow and wrist, and twisted savagely. A sharp crack was audible even over the sounds of the crowd.

Aaron screeched in pain as one of the jagged ends of broken bone tore through his flesh. He went to his knees and tumbled to the side, cradling the injured limb. Sobs and gasps of agony ripped from him.

Just as Zach regained his feet, Clay stepped forward and struck a blow to Zach's jaw. Zach sprawled to the ground, unconscious.

In the meantime, Jeff was using everything Clay had taught him about fighting. His speed and agility had enabled him to strike Pete again and again, while the giant had landed only grazing blows. Pete's nose was flattened, and blood from it covered the lower half of his face. His right eye was also bloody and swollen shut, and the left was not in much better shape. Jeff snapped a hard left and right to that eye, closing it, too. Pete's hands went to his face, and he slumped to his knees, all the fight gone out of him.

Simultaneously, Bartholomew Holt was having trouble with Luther. While Luther lacked the fighting skills of Zach and Pete, he seemed to be fueled by a frenzy of hate that had him flailing blows. Enough of them landed to drive Bartholomew back. As he suddenly lost his footing and tripped, Luther sprang after him and kicked him viciously in the side. Bartholomew curled up on the ground in pain.

At the same moment that Luther swung around to look for a new opponent, Clay was breaking Aaron's arm. Luther saw his younger brother fall and heard the screams of pain. His face contorted with a killing rage, Luther ran toward Clay and slipped a short knife from a sheath under his coat.

Clay was occupied with Zach and did not see Luther lunging toward him, the blade raised to strike. Jeff saw what was about to happen, however, and flung himself toward Luther's legs, trying to stop him any way he could.

Jeff crashed into Luther in a rolling tackle, and Luther fell heavily. Scrambling to the side, Jeff came up on hands and knees, expecting Luther to turn on him, but Luther was still hunched on the ground, and he uttered a high, thin shriek. He fell over onto his side and then rolled to his back, and Jeff gaped in horror as he saw Luther pawing weakly and futilely at the handle of the knife. The blade had been driven to the hilt in his belly when he fell. Luther's back arched up off the ground, and his screams grew louder. Suddenly everything was silent except for Luther's cries and Aaron's muffled whimperings. Blood trickled from the corners of Luther's mouth, and then he went limp, his hands falling away from the knife.

He was dead, and everyone knew it.

A second later Aaron passed out from the pain of his broken arm, and the silence was complete. Clay stepped over to Jeff and helped his brother to his feet. Then the two of them went to help their father. They lifted Bartholomew, whose left hand was pressed to his side, his features pallid.

"Are you all right?" Clay asked Jeff, who nodded as he slipped an arm around Bartholomew's shoulders. Clay left the two of them there and went over to Luther. He knelt beside the body, regarding it grimly.

He straightened and uttered a simple statement: "Dead."

The flintlock pistol was still behind Clay's belt. He slipped it out as he stalked over to Zach. Some of the onlookers gasped, assuming that Clay intended to shoot the oldest Garwood brother. Instead, Clay leveled the weapon at Zach and then prodded him in the side with a toe. After a moment Zach let out a groan and rolled halfway onto his side. Slowly, he pushed himself up into a sitting position as Clay stepped back and covered him.

"On your feet, Garwood," Clay said coldly. "You've got offal to haul away from here."

Jeff shuddered at the callousness in Clay's voice. Yet Clay's anger was justified. The Garwoods had been asking for real trouble for a long time now—and they finally had it.

Zach looked around dazedly, but his expression cleared when he saw Luther's body on the ground a few yards away. He scrambled over to his brother on hands and knees, then caught up one of Luther's outflung hands and clutched it tightly. "Dammit, no," he said. "Don't be dead, Luther!"

No answer came from Luther, of course, and after a few seconds Zach turned to regard the Holts. His gaze fastened in particular on Clay, and he said, "You'll pay for this. By God, you'll pay!"

Clay gestured with the barrel of the pistol. "Aaron's got a broken arm, and Pete can't see. You'd better get them out of here."

"You killed Luther—"

"It was an accident," Clay cut in flatly. "And you brought it on, Zach, you and your hatred for me and my family. If anybody really killed Luther, it was you."

Zach surged to his feet, his face twisted with hate, and for an instant it seemed he was going to charge Clay. But then Clay calmly raised the pistol again and centered the muzzle on him. If Zach did attack, he was going to be charging right into a lead ball. Trembling with the effort to restrain himself, Zach turned away, his shoulders shaking with emotion.

Bartholomew said, "Some of you men give Zach a hand." As a few of the settlers did as he had requested, Bartholomew turned to Norah, who hurried forward, concern etched on her face. Melissa went to Jeff, who drew her into his arms and held her for a long moment, stroking her hair. He was getting her wedding gown dirty, he knew, but at the moment, he didn't care.

Someone volunteered the use of a wagon, and when it had been pulled up close, Luther's body was lifted into it. Then, carefully, Aaron was also placed in the wagon bed. There was a doctor in Marietta who could perhaps set the young man's broken arm and treat his wound. A couple of men helped Pete onto the seat of the wagon. Although he still could not see through his swollen eyes, he had heard that Luther was dead, and sobs of grief and rage shook his massive body.

Zach stepped up onto the wagon, moving somewhat clumsily from the battering he had received. As he bent and picked up the lines, he looked at Clay and Jeff, his gaze moving back and forth between them. His eyes, Jeff thought, no longer looked angry. Instead, they seemed emotionless, even . . . dead.

"This ain't over," was all he said. Then he flicked the reins and got the team moving. With a creak of wheels the wagon rolled away from the Holt farm.

The violence had put an end to any thoughts of celebrating. A few guests sought out Jeff and Melissa and offered weak congratulations one final time, but most just slipped away, mounting their horses or climbing onto their wagons or simply walking off into the night. One of the last to leave was Charles Merrivale, who stalked over to his wife and daughter and grasped Hermione's arm. She had been standing with Melissa, trying to be of some comfort, for the past several minutes.

Now Merrivale tugged her away and said, "We're going."

"Of course, Charles," Hermione replied quickly, knowing that this was not the time to argue with him.

Merrivale paused in front of Jeff and Melissa. As he looked at his daughter, tears welled up in his eyes. He stepped forward and drew her into a close embrace that lasted seconds longer than was usual, his eyes shut tight. Then he held her at arms' length, said, "I love you, sweetheart," and kissed her on the cheek. Before leaving with Hermione, he fixed Jeff with a cold, unfriendly stare.

The man had never liked him, Jeff knew, and tonight's bloody incident would only increase Merrivale's hostility toward him and his family. Jeff was beginning to understand how Merrivale thought, and he knew his father-in-law probably blamed him for all the trouble.

"It's not fair," Jeff said, hardly realizing that he was speaking the words aloud.

Melissa squeezed his arm. "I know. The whole thing was awful. But it's over now, Jeff. And you and I are still married. We have to remember that."

He turned toward her and summoned up a weary smile. "I don't ever want to forget it." He kissed her gently.

"Can we go home now?" Melissa asked a moment later as she rested her head against his chest.

Home. . . . Even with everything that had happened, Jeff liked the sound of that word. He tightened his arms around her. "Yes," he said. "Let's go home."

CHAPTER ELEVEN

U nable to sleep, Jeff stirred restlessly in the bed
in the new cabin. Beside him Melissa shifted,
disturbed by his movements. Her nude body
was snuggled against his, and for a moment he rested
his hand on the curve of her hip, relishing the warmth
and smoothness of her skin. Then he slipped out from
under the heavy quilts and padded across the room to
the doorway. The air in the cabin felt cold on his skin,
and he retreated briefly to pick up a quilt lying on the
floor beside the bed. He wrapped it around himself,
then went back to the door and opened it just wide
enough to step outside. The new leather hinges made
no noise as he swung the door open.

The night was clear and cold, and his breath
fogged the air in front of him as he looked up at the
stars floating in the blackness overhead. From the
nearby woods he could hear the rustlings of small animals, and an owl gave its inquisitive and mournful
cry. Jeff took a deep breath, drawing the chilly air into

his lungs. At that moment he felt at peace, despite what had happened earlier in the evening.

Well, he thought, the wedding night had not gone exactly as planned. The explosion, the fire in the barn, the melee, and then Luther Garwood's death, all had cast a pall over the day, making Melissa and him much more solemn than they would otherwise have been. And yet once they had come to the cabin to consummate their marriage, their lovemaking had been incredibly intense. It was the first time for both of them, so Jeff was not surprised that their passion had been so strong. But their lovemaking had had a bitter-sweet quality to it, as well, perhaps because they realized that under the circumstances they were going to have to snatch whatever happiness they could at every opportunity.

Jeff looked at the stars and listened to the night-time quiet. Things were going to get bad now, he thought. Some people might call a truce rather than risk more bloodshed and death, but not Zach. The worst of it was knowing that he might strike back against innocents—like the children.

Maybe it would have been better, Jeff mused bleakly, if Clay had put a ball through Zach Garwood's head.

They would all just have to be careful. No one would work in the fields alone, and they would not go to town alone either. He and his father could work together most of the time, even though this part of the farm belonged to him now. They would share the chores on both places. The kick in the side that Bartholomew had suffered had resulted in a deep bruise but no broken ribs, as far as Norah could determine. Bartholomew swore by her ability to diagnose such things; Norah had attended to all the family's medical needs for several years after the settlers had first begun moving into the Northwest Territory.

As for Melissa, Jeff had already realized he could not risk leaving her alone in their new cabin. Whenever he was working with his father, he would first take Melissa to the other cabin to stay with Norah and the younger children. Jeff did not know Clay's intentions yet. He knew Clay wanted to get back to the mountains, and that he had remained in Ohio for this long mainly because of the wedding. Now that the wedding was over, he might head for the Rockies again.

It was hard to imagine Clay leaving, though, when things were building to a potentially violent head. He had left almost three years earlier when the question of Josie Garwood's baby had first come up, but Clay was a different man now. Jeff thought he regretted leaving before, especially now that he knew his departure had been seen by many folks as running away from his responsibilities. Clay would not want that to happen again.

These thoughts were running through Jeff's mind, making certain he was no closer to sleep than when he had stepped out of the cabin, when he heard a faint noise behind him. He turned and saw Melissa standing in the open doorway. Her dark hair was a tousled, luxurious mass, and the quilt she had wrapped around her left exposed a tantalizing bit of bare shoulder.

"What are you doing, Jeff? It's cold."

"I couldn't sleep, thought maybe a little fresh air would help me."

"Has it?"

"Not really. But I think I know what might."

"Oh." The starlight was bright enough for him to see how her lips curved softly in a smile. "And what would that be?"

He did not answer in words. Instead, he stepped into the cabin and closed the door behind him. A moment later both quilts slipped to the floor, and neither of them noticed the chill in the air for a long while after that.

Constable Jasper Sutcliffe paid a visit to the Holts the morning following the wedding. He had left the celebration early in the evening, he again explained, because he had felt under the weather, and while plenty of witnesses were available to tell him about the tragedy, he wanted to hear it from the Holts themselves. Bartholomew showed him the hole from the explosion, as well as the other damage the barn had sustained from the fire.

"But you've got no proof that the Garwood boys had anything to do with that," Sutcliffe pointed out. "Your son Clay really started the fight, and Luther Garwood lost his life because of that. I might have a case against Clay."

"I wouldn't advise trying to arrest him," Bartholomew cautioned. "Not in the mood he's in."

Sutcliffe shook his head. "I'm not going to arrest him. I said I might have a case. Too many people say the whole thing was an accident, and there's no getting around the fact it was Luther's own knife that did him in. No, I ain't arresting nobody. But all you Holts had better steer clear of trouble from now on."

At the noon meal Bartholomew told the family about Sutcliffe's visit. He assured them the constable had no intention of arresting Clay for murder, but that did little to ease their minds. Clay did his best to pass the incident off as unimportant, but no one took it lightly.

After the plates had been removed from the table, Melissa herded the children outside for a walk. Norah thanked her for spending so much time with Edward, Jonathan, and Susan. With the threat of retaliation from the Garwoods, they would now be spending a great deal of time together, she realized.

"Melissa is a sweetheart, Jeff," Norah said. "I'm so happy she's a part of the family."

Jeff got up and gave his mother a hug. "So am I. I just wish our wedding day hadn't ended the way it did."

They all were silent.

Finally Clay said, "We're going to have to do something about this, you know."

"What?" Bartholomew asked. "Go skulking over to the Garwood place and start shooting at them? What would that accomplish?"

"Might make them think twice before they try something," Clay said.

"Do you really think so? Knowing Zach Garwood, do you think that's what he would do?"

"I don't reckon he would. It would just make him more determined to get back at us."

"That's right."

Bartholomew got up from the table, his frustration making it impossible for him to remain still. He paced back and forth, his hands clasped behind his back. This was the most incredible mess, he thought. His family was involved in a dangerous situation that they had not asked for, that was no fault of their own. And they had no way out, except through constantly escalating levels of violence. If things continued in this fashion, peace between the Holts and the Garwoods would eventually come, all right—when they all were dead.

Bartholomew could not let that happen.

He reached for his old tricorn hat, plucking it off the peg where it hung by the door. He shrugged into his coat.

Norah looked up from the table, where she was sitting beside Jeff. "Where are you going, Bartholomew?"

"Out," he replied curtly, tucking his pistol under his belt. "Got an errand I need to do."

Norah looked alarmed, and Clay and Jeff shared her concern. "Stay here, Bartholomew," she said. "Please."

He shook his head. "Can't do that."

Norah's face paled. After so many years of marriage, she could often read her husband's mind, but at that moment she had no idea what he planned to do.

All she knew was that it would probably be dangerous.

She stood up and took a step toward him. "Then don't go alone. Take the boys with you," she pleaded.

Bartholomew looked at Clay and Jeff. Jeff stood beside Clay, and at that moment Bartholomew was quite proud of his two sturdy sons. But he said, "I'm not looking for trouble, Norah, and there's no need to take Clay and Jeff with me. I'll be fine."

"You should listen to what Ma's saying, Pa," Clay said. "Doesn't matter whether you're looking for trouble or not. With the Garwoods, that's what you're going to get."

Bartholomew's jaw tightened, and his voice had a seldom-heard ring of command in it when he said, "I won't have any argument from any of you. I know what I'm doing, and I'll thank you to let me get on about my business."

Norah took a sharp breath, and anger made her eyes spark. She was not accustomed to Bartholomew's talking to her like that. She said, "I'll have you know, Bartholomew Holt, that your business *is* my business."

"Not always," Bartholomew snapped. With that, he stalked out of the cabin.

Norah turned to her two oldest sons. "Don't just stand there. Go after your father and talk some sense into him."

Clay was beginning to understand the way his father must feel. "Maybe Pa's right, Ma. Maybe we shouldn't interfere with him."

Norah looked at Jeff, who nodded in agreement. "You boys—" she began angrily. Then, abruptly, her voice softened, and a bittersweet smile appeared on her face. "I was about to say that you boys are just like your father. And then I realized . . . I'm very glad that's true."

Clay put a hand on Jeff's shoulder. "Feel up to taking a walk, little brother?"

Jeff said, "I think so."

Clay gathered up his rifle and pistols. Jeff tucked his pistol into his belt and took his father's long rifle down from the wall pegs. "We'll be back," Clay said to his mother.

The cabin was well behind Bartholomew as he rode around a bend in the road. He checked over his shoulder occasionally to make sure Clay and Jeff were not following him, but so far he had seen no sign of them. Bartholomew hoped they would not come after him; if they did, he would just have to send them back home.

He had been acting on impulse when he left the cabin, but he had thought everything over while he was riding, and what he was about to do seemed to be the only possible way of reaching a peaceful solution. The odds of his being successful were slim, he had to admit, but he could not live with himself if he did not try to find some way to settle this terrible feud.

Since it was a weekday, most people were working on their farms, so Bartholomew saw few travelers on the road. He rode along resolutely, taking the cutoff that led past the Garwood farm. With any luck, he would find Alfred Garwood home alone, with the possible exception of Aaron, who was probably in bed recovering from his injury.

A few minutes later he came within sight of the Garwood cabin. When it was new, it had been as sturdily built as the one Bartholomew had constructed. In fact, Bartholomew had helped with the barn raising and with raising the roof on the cabin. Over the years, however, the Garwoods had not taken care of it, and it had a rather ramshackle appearance, especially since the death of Alfred Garwood's wife. It was in bad need of fresh chinking, and the door hung crookedly on worn hinges. The barn also had an uncared-for appearance.

Bartholomew dismounted, tied his horse, walked up to the cabin, and rapped sharply on the door. The latch string was out, so he could have opened it, but he preferred not to. A couple of minutes went by with no answer, so he knocked again.

This time, after about thirty seconds, trudging footsteps could be heard on the other side of the door. The latch was lifted, and the door swung open a few inches, revealing the pallid face of Alfred Garwood. The man's dark eyes were large and sunken, giving his features a haunted look. His silver hair was in disarray. Even though he and Bartholomew were about the same age, Garwood looked at least ten years older.

"What do you want?" he croaked.

"I've got to talk to you, Alfred. It's important."

"Sure it is. It'd have to be something important to get one of the high-and-mighty Holts over here to talk to a Garwood."

"I'm not here to make trouble," Bartholomew insisted. "I just want to talk to you. Can I come in?"

"Whatever you got to say, you can say it out there," Garwood snapped. "You're lucky ain't none of my boys home 'cept poor Aaron, else you'd be pickin' musket balls out of your hide." Pain showed clearly in his rheumy eyes. "We buried Luther this morning."

Bartholomew hesitated. "I know, Alfred. And I'm mighty sorry for your loss. Your boy's gone, and I'm afraid for my family. Let's work together. Let's put a stop to the hurting and the killing."

Garwood reached to one side of the door, and when his hand came back into view, it clutched a musket. He pointed the barrel at Bartholomew and said, "Damn you! Get off my land, Holt. It may not be much, thanks to you, but by God, it's still mine for now! You and yours took my son away from me, and I'll kill you if you set foot on my place again!"

Bartholomew took a deep breath and said, "I'll go, Alfred." His voice was tinged with sadness as he added, "I can see I'm not going to do any good here."

"No. Nobody can do a damn bit of good now." Garwood lowered the musket, stepped back inside, and slammed the door.

Bartholomew stood there a second longer, then

turned away. He kept an eye out behind him as he mounted his horse and rode away from the cabin, just to make sure that Garwood did not emerge again and come out shooting. Nothing of the sort happened, though, and soon the cabin was out of his sight behind him.

The visit had accomplished absolutely nothing, Bartholomew thought bitterly. But he had had to make the attempt.

A movement in the brush at the side of the trail alerted Bartholomew, and his hand darted to the butt of the pistol in his belt. "Don't shoot, Pa!" came a voice, and Bartholomew recognized it as belonging to Clay. A moment later both Clay and Jeff stepped out of the woods, leading their horses.

"What are you two doing here?" Bartholomew demanded. "I thought I told you to stay at the cabin."

"You told us not to come with you," Jeff replied. "We're just out doing a little hunting. Isn't that right, Clay?"

"That's right."

"A little hunting," Bartholomew repeated. "And you just happened to be doing it in the neighborhood of the Garwood place." Bartholomew shook his head wearily, but he had to smile. He asked, "See any game?"

"Nothing we wanted to shoot at," Clay said. "Thought for a minute we had, but then we decided it'd be better not to."

Bartholomew knew he was talking about the moment when Alfred Garwood had trained the musket on him. Garwood had no idea how close he had probably come to dying. Bartholomew would have wagered that both Clay and Jeff had their sights set on him.

"I tried to talk some sense into the old man's head," he said. "He wouldn't listen. I don't know if he would have been able to do anything to keep Zach and Pete from causing more trouble, anyway."

"Nothing's going to stop Zach," Clay said flatly. "Nothing except lead or maybe cold steel."

And Bartholomew knew with a feeling of utter despair that his oldest son was absolutely right.

Feud or no feud, life had to go on. And when, over the next few days, everything was quiet again, the temptation was to be lulled back into a sense of security. That was probably just what Zach Garwood wanted, Bartholomew thought. Any such sense of security was bound to be a false one. But he let his wife and younger children convince themselves that things had settled down again. They could even hope that the trouble was over.

Bartholomew, Clay, and Jeff knew better, but they kept that knowledge to themselves—and they kept their eyes open.

One afternoon two weeks after the wedding, Norah baked an apple pie, and the smell in the cabin was enough to make a person's mouth water. Bartholomew and Clay had been working in the barn, and when they entered the cabin, Bartholomew stopped in his tracks and inhaled deeply. He looked over at Clay and said, "That's what you've got to look forward to, son, if you ever find a good woman and settle down."

Clay returned Bartholomew's smile and then hugged his mother. "Nobody else could ever hold a candle to Ma's cooking, Pa, and you know it."

Norah flushed in embarrassment while Bartholomew said, "Aye, you're right."

"I haven't heard Jeff complaining about Melissa's cooking," Norah said. "Don't listen to your father, Clay. There are plenty of women who would make a fine wife for you. A man shouldn't be alone all his life."

Clay shrugged, and Bartholomew could see that the conversation was starting to make his son a bit uncomfortable. Quickly Bartholomew said, "Clay's still young yet, Norah. And he's still got some moss to shake off his feet before he's ready to settle down. Right, son?"

"I reckon so, Pa."

Norah picked up the cooling pie. "Well, you can start by taking this over to Jeff and Melissa."

"You mean you didn't bake it for us?" Bartholomew sounded stricken.

"No, I didn't. And don't look so wounded, Bartholomew Holt. I'll make one for you tomorrow."

"I'll hold you to that promise."

Clay took the pie from his mother and picked up his rifle.

"Why don't you hitch up the wagon and take the other children with you?" Norah suggested. "They've been pestering me to go to Jeff and Melissa's."

Clay shrugged. "Sure. That sounds like a good idea."

Bartholomew agreed. It would do Edward, Susan, and Jonathan some good to get away from the cabin for a while. Edward and Susan went to school part of the time, but that was not the same as visiting relatives. Even though Melissa spent most days at the main house, Bartholomew knew that visiting her in her own home was different.

Norah called the youngsters in while Bartholomew hitched a couple of the mules to the big farm wagon. As their parents expected, the children were excited about going to see their brother and his bride. They piled into the back of the wagon, and Susan held the pie while Clay climbed onto the seat, set his rifle at his feet, and took the reins.

"We could all go if you like," Bartholomew suggested quietly to his wife.

Norah shook her head. "I've got more cooking to do. And it doesn't hurt for the children to be out from under our thumbs every now and then. Clay will take care of them."

Bartholomew slipped an arm around her shoulders. "I have to admit, I won't mind spending a little time alone with you, lady. Seems like we don't get much of that anymore." He leaned over and kissed her on the cheek.

"Go on with you," she said sharply. He could tell, however, that she was pleased by the attention.

With the children waving from the rear of the wagon, it rolled away. Bartholomew and Norah watched it go, then stepped back into the cabin. Norah went straight to the big iron kettle where she was preparing stew. Bartholomew settled down at the table and began paring carrots. Some men regarded such a task as woman's work, but he had never minded helping out in that fashion. After all, in the early years, Norah had done more than her share of plowing and planting. As the two of them went about what they were doing, they shared a companionable silence. Every so often one would look up and catch the eye of the other, and they would smile. They had been together for so long that words were no longer necessary for them to know how they felt.

A few moments later, though, Bartholomew glanced up. "Someone's coming," he said. He stood up and started toward the door, and as he did the sound of hoofbeats became more audible. He judged there were at least a couple of riders approaching.

He reached for the door and opened it, then suddenly realized that he had allowed himself to let his guard down, the very thing he had sworn he would not do. Those last few minutes with Norah had been so comfortable that he had relaxed. His muscles stiffened, but it was too late now. The door was already open.

And when Bartholomew saw the two gun-wielding men riding toward the cabin, he started to slam it as fast as he could.

A musket went off with a blast of gunpowder, the ball chipping the side of the door just as Bartholomew thrust it closed. He winced as splinters stung his face. Norah let out a startled cry.

Ignoring the blood dripping down his cheek, Bartholomew dropped the bar across the door. He reached up and snatched the brass-mounted Kentucky rifle and the powder horn from their pegs above the door. "Stay down, Norah!" he snapped. With cool precision he loaded and half-cocked the rifle, not a movement wasted. "I didn't get a good look at the bastards, but I'd wager their name is Garwood!"

"What are we going to do, Bartholomew?"

"Get my pistols and load them." His face was drawn in bleak lines. "We've got to fight back, hold them off. Jeff and Clay will hear the shots and come to see what's wrong." He full-cocked the flintlock. "It's time those young fools were taught a lesson!"

He had confidence they could hold off any attack by Zach and Pete. The walls of the cabin were thick and secure; they would stop a musket ball without difficulty, and so would the door. The only real points of danger were the windows, and as long as Norah stayed down, she would be safe. Bartholomew went to the window to the left of the door and tore aside the paper so that he could see out. He immediately spotted the two riders. They had withdrawn about fifty yards from the cabin after that initial shot. Bartholomew held his fire. He could see now that the men were indeed Zach and Pete Garwood. There was no mistaking Pete's massive frame or Zach's long hair.

Bartholomew frowned. What were they doing? He could see them sitting their horses at the edge of the woods, huddled together as they worked on something.

Then he saw a thread of smoke spiral into the sky, and as Zach and Pete turned around, he spotted flames. Each of them was carrying a torch, which they had lit from a tinderbox. Bartholomew's blood turned to ice as he realized what they were about to do.

Bottled up in the cabin as Norah and he were, they had no place to run. He had to stop Zach and Pete before they got close enough to hurl the torches.

He threw the long rifle to his shoulder and sighted carefully as Zach and Pete galloped toward the cabin, the torches held high in their free hands.

Wind whipped at the fiercely burning brands, and Bartholomew knew they must be soaked in pitch. The Garwoods had come prepared. The lull in the violence had indeed been deliberate; Zach had probably been planning this atrocity all along.

Bartholomew held his breath, sighted the rifle on Pete's broad chest, and squeezed the trigger. The gun blasted and bucked against his shoulder, smoke puffing up and blinding him for a second. When it cleared away enough for him to see, he let out a curse. Pete was still in the saddle, apparently unharmed.

"I need the pistols!" Bartholomew called, turning his head. Norah rushed over to him carrying the weapons. There were two of them, and he had a third in his belt. Three shots with which to stop the Garwoods—or he and Norah would be burned out.

Norah saw what was happening through the tear in the oiled paper at the window. "Bartholomew!" she cried out in fear, clutching at his arm.

Gently he loosened her grip. "I'll stop them," he vowed grimly. On the surface, he was calm, but inside he felt a growing panic. It would be disastrous if Zach and Pete were able to set the cabin ablaze.

He held his fire with the pistols. They were not very accurate except at short range, fifteen or twenty yards at most. He would have to shoot quickly when Zach and Pete approached, or they might have time to throw the torches even if they were hit. Bartholomew could see the hideous grins on their faces, and he realized now he should have let Clay go after them. They were not human beings; they were vicious animals.

He prayed it was not too late to stop them from having their revenge.

Now! Bartholomew extended his right hand, cocked the pistol, and pressed the trigger. No sooner had it exploded than he thrust out the left-hand weapon and fired it. Smoke obscured his vision again for a second, but he heard something strike the roof. Something else hit the wall of the cabin near the door. He dropped the empty pistols and jerked the last one from his belt. A hand seemed to have closed over his heart. He had failed—it had been the torches he heard hitting the cabin. He fired the final shot blindly but was rewarded with the sound of a curse. Perhaps he had at least wounded one of the Garwoods.

"I smell smoke," Norah said quietly. "They set the cabin on fire, didn't they?"

"I'm afraid so. We'll have to take our chances outside now." Bartholomew began reloading the pistol in his hand.

Smoke was drifting into the room, and he could feel the heat increasing. He glanced up and saw smoke coming down through the roof. It was on fire, too, which made their situation even more dangerous. They would have only a few minutes before the blaze engulfed the roof and made it collapse. They had to be out before that happened.

When he had the pistol loaded, he grasped Norah's hand. "We'll make a run for it," he said.

"What about the back way?"

"It won't make any difference. They're on horseback, and from where they're sitting, they can see us from either door. Stay behind me when we go out." He paused for a second and searched her face. Her features were taut and pale, understandably so, but there was no real fear in her eyes. He understood without any words being said, because he felt the same way. As long as they were together, it did not really matter what happened. They had met life side by side for so many years. . . .

They could meet death the same way.

Bartholomew squeezed his wife's hand one last time, then went to the door and jerked it open. Smoke billowed in, and he could see flames leaping up on both sides of the door. He took a step out, Norah close behind him. Muskets roared, and the lead balls slammed into the cabin only inches from them. Bartholomew forged ahead, but suddenly a giant fist crashed against his shoulder, driving him back into

Norah. They both fell, half in the door and half out. More shots sounded. Norah cried out in pain.

Bartholomew twisted frantically to see how badly she was hit. He saw blood on the front of her dress, and his concern for her made him forget the agony of his own wound. He forced himself onto his knees, caught her up with his good arm, and dragged both of them back into the cabin, kicking the door shut behind them. The Garwoods had to have a blasted arsenal out there, he thought. The shots had come too quickly for them to be reloading. They must have had several weapons loaded and ready.

Norah was moaning. Bartholomew laid her gently on the floor and leaned over her. His wounded arm was all but useless, but Norah was hit much worse. Bartholomew was no doctor, but he had seen enough wounded men to know what was going to happen.

Her eyes flickered open, and she said in a thin, weak voice, "Bartholomew . . . ?"

"I'm here, my love." He found her hand and held it tightly. "I'm right here with you."

"You . . . you've got to get out. . . ."

He shook his head. There was no point in it. His shoulder was probably shattered, he was losing blood quickly, and the Garwoods were just sitting out there, waiting for him to try to escape again.

Besides, he would not leave her.

A spasm racked her, and Bartholomew's fingers closed even tighter on hers. She called his name again, and he whispered, "I'm here, Norah. I'm here."

She found the strength to reach up and touch his cheek as he leaned over her, and her lips curved for an instant into a faint smile. Then her arm fell limply to the side.

Bartholomew did not cry. There was no need. She had simply gone on a little before him, but he would be with her again soon enough. He waited, sitting beside her, while the smoke thickened and the heat rose, and finally enough blood welled from his wounded shoulder that he passed out. He slumped forward, lying across the body of his wife.

A moment later the roof of the cabin collapsed, crashing in and sending sparks climbing high into the late afternoon sky. Some of them glowed brightly for long seconds before winking out.

CHAPTER TWELVE

Clay Holt sat at the table in his brother's cabin and listened to the laughter of the younger children. Melissa was good with them, Clay thought. She would make a fine mother for the children she and Jeff would have. At the moment she was dishing out small portions of the pie Norah had baked. It was a little close to supper for such a treat, she had said, but Clay could tell she did not want to disappoint Susan and little Jonathan.

Jeff sat across the table from Clay as the youngsters clustered around Melissa. Jeff looked like a happy man, Clay decided; marriage was agreeing with him. Clay's mind went back to what his mother and father had said to him earlier about settling down. He doubted if that would ever happen. Not many civilized women would ever want a specimen like him, rough as a cob and inflicted with an incurable wander-lust.

Each day he felt more strongly the call of the wil-derness, the lure of the high mountains. He would have been long gone had it not been for the threat the Garwoods posed to his family.

"It's good to see the children happy," Jeff com-mented quietly. "And Melissa, too."

Clay opened his mouth to reply when he heard a faint but familiar sound. He lifted his head, frowning in concentration. "What's that?"

Jeff shook his head. "What's what? I don't hear anything."

"I do." Clay stood up, a deep unease gripping him. He strode over to the door of the cabin and jerked it open. He could hear the distant reports of rifles and pistols more clearly now. "That's gunfire. And it sounds like it's coming from our place."

Jeff was on his feet in an instant, hurrying over to the door, the anxious expression on his face confirm-ing that he heard the shots, too. "You're right," he told Clay. "It must be trouble."

There was no doubt of that in Clay's mind. Too many shots had sounded for them to be Bartholomew hunting or some other reasonable explanation. Clay turned to Jeff and said, "Zach and Pete."

"Come on." Jeff started out the door.

"Wait a minute." Clay's hand closed firmly on his arm. "We can't both go racing over there. Could be that's just what Zach wants us to do. This might be a trick to draw us both away from this cabin."

"You're right. I'll go—"

"The hell you will." With Clay's superior strength, he all but hauled Jeff back into the cabin. "You stay here and look after Melissa and the kids. I'll take your saddle horse." He wished he had ridden over on his own mount instead of in the wagon, but it was too late to do anything about that now.

Melissa and the children crowded near the men,

the pie forgotten. All of them looked frightened. Now that it had been called to their attention, they could hear the gunfire clearly, and it did not take much of a sense of direction to tell that it was coming from the vicinity of the original Holt cabin.

Melissa touched her brother-in-law's arm. "Be careful, Clay."

He tightened his grip on his rifle, glad now that his time in the wilderness with Lewis and Clark had gotten him in the habit of keeping the gun with him. He and Jeff hurried out of the cabin, and Jeff brought his horse from the pole corral in back, fastening a harness into place on the way.

"I'll get my saddle," Jeff said.

"No time." Clay grasped the horse's mane and swung up bareback. He took the reins and turned the animal's head toward the other cabin, then drove his heels into its flanks and sent it leaping into a gallop. He didn't look back as he raced away from Jeff's home.

Clay's heart was thudding painfully in his chest. He and Jeff and their father had known the Garwoods might strike at any time, but Clay had never expected them to attack his parents. Abruptly he realized that he could no longer hear the boom of gunshots over the thudding of the horse's hooves, and the silence frightened him even more. The battle, such as it had been, must be over.

Then, through the trees that were flashing by on both sides of the trail, he caught a glimpse of black smoke rising into the sky.

"No, dammit, no!" Clay was not even aware that he voiced the cry aloud. He leaned forward over the horse's neck, urging it on to greater speed.

His worst fears were realized a few minutes later when he came in sight of the cabin and saw that it was blazing fiercely. The roof was gone, already caved in, and all four walls were on fire. The cabin was beyond saving. Soon it would be nothing but a burned-out, rubble-strewn shell.

He saw no sign of his mother and father.

The horse tried to slow down when it saw the fire. Clay drove it on, and finally, when the animal became too skittish to proceed, he slipped off its back and ran forward, still holding his rifle. As he ran, he looked around for something to shoot at, but there was nothing. The farm and the surrounding fields and woods seemed perfectly peaceful—except for the awful pyre in the center.

"Ma! Pa!" Clay bellowed. "Where are you?" There was no answer, and as he slowed to a stop in front of what had been the cabin's door, he felt a horrible certainty that they were inside that inferno.

And no one could be alive in there, Clay knew.

Even though he had halted some distance away, the heat struck his face almost like a physical blow. He could have turned away, yet something prevented him. Some force held him there, kept his gaze riveted on the leaping flames and the billowing smoke. His mouth hung slightly open in a mixture of awe and grief.

Clay had no idea how much time passed while he stood there watching the fire. One by one the walls collapsed, and the flames gradually began to die down. He felt a hand touch his shoulder, but his senses were so numbed by now that he did not flinch or jump. Instead, he looked over slowly and saw Jeff standing beside him, the same stunned, horror-stricken expression on his face. Behind Jeff, Melissa was doing her best to keep the children in the wagon that had brought them back to their home. Clay wished Jeff had been able to keep Melissa and the youngsters at the other cabin so that they would not have had to see this, but it was too late now.

Too late for a great many things, Clay thought.

Other people—neighbors, Clay realized vaguely —were showing up, drawn by the smoke. Whenever fire broke out, settlers came from miles around to see if they could help. Men came up and spoke to Clay, and he supposed he answered, but late. he could not have repeated any of what was said. His mind was too overwhelmed by what had happened. Finally, he realized that Jeff was asking him, "What about Ma and Pa?"

"I didn't see them anywhere around," Clay replied. "I think they're . . . in there."

Jeff grasped his shoulders tightly. "You don't know that!" he said angrily. "Maybe they got away."

Clay shook his head. "Zach wouldn't have let them get out. When it burns down, we'll find them in there." His voice was flat, filled with a terrible conviction.

Some of the men were working to keep the fire from spreading, and they seemed to have it contained to the cabin itself. Soon, the flames died down and then went out, although the ashes and the blackened remains of the building continued to smolder. Clay strode forward, with Jeff hanging a little behind him. Jeff plucked at his arm and said, "It's too hot in there, Clay," but Clay shrugged him off.

He did not have to go all the way into the cabin to see what he needed to see, he discovered a moment later. The front wall had collapsed like the others, and what he saw between the fallen timbers was enough to tell him the grim truth. He turned away, his face stony.

Jeff peered past him, saying, "Oh, God . . . oh, my God. What are we going to do?"

"Take Melissa and the kids back to your cabin," Clay snapped as he strode away. "Take care of them."

Jeff caught up with him. "What are you going to do?"

"Take care of everything else."

"Clay!" Jeff grasped his arm. "You can't—"

Clay jerked free of his brother's hand and went to the horse. He mounted up and kicked the animal into a run, ignoring Jeff's shouts behind him.

It was too late for talking, too late for anything now except more blood and death.

It had been too late, Clay realized grimly, the day he left for the mountains, three years earlier.

He rode first to the Garwood farm, and when he got there, he went in fast and hard, throwing caution to the wind. He kicked the door open and stalked into the cabin, the long rifle in his hands ready to fire. No one challenged him, though, and it took only a few seconds to determine that no one was at home. The whole family was gone, even the recuperating Aaron.

When he went back outside, he could see all the Garwood fields, but no one was working. That left Marietta as the most likely place he would find them. He swung up onto the horse again and headed toward town.

Behind him to the northwest, a faint pall of smoke still hung in the sky from the fire. It made the rays of the setting sun look garish.

Clay slowed the horse to a walk as he reached the outskirts of the settlement. That late in the day, not many people were on the street. His eyes flicked over them, searching for the Garwoods. The people he passed looked at him with a mixture of curiosity and fear. Clay's face expressed his rage and hate.

Up ahead of him, Pete Garwood stepped out onto the porch of Steakley's trading post. Pete had a sliver of wood dangling between his teeth and was chewing on it casually when Clay rode up and stopped directly in front of the porch.

The sliver snapped sharply as Pete's jaw clenched. He spat out the remains of it, and his features paled. On his cheek a red mark stood out. Clay recognized it as a burn from a musket ball, and he felt a surge of satisfaction that his father had at least marked one of the bastards. It was too bad the ball had not landed a couple of inches to the side.

Well, he would take care of that now, Clay vowed.

He centered the flintlock on Pete and said, "My parents are dead."

Slowly Pete lifted his hands and extended them

toward Clay, palms out. "I swear to you, Holt, I didn't have nothing to do with it," he said shakily. "I never hurt nobody—"

"Don't bother lying, Pete, because I just don't give a damn anymore. I'm going to kill you."

People nearby were scurrying for cover. Clay's voice carried clearly to the few customers in the store, and they headed for the back of the building, where they ducked behind the counter with the frightened proprietor.

"Where's your brother?" Clay asked.

"You mean Zach? I—I ain't seen him all day—"

"It doesn't matter. I'll find him after I've killed you."

Despite his great size, terror made Pete quake as what little nerve he had broke. "Good Lord, Holt, you can't just—just shoot me down like a dog!"

Clay's finger tightened on the trigger of the rifle. "Why the hell not?"

The strange smile on Clay's face frightened Pete even more than the rifle. Suddenly Pete went to his knees. "Please don't kill me," he blubbered. "Oh, God, please don't . . . please—"

"Shut up!" Clay snapped. Carefully he uncocked the flintlock. "I'll give you more of a chance than you bastards gave my ma and pa." He slid down from the horse's back, put the rifle carefully on the ground, and as he straightened, pulled his hunting knife from its sheath. He stepped toward the porch and the terrified man who knelt there.

And then, as Pete glanced up, Clay saw the look of sly triumph in his piggish eyes.

With surprising speed Pete's hand darted toward the butt of the flintlock pistol tucked in his belt. His fingers closed on it, and he jerked it free. Clay lunged forward, leaping onto the porch and lashing out with his free hand. His arm hit Pete's wrist, knocking the barrel of the gun aside as it discharged. The blast of powder was deafening.

Clay drove the knife forward and felt the blade go

smoothly into Pete's belly. He ripped it up and down, then twisted it and tore it from side to side before yanking it out and stepping back. Pete screamed as blood and entrails spilled out of the hideous wound. Clay watched without expression as Pete hunched over and tried to hold himself together for a few seconds before he collapsed and died on the porch.

Bending over the body, Clay wiped his knife clean on the back of the dead man's coat. Then he slipped it back in its sheath and turned away.

He felt strangely calm. And why not? he asked himself. There was still work to do.

The pounding of hoofbeats made him look up, ready to meet any new threat.

Jeff felt a wave of sickness wash over him as he saw Clay standing beside the body of Pete Garwood. Pete was lying facedown, and judging by the pool of blood, Jeff did not want to see what Clay had done. Jeff reined up in front of the trading post.

"What are you doing here?" Clay asked. "I told you to look after Melissa and the kids."

"Melissa convinced me that she would be fine. She's a good shot, and Edward can reload for her. I had to come after you, Clay. I had to stop you—"

"Stop me from what?" Clay broke in. "Settling the score? Avenging what the Garwoods did to Ma and Pa?"

Jeff took a deep breath, praying that he could make his brother understand. He was as grief-stricken and filled with rage as Clay, but as he had stood there in front of the burned-out husk of the cabin where he had grown up, a thought had come with startling clarity.

The feud had to end, and it had to end now.

He had talked to Melissa for a few moments, brushing aside her attempts to comfort him. There would be time for that later. His grieving, Jeff suspected, would not be finished for a long time. But right then, it was more important to put a stop to the killing.

She had agreed with him, and after arranging for his parents' bodies to be removed from the smoldering timbers, he had, like Clay, ridden first to the Garwood farm and then, finding the cabin empty, to Marietta.

But he had arrived too late to prevent another death, and he felt a pang of regret at that, even if the victim was Pete Garwood.

"This has got to stop," Jeff said to Clay. "It can't go on. Yes, Ma and Pa are dead, but so are Luther Garwood and now Pete. Who's next, Clay? Edward? Little Susan or Jonathan? Maybe Matthew Garwood? For God's sake, where does it all end?"

Clay looked up at him sharply. "Zach's still alive," he said. "You know he was there."

"Well, after he's dead, you'd better kill Aaron, too. And old man Garwood. And Josie and that little boy. Because if you don't, Clay, it just keeps going. *It just keeps going!*"

Clay drew a long, ragged breath, and Jeff thought he was finally getting through to his brother. After a moment Clay asked quietly, "What can we do, then?"

"I've thought about it, and there's only one way to stop this. We've got to leave."

Clay looked up at him. "Leave Marietta?"

"You were going to anyway," Jeff said quickly. "I'll go with you. We'll head west, far away from the Garwoods. You and I are the ones they'll be after next. If we're gone, there won't be any reason to fight anymore."

"What about the children? And Melissa?"

"The youngsters can't stay here, not with Ma and Pa . . . gone. But we can send them to Uncle Henry and Aunt Dorothy in Pennsylvania. They'll take good care of them. It's what Ma and Pa would have wanted."

"What about Melissa?"

That was the hardest part for Jeff, the thought of being separated from his wife. He forced himself to go on. "She'll go with the kids. They'll need somebody to make sure they get to Pennsylvania all right, and that way I can be sure she's safe, too. Later, after things settle down, I can either send for her or come back myself."

Clay rubbed his jaw in thought. At least the killing rage had gone out of him, Jeff observed, and that was a small victory. He was not ready to celebrate, though, especially with Pete Garwood's body lying only a few feet away and the townspeople looking on warily from hiding.

"And you'd go to the mountains with me?" Clay asked.

"From what you've said, the West is a mighty big place. Too big for the Garwoods to ever find us."

"You're right." Clay's features took on a stubborn cast. "But that'd be letting the Garwoods win. That'd be running from them."

"It would be saving the lives of the people we care for," Jeff said. "And I don't give a damn about anything else right now. There's been enough pain and death already."

"Don't reckon I can argue with that," Clay said softly. He looked up at his brother and extended a hand. "All right. We'll go to the mountains."

Before Jeff could reach down from the saddle to shake Clay's hand, a voice called out, "What the hell happened here? Don't move, either of you Holts!"

Jeff glanced back and saw the constable striding toward them in the road, a cocked musket in his hands. Sutcliffe's face was red with fury.

In a low voice Clay said quickly, "You and I both know Pete helped Zach burn down that cabin, but Sutcliffe'll never believe it without proof. Rear that horse in the air."

"What?" Jeff asked, unsure what Clay had in mind.

"Just do it, dammit!" The urgent command was hissed.

Jeff yanked back on the reins and dug his heels in

the horse's flanks. It let out a whinny of displeasure and came up on its rear hooves, blocking Clay from Sutcliffe's view. Clay snatched up his rifle and sprang onto the other horse.

"Stop right there, Holt!" the constable cried. He brought his weapon to his shoulder.

Jeff shouted as if he were trying to bring his mount under control. In reality, he turned the horse toward Sutcliffe, who had to flinch back from its pawing hooves or risk being kicked. Jeff heard the rattle of hoofbeats and glanced over his shoulder. Clay was galloping away.

"Damn you!" Sutcliffe shouted. He dashed out into the road where he could get a clear shot at Clay, who was already at least fifty feet away. The constable fired.

Jeff felt a stab of fear at the sound of the shot, but then he saw Clay look back, and he knew that he had not been hit. By the time Sutcliffe could reload, Clay would be well out of range.

Sutcliffe knew that, too, and instead of trying to reload, he threw the gun aside, reached up to grab Jeff's shirt, and hauled him out of the saddle. Jeff landed heavily in the dirt, and when he tried to get up, the constable slammed a fist into his jaw. "You helped him get away!" Sutcliffe accused.

Jeff fought down the impulse to spring up and strike back at the man. Instead, he propped himself up on one elbow and rubbed his jaw with the other hand. "Sorry, Constable. I don't know what got into my horse."

"You won't get away with that story, Holt! I've got witnesses—"

Sutcliffe broke off as someone up the road cried out. Jeff looked that way and saw a grim procession coming into town. The wagon that Clay had brought to his cabin earlier was in the lead, with Melissa driving it. The children were huddled beside her on the seat, sobbing. Several of the Holts' neighbors grimly rode along behind.

Jeff knew what was in the back of the wagon that had prompted the cry from one of the bystanders—the blanket-wrapped bodies of his parents. He got slowly to his feet and waited for the wagon. Behind him he heard Sutcliffe mutter, "What the hell—?"

"My parents are dead, Constable." He turned cold eyes on Sutcliffe. "And if you're determined to arrest me, you can do it after I've seen to the burying."

Two days later Jeff looked down at the fresh graves in the cemetery behind Marietta's Congregational Church. He had thought about burying Bartholomew and Norah on the farm, but although that was legally Holt land, in Jeff's heart it no longer belonged to the family. It had been taken from them by the terror and death that had visited there. By laying his parents to rest here, he had decided, their graves would be cared for. And besides, the burial ground was on a slight hill overlooking the sweep of the Ohio River that had brought Bartholomew and Norah Holt to the Northwest Territory. Jeff thought they would be content to rest here.

The minister was praying, but Jeff had not really heard much of what Crosley had to say. Quite a few people were in attendance at the service, and most of them had spoken to him. Jeff did not recall much of that, either. Melissa stood beside him, holding tightly to his arm as she wept. Edward was on his other side, his young face pale but composed as he strived mightily to be a man, despite his tender age of ten years. Susan and Jonathan, both sobbing, stood in front of Jeff, and he had his hands on their shoulders.

Suddenly Jeff wanted to shout for everyone to be quiet, to stop weeping and looking so sad. He remembered all the happy, joyous times, all the laughter that had rung in the Holt cabin when he was growing up. The happiest laughter of all, he thought, had belonged to his mother and father. If they were looking down on this service, they were probably downright depressed by now.

But Jeff remained silent, his lips pressed firmly together, and finally the ordeal was over. The mourners filed away. Jeff shook hands with some of them as they left, and he thanked the neighbor who had agreed to keep an eye on the Holt farm in exchange for the use of the animals. Then he looked down toward the river.

The boat was there, the boat that would carry his wife, his brothers, and his sister, to Pennsylvania—and out of his life.

No one had seen Zach Garwood since the deaths of Pete and the Holts. Clay seemed to have dropped completely out of sight as well. Alfred Garwood, along with Aaron and Josie, had taken Pete's body to the churchyard to bury him there. No other threats had been made, but Jeff had seen the look in Aaron's eyes. It was a look he had seen too many times before, and it told Jeff what he already knew.

The killing would not end unless Clay and he left Ohio.

Sutcliffe wanted to arrest Clay for murdering Pete, although plenty of people who had seen the fight told him that it had been fair, that if anything Pete had had the advantage, his pistol against Clay's knife. The constable insisted that Clay be tried by a judge, however. He wanted to arrest Jeff as well, but public sentiment had been against him, considering the losses that the Holt family had suffered. Besides, Sutcliffe had no proof that the horse Jeff was riding had not shied on its own.

Jeff was the last one to leave the cemetery, and as he strode out its gate, he paused and looked back. For an instant he saw a shadowy figure at the edge of the trees beyond the burial ground. Then the shape disappeared. Clay had been there, Jeff thought, to say his own good-byes.

Soon there would be more farewells. Later that afternoon Charles Merrivale would take Melissa and the Holt children to the riverboat that would carry them up the Ohio to Pennsylvania. Jeff would already be gone by then, having slipped away earlier to throw Zach Garwood off the scent, if indeed Zach was still lurking somewhere in the vicinity. Jeff was convinced he was.

All the details had been worked out. Melissa would accompany the children to Pennsylvania, to the home of Henry and Dorothy Holt in Pittsburgh. Once they had arrived safely, Melissa would send a letter to Jeff in St. Louis to let him know that everything was all right. He had given her the name of the inn where Clay had stayed upon his return with the Corps of Discovery, a name Jeff knew from the many stories Clay had told about the expedition. The brothers would have to outfit themselves for their journey west, and St. Louis was the logical place to do that.

Since the deaths of Bartholomew and Norah, Jeff and Melissa and the children had been staying with Melissa's parents—much to the annoyance of Charles Merrivale, Jeff suspected, although Merrivale had not been able to complain much under the circumstances. All of them returned to the Merrivale home following the funeral, and Jeff began getting ready to leave. He dressed in his sturdiest clothes, and Melissa packed some of the food that had been brought to the house by friends and neighbors of the Holts. Jeff had his Harper's Ferry rifle, a couple of .54 caliber flintlock pistols, and a knife. He was almost as well armed, he thought with a grim smile, as Clay had been that first day when he had rescued Jeff from the Garwoods in the brawl at Meaghan's tavern. All he needed was some buckskins, a 'hawk, and a coonskin cap, and he would look every bit as much the frontiersman as Clay.

Looking the part and being it were two different things, however, as Jeff well knew. He had a great deal to learn, but he would have a good teacher.

His horse was behind the house where it could not be easily seen. He loaded his gear on the animal, then knelt in front of his younger brothers and sister. Susan and Jonathan were crying again, and tears shone in Edward's eyes. Jeff hugged all three of them and whispered, "I'll be back. I'll see all of you again, and so will Clay. Remember that. And remember . . . I love you."

A broad band seemed to be tightening around his chest as he said good-bye to them, and he had to blink back tears. He stood and took Melissa in his arms, then kissed her with a passion that shook both of them to the core. "I'll always love you," he said huskily. "I'll be back."

She tried to be brave. "I know. I'll take care of the children."

"I know you will. I—God, I don't want to leave you! I'm only doing it—"

"You're doing the right thing, and we both know it," she told him firmly. "Now, you'd better go. You don't want to waste any time." A pair of tears rolled down her soft cheeks. "You've got a long way to go, and so do I."

Jeff looked into her eyes for a second, then turned away and climbed into the saddle. He gave them all a wave, then urged the horse into a trot. After that, he was afraid to look back.

Jeff stuck to the woods and the back trails he had learned as a youngster with Clay. He was convinced no one had seen him leaving Marietta. Zach Garwood had been cheated of his revenge. At least, Jeff hoped that was the case.

He had covered several miles when a sudden movement made him rein in and lift his rifle. He had been riding through a thick stand of trees, and someone else on horseback was emerging from the undergrowth. Jeff relaxed when he saw the ringed tail of the coonskin cap.

"Everything all right back in town?" Clay asked.

"Hard saying good-bye."

"It always is."

They rode together in silence for a while. Then Jeff asked, "What are the mountains like?"

Clay smiled. "Like nothing you've ever seen before, little brother. They reach up to the sky like they're going all the way to heaven. When you first see them, they seem to be only a few miles away, but a week later you're still riding toward them, and they don't look a damn bit closer. Some of them are so high the snow never melts, and when the sun hits them, you know why the Indians gave them that name."

"You mean the Rockies?" Jeff asked.

Clay shook his head. "Nope. The Indians call them the Shining Mountains."

Together, the Holts rode on, heading west.

PART III

We prepared a speech and some presents, and then sent for the chiefs and warriors, whom we received, at twelve o'clock, under a large oak tree, near which the flag of the United States was flying. Captain Lewis delivered a speech, with the usual advice and counsel for their future conduct. We acknowledged their chiefs, by giving to the grand chief a flag, a medal, a certificate, and a string of wampum; to which we added a chief's coat—that is, a richly laced uniform of the United States artillery corps, with a cocked hat and red feather. One second chief and three inferior ones were made or recognized by medals, a suitable present of tobacco, and articles of clothing. We smoked the pipe of peace, and the chiefs retired to a bower formed of bushes by their young men, where they divided among one another the presents, smoked, eat [sic], and held a council on the answer which they were to make us to-morrow. The young people exercised their bows and arrows in shooting at marks for beads, which we distributed to the best marksmen. In the evening the whole party danced until a late hour, and in the course of their amusement we threw among them some knives, tobacco, bells, tape, and binding, with which they were much pleased. Their musical instruments were the drum, and a sort of little bag made of buffalo-hide dressed white, with small shot or pebbles in it and a bunch of hair tied to it. This produces a sort of rattling music, with which the party was annoyed by four musicians during the council this morning.

—from "The History of the Lewis and Clark Expedition"

CHAPTER THIRTEEN

In the little more than forty years since the French fur traders Pierre Laclede and his stepson René Auguste Chouteau had first established a trading post on the site of what would become St. Louis, the settlement had grown steadily. Control of the area had passed through the hands of the Spanish and the British, as well as the French, but with the Louisiana Purchase, St. Louis and its environs had become firmly American, although the population of the city itself remained a mixture of nationalities. Now, in the spring of 1807, the Chouteau family still controlled much of the fur trade. Keelboats plied the waters of the Mississippi between St. Louis and New Orleans, and there was talk that someday soon, river traffic would extend along the Missouri to the north and west. Men of all stripes came to St. Louis, some passing through, others remaining as permanent settlers. Most were adventurers or entrepreneurs or criminals, bent on heading farther west.

Jeff Holt was not sure which category he and his brother Clay fell into.

They had arrived in the city soon after the first of the year; the trip from Ohio had been a miserable one for the most part. Just days after their departure, winter had descended in earnest, bringing with it cold rain, ice and snow, and wind so bitter it seemed to shrivel a man's insides. Even the buffalo-hide capes that Jeff and Clay wore did little to block the fierce wind and rain, so the brothers had been forced to hole up for days at a time. Sometimes they had stayed at inns or taverns along the way, but for the most part they had sought shelter in caves or under the overhang of bluffs. It had been a rugged existence, but Jeff knew it was nothing compared to life in the mountains. Clay could survive, Jeff was certain of that; he was less sure about himself.

But it would be better than going back to Marietta, he told himself many times. At least he could take some comfort from the knowledge that Melissa and the children were safe.

In the space of the few short months since Clay had last been to St. Louis, word of the success of Lewis and Clark's expedition had spread throughout the country, attracting a wide variety of people to St. Louis. No rooms were available at the inn owned by Major Christy, Captain William Clark's old friend and comrade. Jeff had given Christy's name to Melissa and told her to write to him in care of the major's establishment, and he was upset by the lack of accommodations there until Christy assured him that he would hold any letter that arrived for him. The Holts would check at the inn every day, Jeff promised.

The brothers found rooms at a much smaller and less impressive lodging than Christy's. It was, in fact, downright squalid, but at least they had a bed and a roof over their heads. And their money would last longer here than it would have at Christy's.

The weather worsened. Snow and ice stayed on the ground, and Jeff and Clay could do nothing except sit in the tavern that occupied the ground floor of the inn. Clay did not seem particularly bothered by the many days of sitting on a bench before the fireplace, his long legs and booted feet stretched out to the welcome warmth of the blaze. Jeff, on the other hand, grew more anxious with each day that passed, especially when he did not hear from Melissa. He had halfway expected that her letter from Pittsburgh, assuring him that she and the children had gotten there safely, would be waiting for him when he and Clay reached St. Louis. That had not happened, and by the middle of February, he was worrying himself to distraction.

Then one day when he checked at Christy's, the letter was there, his name written on the envelope in Melissa's hand. The sight of it caused an almost unbearable pang of longing.

Unfortunately, the letter itself had done little to ease his mind.

Now the snow and ice had been melted by a warm breeze from the south, and the sun shone nearly every day. It was March, with spring not far off. The improvement in the weather had cheered up most of the city's inhabitants.

Jeff Holt, however, still spent most of his days in the tavern, staring broodingly into the fire.

That was where he was when he took Melissa's letter out of the pocket of his jacket and unfolded it. The paper was heavily creased and growing tattered from a month's worth of folding and unfolding. He had read it at least a hundred times, and each time he hoped that somehow it would say something different.

His eyes scanned the words now, words so familiar they might as well have been burned into his brain.

Dearest Jefferson,

I take pen in hand to inform you that your brothers and sister should be in Pittsburgh by now, safely ensconsed with your aunt and uncle. I know you were anticipating that I would accompany them and that we did in fact agree on such a course of action, but my father has prevailed upon me to remain here in Marietta with him and my mother. You know how persuasive Father can be.

Please, do not trouble yourself about the children. The captain of the riverboat which bore them east assured me that he would watch out for them and make certain they reached their destination safely. In addition, I instructed Edward to tell your aunt and uncle to write to you at the address you gave to me, so you will know that the children have arrived in Pittsburgh. You should be receiving this communication shortly, if you have not already.

I know you may be upset that I did not accompany them as we planned, and I beg your forgiveness. Father insisted that I remain, and I could not argue with him.

All is quiet here. There has been no trouble from the Garwoods. And at any rate, Father says, "I can take care of my own family, and I'm not afraid of any Garwoods." I am certain he is right.

I miss you terribly, Jefferson, and I long for the day when we can be together again. I pray that this letter finds you happy and healthy.

> Your loving wife,
> Melissa

Jeff felt tears forming in his eyes as he read the letter yet again. A familiar upsurge of confusing emotions gripped him. He loved Melissa and missed her as badly as she said she missed him. But at the same time, he was angry with her for allowing her father to browbeat her into staying in Ohio. Maybe there had not been any trouble so far from the Garwoods. That did not mean Zach had forgotten about the deaths of

Luther and Pete; Zach would seek vengeance—on any target that happened to be handy.

Jeff drew a deep, shaky breath, refolded the letter, and slipped it back into his pocket. He could almost hear the pompous, arrogant Charles Merrivale making his claim that he could protect his family. Merrivale just did not understand the kind of person he would be dealing with in Zach Garwood.

At least Edward, Susan, and Jonathan were safely beyond Zach's reach. Jeff had indeed received a letter from his uncle Henry informing him that the children had arrived in Pittsburgh and were more than welcome. His uncle and aunt would give them a good home, Jeff knew. He was thankful for that.

Lost in his thoughts, he did not hear the footsteps coming up behind him, did not know anyone was around until the hand fell on his shoulder. Jeff started, his hand going to one of the pistols in his belt out of habit. He looked up and saw Clay standing beside the bench.

"Take it easy, little brother. I just wanted to tell you that you ought to step outside and get some sun. You've been brooding in here long enough, and it's a glorious day."

Jeff shook his head. "I don't feel much like it. You go ahead if you want to."

"I've already been out. And I heard something that's pretty interesting." Clay straddled the other end of the bench and sat down. "You ever heard of a man named Manuel Lisa?"

"The name's a little familiar. I don't recall who he is, though."

Clay took off his coonskin cap and tossed it onto the table next to him. "He's a Spaniard, up from New Orleans. Doesn't have the best reputation in the world, but he's a pretty sharp character. I never met him, but he helped outfit the Corps of Discovery for Lewis and Clark, and I heard talk down by the riverfront that he plans to take some men back up the Missouri after beaver."

Jeff felt a tingle of interest. "I thought men were already going into the mountains after beaver. Your friend Colter from the expedition went back, didn't he?"

"Some fellows headed into the Rockies last year, all right, but they went in twos and threes, sometimes alone. This Spaniard is going to take a big bunch, maybe build a fort somewhere up the Missouri and set up a trading post." Clay paused, then said, "He's hiring a lot of corpsmen, men with experience out there on the frontier. I reckon he'd take me on, and I'd vouch for you. It's a way of getting out of this godforsaken town."

Jeff made an effort to pull himself out of the gloomy, lethargic state into which he had settled. Clay's news was important. They had left Ohio in a hurry, without making plans for what they would do when they reached St. Louis. For a while the weather had taken the decision out of their hands; nobody with any sense was going to start up the Missouri in the dead of winter. But spring was rapidly approaching now, and they would have to figure out how to proceed. They lacked the finances to outfit themselves properly for a trapping expedition, and Clay had already said they would probably have to find someone willing to back them in return for a share of the profits.

The expedition being put together by this Manuel Lisa could really simplify matters, Jeff realized. Clay and he could join it and not have to come up with a great deal of money before they started. The idea sounded made-to-order.

"When is he leaving?" Jeff asked.

"As soon as he can get all his men and supplies together. Early next month, I'd say. Why don't we go see him?"

Jeff hesitated. They could not sit in St. Louis forever. "All right, let's go."

Clay stood up. He put his cap on and led Jeff out of the tavern.

The streets were bustling with activity. Everyone was glad to be out and moving around again after the long winter.

Manuel Lisa had a small office in a nearby building. Most of the space in the building, Clay explained, was being used to store the goods and supplies Lisa intended to take upriver. The Spaniard had no secretary; he greeted the brothers himself as they stepped into his office. He was a sturdily built man with a dark complexion, an aristocratic mane of gray hair, and thick, startlingly black brows.

He extended his hand to his visitors, and those striking brows lifted in curiosity as Clay said, "Howdy, Señor Lisa. I'm Clay Holt, and this is my brother Jeff."

"I am quite pleased to meet you, Mr. Holt," Lisa said in excellent English. "Your name is familiar to me, of course, from tales I have been told by your former companions in the Corps of Discovery. It seems they think highly of you."

Clay looked slightly uncomfortable at the praise. Lisa went on, "I hope you have come to tell me that you wish to join my little excursion up the Missouri."

"That's what we were thinking of," Clay admitted.

Lisa turned toward Jeff. "And you, sir? You would like to go along, too?"

Jeff said, "Clay and I figured to stick together."

"I do not recall your name as being among those who undertook the journey with Captain Lewis and Captain Clark."

"I wasn't with them," Jeff said. "But I can take care of myself, sir. I'm ready to learn whatever I need to know."

Lisa regarded him dubiously. "No offense, young man, but the expedition I propose is no place for learning. It is a very serious business. If I am to get ahead and stay ahead of those damned Frenchmen, I must have only the best men working for me."

"Jeff will be one of the best before you know it,

señor," Clay said. "He's smart, and rawhide tough. You won't regret taking a chance on him."

"Besides," Jeff added boldly, "if you don't hire us, we'll just go out there to the Shining Mountains and get a jump on you."

Lisa looked intently at him for a long moment, then chuckled. "Yes, I believe you would. Very well, Mr. Holt—both Mr. Holts—I welcome you to my company. I warn you, though. The life will not be easy."

"Wouldn't want it to be." Clay put his hand on Jeff's shoulder. "We'll be ready to go whenever you say the word."

"Excellent. In the meantime . . ." Lisa regarded them shrewdly for a second, then opened one of the drawers in his desk and withdrew a small leather pouch. He opened it and took out a couple of coins. "Here." He flipped the coins to Clay and Jeff, who plucked them out of the air. "Consider that an advance on your earnings, gentlemen. Eat well and try not to drink too much. Get plenty of rest and sleep. Enjoy yourselves while you can, for soon you will be entering a life where the hardships will be many and the rewards few, at least for a time. Remain diligent, though, and someday you will be rich men."

"I'll settle for being free," Clay said.

Those words echoed in Jeff's mind as he and Clay went back to their lodgings. That was really why they were there, he thought—to be free. Free from the violence and hatred that had plagued the Holt family back in Ohio. Free from the likes of Zach Garwood.

Despite Manuel Lisa's warning about not drinking too much, both Holt brothers celebrated that evening. Living over a tavern meant that beer and whiskey were readily available, and after they had eaten supper, they carried full mugs to one of the tables near the fireplace. The evening air still had quite a chill in it, and the heat from the fire felt good. The establishment was busy that night. Burly riverboaters and buckskin-clad frontiersmen rubbed shoulders at the bar, and quite a few people sat at the tables. A fiddler was scratching out a tune, trying to make up for his almost complete lack of talent with his zeal. Several couples danced clumsily but enthusiastically. Most of the women in the room were unabashed trollops, wearing low-cut linen gowns and shawls that furnished some warmth without interfering with the display of creamy, rounded breasts.

Jeff paid little attention to the women at first, not even the serving girl who refilled their mugs, bending over as she poured from a pitcher to give him an unobstructed view down the front of her gown. He ignored her and wondered why she gave him a look of disappointment and then flounced away with the coin Clay gave her.

The only woman Jeff was interested in was back in the Ohio River valley. He saw her in his dreams at night, and her image filled his mind now. He lifted the mug and swallowed almost half the brew without really tasting it.

"Better go easy on that," Clay cautioned him. "You've already had more than you're used to drinking."

Jeff smiled crookedly. "Well, we're celebrating, aren't we? We're about to embark on a great adventure."

"A hell of a lot of hard work is more like it. The trip out here to St. Louis was easy compared to what we're facing now, Jeff."

"I'll worry about it when we get there."

In the back of his mind Jeff knew he was being unreasonable. He should have been happy that he and Clay had a purpose again at last, but instead the day's developments seemed to have thrust him even deeper into depression. Marietta was only a few hundred miles away, and now that the weather had improved, he could cover that distance fairly quickly. It would have been simple to go back home, back to his wife.

If only Melissa had gone with the children to Pennsylvania the way she was supposed to! If she had done that, Jeff thought, he wouldn't be sitting worry-

ing about her still being in the same community as
Zach Garwood. He would have known she was safe,
and he could have concentrated on the expedition of
which he was now a part.

Instead he was drinking and brooding, and that,
he knew, was a bad combination. His mood was so
dark, though, that he seemed unable to do anything
about it.

He drained the mug and signaled for more, paying no attention to the dark look Clay gave him. Clay
had always been the impulsive brother, while Jeff had
been considered levelheaded. Perhaps it was time to
do something about that, Jeff thought. Clay knew
more about surviving in the wilderness, and Jeff
would follow his orders to the letter once they got
there. But here in civilization, Jeff didn't think he had
to worry about pleasing his older brother. He was a
grown man, after all, not a child tied to his mother's
apron strings.

Thinking of Norah made Jeff feel a sharp pain. He
missed her, missed his father as well. Not a day went
by that he did not think of them. They were gone,
though, and he had to live with that knowledge, just
as he had to live with the fact that he was separated
from his wife and probably would be for months, perhaps years, to come.

"Here," a voice said curtly beside him.

Jeff looked up at the woman this time. At first
glance she seemed as sluttish as the rest of the women
in the tavern. The neckline of her dress swooped low
enough to reveal much of her full bosom. As she
leaned over to pour more beer into his mug, he saw
the edge of one brown nipple peeking out from the
garment. Her hair was the color of corn silk and was
curled into tight ringlets that fell to her shoulders. She
wore a thick layer of powder on her face, making her
dark blue eyes stand out that much more. No, Jeff
thought, revising his opinion as his gaze dwelled on
her, she did not look like the other hoydens after all.
She was much more striking.

He reached up and put a hand on her wrist. "Why don't you sit down?" he asked. "You've been scurrying about this room all evening. You must be tired."

The woman shrugged. "Serving drinks is my job, mister. If I get tired, I don't think about it."

"Still, it won't hurt you to rest your feet."

Clay spoke up. "She doesn't want to sit down, Jeff."

"I didn't say that." The woman set the pitcher on the table and sat on the bench. "I wouldn't mind. For a few minutes."

"My name is Jefferson Holt, and this is my brother Clay. And you are. . . ?"

"Estelle."

"Won't you have something to drink, Estelle?"

She shook her head. "The owner doesn't like it."

"Those other women are drinking," Jeff pointed out. As a matter of fact, they were guzzling down just as much liquor as their male companions.

"They don't work here. I do. They're just here to find men to take back to their rooms for a quick tumble in exchange for a few coins."

"And you've never done the same thing?" Clay suggested.

Jeff felt his face flush with anger. "You've no right to speak to the lady that way, Clay," he said. "Anyone can see she's respectable, not like those—those harlots!"

Clay's mouth quirked in an ironic grin. "Sure, little brother. Whatever you say." He got to his feet. "But if you're determined to make a fool of yourself, I'd rather not be around to witness it. Just remember one thing."

"What's that?" Jeff challenged.

"Remember Melissa." With that, Clay turned and walked off, heading for another corner of the room.

Jeff caught his breath, and his eyes narrowed in anger. Clay had a hell of a nerve, speaking to him like that about Melissa! Of course he remembered her. He was married to her.

Estelle leaned toward him. "Who's Melissa?"

"My wife."

"Oh." The knowledge that Jeff was married did not seem to bother her. As if out of idle curiosity, she asked, "Where is she?"

"Back in Ohio."

"I'm not surprised. Not many men bring their wives out here." She gave a low, throaty laugh. "St. Louis may be civilized, but it's not yet a place for a proper woman."

"What about you?" Jeff asked.

"No one said I was proper, darlin'."

Jeff shifted uncomfortably on the bench. Estelle had slid even closer to him, and although they were not touching, he could feel the warmth of her body. He said, "I meant how did you come to be here on the edge of the wilderness?"

"My man brought me. He didn't have as much sense as you."

"What happened to him?"

"He got in a fight with some men off a riverboat. He'd been in a tavern a lot like this one, drinking too much. They beat him to death."

The matter-of-fact way in which she said it made Jeff shiver. Obviously, Estelle had seen more than her share of trouble since her husband had been killed. That would account for the hardness he could see in her eyes.

She went on, "If you're wondering, yes, I've done what I had to do in order to survive since then. There was no money, no way to go back home. This life is all I have now."

"I'm sorry," Jeff said sincerely. "I was sitting here feeling sorry for myself, and I had completely forgotten there are people much worse off than me."

"Well, don't feel sorry for me." Her voice was edged with anger. "Don't waste your sympathy. I'm better off. Can you imagine what it would have been like if he'd lived and taken me on into the wilderness? I'm glad he's dead. He was a damned fool."

Jeff did not argue with her. Instead, he reached into his pocket and groped for a coin. "I want to give you something."

She put a hand on his arm. "Not unless I earn it. I've got my pride, you know."

"You mean—"

"You know good and well what I mean. You're a long way from home, a long way from your woman. Are you staying in St. Louis for good?"

"No, my brother and I—we're going west. Going to the mountains."

"Then we'll probably never see each other again. You see, it's not complicated at all, is it?"

Jeff was aware that his brain was a bit fuzzy from all he had drunk. Her words made sense to him, though, and he could not deny that she was attractive. He had no idea how long she had been making her living this way, but it could not have been a lengthy period of time. Despite what she had said, there was still a veneer of respectability about her.

"All right," he said abruptly. "Do you have a room here?"

She said, "I just serve drinks here. I live close by, though. We can walk over there in minutes."

"What about your job?"

"I come and go as I like. Old Phineas, who runs the place, doesn't mind." She stood up and held out her hand to Jeff. "Are you coming or not?"

He swallowed the last of his beer and came to his feet. "Aye."

They headed for the exit, ignored by the other carousers in the tavern. Jeff glanced around, thinking that he would probably see Clay watching with a look of disapproval, but he did not see his brother anywhere in the smoky, low-ceilinged room.

Maybe Clay had found a woman of his own, Jeff thought. He had no ties, no reason not to take his pleasure as he found it.

Guilt began to gnaw at Jeff's insides—an all too familiar feeling. He had lived with the nightmare of his parents' death and the feeling that he should have done something—anything—to prevent the situation from coming to such a tragic conclusion. Now, as he and Estelle stepped out of the tavern and started down the dark street, he asked himself if he really wanted to add to his guilt by going along with what she had suggested.

"What's wrong?" she asked sharply as Jeff paused. They had gone less than a block from the tavern, but already the shadows were thick and dark around them. The only lights came from taverns and grogshops such as the one they had just left.

"I'm not sure this is a good idea." Jeff's head was beginning to hurt, and he knew he had drunk too much. "I think I should go back."

"You don't want to do that." She moved closer to him, put her hands on his arms, and rubbed gently up and down. He felt the softness of her breasts pushing against his chest. "Come along with me. I'll take care of that dark mood that's plaguing you."

Waves of pain echoed through his skull. Jeff winced and said, "I—I've got to go. . . ."

He was getting dizzier by the second, he realized, and instinct began screaming a warning in the back of his head. The blonde had put something in that last mug of beer, he thought, some sort of potion that was making him groggy. And the only reason for her to do that, he figured out abruptly, was that she intended to rob him, either alone or with the help of a confederate.

He took a quick step away from her, muttering, "Lemme 'lone," but his balance deserted him, and he stumbled. Estelle came after him and clutched at his arms again.

"What's wrong?" she demanded, a note of desperation in her voice. "Where are you going?"

Jeff twisted out of her grasp, and again the world spun crazily around him. He felt himself falling, then landed heavily on the packed dirt of the street.

"Bert!" the blonde hissed. "Come on, Bert. He's out!"

She was mistaken, however; Jeff was not unconscious. As her partner in crime darted from an alley and hurried toward them, Jeff tried to push himself up on his hands and knees so that he could get to his feet once again. He did not make it.

In low-pitched tones a harsh male voice said, "He's still awake, dammit! Ya got to start makin' that dram stronger!"

"Strong enough to kill somebody?" Estelle replied. "Then we'd be murderers instead of just thieves, Bert."

"Murderin', thievin', it don't make a hell of a lot of diff'rence, lass. Stand aside. I'll thump this fella a good'un, and he won't bother us while we're lookin' through his gear."

Jeff let out a groan. This was absurd! He was in the middle of a town, less than a block from his lodgings, yet he was going to be attacked and robbed, perhaps even killed. He might die before he ever saw the Shining Mountains. . . .

"Stand away from him," a new voice ordered.

Clay! Jeff recognized his brother's voice, and hope shot through him. Clay would put a stop to the robbers' plans. Jeff blinked his eyes and tried to see through both the shadows and the drug-induced fog that shrouded his brain.

He heard the man called Bert curse in surprise, then say, "Go back inside, mister. This don't concern you."

"The hell it doesn't," Clay replied flatly. "That's my brother."

Suddenly there was a rush of footsteps, the sound of blows being struck, and grunts of effort from the men engaged in combat.

"Stick him, Bert, stick him!" Estelle cried.

Jeff wanted to shout a warning to Clay to watch out for a knife. Evidently, though, Clay was well aware of the threat, for a second later Jeff heard a sharp crack, followed by a shrill bellow of pain. He identified the sound as that of a bone breaking, and he knew that the bone in question did not belong to Clay.

Another crack split the night, but this time it came from a pistol. It was followed by a disappointed "Oh, no!" from the woman, then a thud as a fist struck home.

Silence fell over the street for a few seconds. The man with the broken bone must have passed out, Jeff thought, because he had stopped screaming. And the woman was quiet now, too. St. Louis was still sufficiently wild that a few screams and a single gunshot would not attract much immediate attention.

"Damn, I hate to have to hit a woman," Clay said after a moment. "Riles me up whenever anybody shoots at me, though, even a female." He loomed over Jeff, blotting out some of the stars that seemed to be dancing a jig, at least to Jeff's eyes. Strong hands gripped Jeff and lifted him to his feet.

"Can you walk?" Clay asked.

"Not . . . very well," Jeff managed to say.

"Well, I'm not in much of a mood to carry you, not after that gal took a shot at me and her man tried to carve me up with a knife."

"She said her man was dead."

"Reckon she lied," Clay said curtly. "Or else this fellow is somebody different she hooked up with. Doesn't really matter, does it? What's important is that they planned to rob you, maybe even slit your throat for good measure."

"She didn't want any killing."

"That wouldn't have stopped him." Clay put an arm around Jeff's waist and draped Jeff's arm across his shoulder. "Hang on. I'll get you back to the room."

"Thanks for—for helping me," Jeff said as they started awkwardly down the street. "Don't know how you figured it out."

"I've seen such things happen before. It's an old trick. When I got back from stepping outside for a minute and saw you were gone, I was pretty sure what was in the wind."

Jeff's stomach was starting to roil around now, and he winced as a particularly strong wave of queasiness rolled over him. "I'm sorry. I—"

That was as far as he got. He went to his knees, and Clay allowed him to fall. Bending forward, Jeff let the nausea overwhelm him and began to retch.

"Seen that happen before, too," Clay said with a dry chuckle.

At that moment, despite his gratitude for what Clay had done to help him, Jeff almost hated him. He was too busy being sick to worry about such things for long, however. He felt so terrible, in fact, that he barely heard Clay say softly, "I'll be glad when we get out of this damned city and only have to deal with Indians and wild animals."

The events of that night—plus the pounding head and sick stomach Jeff had to deal with all the next day —taught him a lesson. He had let his depressed state of mind blind him to what was going on around him. If that ever happened once he and Clay got to the mountains, it could cost not only his life, but Clay's as well.

Jeff stayed completely sober for the next few weeks, while the weather improved and, according to Clay, the last of the ice on the upper reaches of the Missouri was likely breaking up. They stayed in touch with Manuel Lisa and finally, on April 19, 1807, boarded keelboats along with sixty other men, including the Spanish entrepreneur himself. The fur trading expedition was under way at last.

Spirits were high. Lisa spent his days walking up and down alongside the squatty cabin of one of the keelboats, exhorting the men who were poling the craft upriver. Jeff and Clay took their turns at the strenuous task, and Jeff could almost feel his muscles hardening daily from the work. Ahead of them the Missouri River coiled like a brown snake, giving am-

ple evidence of why it was known among frontiersmen as the Big Muddy. The land around it was
alive with the new greens of spring, high bluffs and
gently rolling prairie stretching as far as the eye could
see. Jeff looked west every day but saw no sign of the
mountains, only more of the endless flatland. He had
heard that some of the politicians in Washington City
had started calling it the Great American Desert and
claiming that it did the country no good to try to cross
it, that expeditions such as this were just a waste of
time, energy, and money.

Jeff did not believe that. He had heard Clay talk in
unguarded moments about the call of the West, and
Jeff was beginning to understand what he meant.
Something was out there, something that summoned
him onward.

By the time they had covered three hundred
miles, the days had settled into a monotonous routine
for Jeff. He worked, he ate, he collapsed in exhaustion.
It was the same for the other men. Even the indomita-
ble Manuel Lisa was beginning to look a bit ragged.

After two more days had passed, they sighted a
line of trees snaking across the trackless wilderness to
the west and then intersecting the thicker growth that
marked the course of the Missouri up ahead. "That'll
be the Platte," Clay told Jeff as they planted their long
poles in the bottom of the river and walked forward,
propelling the keelboat against the current.

As they drew nearer the junction of the rivers, Jeff
spotted a thin curl of smoke spiraling into the clear
sky. He pointed it out to Clay.

Clay frowned and rubbed at his jaw. "Wonder
who the hell's out here in the middle of nowhere?"

They were not the only ones to see the smoke.
Manuel Lisa noticed it, too, and called out for the
boats to put in at the shore. They had seen few Indians
during the journey so far, and those they had seen had
stayed well away from the river and had not at-
tempted to contact the white men. The smoke might
be coming from an Indian camp, and the natives

might have beaver pelts—what the fur traders called plews—to swap for whiskey or beads or cloth.

Instead of an Indian camp, however, the travelers saw a lone man sitting cross-legged next to his small fire. He stood up and lifted a hand in greeting as the boats drew in sight, then crossed his arms and waited as they came to shore.

Clay's eyes narrowed as he studied the tall, lean, buckskin-garbed figure. "I know that man!" he exclaimed. "That's John Colter!"

Shouts of recognition rang out from the other former members of the Corps of Discovery as the boats grounded just below the mouth of the Platte River. Several men, including Clay, leapt agilely to the shore and surrounded Colter. They slapped him on the back and immediately volleyed questions at him. The other members of the party disembarked as well, and after a few minutes, Clay took Colter to Manuel Lisa, his arm around the Virginian's shoulders.

"Señor Lisa, this here is John Colter," Clay said. "You won't find a white man who knows more about the mountains, and I reckon not many red men do, either. John, this is Manuel Lisa. We're going up the Missouri after beaver."

"Plenty up there to be had," Colter said as he shook hands with Lisa. "Watch out that the Blackfoot and the Rees don't lift your hair and take you under, and you'll make out all right."

"We have trade goods with which to placate the savages," Lisa told him, "and I intend to build a fort to protect us from those who will not be reasonable. We shall indeed make out all right." His voice was full of his usual confidence.

Clay asked, "What happened to those two fellows you went back with, John? What were their names? Dickson was one—"

"The other was called Hancock," Colter replied. "I'm not rightly sure where they are, Clay. We took some plews and traded them off to some Frenchman we ran into, and I reckon Dickson and Hancock figured there weren't enough profits in this game for them after all. They went off on their own, heading east. May be back in civilization by now for all I know. Myself, I been wandering around for a bit, seeing the country."

Jeff remembered what Clay had told him about John Colter. The Virginian had been in the wilderness for more than three years now, and he seemed to have no desire to return to civilization. Since leaving the Lewis and Clark expedition, Colter had seen even more of the rugged country to the west, probably more than any white man had ever seen.

Lisa seemed to be thinking along the same lines. He asked, "How would you like to join us, Mr. Colter? We could use an ally such as yourself."

Colter squinted. "Where is it you're heading, exactly?"

"That has not been determined." Lisa raised a dark eyebrow. "I would certainly be willing to listen to the advice of a man such as yourself, though, and would give anything you had to say great weight."

"Well . . . I reckon I could go along for a spell. I been sitting here by the Platte for a week, trying to figure out what to do next. Reckon you fellas coming along the way you did must be a sign." Colter grinned. "Don't seem like I was meant to get too far from the Stonies."

Clay slapped him on the back. "Glad to have you with us, John."

Colter shook hands with Lisa again. Then the group settled down on the shore of the river. Not much of the day was left, so Lisa declared that they would camp there. Jeff and Clay and he sat by the fire with Colter, listening intently as the mountain man described the country he had been through since the previous spring. Colter drew crude maps in the dirt with his finger, and Jeff leaned forward to study them, committing them to memory as much as possible. Clay was doing the same thing. Out here, Jeff realized, you listened and listened good when a man like John

Colter was talking. Your life might depend on the things he could tell you.

With Colter enlisted as one of the group, they pushed on as the weather warmed even more. Wildflowers bloomed on the banks of the river in a riot of color. The white men passed a few villages with tipis clustered near the shore, but they were not challenged. The Indians seemed curious about them but not openly hostile.

That changed abruptly, however, when they reached the mouth of a small river, where a crowd of several hundred painted Indians waited. The Indians must have heard about the white men coming upstream, for they had gathered to wait for them. Colter studied the natives through a spyglass that Lisa handed him, and as he lowered the instrument, his face was grim. "Them's Rees," he told Lisa, while Clay and Jeff stood nearby, listening. "Some call them Arikara. Don't matter what you call them. Most of the time they're bad medicine."

"I see only a few canoes drawn up on shore," Lisa commented. "I don't think they can stop us."

"Wouldn't be so sure. They got guns."

As if to emphasize Colter's words, a ragged volley of shots rang out from the shore, and splashes in the water ahead of the keelboats showed where the balls were falling. "Good Lord!" Lisa exclaimed.

"They're wavin' us in," Colter pointed out. "Better do as they say. They ain't very good shots, but there's enough of them to do some damage, even if it's accidental."

Lisa's face was set in stern, angry lines. He signaled for the other boats to follow his lead, then had his men pole for shore. "Mr. Holt," he said quietly to Clay, "can you fire a cannon?"

Jeff saw his brother glance at the long gun mounted on a swivel on the bow of Lisa's keelboat. "Well, I never have before," Clay answered slowly.

"No matter," Lisa said with a casual flip of his hand. "Light a torch and stand beside the gun. If I command you to do so, thrust the flame against the touchhole. That's all there is to it. The cannon is already loaded."

"All right," Clay agreed, but Jeff could see the uncertainty in his eyes. Nobody was better with a rifle than Clay Holt, but firing a cannon was new to him.

Clay used flint and steel to light one of the pitch-soaked torches carried in the keelboat's cabin, then planted himself next to the cannon. The boats were nearing the shore now, close enough for the men to see the painted faces of the Arikara. Jeff's .54 caliber rifle was lying at his feet, and he badly wanted to pick it up, but he kept poling as Lisa had ordered. A few moments later the keelboats grounded.

At least three hundred Arikara stood there, Jeff estimated. His heart pounded wildly in his chest at the awe-inspiring display.

As soon as the boats had touched the shore, the Indians surged toward them. Manuel Lisa stepped up beside Clay and the cannon and roared, "Stop right there, gentlemen!" He reached down, grasped the barrel of the cannon, and swiveled it so that the black, gaping mouth of its muzzle faced the warriors. "If any of you so much as set foot on any of my craft, I'll fire this gun and blow you all to Hades!"

Not all the Indians understood English, but enough of them did that the group moved back immediately. Some of them almost fell over their own feet to get out of the line of fire, so terrified were they of the cannon.

"Pick up your rifles, men," Lisa ordered.

Jeff gripped his rifle tightly, hoping he would not have to use it. He knew Lisa was running a bluff. The cannon and rifles could do a lot of damage, but not enough to wipe out all the Arikara. The white men could take their best shot and still be overrun in a matter of minutes.

That was not to be, however. Two chiefs stepped forward and addressed Lisa. Colter kept his face carefully emotionless as he translated, but Jeff could hear the relief in his voice. "They've decided they'd rather trade than fight, Captain. They want to smoke the peace pipe with you."

Lisa allowed himself a slight smile. "Very well. Tell them I'd be happy to smoke with them."

Jeff caught Clay's eye and saw how relieved his older brother was as well. Clay stayed where he was beside the cannon, holding the torch at the ready, while Lisa stepped down from the boat and negotiated with the Arikara chiefs. Colter translated as the Spaniard drove a sharp bargain with the natives. By the middle of the afternoon, as the keelboats headed upstream again, they had not only successfully passed the danger of the Arikara, but they had several dozen beaver pelts stored in the cabin of the lead boat, received from the Arikara in exchange for a length of bright red cloth, a handful of blue beads, and a tin cup.

"Quite an auspicious beginning, gentlemen," Lisa told his men proudly. "Quite an auspicious beginning indeed."

Jeff had to agree. He just hoped that the next meeting with the Indians would not be quite so nerve-racking in the bargain.

CHAPTER FOURTEEN

The winter of 1807 had been as harsh in Marietta as it had in St. Louis, perhaps even more so. Melissa Holt had never known such despair as she felt when she looked out the windows of her father's house and saw the ice-coated trees and the thick gray clouds scudding low in the sky. The whole world seemed to have closed in around her.

She missed Jeff with a longing that was more painful than any physical hurt.

Hermione had done what she could to ease her daughter's dark mood. Melissa had always loved to cook, ever since she was a little girl, and the large cast-iron stove nearly always had a fire in it as Hermione seemed to bake from morning to night. She tried to involve Melissa in what she was doing, but although Melissa was willing to help out, the work did not really seem to interest her.

Her daughter was pining for Jefferson Holt, Hermione knew, and she could do nothing to remedy the situation. It was entirely possible—although Hermione shuddered to think such a thing—that Melissa might never see Jeff again. All sorts of things could happen out on the frontier.

Melissa wished she knew how Jeff had taken the news that she had not accompanied the Holt children to Pennsylvania. She was sure he was disappointed when he read her letter. Her father had been adamant, and she had never been able to stand up to him when he was determined to have his way. Her mother had not interceded on her behalf, either; Melissa knew that Hermione had not really wanted her to leave, despite the possible danger from the Garwoods.

At least that problem had not reared its ugly head again. The Garwoods still lived on their farm, Melissa knew, since she occasionally saw Josie and Matthew or old Alfred in town. But she had not seen Zach or Aaron even once since Jeff and Clay had left the area; evidently the two Garwood brothers were staying close to home most of the time.

She wanted to believe that Zach Garwood's desire for revenge had died along with Pete, but she knew better. Zach was not the type of man to let go of something he cherished as much as he did his hatred of the Holts.

And she was one of the Holts now, the only one at whom Zach could strike. Even through her depression that knowledge was always with her, and she never left the cabin unless her father accompanied her.

Gradually, the snow and ice had melted, and the cold winds had stopped howling from the north. The sun returned, bringing with it warm breezes from the south and green shoots of grass. Leaves had begun to bud out on the trees. It was a time of rebirth, a time that Melissa had always enjoyed.

That year was different, however. She was too sick to appreciate the advent of spring. Her features were pale and washed out, and nearly every morning she was seized by a violent bout of nausea. She tried to conceal the way she felt from her parents, but she thought her mother suspected. Her father, of course, did not. Charles Merrivale paid little attention to anything that did not affect him directly.

Toward the end of April, Melissa's illness eased somewhat, but by then she knew very well what was wrong with her: She was going to have a baby—Jeff's baby.

She knew she should have been happy and excited, but instead she became even more depressed. How could she be glad about such a development, she asked herself more than once, when she did not even know if Jeff was still alive?

Then the letter arrived.

Charles Merrivale brought it back with him when he returned from Steakley's trading post, which also served as Marietta's post office. "This came for you today," he said with ill grace as he held out the envelope to Melissa.

She recognized the writing on it and snatched it out of his hand, too excited to be polite. She tore open the envelope, then unfolded the sheet of foolscap inside and scanned the words. Hermione came over to stand beside her, almost as anxious for news of her son-in-law as Melissa was.

"He and Clay have joined a group going up the Missouri River to trap beaver," Melissa announced. "They're both well, thank God. He—he doesn't say anything about when he'll be back, though, or if he wants me to join him."

"Of course you won't join him," Merrivale snorted. "A girl such as yourself going out into that godforsaken wilderness—that's the most ridiculous idea I've ever heard! I wouldn't permit it." Merrivale put his pipe in his mouth, clamped his teeth down on the stem, and said around it, "A pitiful excuse for a husband, if you ask me."

Melissa looked up from the letter, her eyes flashing with anger. "I won't have you talking about my husband that way, Father!"

"He has run off to the wilderness to hunt beaver and live with the Indians. He'll probably take himself a red-skinned squaw."

"Charles!" Hermione exclaimed. "What a way to talk! You can't mean that." She glanced at Melissa and saw the stricken look on her daughter's face.

"I most certainly do mean it," Merrivale insisted as he sat down. "Mark my words, Melissa, you'll never see that wastrel again."

"That wastrel, as you call him," Melissa said, her voice shaky, "is the father of your grandchild."

Merrivale's head snapped up, his eyes widened, and the pipe dropped from his mouth. Only the fact that he had not yet lit it kept him from setting fire to his breeches.

"What?" he said in astonishment.

Melissa glanced at her mother and saw no surprise on Hermione's face. As she had suspected, her mother had been well aware of what was going on. "I said I'm going to have a baby, Father. Jeff's baby."

Merrivale's features were slowly turning red from embarrassment.

Melissa smiled, but the smile did not reach her eyes. "What's the matter, Father?" she asked. "Surely you're not surprised?"

"I—I just fail to see the point in discussing it further."

Hermione shot a meaningful glance at her husband. "Don't trouble yourself, Charles. Melissa will be just fine. Won't you, darling?"

"Of course," Melissa replied, but suddenly she did not feel so sure of that. Now that the news of her pregnancy was out in the open, she felt an unexpected surge of fear. She had her mother to help her, but her husband—the one who should have been at her side at a time like this—was hundreds, perhaps thousands of miles away. In the time it had taken for the letter to reach her from St. Louis, Jeff and Clay had surely left the city and begun their voyage up the Missouri.

There was no way of knowing how far into the wilderness they had penetrated by now.

Hermione patted her daughter's shoulder. "I know you're frightened. But everything will be all right, Melissa. You just wait and see."

Melissa wished she could share her mother's optimism.

Charles Merrivale spent the rest of the afternoon sitting in his chair and brooding. He paid no attention as his wife and daughter bustled around the kitchen preparing supper.

In the back of his mind had been the hope that something had already happened to Jeff Holt, that the young whelp would never return to plague them again. That was still possible, of course, but the arrival of the letter from Jeff had gotten Melissa all stirred up again. She was still thinking of herself as Jeff's wife, as ludicrous as that idea was.

Even if nothing happened to Jeff in the West, Merrivale thought, even if he did come back someday, he would no longer be a suitable husband for Melissa. He would be little better than a savage, accustomed to living in the wilderness, probably with an Indian squaw. The thought of such a man touching his daughter made Merrivale burn with anger—anger he was careful to conceal, however.

He had realized that he could not allow Hermione and Melissa to see just how deeply he hated Jefferson Holt. If they knew the plan that was beginning to form in his head, they would try to stop him. . . .

By evening he had made up his mind. He would announce his decision when they had finished eating, and there would be no argument.

When the meal was over, having been eaten for the most part in an uncomfortable silence, Melissa and Hermione stood up to begin clearing the china off the linen-covered table. Merrivale said sharply, "Both of you sit down. There's something we need to discuss."

Hermione glanced at him in surprise, and Melissa felt a tingle of dread. She did not like the way her father sounded. His tone seemed even more obstinate than usual.

Mother and daughter sat down at the table again and waited for Merrivale to continue. He placed his palms flat on the table, looked at them for a long moment, then said, "We're going back to North Carolina. We're going home."

"No!" The exclamation was jolted out of Melissa. "This is our home now!"

"You can't mean it, Charles," Hermione added, her distress evident.

"Indeed I do mean it," Merrivale said heavily. "It's time to return to civilization."

"But Ohio *is* civilized. It's a state now, Charles."

Merrivale dismissed his wife's point with a wave of his hand. "No society that would tolerate ruffians like the Garwoods—and the Holts—can truly call itself civilized. We're going to leave this farm and go back to a place where decent people can live in peace. A suitable place for our grandchild to be reared."

Melissa was on her feet now. "I won't go!" she said raggedly, her chest heaving with emotion. "The Garwoods haven't caused any trouble for a long time. There's no reason to run from them!"

That might not be strictly true, she realized, but she was going to stick by her guns anyway. She could not allow her father to browbeat her into meekly accepting the insane notion of returning to North Carolina.

Merrivale would not be swayed. "No grandchild of mine is going to be born in this godforsaken wilderness. We're going back, and that's final."

Hermione slumped in her chair. "Please, Charles—" she began wearily.

He shook his head.

With a sigh of defeat Hermione lowered her eyes. Melissa's gaze darted back and forth between her mother and father. She saw a slight smile of triumph on her father's lips.

How could she stand up to him without her mother's help?

It was simple—she could not. Melissa felt a wave of despair, stronger than any that had come before, wash through her. Her father had won again. He was going to get his way, as usual. Had there ever been any doubt?

This time, Melissa vowed, it would be different. Charles Merrivale might think he had won, but sooner or later the tables would be turned. Melissa was already thinking of a way to foil his plan, at least in the long run.

She had to be successful. For her sake, for Jeff's sake, and for the sake of their child.

All through the summer and into the fall the expedition led by gray-haired Manuel Lisa pushed on, heading steadily up the Missouri. They were in wild country and might as well have been a million miles from St. Louis, rather than hundreds. The terrain was varied in color and texture, from lush green forested hills to steep rocky bluffs, sometimes rising high above the water on both sides of the river. Frequently Indians were standing on the pinnacles, watching the passage of the keelboats. Jeff had almost given up hope of ever seeing the mountains, but Clay told him to be patient.

"The Rockies haven't gone anywhere," Clay assured him. "They'll be there."

Jeff could pole the boat from dawn to dusk now without tiring too much. He was stronger than he had ever been in his life. His years on the farm had been filled with hard work, but nothing to compare with this. The faces of the travelers were now a deep bronze, and in their buckskins Jeff supposed they did look somewhat like Indians. He had traded a small mirror that had been cached in his gear for a fine set of buckskins in one of the Mandan villages they visited.

The woman who had made the breeches, tunic, and capote had decorated them with beads and painted porcupine quills, so Jeff looked like an honored warrior from her tribe. She would have shared her blanket with him as well, he was sure of that, and he had to admit that he was tempted by her dusky, round-faced beauty. It had been a long time indeed since he had left Melissa. But in the end he was satisfied with the buckskins, and the woman seemed happy enough to switch her attentions to another man in the party.

Lisa had brought along plenty of trade goods—silk, calico, thread, kettles, pots, beads, brass rings, looking glasses, tin cups, crockery, thimbles—anything that might catch the eye of an Indian. Some of these goods had been useful as the group traveled along especially dangerous stretches of the river. Lisa, in the company of several other men, would leave the boats and proceed on foot with a selection of trade goods to the villages, where they would spend an hour bartering with the natives while the keelboats drifted quietly by on the river. Jeff went with Lisa on a couple of these visits, and by the time he and the others had returned to the boats, his nerves were stretched almost to the breaking point. The only real trouble came when Lisa was forced to fire the cannon over the heads of a large group of Assiniboin, who had gathered on the shore to try to stop the white men. Faced with the threat of the long gun, they had quickly scattered and proved to be no real threat.

John Colter turned out to be an invaluable addition to the party. Not only was he knowledgeable about the river and the land through which it passed, but he also knew all the Indian tribes: which ones were to be avoided at all costs and which ones could be trusted—to a point. Acting on Colter's advice, the boats followed the Yellowstone River when it forked off from the Missouri. According to Colter, the valley where the Yellowstone and the Big Horn came together would be a perfect spot for the fort Lisa intended to build. "It's right in the heart of beaver country," Colter told his companions, "far enough south of the Blackfoot's usual stomping grounds that we won't have to worry overmuch about them. Mostly Crow and Sioux around there, and they're friendly enough if you treat them right."

Jeff could see something in the distance now when he stared toward the west, although it was only a low blue line on the horizon. One morning Clay noticed where Jeff was looking and said, "That's them."

"What do you mean?"

"The Rockies. The Shining Mountains. You've been wanting to see them for months, Jeff. Well, there they are."

Jeff's heart leapt. At long last he was looking at the majestic range that ran down the spine of the continent. Only a limited number of white men had ever seen those mountains, and now he was one of them. It was a good feeling.

Day by day, as the expedition drew ever nearer to the mountains, summer fled with surprising quickness. Autumn closed in with its chill wind and rain, and Jeff began to worry they would not reach the spot where Lisa planned to build the fort before winter arrived. By early November, though, they were closing in, and a few days later, Colter pointed out where the Big Horn River merged with the Yellowstone. "Right there," Colter said, standing on the bow of the leading keelboat and pointing. "That's the spot."

It was indeed an impressive location, lying in a valley that would be lush with grass during the summertime. Trees covered the hills surrounding it, and over it all loomed the mountains, still a good distance off but close enough for their gray peaks to seem to reach all the way to the heavens.

"This will be our home, gentlemen," Lisa told his followers. "As soon as we have built it, the fort will be named after me," he said. "Rather immodest of me, I admit."

And the sooner the better, Jeff thought. The other men were probably echoing the same sentiment in their heads. Everyone set to work with a vengeance, felling trees and notching and stacking the logs to form walls for a stockade. The fort seemed to take shape slowly, but Jeff knew they were actually making good progress. At night, as he rolled into his blankets and tried to sleep, he found himself staring up at the brilliant points of light that were the stars. He remembered Clay talking about how much brighter and compelling the stars were in the mountains, and now he could see for himself what his brother had meant.

Despite the dangers they had encountered, Jeff was struck by the rugged beauty of the country. He was beginning to understand why Clay preferred it to the more civilized areas in the East. Out here a man was truly free—free to survive and prosper if he had the necessary luck and skill, free to die if he did not. But either way . . . free.

It was almost enough to deaden the dull ache he felt inside every time he thought about Melissa, so far away, back in Ohio. And just before he drifted off to sleep, he found himself wondering about her. Was she well? Was she safe? Was she happy?

Melissa was miserable.

Her father had wasted no time in making preparations for the family to leave Ohio and go back to North Carolina. With the steady tide of immigration into the fertile Ohio River valley, it had not been difficult to find a buyer for their farm. The land was good, and the house was well built. Charles Merrivale asked a high price for his property, but he got a suitable offer very quickly. Almost before Melissa knew what was happening, the transaction had been concluded, and the day had been set for her parents and her to begin their pilgrimage.

It was early June, and her belly was swollen. In a way she was glad things were moving quickly. She wouldn't have wanted to travel much later in the summer. Already she seemed to be more uncomfortable with each passing day. Her mother was a great deal of help and comfort, of course, since she knew what to expect and did her best to prepare Melissa for the annoyances and unpleasantness that sometimes were part of having a baby.

Charles Merrivale was happier than his wife and daughter had seen him since before they came to Ohio. He was convinced it had been a mistake ever to leave his successful mercantile store in North Carolina, and it was a mistake he was now going to rectify. He had listened to the tales of how much money was to be made farming on the edge of the frontier, but for him those predictions had not come true. Now, with a great sense of relief, he made ready to return to something he knew and with which he was comfortable. He would start another store, he declared, and it would be even more successful than the old one.

Melissa hated his smug look as he watched Hermione and her pack their belongings for the trip. He was convinced that he was in total control, that he had the whole world under his thumb.

He would find out he was wrong this time, Melissa thought. When Jeff came back, everything would be different.

Melissa went with her father into Marietta to arrange passage on one of the riverboats that plied the Ohio. It would be an expensive voyage because they were shipping a great deal of heavy baggage. The furniture would be left in the house, but everything else would go back to North Carolina with them. They would travel by river, then buy a wagon or perhaps even two, Merrivale had decided.

While he paid a visit to the office of the riverboat company to settle the details of the trip, Melissa went across the street to Steakley's store. She looked around carefully as she entered, checking to make sure that Zach Garwood was not in the trading post. Then she went to the counter in the rear and waited patiently until the proprietor had finished with a customer.

Steakley smiled at her when he finally turned toward her. "Hello, Mrs. Holt. What can I do for you?"

Melissa reached inside her bag and brought out an envelope. She had labored over the letter inside it for almost an hour the night before, writing by the light of a single candle after her parents were asleep. She held out the envelope to the storekeeper. "Can I leave this with you, Mr. Steakley?"

"If that's a letter you want to mail, I reckon I can take it as the postmaster, Melissa."

Quickly she shook her head. "I don't want to mail it," she said. "I-I wouldn't know where to send it."

Steakley glanced at the name written on the envelope: Jefferson Holt. His bushy eyebrows lifted. "This is to your husband."

"Jeff will be coming back to Marietta, and when he finds that I'm gone, I'm sure he'll come here to find out where. I want you to give that to him when he does."

Steakley rubbed his jowls and frowned in thought. Slowly he said, "Your pa told me that you all were leaving this part of the country, Melissa. I'll be sorry to see you go. Your pa was always a good customer."

Melissa felt her impatience getting the best of her. "Will you keep that for Jeff or not?"

"Oh, sure, I reckon I can do that. It's not really part of my job as postmaster, but as a favor, you know."

She thought she knew what he was hinting at, and she delved into her bag again, brought out a gold piece, and laid it on the counter. "Will that be enough?"

"Why, you don't have to do that!" Steakley exclaimed, gesturing at the coin. "I said I'd be glad to do it as a favor."

Despite his protest, Melissa noticed that the eagle disappeared smoothly as his hand passed over it.

"Thank you, Mr. Steakley," she said. "I really appreciate this."

"Glad to do it. You be careful now, on your way back to North Carolina."

Melissa managed to smile and thank him again. Then she ducked out of the store and went back across the street just in time to greet her father as he emerged from the office of the riverboat company. "Where did you go, sweetheart?" Merrivale asked.

"I was right out here, Father," Melissa lied. "I just needed some air."

Merrivale put his arm around her shoulders. "How's my girl feeling?"

"I'm fine."

"I know all this activity must be hard on you, Melissa, but I truly believe it's for the best."

"I know you do, Father. I wish I could be so confident."

He gave her shoulders a squeeze. "Now, don't you worry. You're going to be very happy to be back home in North Carolina when that baby of yours arrives."

They walked back to the buggy that had brought them into town. Though her father might still have quite a few tasks before him, Melissa was relieved to have taken care of her most important one.

When Jeff returned from the mountains, as Melissa believed with every ounce of conviction that he would, he would be able to find her. He would go to North Carolina, reclaim his wife and child, and take them with him to wherever he wanted to make his home. Melissa did not care where that might be. As long as she and the baby were with Jeff, that was all that would matter.

Lost in those thoughts, she swayed slightly in the buggy seat as she rode beside her father. Her lips curved in a faint smile. Jeff would come for her—and there would not be one damned thing that Charles Merrivale could do about it.

That evening, Rathburn Steakley was hard at work on his favorite task—counting money. He had not yet locked the door of the trading post, but it was late and he did not expect any more customers to appear. Business had been brisk that day, and Steakley had a considerable pile of coins on the counter in front of him. He counted them in the light from a single candle, drawing them one at a time off the edge of the counter and letting them fall into the open neck of the drawstring bag he held in his other hand. The clinking they made as they joined their fellows was a lovely sound, as far as Steakley was concerned.

The front door of the store opened.

Steakley looked up sharply and at the same time raked the rest of the coins into the bag. He would lose count, but he could always start over later. He did not want anyone seeing how much money he had on hand.

Charles Merrivale strode into the store and marched down the center aisle toward the counter at the rear. "Good evening, Steakley," he said, his voice and demeanor as stern and dignified as always.

"Hello, Mr. Merrivale," Steakley greeted him. "Kind of late for you to be out, isn't it?"

"I need to take care of some last-minute business before my family and I take our leave. You knew we were moving back to North Carolina, didn't you?"

Steakley bobbed his balding head. "Yes, sir. You came in here a few days ago and settled up your account with me, remember?"

"Of course I remember," Merrivale snapped, and Steakley almost winced. He had forgotten how easily Merrivale could take offense. He was about to mumble some sort of apology when Merrivale went on, "Was my daughter in here this afternoon?"

Steakley hesitated before answering. Melissa had not said anything about not mentioning her visit to her father, but the storekeeper had a feeling that she would have preferred it to be a secret. However, with Merrivale standing right there glowering at him and waiting for an answer, Steakley found that any resolve he might have had to be discreet was rapidly fading.

"Yes, I believe Melissa did stop in here for a minute," he said.

"And she gave you a note or a letter of some sort, didn't she?"

Steakley knew the surprise he felt was visible on his face. There was no point in denying it. "Why, yes, she did," he admitted. "A letter for her husband."

Merrivale held out his hand, palm upward. "I want it."

Steakley began to hem and haw. "I, ah, I don't know if I can do that, Mr. Merrivale. I mean, she entrusted me with it, and I'm the postmaster now—"

"She didn't mail it," Merrivale cut in. "She merely left it with you to give to young Holt if he ever comes back here, am I correct?"

"I . . . I reckon that's right."

"Then you have no official responsibility for it. Hand it over, man."

Blinking his eyes rapidly, Steakley pondered his dilemma. He had taken money from Melissa to see that the message was safely delivered to Jefferson Holt, should Jeff ever return to Marietta. Steakley was well aware of his own avarice, but he liked to think of himself as an honest man, within his own limits. He was not above hinting for a little bribe under certain circumstances, but he always gave fair value for money received.

It was difficult to stand up to a man such as Charles Merrivale, however. Merrivale was accustomed to getting whatever he wanted.

And anyway, Steakley told himself, it was pretty unlikely that Jeff Holt would ever come back. He would probably get himself killed by Indians somewhere out there in the wilderness, the storekeeper thought.

"I'm not sure I should do this," Steakley said.

"What if I told you that Melissa changed her mind, that she no longer wants you to hold the letter?"

Steakley felt a surge of relief. "Well, in that case— and since I'm sure she'd want me to have something for my trouble . . ."

Merrivale looked disgusted, and for a second Steakley thought he had pushed the man too far. Then Merrivale reached into his pocket and brought out a coin. He dropped it on the counter and said between gritted teeth, "Of course she would."

With practiced dexterity Steakley scooped up the coin with his left hand while his right took the letter from a shelf under the counter. "There you are," he said pleasantly.

Now that money had changed hands, there was no longer any need for pretense. Merrivale tore open the envelope and unfolded the sheet of paper inside. His expression darkened as he read what was written there. Then he tore the letter in half with what appeared to be savage pleasure. He tore the paper again and again, until Melissa's message to her husband was reduced to so many shreds of tattered foolscap. The pieces fell in a pile on the countertop.

Steakley was somewhat surprised by his visitor's vehemence in destroying the letter, but he did not say anything. That was Merrivale's business and none of his. After he had ripped the letter to pieces, Merrivale looked up at Steakley and said, "If any more letters come here from my daughter intended for Jefferson Holt, I trust you'll destroy them. Because they will be mistakes, too."

"I can't—"

Merrivale reached into his pocket and slapped another coin on the counter. This time it was an eagle instead of a half eagle.

"Well, ah, I suppose . . ."

"Just do it." Merrivale added another eagle to the first one. "And if Jefferson Holt ever shows up here looking for my daughter—"

"She left with you and her mother, and I don't know where the three of you went."

For the first time Merrivale allowed himself a tight smile. "Now you're beginning to understand, Steakley. I trust I can count on your discretion in this matter?"

"Yes, sir. You certainly can," Steakley promised. All it took was simple ciphering, he thought, to see that a larger payment took precedence over a smaller one.

Merrivale scooped up the pieces of paper from the counter and wadded them into a ball. After nodding to Steakley, he turned on his heel and walked out of the store. Steakley saw him pause on the porch and throw the remains of Melissa's letter into the street.

With a sigh and a shake of his head, Steakley picked up his money bag and dumped the coins on the counter again, adding to the pile the three that Merrivale had given him. Too bad about Melissa and Jeff, he thought. All that bad luck with the Garwoods, and now it looked as if fate and Charles Merrivale were conspiring to keep the young people apart for good. It was a shame; they had made a nice couple. But it was really none of his business, and he had been well paid to keep it that way.

After a few moments, he whistled to himself as he counted the coins.

Fletcher McKendrick turned up the fur-lined collar of his coat and shivered. Although it was not yet officially winter, in the Canadian province of Manitoba the cold winds had already arrived. McKendrick buried his hands deep in his pockets as he tramped across the open space in the center of Fort Rouge. The fort, which had been built some sixty years earlier by one of the first French fur trappers to penetrate the Canadian wilderness, was laid out in the usual way, a high log stockade with several sturdy buildings inside the walls.

McKendrick was on his way to a meeting in one of those buildings, and he was a bit nervous about it. In the months since the dour Scotsman had been sent there from London, he had grown accustomed, to a certain extent, to the rough-edged Canadians. The company for which he worked, the London and Northwestern Enterprise, was in the fur business, which meant he spent his days dealing with French voyageurs and British trappers, and a more rugged breed McKendrick had never encountered. At first the men had taken him lightly, he knew, thinking that anyone sent from London would be a novice and perhaps even something of a weakling.

They had learned differently. Fletcher McKendrick bowed to no man.

Flurries of snow spiraled down from the gray sky. Some of the flakes caught in McKendrick's bushy red eyebrows and melted. He wiped them away with a rough, big-knuckled hand and hurried on, eager to be out of the biting wind. He hoped the meeting would be successful, but considering everything he had heard about the man called Duquesne, he had his doubts.

As the representative of the London and Northwestern Enterprise, McKendrick had been charged with making the company a success in Canada. It was a bit like David and Goliath, he thought, remembering the stories he had heard in church when his mother dragged him there as a child. The Hudson's Bay Company and the recently formed North West Company were the Goliaths of the fur-trading industry, and the London and Northwestern Enterprise was an upstart competitor. That situation only made the company's directors in London more desperate for some measure of success, however. The task with which they had charged McKendrick had been stated simply: Make the company profitable—or else.

McKendrick had not asked what the alternative was if he failed. He did not intend to do so.

It had taken him a while to size up the situation when he arrived. Trappers and traders working for the Enterprise had come to the area of Fort Rouge and gotten a foothold, but the larger companies were still much stronger and took the lion's share of the beaver plews. Upon McKendrick's arrival at the fort, he had studied the problem from every angle and had finally come to an inescapable conclusion: As vast as it was,

Canada simply was not big enough for another fur company to achieve the success of the two giants in the field.

Therefore, McKendrick had decided, the London and Northwestern Enterprise would have to expand in other directions. To the south was an even larger area full of beaver ripe for the taking. The Americans had shown little interest in exploiting it, McKendrick had learned from questioning trappers who had ventured there from time to time.

Well, if the Americans did not want the beaver in those mountains, Fletcher McKendrick certainly did. He immediately issued orders for the trappers and traders in the employ of the Enterprise to head farther south. No one would ever know where the furs they brought in came from.

Then, like a deliberate slap in his ruddy face, McKendrick had received word through his Indian contacts that an American fur trader—a Spaniard, really, but still an American as far as McKendrick was concerned—was leading an expedition up the Missouri River to establish his business in the heart of the country that McKendrick so coveted.

This man Lisa could not be allowed to succeed, and McKendrick was prepared to take steps to ensure that outcome.

Since Fort Rouge was not a military post but a commercial one, McKendrick had had no trouble securing lodging there. Earlier that evening, one of the trappers who worked for the Enterprise had stopped by McKendrick's cabin and told him that the man he wished to see had arrived. Duquesne was waiting for him in the tavern, the man had said.

McKendrick had bundled up right away and started across the compound to the log building that served as the post's tavern. When he reached it, he shoved the door open and stepped in, wincing a bit at the warmth of the overheated room.

Glancing around the room, McKendrick picked out Duquesne, sitting alone at the end of a long, rough-hewn table. The man wore greasy buckskins and was the only one in the room McKendrick did not recognize. The French trapper sat hunched over, staring into a cup of whiskey.

McKendrick took off his beaver hat, knocked the snow from it, and went over to the stranger. "Monsieur Duquesne?"

The man looked up at him. "Oui. And you are McKendrick?" His accent was rather heavy, but McKendrick had no trouble understanding him.

"Aye. Do ye mind if I sit down?"

Duquesne waved a hand. "Help yourself."

McKendrick studied him as he settled on the bench a few feet away. Duquesne was not an overly impressive physical specimen. In fact, he was rather short and unimposing—scrawny, to put it bluntly, McKendrick thought. His dark hair was touched lightly with silver and was cut in a ragged bowl. He wore a short beard, made scraggly looking by several bare patches of skin. His eyes as he glanced at McKendrick were a startling blue, however. They reminded the Scotsman of two chips of ice, and they were about as warm as ice, too.

"Do ye know why I wanted to see ye, Monsieur Duquesne?" McKendrick asked in a low voice. The other trappers in the tavern were gathered at the far end of the room and would not be able to hear the discussion. They knew Duquesne's reputation and preferred to leave him alone, McKendrick supposed.

Duquesne shook his head, then sipped the whiskey. He did not seem particularly enthusiastic about the meeting, but McKendrick thought that the Frenchman probably did not want to appear overeager.

"I work for the London and Northwestern Enterprise," McKendrick went on. "Ye be familiar with the company?"

"Oui."

"We've bought some of your furs in the past, and now we want to hire ye again."

"To bring in the beaver plews?" Duquesne shook

his head. "I am a free trapper, Monsieur McKendrick. I do not wish to work for your company."

McKendrick leaned forward. "That's not what I meant. Have ye heard of a man called Manuel Lisa?"

For the first time interest flared in Duquesne's cold eyes. "I know of him. It is said he intends to take men to the mountains to trap beaver."

"Aye," McKendrick agreed sourly. " 'Tis more than an intention, though. I've had word that he is already on the way up the Missouri River."

"What has that to do with me—or you?"

McKendrick took a deep breath. He was going to have to be honest with Duquesne, and that made him a bit nervous. From everything he had heard about Duquesne, the man was unpredictable. He might accept McKendrick's proposition, or he might be offended by it and ruin everything. Still, Duquesne was undoubtedly the best man for the job, so McKendrick knew he would just have to take the chance.

"I want you to stop Lisa from succeeding," the Scotsman said bluntly.

The mildly curious expression on Duquesne's face did not change. He regarded McKendrick in silence for a long moment, then took another drink. He wiped the back of his hand across his mouth, then finally smiled slightly. "And how would I accomplish this?" he asked, a trace of mockery in his voice.

"I do not give a damn about that. Your methods are your business."

"You want Lisa stopped so that there will be more beaver for your company's trappers to take, no?"

"That is correct. The Americans have no right to take over the mountains."

Duquesne raised an eyebrow quizzically. "They own that territory now. They bought it from my former emperor."

"Former?" McKendrick echoed.

Duquesne said, "I swear no allegiance to Bonaparte." He leaned over and spat contemptuously on the tavern's dirt floor. "The little corporal had me thrown out of his army. I barely escaped a firing squad, in fact. They said I was mad. Bonaparte is the madman.''

McKendrick could not help but wonder what Duquesne had done to get cashiered from the French army, but he decided it might not be prudent to delve too deeply into the matter. He cleared his throat and said, ''All I care about is that Manuel Lisa be stopped. It may be too late to prevent him from building his fort, but he can still be persuaded 'tis not a good idea to trap in the Rockies or to trade with the savages who live there. Make him go home, Monsieur Duquesne, and the London and Northwestern will make it worth your while.''

Again Duquesne was silent, a silence that stretched out uncomfortably for McKendrick. Finally Duquesne nodded and said, ''I will take the job. Lisa will be defeated, and his fate will make other Americans think twice before they attempt to trap in the Rockies. This is what you wish, no?''

''That is exactly what I wish,'' McKendrick said, trying not to sound too relieved that Duquesne had accepted the assignment. He did not want the Frenchman to sense the degree of desperation that gripped him—otherwise, Duquesne might ask for too much money.

''And the payment?'' Duquesne asked, following up on that very subject.

McKendrick shrugged. ''What do ye think is fair?''

Duquesne named a sum, and for a few seconds McKendrick's eyes threatened to bulge out of his head. The Scotsman swallowed uneasily, found his voice, and said, ''I do not know if I can authorize that much—''

''You can,'' Duquesne cut in smoothly. He was smiling again. ''Or you can find someone else to do your dirty work for you, monsieur.''

McKendrick swallowed again, and he felt as if he had a stone in his throat. His head jerked in a nod.

"Aye," he said hoarsely. "The company will meet your price."

"I thought as much." Duquesne downed the rest of the liquor in his cup. "I will need money for expenses, to hire men to help me. They will not work cheaply, either."

"Just tell me what ye need," McKendrick said. The words required an effort.

Duquesne stood up. "I will be in touch. You are staying here at Fort Rouge?"

McKendrick said, "I'll be around."

The Frenchman gave him a languid, mocking salute, then strode out of the tavern. McKendrick watched him go and tried to suppress the shudder that ran through his body. Duquesne was more than simply irritating with his arrogance; there was something truly frightening about the man, even to someone who had come up the hard way like Fletcher McKendrick.

He motioned for the tavern keeper to bring him a beer, and when the man came over a few moments later, he said to McKendrick, "Do you know who that was you were talking to?"

"I am aware of his identity, yes," McKendrick replied.

"He's a bad one, Duquesne is. Heard tell he's killed nigh on to a dozen men. Too bloodthirsty even for that Napoléon fella."

"Perhaps he's only—misunderstood." McKendrick did not believe that for a second, though. He had looked in Duquesne's eyes and seen the evil there. But the Frenchman was not insane; McKendrick was convinced of that. Duquesne genuinely liked doing the things that had given him his reputation.

He had unleashed a monster on Manuel Lisa and the men with him, McKendrick thought. But if that monster got the job done, that was all that really mattered.

CHAPTER FIFTEEN

We saw many otter and beaver to-day. The latter seem to contribute very much to the number of islands and the widening of the river. They begin by damming up the small channels of about 20 yards between the islands; this obliges the river to seek another outlet, and as soon as this is effected the channel stopped by the beaver becomes filled with mud and sand. The industrious animal is then driven to another channel, which soon shares the same fate, till the river spreads on all sides, and cuts the projecting points of the land into islands.

—from "The History of the Lewis and
Clark Expedition"

At the meeting place of the Yellowstone and Big Horn rivers, winter lashed at the sturdy little fort that had been constructed by Manuel Lisa and the men who worked for him. Storm after storm roared down out of the northern latitudes, bringing with them snow and ice in such generous proportions that drifts reached nearly to the tops of the cabins that had been built inside the stockade. The year 1807 turned into 1808 during one such blizzard, and the men did little to mark the passing. They were more concerned with staying alive.

The fort had been finished late in the fall. Lisa knew there was no point in trying to begin his fur trapping and trading operation until spring, so when the buildings were nearing completion, he had relieved several of the men from their construction duties and sent them out to hunt. A good supply of staples had been brought upriver on the keelboats, but it would be necessary to lay in a store of meat for the winter. Clay and Jeff Holt, along with John Colter and several of the other men, had been given that task.

As Clay tramped through the woods, often with Jeff alone but sometimes with Colter accompanying them, he felt his spirits lift. During the expedition with Lewis and Clark, there had not been as much time to savor the beauty of the wilderness. Now, although it was imperative for the hunters to perform their job before winter closed in, a man stood more of a chance to be still and drink in the majesty of the mountain scenery. Since he had returned to the frontier, Clay had often wondered how he had ever managed to stay cooped up in civilization all those months back in Ohio.

Colter had covered quite a bit of ground during his foray with Hancock and Dickson, and he spent part of his time with the Holts spinning yarns about the things he had seen. Each story fueled Clay's desire to penetrate deeper into the wilderness. Even Colter's tales about his encounters with hostile Blackfoot and Arikara did not blunt the growing wanderlust in Clay. It was wonderful, Clay thought, to see things that few had ever seen before, to tread on ground that had never known the touch of a white man's foot. Even if he had not been part of the Corps of Discovery, he knew he would have come out to the frontier sooner or later. It was fated.

More than anything else, he felt as if he had come home.

The long rifles of the hunters brought down deer, elk, and antelope, and the carcasses were butchered where they fell. The meat was taken back to the fort, where it was jerked, dried, and salted. Subsisting on such fare was not as good as having fresh meat, but in the dead of winter when it was impossible to get out and hunt, when game was scarce to start with, it was certainly better than doing without any kind of meat at all.

The men holed up in the cabins from late December until March, leaving the log buildings only when it was absolutely necessary. The rest of the time they sat in front of the fires, which were carefully banked to conserve firewood. Lisa forbade gambling, a wise decision considering the cramped quarters but not a particularly welcome one. The men whittled, swapped yarns, and slept a great deal. Clay could feel himself becoming more restless with each passing day, and he wished spring would hurry, sweeping winter away with its arrival. The enforced idleness was bothering Jeff, too, Clay sensed. As long as Jeff had been busy with hard work, he had not had the time and energy to worry about Melissa and miss her. He had plenty of opportunity for that now, and Clay could see his brother sinking into the same brooding melancholy that had gripped him back in St. Louis. Luckily, there were no whores and robbers in the middle of the wilderness to get Jeff into trouble.

Eventually the weather began to warm, and some of the snow melted away. Manuel Lisa sent Clay, Jeff, and Colter out to hunt again, and for the first time in weeks the company had fresh meat. That did as much to lift the spirits of the group as the sunshine, which was becoming more frequent.

A few times during the winter, Indians had appeared at the fort, drawn by curiosity, and Lisa had welcomed them heartily, making presents to them of blankets, salt, and the gaudy trinkets that seemed to hold for them an endless fascination. With Colter translating, Lisa had told the visitors to return in the spring and bring beaver pelts with them. He promised more trade goods in return for the plews. As winter made way for spring, many of those Indians returned, accompanied by others who had heard about the white men in the strange lodges made of logs. Most of the Indians had pelts with them, and to Lisa's delight the furs began to pile up in the square building constructed for storage. On sunny days the frames that had been built for stretching and drying the hides were always in use. It was a busy time, and after the months of inactivity, the hustle and bustle that filled the camp was quite welcome.

One day in the middle of March, Lisa called Clay, Jeff, Colter, and several of the other men into his cabin, which was somewhat larger and better furnished than the others, in keeping with the Spaniard's basically flamboyant personality. Given what he knew about Lisa's background, Clay had been a little surprised that the man had accompanied his employees into the wilderness. Lisa would have seemed more at home in a drawing room. However, Clay could not fault the man's courage, determination, or willingness to share the load. He had been right there with them in good times and bad.

When Lisa had assembled the men who had become his chief lieutenants, he said, "As you know, gentlemen, we did not make the long pilgrimage from St. Louis merely to sit here and collect pelts from the Indians. We will be doing a good bit of trapping ourselves. I also want a man to spread the word among the tribes that we are trading for hides. I think that would be a suitable task for you, Mr. Colter. You know the terrain, and you know the natives. What do you say?"

Colter shrugged. "You want me to just wander

around and tell the redskins you're in the market for furs?"

"Indeed."

Clay could see the interest in his friend's eyes. To a man like Colter, the opportunity to see some fresh country and do his job at the same time was a chance not to be missed. He was not surprised when the Virginian said slowly, "I reckon I could do that."

"Very good." Lisa turned to the others. "And you men will be in charge of trapping on your own. The rest of the company will remain here at the fort to handle day-to-day chores. You trappers, though, will be free to come and go as you please. Stay out as long as you like and return when you need supplies, or, as I hope will be the case, when you have so many plews that you can no longer carry them."

Clay and Jeff exchanged a glance. Lisa was giving them quite a lot of responsibility, but they would be able to explore and truly live free in shouldering it. Clay could tell that his brother was looking forward to it; so was he.

Less than a day later, the trappers started out from the fort, taking the time only to gather the supplies they would need. Clay and Jeff would trap together, and they filled their packs with the necessary items. The most important pieces of equipment were the beaver traps, and Clay and Jeff took eight of them. They would set out only half a dozen at a time, holding a couple of traps in reserve. In addition they took along extra food to supplement what they would forage for themselves; cold weather gear, including snowshoes, in case of a late-season storm; a few trade goods so they would be prepared should they run into any friendly Indians; plenty of powder and balls for their rifles and pistols; skinning knives; flint and steel for making fires; and a hollowed-out, stoppered horn similar to a powder horn, in which they carried the castoreum, the "beaver medicine" that would serve as bait to lure the animals into the traps. Altogether, the gear added up to some fifty pounds, divided into two packs that could be carried on a man's back or in the bottom of a canoe without great difficulty.

The Holts left the fort in a birchbark canoe, the sections sewn together and sealed with pine pitch. John Colter had shown them how to make the canoe and assured them that it was not only quite waterproof but also lightweight enough to portage.

Neither Clay nor Jeff had ever trapped beaver before, of course, but they had been given lessons in the art by Colter, who had spent some of the winter months teaching the other men what he knew about the endeavor that had brought them all there. As he and Jeff set out from the fort, paddling upstream along the Big Horn, Clay believed they were as well prepared as they could possibly be.

They made only a few miles the first day. Colter had suggested they start their trapping on one of the smaller creeks that flowed into the river, since it would be easier there to spot still stretches of water created by beaver dams. Clay and Jeff passed several likely looking creeks during the first few days of their trip, but they decided to continue on upriver. Once they had gone far enough, in their opinion, they would then start working their way back, trapping on each of the little streams as they came to them.

During the afternoon of the fourth day out from the fort, Clay angled the canoe toward the mouth of a creek flowing into the Big Horn from the west. "We'll try that one," he said.

They paddled several miles upstream until it became too shallow even for the canoe. A nearby clearing on the bank would make a good campsite, Clay decided. Since leaving the river, they had spotted several beaver dams, and in the morning they would begin setting out their traps.

When they had pulled the canoe up onto the bank and were unloading their gear from it, Jeff said, "Why do you think we haven't seen any Indians since we left the fort? I thought this part of the country was supposed to be full of them."

"Maybe we haven't seen them, but I'd wager they've seen us. Could be we're the first white men to paddle up this creek, but we're not the first ones to visit these parts. You'd be surprised how quick word gets around among the natives. Lewis and Clark came through the Rockies, then Colter and his partners, maybe some more trappers we haven't heard about. The Indians know white men are starting to stir around here. You can be sure they're curious about us, but they're being cautious. We'll see them sooner or later. If they're Blackfoot or Rees, we may wish we hadn't."

"Those two tribes aren't common around here, though, are they?"

Clay said, "Not according to Colter, and if anybody would know, it'd be him. This is Crow and Sioux country. Doesn't mean a band from some other tribe couldn't pass through every now and then, looking for some better hunting—or just looking for trouble."

They built a small campfire that night to cook a pot of beans. That, along with some of the dried meat they had brought from the fort, served as their evening meal. The warmth of the flames was welcome. Even though winter was officially over, the nights were still chilly. Once the fire had burned down to glowing embers, the two men rolled in their blankets and settled down to sleep.

Before he dozed off, Clay reflected that he might be lying on cold, hard ground in the middle of a wilderness thousands of miles from civilization, but he was perfectly content.

The next morning their work began in earnest. Carrying their traps, Clay and Jeff walked downstream along the bank, their eyes scanning the water for signs of beaver. Each time they came to a calm stretch of water, indicating the presence of a dam, they went on downstream a hundred yards or so, then entered the water and waded back toward the spot they had selected. "Doing it that way kills the man-smell and don't warn the beaver you're around," Colter had told them, and both of the Holts remembered his words quite well.

When they found a suitable shallow place in the creek, they opened the traps and set them on the bottom, then laid the heavy chains attached to the traps in deeper water and drove a stick down through one of the links, fastening the chain there. All that was left was to bait the trap.

Clay unstoppered the horn of "medicine" and grimaced when he caught a whiff of it. The stuff had been made by pulverizing dried perineal glands of beavers with a nutmeg, a dozen cloves, and thirty grains of cinnamon, to which some kind of spirits had been added. The mixture had the consistency of mustard, and its vile odor had by now reached full potency and would attract beaver from as far as a mile away. He dipped a stick into it, then shoved the lure into the creek bed near the trap. When a beaver came to investigate the irresistible scent, it would trigger the trap and the animal's leg would be caught by the snap of the heavy jaws. Held down by the trap, the animal would drown. It was all brutally efficient. The beavers were caught and killed without any marring of the pelt, which would eventually find its way back East to be used for a gentleman's top hat or a lady's fancy muff.

Setting the traps took most of the morning, and then Clay and Jeff headed back to their camp. They would check the traps in the late afternoon. In the meantime, they could hunt, explore, or just take it easy around their camp.

Evidently, Jeff felt like talking because as they heated the beans left over from the night before, he said, "I wonder how everybody's doing back home."

As far as Clay was concerned, home was right where he was at the moment, but he knew what Jeff meant. Jeff still thought of Ohio as his home because that was where Melissa was. Clay supposed he could understand that. "I reckon they're all fine," he said.

"How do we know that? We'd never hear otherwise, out here in the middle of nowhere."

Clay shrugged. "You're right, but there's nothing we can do about it. Lisa's planning to go back to St. Louis next fall. We can go with him if you like, even go all the way back to Ohio. Maybe Zach will have calmed down by then."

"You don't really believe that, though, do you?"

"Do you?" Clay asked in return. "You really think Zach's ever going to give up hating us?"

For a moment Jeff did not reply. Then he said solemnly, "No, I don't. As long as he's alive, Zach will still want to even the score."

Clay didn't say anything, but he knew Jeff was right. He wondered if he was still wanted by the law for Pete Garwood's death. If that was the case, he thought, he should have gone ahead and killed Zach and Aaron, too. If he was going to live the rest of his life as a fugitive, he might as well deserve it.

But that was over and done with, he told himself. Now that he thought about it, he probably wouldn't go back to St. Louis with Lisa in the fall. The Spaniard planned to leave a contingent of men at the fort throughout the winter, and Clay decided he would volunteer to be one of those men. That would be better than returning to Ohio, even if it meant Jeff and he would have to split up.

For the first time the possibility of never going back suggested itself seriously to Clay. He could spend the rest of his life in these mountains, he thought. To most men, that would have been an unappealing prospect, but it was strangely inviting to Clay.

Abruptly he lifted his head, his reverie broken. Jeff noticed and immediately tensed. "What's wrong?" he asked as he reached for the long rifle lying close at hand.

Clay stopped him with a gesture. "Wait a minute." He peered around the camp. "Don't know if anything's wrong. There was just something . . ."

He was not sure how to explain it. Some instinct

had suddenly sprung to life inside him. If he had been forced to put it into words, he would have said that he felt the touch of eyes on him—and yet no one else was in sight, no sounds of movement in the woods. They seemed to be completely alone.

After a few seconds, Clay relaxed. "I don't know what it was," he told Jeff, "but it's gone now."

"Indians?"

"More than likely. If it was, I'm not surprised we didn't hear them."

"They must have been friendly."

"I'd say so," Clay agreed dryly. "Otherwise, we'd probably be stuck full of arrows by now."

Jeff grimaced. "Maybe this wasn't such a good idea."

"Coming out here to the frontier, you mean?" Clay shook his head, serious again now. "A man's got to die someplace. I don't know of anywhere better than in the middle of all this."

"You don't have a wife waiting for you," Jeff snapped.

Clay felt a surge of anger, then decided it was unreasonable to feel that way. Jeff was just telling the truth. "That's right, I don't have a wife. But I've got brothers and a sister back there, just like you. Don't you think I want to see them again sometime?"

"Do you?"

Clay took a deep breath, then realized he did not know how to respond to his brother's question. He had just been thinking about staying in the mountains from now on, and if he did that, it would mean, in all likelihood, that he would never see Edward, Susan, and Jonathan again. Could he live with that, if it meant remaining in the one place where he had known true contentment?

That was something he could not answer.

For a week and a half Jeff and Clay were away from the fort, slowly working their way back along the Big Horn and the many smaller streams that ran into it. On several different occasions Clay had felt the same uneasy sensation that had gripped him at their first camp. He was convinced now that Indians were watching them. Neither Jeff nor he could see anyone, though, so he continued to share Jeff's assessment of the situation: The Indians were curious and shy but not hostile.

When the Holt brothers returned to the fort, they brought with them several dozen beaver plews. Manuel Lisa was very pleased with the results of the first trip. Some of the other men had also brought in pelts, and Indians were still paying visits to the fort with hides they wanted to trade. Colter was off on his jaunt through the wilderness to spread the word about the white men and their need for furs. All in all, the expedition was going exactly as Lisa had hoped and planned it would.

Clay and Jeff stayed at the fort for a couple of days, resting from their journey, and then were ready to go again. Such was the pattern that developed over the next few months as spring passed into summer. Clay and Jeff went out on forays lasting from one to three weeks, going as far down the Big Horn as the Wind River and also along the Yellowstone, deep into the Absaroka range. It was magnificent country, and each trip increased Clay's feeling that he was destined to spend the rest of his life there.

On each trip, though, he also had the same strange sensation that he had noticed during the first one. Someone was watching them, and he was not sure if it was the same band of Indians or a different bunch each time. That was more likely, he decided. No one group would have a reason to trail them all over the country.

One day, when Clay and Jeff had just returned to the fort from two weeks in the wilderness and were walking into the stockade with a load of pelts slung over their shoulders, they saw a group of Indians sitting in front of the makeshift trading post that Lisa had opened. The Spaniard was talking to them, hav-

ing learned enough of the various tribal dialects by
now to be able to carry on a rudimentary conversation. All that really mattered was being able to strike a
deal for the plews, and Lisa had proven a quick study
where that was concerned. The sight of Indians inside
the stockade dealing with Lisa was not an unusual
one, so Clay and Jeff started past the group without
really paying much attention to them.

Suddenly, Clay stopped in his tracks. One of the
young men—little more than a boy, really—was looking over his shoulder at them, a strangely intent expression on his face. He seemed to be a well-built
youngster, and from the beadwork on his moccasins,
Clay tentatively identified him as a Teton. When the
young man saw that Clay had noticed his stare, he
turned his attention back to Lisa, acting as if the other
white men were not even there.

"What was that all about?" Jeff asked, puzzled.

Clay shook his head. "Damned if I know. That
youngster seemed mighty interested in us, and then
he seemed to forget we even existed. Could be today's
the first time he ever saw white men."

Indeed, Clay did not remember seeing any of the
band around the fort before. Nothing unusual about
that, though. Strange Indians showed up fairly often,
drawn by other tribes' gossip about the white men.

Clay dismissed the incident, and he and Jeff took
their pelts to the warehouse. The original storage
building was already full, so Lisa had instructed the
crew at the fort to build an even larger one. From the
looks of it, this was going to be an extremely profitable
venture for the Spaniard.

By that evening the little band of Teton was gone,
their transaction with Lisa concluded, and if Clay
thought about them at all over the next few days, it
was only fleetingly. He and Jeff restocked their supplies and got ready for another trip into the wilderness.

This time they headed southeast into the Big
Horn Mountains, in the direction of the Tongue and

Powder rivers. This country had not yet been extensively trapped, and while Clay and Jeff did not intend to trek all the way to those rivers, they knew that many creeks in that region would be likely homes for beaver. Now that it was summer, the pelts they were taking were thinner, not as prime as the ones they had accumulated during the spring. Clay could see that fur trapping was going to be a seasonal business, with the best times being spring and late fall, after the animals began to put on their winter coats. At this juncture, however, the trappers would take what they could get.

They made good time tramping across the broad, flat valley of the Yellowstone, then striking out into the mountains. Those peaks were not as high as the main range of the Rockies to the west, but they were rugged enough. A few days later, they reached a good-sized stream, and as they stood on the bank, Jeff asked, "Did we get all the way to the Tongue without knowing it?"

Clay shook his head. "I don't think so. I reckon this is Rosebud Creek. It fits Colter's description. We should have good trapping here." He looked around at the clearing where they had stopped. "And this'll make a fine camp. We're in business again, little brother."

It was too late in the day to set out their traps, so they contented themselves with making camp. They would do without a fire that night, Clay decided. So far they had not seen any Indians, but he wanted to familiarize himself with the area before they announced their presence with smoke from a campfire. Their supper consisted of dried meat from the fort, washed down by creek water that was bitingly cold even at this time of year, since it was partially fed by melting snow from the mountaintops.

They were up early the next morning and headed along the creek on the lookout for beaver dams. Most were formed of willow brush, mud, and gravel, all tightly woven together to resist water. Some dams were as tall as five feet and would cause the stream to back up and flood several acres of land. Spotting a few of a smaller size, Clay and Jeff set their traps and continued on. It was a beautiful day, with birds flitting from branch to branch in the trees, small animals rustling in the brush, bright sky arching overhead, and a faint breeze touching the bearded faces of the two men. Clay looked over at Jeff as they walked along the stream. His younger brother was as lean and tan as Clay himself, and Jeff wore a full brown beard. In his weathered buckskins, with a pack slung over his shoulder, a coonskin cap perched on his head, and his Harpers Ferry rifle cradled in the crook of his arm, primed and loaded, he bore little resemblance to the young man who had left Ohio some sixteen months earlier. Prissy old Charles Merrivale would be shocked and horrified to see his son-in-law now, Clay thought with a smile. It would almost be worth going back to civilization just to witness that reunion.

"What are you grinning about?" Jeff asked, noticing Clay's expression.

"Just thinking about the way you've turned into a mountain man. I wasn't sure you had it in you. Reckon you know the way the stick floats, though."

That was a high compliment, and Jeff knew it. Only an experienced trapper could spot where a beaver had pulled a trap loose from a streambed by the way the stick that had pinned down the chain was floating. But the saying had recently come to have a more general meaning—that someone knew his way around the mountains. The only higher praise was to say that a man had the "ha'r of the b'ar" in him. The Indians believed that a man could attain the strength and bravery of a grizzly bear by eating its hair. Few men ever reached that level.

Clay could tell that Jeff was pleased by his assessment. He knew that Jeff was beginning to share his enthusiasm for the mountains and the frontier way of life, but he also knew his brother yearned to be back in Ohio with Melissa. Clay understood that and was grateful Jeff didn't let his emotions interfere with their work. In fact, Clay couldn't have asked for a better partner.

They walked along in companionable silence for a time. Only when Clay realized that the silence had become a bit too pervasive did he stop.

"Hold on," he said suddenly, reaching out to put a hand on Jeff's arm.

"What is it? That feeling of yours back again?"

Clay had told Jeff about the uneasy sensation that had bothered him at one point or another on every one of their trips. Jeff had not experienced it, but he was not going to discount Clay's instincts.

"Listen," Clay said, his voice little more than a whisper.

"To what?" Jeff asked in the same tone of voice. "I don't hear a thing."

"Neither do I. The birds have hushed, and the varmints have gone to ground. Something's spooked them." Slowly Clay turned, his keen eyes searching the terrain around them on both sides of the creek. He didn't see anything—

There! In the trees across the stream, he had spotted the faintest flicker of color and movement. Somebody was over there.

Every nerve in his body screaming a warning, Clay threw himself at Jeff. He struck hard, slamming into Jeff's shoulder with his own, and both of them went down. At that instant, over his startled exclamation, Jeff heard the rush of an arrow passing close by. He rolled over and saw the shaft quivering in the trunk of a tree some ten yards away.

On the other side of the stream, warriors on horseback burst from the woods, whooping and howling. More arrows cut through the air around Clay as he got to his knees and lifted his rifle. "Rees!" he shouted to Jeff, using the mountain man's name for the Arikara. He had recognized their distinctive markings right away.

Clay fully cocked the flintlock and centered its

sights on the chest of one of the charging men. He pressed the trigger. The rifle went off with a roar of exploding powder, smoke and flame spewing from its muzzle. The Arikara was knocked backward off his horse, as though he had run into a wall. The blast of the rifle stung Clay's ears, yet he heard the dying man's shriek of pain.

Beside him, Jeff fired, and another Arikara tumbled from his horse. The band of warriors pulled up short, still on the far side of the creek. Obviously, they had not expected this much resistance from the white men.

Clay jerked one of his pistols out of his belt and ordered, "Run for the trees!" as he lined the weapon on the Indians. Jeff hesitated for a split second, then realized what Clay had in mind. If he could reach the woods, he could cover Clay's retreat from there. Jeff surged to his feet and sprinted toward the trees.

Out of the corner of his eye Clay saw his brother's dash for safety. Then he concentrated his attention on the attackers again. Another arrow whipped past him. He fired one of his pistols, bracing his wrist against the recoil, and was rewarded by the sight of an Arikara sagging against the neck of his mount and feebly clutching at a bloody, shattered shoulder. In less than a minute Jeff and he had put three enemies out of the fight; that went a long way toward evening the odds.

Not enough, though. Seven or eight of the Rees were still alive and out for blood.

"Come on, Clay!" Jeff shouted from the woods. Clay spun around and ran for the shelter of the trees, an empty weapon clutched in each hand. Jeff sent a pistol ball toward the Arikara to keep them off-balance. With each desperate step, Clay expected to feel an arrowhead slam into his back between his shoulder blades. That did not happen, although he felt one of the arrows strike a glancing blow on his thigh. It threw him off stride but did not penetrate the tough hide of his buckskins.

He reached the trees and swung around, turning sideways to present the narrowest possible target as he took cover behind a tree. Nearby, Jeff's second pistol roared. Clay jammed his empty pistol under his belt again, set the empty flintlock rifle on the ground, and drew his second pistol. The range was a little extreme, but he fired anyway, biting off a curse as he saw that the ball had not hit anything. The Arikara were regrouping and getting ready to charge again.

Clay glanced around. He did not know how deep this stand of trees was, but one thing was certain: The attackers would not be able to gallop their horses through it. He picked up the empty rifle and called to Jeff, "Run for it! Stay in the trees! That'll slow them down!"

Jeff nodded and darted away from the edge of the grove, heading deeper into the woods. Clay followed. Around him arrows rattled through the branches, but none of them came close to hitting him. Jeff was several yards away, and while Clay could not always see him because of the undergrowth, the sound of Jeff's crashing progress through the brush was always audible. Clay leapt over fallen logs and bulldozed his way through bramble thickets, the stickers clawing at his hands and face but rarely tearing through his buckskins.

His heart was pounding loudly, but not loud enough to prevent him from hearing hoofbeats and angry shouts behind them. The Arikara were trying to make their way on horseback through the dense woods. They would abandon that tactic soon enough, he knew, and leave one man to watch the horses while the others tracked their prey on foot. Clay was grateful for each second that passed, for it allowed Jeff and him to build a lead that might give them a slim chance of getting out of this alive.

The trees began to thin out, and with a sinking feeling Clay realized that they were coming to a clearing. If it was large enough, it would allow the Arikara to close the gap between them.

Maybe Jeff and he could find a place to fort up, Clay thought. They had plenty of powder and shot, and if they could locate some good cover, they might be able to stand the Arikara off. They could certainly inflict more damage and make their opponents think twice about charging them.

But as Clay emerged from the trees and spotted Jeff several yards to his left, he also saw to his dismay that they were facing a broad stretch of open ground that led to a rather steep ridge. The slope itself was dotted with bushes, but the growth would not provide adequate cover. And the ridge was too high for the white men to reach its crest before the Arikara caught up to them.

Clay angled over toward Jeff and waved him on. "Keep going!" he said, reaching for the 'hawk in his belt. "I'll hold them off!" That was the only hope for either of them. If he could delay the Arikara long enough with hand-to-hand fighting, Jeff might have time to reach the top of the slope. From there, Jeff could hold them off.

Clay, however, would certainly lose his life. Jeff knew that as well as his brother did.

"No!" he exclaimed, slowing his stride as he ran alongside Clay. "We'll stand together!"

Clay hated to waste his breath arguing, but that was what he was about to do when he saw movement up ahead, just above the base of the slope. An Indian, wearing breechclout and moccasins, had stepped into view beside a thick clump of brush. Instinctively Clay shifted his grip on the 'hawk and drew back to throw the weapon.

He lowered it abruptly, though, when he realized that the Indian was gesturing frantically at them. Darting a glance at the woods, Clay saw that their pursuers had not yet appeared. Clay looked back at the lone Indian. He was young, and something about him was familiar. . . .

Suddenly Clay remembered. He was the young Teton who had studied the two of them so intently back at the fort several days earlier. Acting on a hunch, Clay pointed him out and snapped to Jeff, "Come on!"

They raced toward the youngster, reaching him just as they heard the howls of the Arikara. The boy pushed back the brush and pointed toward an oval of darkness in the side of the ridge. It was a cave, Clay realized. The Teton was showing them a hiding place.

Or trapping them for the Arikara to kill at their leisure.

There was no love lost between the Teton and the Arikara, Clay recalled. In fact, the tribes were long-standing enemies. This boy had no reason to help the Arikara. So far in their dealings with white men, most Teton had been friendly.

"We've got to take a chance!" Bending over, Clay pushed into the opening, which was so narrow that his shoulders scraped its sides.

Darkness closed in immediately, and with it a feeling of panic. Clay hated being shut in anywhere. This was the worst sensation he had ever felt. But he continued into the cave, bumping his head painfully on the rough rock ceiling. When he looked back over his shoulder, twisting awkwardly to do so, he saw Jeff and the lad silhouetted against the mouth of the cave. The boy was pulling brush back into place against it, to conceal the entrance.

Clay stopped when he estimated he was fifty feet inside the ridge. He managed to turn around and then sank cross-legged on the floor of the tunnel. A thick darkness enfolded him, relieved only by the faint light filtering in through the brush over the cave mouth, though much of that illumination was blocked by the bodies of Jeff and the Indian youth. Clay did not need light to reload his weapons, however; he worked by touch. Laying his rifle aside because it would be too awkward to use in such close quarters, he began to reload his pistols. Jeff crouched just in front of him, and Clay whispered for him to do the same. That was the only sound, other than their ragged breathing. The

Teton boy was not winded, and he knelt in complete silence.

Confident now that they had not entered a trap, Clay finished loading his pistols, then waited to see what would happen. He heard faint noises, and after a moment he recognized them as the puzzled exclamations of the surviving Arikara warriors. They must have emerged from the woods expecting to find their quarry struggling up the rugged ridge, only to discover the two white men were gone.

If they mounted a diligent search, they would probably find the cave, Clay thought. In that case the Arikara could send arrow after arrow into the blackness until whoever was inside was riddled. He and Jeff would not make it easy, though. If the Teton youngster got down low to the ground, they could pepper the opening with gunfire every time one of the Arikara showed his face.

It might not come to that. The enemy might not find the cave. Even if they did, there was no telling how far into the hillside the tunnel extended. The fugitives could pull back even farther, perhaps out of arrow range.

Then, if Jeff and he could find no other way out of the cave, it would become a waiting game to see who would be the first to give up.

The voices from outside grew stronger, faded away, and came back again accompanied by hoofbeats. Clay, Jeff, and the young Teton crouched in the cave, silently waiting. Finally, after what seemed an eternity, came a sound that told them what they wanted to know—the birds were singing again.

The Teton lad shifted and turned toward the two white men. He surprised his companions by saying, "Rees do not know about cave, I think. They are long way from home."

"You speak English!" Jeff exclaimed.

"Yes, Proud Wolf speaks white man's tongue."

"Proud Wolf, eh?" Clay said. "Pretty big name for a youngster."

He heard a sound that he identified as the boy striking himself on the chest with a clenched fist. "Proud Wolf does not have as many summers as other warriors, but just as brave. Proud Wolf has already had vision. In it came men with pale skins, seeking to trap animal you call beaver. You are first, but many white men will come after you."

"Reckon there's a good chance of that, all right." Clay shifted his cramped shoulders. "Think it would be safe to get out of this hole now?"

"Rees are gone. Safe to go."

With Proud Wolf leading the way, the three of them emerged from the tunnel, and Clay grimaced at the stiffness of his muscles as he stood up. Jeff was experiencing the same thing, and he let out a groan as he stretched.

Clay looked around carefully, but as Proud Wolf had indicated, the Arikara were gone. Meeting the boy's level gaze, Clay said, "We appreciate the help, Proud Wolf. I've got another question for you, though."

The Teton stood silent, waiting.

"Why have you been following us ever since we started trapping?"

The question was strictly a hunch on Clay's part, but the flash of surprise in Proud Wolf's eyes confirmed his guess. The youngster tried to hide his reaction, but he was not completely successful.

"My people live in this land for many seasons," he finally said, not answering the question directly. "It is our land. But we do not mind sharing if white men are worthy."

Clay had heard John Colter talk a little about the visions the Indians sometimes had. Such visions were powerful, and if Proud Wolf had seen white men in his vision, he would naturally be interested in seeing how close the reality came to what he had in his mind. It looked as if the boy had fixed on Jeff and him as representatives of their kind. Obviously, Proud Wolf had not been too displeased with what he had seen, or he would not have helped them.

"Well, like I said, we appreciate the helping hand, son. But we need to get on about our business now—"

Proud Wolf said, "No. You come with me. We go to my village."

Clay and Jeff exchanged a glance. One of Manuel Lisa's policies was to establish and maintain good relations with as many Indians as possible, and here was an opportunity to do just that. They had a friend in Proud Wolf already, and a visit to his village might make the bond even stronger. Jeff nodded his agreement, and Clay turned back to the boy.

"We'd be honored to visit your home," he said simply.

Proud Wolf turned and broke into a jog away from the ridge and back toward the creek, although the path he took would lead them to a different part of the stream from the spot where they had encountered the Arikara. Clay and Jeff trotted after him.

CHAPTER SIXTEEN

It is the custom of all the nations on the Missouri to offer to every white man food and refreshment when he first enters their tents.

—from "The History of the Lewis and Clark Expedition"

Zach Garwood leaned forward, curling his fingers around the mug of ale on the table in front of him. He was in Meaghan's tavern in Marietta, and his brother Aaron was sitting across from him, staring gloomily into his own mug.

Aaron broke the silence by saying, "I never thought Pa would die. I thought he'd just go on somehow."

"You mean you figured he was too ornery to die," Zach said.

"That's not what I mean at all!" Aaron looked up. "I just never really thought about him . . . not being here."

"Well, you'd better get used to it, 'cause he's sure as hell dead. In a little while, he'll be in the ground."

The brothers were dressed in their best clothes, which nevertheless were rather threadbare. The funeral for Alfred Garwood was supposed to begin in a half hour, and they had come into town to have a drink beforehand, a bracer to get through the ordeal.

Zach had argued against even having a service. "Dig a hole and plant the old man out back," he had said. But Josie had been firm in her determination to do everything right and proper, and that meant a funeral with the preacher saying words over their father. It was all a lot of damned foolishness as far as Zach was concerned.

Deep down he felt the way Aaron did—he had never really expected the old man to die. Alfred Garwood had not been in good health for years, but he never seemed to get any better or any worse; he just stayed the same. Four days earlier, however, Garwood had taken to his bed with a fever. Josie had tried to nurse him, but her efforts had not done any good. Garwood had gotten worse and worse, finally slipping into unconsciousness and never waking up.

Still, Zach thought, he shouldn't have been too surprised by his father's death. The going had been rough for all the Garwoods lately—the surviving Garwoods, that is. Pete and Luther did not have to worry about crops failing or wells drying up or the farm being seized because the taxes on it could not be paid. Those were concerns for the living.

None of them were really cut out to be farmers, Zach thought. Never had been. When his mother was alive, she had kept the family going out of fear; none of them had wanted to face the wrath of an angry Ma Garwood. After her death, things had really begun to go downhill.

While the damned Holts got richer and richer and ran roughshod over anybody who happened to be in their way, Zach told himself.

The past few months had been especially frustrat-

ing where the Holts were concerned. Clay had disappeared after killing Pete, and Jeff had slipped away
shortly thereafter. The younger children were gone,
too, and Zach had heard rumors that they had been
sent to live with relatives. That left only Jeff's wife,
Melissa—pretty little Melissa—as a potential target for
Zach's rage. He had been biding his time, trying to
figure out the best way to get at her, when suddenly
she and her parents up and disappeared, too. Again,
Zach had heard gossip to the effect that they had gone
back where they originally came from, but he didn't
know where that was. Besides, he couldn't afford to
go traipsing around the whole eastern half of the
country looking for them.

His anger had grown so great that if one of the
Holts had appeared magically in front of him, Zach
would have cheerfully clubbed him or her to death
with his bare hands, even one of the little ones.

"Well, I guess we'd better be going," Aaron said,
breaking into his brother's thoughts.

Zach looked up. "That time already?"

Aaron nodded solemnly, drained the last of his
ale, and stood up. He moved a little awkwardly. The
arm that had been broken by Clay Holt had never
healed properly, and he held it close to his body. Most
of the time the old injury did not hamper him, but he
was unable to move the arm into certain positions,
making it difficult for him to do chores on the farm—
which had led to more work for Zach. That only
added to the resentment and hatred Zach felt for the
Holts in general and Clay in particular.

Zach tossed down the rest of his drink and followed his brother out of the tavern, wiping the back of
his hand across his mouth as he emerged. They
trudged toward the church at the other end of town. A
shower earlier in the day had left the street muddy,
and the sky was still gray and overcast. Just the right
kind of weather for a funeral, Zach thought.

Josie and Matthew were waiting at the door of the
church. The little boy wore a dark blue suit with

knickers and a cutaway coat. It had probably cost
more than the gown that Josie wore, Zach thought. For
a moment he wondered where Josie had gotten the
money to buy the new suit, but then he smiled crookedly as he realized the foolishness of that thought.
Josie had gotten the money the only way she ever got
money—she had whored for it.

She frowned darkly at her brothers as they
walked up to the church entrance. "I thought you
weren't coming," she snapped.

"I told you we'd be here, didn't I?" Zach said.
"Come on. Let's get this over with." He took Josie's
arm and led her into the church while Aaron held little
Matthew's hand.

Not surprisingly, there were few mourners. Many
of the people in the community might believe that
Clay Holt had done wrong by Josie, and they might
even blame Clay for Pete's death, but that didn't mean
they were particularly fond of the Garwoods. The
plain pine coffin sat at the front of the room, and as
the mourners sat down, Reverend Crosley stood beside the casket and gave a short sermon. He seemed to
be having trouble finding many good things to say
about Alfred Garwood, Zach noted. Zach looked
down at his lap and let a slight smile tug at his lips.
He would have had a hard time coming up with anything good to say about the old man, too.

Finally it was over. Zach and Aaron carried the
coffin out to the churchyard and said good-bye to their
father. After they had lowered the coffin into the
ground, next to their mother's grave, Zach tossed a
clump of dirt onto the closed lid and turned away, no
longer interested. He was ready for another drink.

The remaining members of the Garwood family
rode back to the farm together in the wagon that Josie
had driven to town. The horses Zach and Aaron had
ridden into Marietta earlier were tied on the back.
Zach handled the reins on this trip, Josie sitting beside
him on the seat while Aaron and Matthew rode in the

back. Aaron smiled and played with his nephew during the short journey, but his thoughts were on other matters.

He wondered how Zach could be so cold, so heartless. Didn't Zach realize that their father was dead, that they would never see him again? The family was down to only four members now.

Zach took off his cravat and tilted his hat back as he drove. "I'm for some whiskey when we get back to the cabin. How about you, Aaron?"

Before Aaron could answer, Josie said in a peevish tone, "There are still crops to be harvested, you know."

"Mighty poor ones," Zach grunted.

"And whose fault is that?"

"I don't know. God's?"

"Don't blaspheme," Josie said coldly.

Zach laughed. "Getting religion, Josie? That's mighty odd, considering how you spend your days—and nights."

Josie's lips compressed into a thin line, and her features paled with anger. She made no reply, though, evidently preferring to ride in silence rather than prolong the argument.

Aaron grimaced. He wished Zach wouldn't talk to Josie that way. It wasn't her fault that her life had worked out so badly. She just wanted to do the best she could by Matthew, Aaron thought. Of course, it wasn't proper the way she went about it, but she was a grown woman, and he had no right to tell her how to live her life.

The cold silence continued. Aaron pulled Matthew onto his lap and started telling him a story, and although the boy squirmed around at first, he settled down eventually and seemed to be paying attention. Aaron liked his nephew, but he had to admit that Matthew was a handful most of the time, as rambunctious as most young boys and worse than many. Josie was too busy to keep up with him much, and without a father to watch over him, Matthew just naturally ran wild. Aaron did what he could to help, but he was occupied most of the time, trying to help Zach keep the farm going.

Zach brought the wagon to a stop in front of the ramshackle cabin and hopped down. He went inside without helping Josie down or unhitching the team. Aaron did both of those things, and he also caught Matthew under the arms and swung the child down from the wagon bed. The weight made a twinge of pain go through his bad arm, but he ignored it. He was accustomed to such minor annoyances. Working one-handed part of the time, he got the horses unhitched and situated in the barn.

As he walked from the barn to the cabin, rain began to fall again, large drops that struck bitingly against his face. He ducked his head and hurried on inside.

Josie had started a blaze in the fireplace and was carrying a kettle of stew over to it to suspend above the flames. Zach was sitting at the table, a tin cup of whiskey in front of him. In one corner of the room, Matthew was playing with a couple of the small wooden figures that Luther had once carved for him.

"Been thinking," Zach announced suddenly as Aaron was shaking the water off his coat. "The Holts are still out there somewhere. I reckon it's time we caught up to them and settled the score for Pete and Luther."

Aaron stared at his brother, taken completely by surprise by Zach's statement. "What?" he finally said.

Zach sipped the whiskey and then looked up at him. "I said we ought to go after those goddamned Holts. I've heard tell that they went west. They're somewhere out there now, working as fur trappers."

"You don't know that for certain," Aaron said, frowning. "Some people said they might have done that after they left town, but nobody knows."

"I do," Zach insisted. "They ran like the damned cowards they are."

Josie spoke up, not looking at her brothers as she

stirred the stew. "I imagine they left because there was nothing to hold them here after their parents were killed in that awful fire."

Zach sneered. "You almost sound like you feel sorry for those old bastards."

"Norah and Bartholomew Holt never did me any wrong," Josie replied. "It was just Clay. . . ."

"Their son," Zach snapped. "They got what they deserved."

Aaron sat down at the table, leaned forward, and rubbed his temples with the balls of his hands. In his skull was a pounding ache that hadn't been there a moment earlier. He knew why it had appeared; the headache came every time someone mentioned the fire that had taken the lives of Bartholomew and Norah Holt.

Over the past months Aaron had thought about that day time and time again. He had searched his memory for any tiny detail that would contradict the awful suspicion he had, but try as he might, he still could not account for the whereabouts of Zach and Pete during the time when the Holt cabin had been set afire and destroyed. Zach had shown up at home not long afterward and mentioned offhandedly that Pete had gone into Marietta, but he had never offered any explanation of where they had been earlier.

Aaron believed he knew, and he hated himself for what he thought about his brothers. As the youngest one in the family, he had always wanted desperately to impress his older brothers and be liked by them. So he had gone along, doing whatever they had told him to, being one of them whenever they would allow it. If that included fighting with the Holts, so be it. Aaron could not deny that he had jumped right in every time a brawl broke out. He had dealt out some punishment of his own, and he had taken some, too. His bad arm was a constant reminder of that.

But in those days leading up to the wedding of Jefferson Holt and Melissa Merrivale, Aaron had begun to question some things for the first time in his life. He had known about Zach's plan to set off a keg of powder during the party after the wedding. Zach had assured him that no one would be hurt, that he just wanted to throw a scare into the Holts and ruin what should have been a happy day for them. So, once again, Aaron had gone along with Zach's plan.

Things had not worked out the way Zach had said they would, though. Luther had died.

And the Holts' barn had burned down in a fire that was a precursor to an even more deadly blaze. By this time, Aaron had no doubt that Zach had been behind that fire, also. Zach and Pete had murdered the Holts. Aaron was sure of it.

But there was nothing he could do. Zach was his brother, the only one he had left. Besides, he had no proof that Zach and Pete had intended for Bartholomew and Norah to die. They could have just been trying to scare the Holts. Aaron knew how things could go wrong, how quickly everything could get twisted around. He did not want to believe the worst about his brothers—and yet it was hard not to.

"Well, what do you say?" Zach demanded, breaking into Aaron's morbid thoughts. "Are we going after those bastards or not?"

Before Aaron could answer, Josie let out a snort of contempt. "I say you're crazy," she told Zach. "The two of you don't have any business running around the Rocky Mountains. You'd just get yourself killed."

"Josie's probably right, Zach," Aaron said, although he had to work up some courage to disagree with anything his brother said. "Besides, if we took off, that would leave Josie and Matthew here alone. How would the taxes get paid?"

Zach gave a derisive laugh. "Hell, Josie knows how to make enough money to pay those taxes and take care of herself and the boy. There's plenty of men around here who'll pay to have her—you know that. She'll get by."

Aaron glanced at his sister and saw how pale she was. She was furious with Zach, and with good reason. Aaron swallowed and looked down at the table. Despite Zach's crudity, he was telling the truth. Everybody in the area knew that Josie was a prostitute.

When Aaron glanced up again, she was looking at him coldly. "Have you got something to say, Aaron?" she asked.

She was waiting for him to defend her, to stand up for her honor. That was what he should do, he knew. Whether she was a trollop or not, she ought to be able to count on her brother for something.

But old habits were hard to break, and Zach was glowering at him, waiting for him to make a decision.

"I . . . I reckon Zach's right," Aaron finally said in a choked voice. "Clay Holt got away with killing Pete, and that's not fair. And you . . . well, you'd make out all right."

Zach grinned broadly. "So you're going with me? We're heading west?"

Aaron shrugged, miserable. "I suppose we can give it a try."

The long-handled spoon Josie had been using to stir the stew rattled against the side of the kettle as she threw it into the steaming mixture. "Go west, then, damn you!" she said bitterly. "Go to hell while you're at it!"

Aaron got to his feet and said tentatively, "Now, Josie, don't be like—"

"Hush your mouth, Aaron Garwood! I don't want to hear anything else from you." She swung her angry gaze toward Zach. "And you! If you think I want you around here anymore, you really are out of your mind! Just go on—leave your sister to fend for herself . . . and your son!"

Zach turned as pale as milk. "What the hell are you talking about?"

"You know good and well what I'm talking about." Josie crossed her arms over her heaving chest, glared at Zach for a moment longer, then slowly turned her head and looked at Matthew, who was still

playing in the corner, seemingly unaware of the tur-
moil going on around him.

Aaron blinked rapidly, trying to make some sense
out of what Josie was saying. What she had implied
was impossible, unless . . .

But that was too horrible to even think about,
Aaron told himself. It could not be true. Zach had his
faults, true enough, but Aaron would not allow himself to believe such a thing about his brother.

He just wished he had not noticed suddenly that
except for Matthew's dark hair and eyes—which were
also Garwood traits—the boy looked nothing at all
like Clay Holt.

"I'm not going to listen to any more of this," Zach
declared. He drank another cup of whiskey, then
stood up. "Come on, Aaron. We've got plans to make.
I want to leave as soon as we can."

"Sure, Zach," Aaron mumbled and got to his feet.
He glanced at Josie and saw that she was still furious.
He wished he could say something to make things
right, to bring some peace back to the family, but he
couldn't find the words to accomplish such a thing.

The two men left the cabin, Zach striding along
confidently, Aaron following with a hesitant, sheepish
expression. The rain had stopped again. When they
were outside and the door was closed behind them,
Aaron asked, "Are you sure we're doing the right
thing?"

" 'Course we are," Zach replied. "Can't let the
Holts get away with what they've done. And listen,
don't worry about Josie. She'll be fine."

"Zach, about what she said . . ."

Curtly, Zach waved his hand. "You can't pay any
attention to what Josie says. Hell, she's out of her head
part of the time, you know that. And she's just mad
right now. Forget about it."

"But what she said about Matthew—"

Zach spun toward his brother, and Aaron
flinched from Zach's fierce glare. "Goddamn it, I said
forget about it! She's a whore and a slut, and she's

liable to say anything!" He grimaced. "Hell, she's been with so many men she probably doesn't even know who the brat's father is. Clay Holt was just a handy scapegoat."

Aaron frowned in confusion. "But if that's the way it is, then why do you hate Clay so bad? Why are we going after him and Jeff?"

"Because they killed Luther and Pete," Zach snapped. "Because their pa stole land that should've belonged to us. Because maybe Josie's been telling the truth about Clay all along. Hell, boy, we're going after them because they're Holts! That's enough reason for me."

It was at that precise moment, Aaron realized later, that he began to believe that maybe Zach really was insane.

After the ordeal of fighting and then fleeing from the Arikara, Clay and Jeff Holt were understandably tired, but Proud Wolf did not slow down. He maintained his steady jog as he led them over forested ridges, through parklike meadows, and across tiny, icy-cold streams on the way to his village. Clay was hurting and struggling for breath before they got there, but he was stubborn enough not to want the youth to see that. Jeff was exhausted, too, but like Clay he kept going. Finally Proud Wolf took them down into a beautiful valley, where the tipis of the Teton were clustered beside another creek.

Dogs and children ran out to greet the visitors and trail closely at their heels. Clay smiled at the youngsters and tried not to look threatening. Jeff followed his example. Women stopped working at their chores to look at the two white men, and several men stepped out of the tipis, pushing aside the flaps of buffalo hide over the entrances. The braves did not seem particularly hostile as they watched Clay and Jeff with expressionless faces, but they were not overly friendly either. Clay felt a tingle of unease. He had learned never to take any of these deceptively simple people for granted.

Proud Wolf came to a stop in front of a tall, powerful-looking warrior wearing breechclout and moccasins, with several feathers braided into his long, dark hair. The youth stood silently until the tall man said something to him, and Clay guessed that Proud Wolf had been waiting for leave to speak. For the next few minutes Proud Wolf talked in his native tongue, throwing in quite a few gestures.

Jeff leaned closer to Clay and whispered, "What's he saying?"

From what he could follow of the conversation—and Clay was no expert on Siouan dialects—he thought Proud Wolf was explaining how he had hidden them from the Arikara. "I think he's talking about how he saved our skins. Says we're the white men he saw in his vision. I reckon that makes us special."

"Like gods or something?"

One corner of Clay's mouth quirked in a smile. "Not *that* special," he said dryly. "I'd settle for them not wanting to put us under."

The tall man, who Clay figured was a chief of some sort, occasionally interrupted Proud Wolf's story to ask a question. As the boy talked, the chief stared solemnly at the two white men. Finally, with a gesture, he called a halt to Proud Wolf's tale and stepped over to them.

"You are from the fort where the white men trade for beaver?" he asked in more than passable English.

Concealing his surprise, Clay nodded and replied, "That's right. We were out trapping beaver when those Rees jumped us. They would've caught us had it not been for Proud Wolf here."

"Then you come to these mountains in peace?"

"That's right," Clay assured him, trying to sound as sincere as he could.

"You are not friends to the Blackfoot or the Rees?"

Clay shook his head. "I'd just as soon stay as far away from those sons of Satan as I can."

He thought he saw a faint flicker of amusement in the chief's eyes, but it was rapidly veiled. "The man who taught us your tongue said that we are all sons of God, not Satan."

"Well, that may be true," Clay said slowly. "I still don't want to do any psalm singing with a bunch of Blackfoot."

This time the chief definitely looked amused. "I am called Bear Tooth, and these are my people."

"Clay Holt," Clay introduced himself, thumping his chest. "And this is my brother, Jefferson Holt."

"You are welcome in the Hunkpapa village of Bear Tooth," the chief said, then walked over to the nearest campfire and sat down cross-legged beside it. Clay and Jeff, unsure of how they were supposed to proceed, glanced at each other. Acting on a hunch, Clay joined the chief and sat beside him. Jeff followed suit, sinking down beside Clay. Then other warriors advanced and sat down around the fire, completing the circle.

"We will eat now," Bear Tooth said gravely.

The next hour was rather harrowing for the Holts, as they shared a meal and then a pipe with Bear Tooth and the other warriors. They were nervous that they would offend their hosts inadvertently. Evidently the Hunkpapa were satisfied with their behavior, and gradually the feeling of tension in the air lessened. Clay didn't ask what was in the stew that an Indian woman served to him in a wooden bowl. He just ate it and had to admit to himself that it was good, if a little bit gamy. A couple of times, he noticed Proud Wolf loitering in the vicinity of the fire, frowning as if he was displeased at being excluded from the circle of warriors. For all the boy's boasting to the white men, it seemed the other Hunkpapa did not hold him in as high a standing as he did himself.

Finally Clay felt at ease enough to ask, "How is it that you speak such good English, Bear Tooth?"

"Not only English," Bear Tooth said, giving Clay a slight smile. He spoke rapidly in another tongue, and although Clay and Jeff could not understand what he was saying, they recognized the language.

"That's French!" Jeff exclaimed.

Bear Tooth nodded. "The man who taught us came from the Great White North and wore a long, dark robe. He spoke of many things which we did not understand—the power and the glory and the blood of the lamb. He told us he was sent by the Great Spirit. This we did understand, though we call it Wakan Tanka. He was very discouraged when he left us, but he swore he would continue on until he found a people who would believe the message he bore. We were sorry to see him go. He taught us much, even though we could not believe everything he said about the Wakan Tanka."

Jeff said to Clay, "A French-Canadian missionary. Had to be."

"Reckon you're right," Clay agreed. "I've heard that some of them came into this country even before Lewis and Clark." He looked back at Bear Tooth. "You've made us mighty welcome, Chief, and we appreciate it. But we ought to be getting back to our business—"

"You will stay," Bear Tooth said. His tone told them he had not even considered the possibility that anyone would ever dare to argue with him.

Clay and Jeff exchanged another glance. They did not want to insult the Hunkpapa by declining their hospitality. Making friends among the Indians was as important in the long run as any beaver they might trap. Clay inclined his head toward the chief and said, "Thank you. We will be pleased to visit with our new friends, the Hunkpapa, part of the Teton Sioux."

In one lithe motion Bear Tooth uncoiled from his sitting position. Clay and Jeff followed a bit more awkwardly. As the other men got to their feet, Bear Tooth turned his head and spoke sharply to one of them. To Clay and Jeff he said, "Elk Horn will take you to the tipi you will use while you are here."

The man called Elk Horn stepped forward. He was a couple of inches shorter than Bear Tooth, but his shoulders were equally as broad, and his muscular bare torso shone from the grease that had been rubbed on it. His hair was also greased and had several feathers woven into the two braids that hung over his shoulders. His features were too stern and arrogant to be called handsome, but he had a compelling air about him that suggested that while he might be subordinate to Bear Tooth, he was still one of the leaders of the band.

He lacked his chief's flair for languages, however. He grunted, "You come," to Clay and Jeff. They followed him to one of the cone-shaped, buffalo-hide tipis, its sides decorated with drawings. The narrow door opening faced east, and over it hung a skin curtain suspended from a stick and weighted at the bottom by another stick, parallel to the top one. Elk Horn pushed aside the door covering and stood back to let them enter. Ducking their heads, Clay and Jeff stepped inside. The tipi was roomier than it looked from the outside. A small fire pit was located in the center, but even with it Clay and Jeff would have plenty of room for stretching out in their blankets.

Elk Horn put his head in through the opening and said, "Woman will come." Before either Clay or Jeff could say anything in reply, he ducked back out and disappeared.

"What the devil did he mean by that?" Jeff asked.

Clay shrugged. "Maybe Bear Tooth figures to give us a woman to cook and clean and such for us while we're visiting. Indians do that. Every time we stayed with the Mandan or the Shoshone while I was with Lewis and Clark, they went out of their way to make us feel at home."

Sometimes even giving us squaws to share our blankets at night, Clay thought. Many of the Indian women they had encountered, in fact, had been eager to give themselves to the white men. The men of the tribes often encouraged the practice as well. It seemed to be a point of honor for them to have a wife or daughter bedded by a visitor. If that was what was going to happen here, Clay wondered how Jeff would take to it. Fidelity to the marriage vows was one thing; insulting your hosts was quite another, especially when they were armed with knives and 'hawks and arrows.

No point in worrying about something that might not even come about, Clay told himself. Besides, the woman that the Hunkpapa sent would probably be some toothless, withered old crone who would cook for them and nothing else.

That was what he was thinking when the door flap was pushed aside and damned near the most beautiful woman he had ever seen stepped into the tipi. Like the other women they had seen in the camp, she was wearing a long, one-piece skin dress tied with belts, short leggings, and beaded moccasins. She smiled at them for a second, then lowered her dark eyes to the ground and said shyly, "I am Shining Moon. Bear Tooth has sent me to you for as long as you stay with us. What do you wish me to do first?"

Clay could not answer. Not with his mouth hanging open in amazement.

As it turned out, Shining Moon was Proud Wolf's sister, and she already knew all about the boy's vision concerning the white men. She was there to cook and clean for the visitors, as Clay had supposed, but if her duties were to include anything else, he could not tell it from her dignified demeanor. She spoke English as well as her chief, Bear Tooth, so she was obviously intelligent. Her hair was the color of midnight, and although it was parted in the middle and wound in a tight braid, Clay had a feeling that if it were unloosed, it would cascade down her back in a fall of loveliness. He was unsure how old she was; around eighteen or twenty, he guessed. She was a woman, though, not a girl. Her amply curved body, though slender, was more than enough proof of that.

The stew she prepared for their supper, made with prairie turnips, potatoes, and onions, was as good as that they had eaten earlier in the day. They were also given pemmican, a nourishing, portable food made of dried chokecherries mixed with dried and pounded meat that would keep for several years, according to Shining Moon. This meal was not as tense as the other one, since they ate by themselves in the tipi, with only Shining Moon in attendance. Clay tried to get her to share in the food, but she refused politely.

"It is not my place to eat with you," she said, eyes downcast again. "Shining Moon will eat later."

Jeff started to protest, but Clay put a hand on his arm and gave a little shake of his head. As long as the Hunkpapa were friendly, it was better not to push them about anything.

Clay did, however, try to draw Shining Moon into a conversation, and that was how he discovered Proud Wolf was her brother. The boy was older than he looked, too.

"He has seen fifteen summers," Shining Moon told them. "As a baby, he was very sick. We thought he would die, but he did not. Since then he has grown slowly and never as much as the other young men. It has been . . . difficult for him."

Clay nodded. He would have figured that Proud Wolf was a good three or four years younger. In a society that placed as much emphasis on physical prowess as the Teton did, a boy who was small for his age would have a pretty hard time of it. Proud Wolf did not seem to have allowed it to bother him, but deep down it must have. As far as Clay was concerned, the lad had nothing to be ashamed of. He was smart and quick thinking—the way he had rescued them from the Arikara proved that—and he had demonstrated his stamina during the long run back to his village.

That night Shining Moon announced that she would be sleeping in their tipi, then stepped outside to fetch her buffalo robe.

"I'm not used to such as this," Jeff hissed to Clay after she was gone.

"Don't worry about it, little brother. If you're going to live in the mountains, you'd better get used to Indian ways, even when they seem mighty strange to you."

Jeff shook his head. "If Melissa knew what was going on here—"

"In the first place, there's not a damn thing improper going on here, not the way the Indians see it," Clay cut in. "And even if there was, I reckon Melissa would be too thankful that you're safe and sound to be worrying about some civilized notion of propriety."

"Are you saying that if that girl offers herself to me, I ought to take her?"

Clay shrugged. "Up to you."

"Well . . . what would *you* do?"

A grin spread slowly across Clay's face. "I'm not sure you really want to hear the answer to that question, Jeff. Maybe you'd best just go to sleep. She's coming back."

They fell silent as Shining Moon slipped into the tipi carrying her buffalo robe. She said nothing as she laid it across the entrance to the tipi and curled up in it. The fire was dying down, and Clay could not see her very well now. She had her face turned toward him, he could tell that much, but he could not read her expression.

It took a while for Clay to fall asleep, but when he finally did, his slumber was deep and dreamless. When he awoke the next morning, Jeff was still snoring quietly on the other side of the fire pit, and Shining Moon was gone.

Clay sat up, ran his fingers through his hair, and scratched his jaw through the bristly black growth of beard. Evidently Shining Moon had stayed near the entrance of the tipi all night. She had certainly not paid a visit to his blankets; he could not have slept through that. And if she had approached Jeff, Clay's brother would have made enough of a commotion to wake him, too.

He got to his feet, stretched, and stepped outside. The sun had not been up long, he realized. The village was already bustling with activity, however. Clay spotted Shining Moon walking toward the tipi, carrying a gourd filled with water. He stepped forward to meet her and take the water from her, but she shook her head. "I am to care for you," she said. "This is my task."

Clay shrugged, then grinned. If that was the way she wanted things, it was fine with him.

Over the following days he grew somewhat accustomed to having Shining Moon there nearly every time he turned around. She was an excellent cook, and she kept the tipi spotless—or as spotless as a buffalo-hide dwelling erected on dirt could be. She was not very forthcoming about herself, even though Clay tried to get her talking on several occasions. He told Shining Moon of his admiration for a strong, young Shoshone Indian woman named Sacajawea.

Gradually, he learned that Shining Moon and Proud Wolf were the children of a well-respected warrior who had been killed in a clash with the Blackfoot several years earlier. As was customary, Bear Tooth had taken the man's widow and children into his own family.

Clay also discovered that despite her beauty, Shining Moon was not betrothed to any of the young men in the tribe. That admission slipped out while she was preparing a meal while Proud Wolf and Jeff were away, leaving her alone with Clay. When he heard her say that she was not engaged, Clay frowned in surprise. He would have thought the men would be falling all over themselves to court her, and he said as much.

Shining Moon allowed herself a tiny smile. "The

young men say that I speak too much and too sharply. They think I would not make a good wife for them because of this."

"Well, then, I'd say they're damn fools," Clay replied. "Nothing wrong with a woman having opinions of her own."

"You say that now," Shining Moon said without looking at him. "You might believe differently if I were your woman."

Clay's pulse was thumping a little harder than usual for some reason. "I don't think so. I like people being straight with me, no matter who they are."

Shining Moon nodded, but Clay was left with the feeling that she was not convinced.

Standing beside a clearing near the village, Jeff and Proud Wolf were watching a number of young Hunkpapa men competing in some sort of game. Jeff had been trying to figure out the rules of the competition, but so far he had been unable to fathom them. To him it appeared that the Hunkpapas were running around aimlessly, chasing some sort of round object made out of buffalo hide and stuffed with dry grass. The game didn't make sense to Jeff, but its participants were obviously enjoying it, for they were whooping and waving their arms as they dashed around.

Jeff inclined his head toward the playing field. "Looks like they're having a good time," he said to Proud Wolf. "Why don't you get in there with them?"

Proud Wolf shrugged his narrow shoulders and did not look at his companion. "I am too small," he said. "The other young men do not allow me to join them."

"Well, that doesn't hardly seem fair," Jeff said. "You ought to have a chance, just like anybody else."

"That is the way the young men believe, and nothing can change their minds."

"I'd sure let you play, if it was me."

"Yes, but I saved you and your brother from the Rees," Proud Wolf said with a little smile.

"Yeah, that's right. Tell you what, why don't you show me more of what goes on around here? The man I work for wants us to befriend your people, and I reckon that means learning as much about you folks as we can."

Proud Wolf looked at Jeff steadily for a few moments, and then his smile widened. "Yes," he said at last. "I will teach you about the Hunkpapa."

Later in the day, as Proud Wolf and Jeff were strolling past the tipi that had been given to the white men for their use during the visit, Clay and Shining Moon emerged. Jeff began telling his brother about all the things Proud Wolf had shown him. "It takes a dozen or more buffalo skins to make one of these tipis," Jeff explained, "and they belong to the women, not the men. The men hunt the beasts, but from there on the women do everything—even butcher the carcasses and carry them back to camp!"

Clay shook his head. "I can't see many of the women I've known doing anything of the sort, that's for sure."

"Neither can I. And then the squaws put every bit of the animals to use. They use the hides for everything from shelter to clothing, and with the horns they make spoons and ladles. They even use the hair, for weaving bags and belts."

"Is that what your belts are made of, Shining Moon?" Clay asked. He felt a momentary chill, as if just saying her name gave him a physical reaction.

"Yes, Clay Holt," she said, smiling almost shyly.

Clay longed to touch her, but he had to be satisfied with drinking in her beauty.

None of the four people noticed a Hunkpapa warrior standing near his own tipi, his arms crossed over his chest and a scowl on his face. Elk Horn, his features darkened with anger, watched the two white men talking to Shining Moon and Proud Wolf. He saw the way Shining Moon carried herself with deference around the white men, especially the older one. Never had she exhibited such an attitude toward him, he thought bitterly. She never seemed to hold him in high regard, despite his standing as a warrior and sub-chief of the band. And she certainly never smiled at him as she smiled at the white man when he was not looking.

Elk Horn's anger grew until he was forced to turn away, thrust aside the entrance flap of his tipi, and step inside. Otherwise, his rage might have made him forget how Bear Tooth had made the visitors welcome. He might have challenged the tall man to fight for Shining Moon.

Shining Moon's beauty was such that he burned for her in the night. Some of the braves thought Shining Moon was too sharp-tongued to be a proper mate for a warrior. Elk Horn disagreed. If she became his wife—and he firmly intended for this to happen—she would rapidly learn to afford him the proper respect. He would see to that. She would cook for him and please him in his sleeping robe, and she would do this in silence, as was befitting. If she did not, she would greatly regret her audacity.

Elk Horn grinned cruelly. Shining Moon might not know it yet, but soon she would be his for the rest of time. And if the white man was foolish enough to try to interfere . . .

Elk Horn slipped his 'hawk from his belt and ran his thumb along the sharp edge of its blade. If the white man got in his way, he could do something about that, too.

CHAPTER SEVENTEEN

While on shore to-day we witnessed a quarrel between two squaws, which appeared to be growing every moment more boisterous, when a man came forward, at whose approach everyone seemed terrified and ran. He took the squaws and without any ceremony whipped them severely. On inquiring into the nature of such summary justice, we learned that this man was an officer well known to this and many other tribes. His duty is to keep the peace, and the whole interior police of the village is confided to two or three of these officers, who are named by the chief and remain in power some days, at least till the chief appoints a successor.

—from "The History of the Lewis and
Clark Expedition"

Summer rolled on, and the trappers from the fort
built by Manuel Lisa and his men continued to
spread out over the valleys of the Yellowstone
and the Big Horn. Clay and Jeff Holt had returned to
the fort from the Hunkpapa village, along with Bear
Tooth, Shining Moon, Proud Wolf, and several other
men. Bear Tooth and Manuel Lisa had formalized
their friendship by smoking a pipe and exchanging
gifts. Lisa was pleased with Clay and Jeff's efforts to
get along with the Indians.

After the Hunkpapa had returned to their village,
Clay found himself thinking often of Shining Moon.
During the time Jeff and he had stayed with the tribe,
she had continued to be the same shy, sweet young
woman he had first taken her to be, showing no sign
of the tartness of tongue that she claimed had kept her
unmarried. Clay didn't know if that was significant.
Perhaps she had never met anyone like him before, he
allowed himself to think in his more immodest moments.

In the vicinity of the fort were other Teton villages, primarily to the southeast, most of which the
trappers had visited by now. They had also become
acquainted with the various bands of Crow that lived
to the north and west. It had been months since the
white men had begun to scatter out from the fort on
their trapping missions, and the Indians had gotten
over much of their curiosity. For the most part the
mountain men were accepted and made welcome by
them.

Every time Jeff and Clay were anywhere near
Bear Tooth's village, Clay made sure they stopped
there. Jeff's friendship with Proud Wolf had grown
stronger, and Clay was always glad to see Shining
Moon.

As the summer months went on, the trapping had
gradually gotten worse. The pelts were thinner, and
while the rivers and creeks in the area were a far cry
from being trapped out, there seemed to be fewer beaver around. Clay speculated that some of the animals

had moved farther north in search of cooler weather, although he had no real evidence to indicate that such a migration had taken place. All he knew for certain was that Jeff and he and the others were having to venture farther from the fort on each trip to harvest a suitable number of plews.

One mid-August day Clay and Jeff were with three other men named Scott, Curry, and Tompkins, moving along a stream called Ten Sleep Creek in the Big Horn Mountains. The trappers traveled in larger groups now, and they always kept their rifles and pistols primed and loaded. The rugged, heavy woods sloped down almost to the banks of the creek, making traveling difficult. The men had been away from the fort for two weeks, and they were finally having good luck. Along one stretch of the stream the beaver were plentiful. Not too far away, Clay recalled, was an Oglala village he and Jeff had visited once. The people there were led by a chief called Wind-in-Hair, and while Clay and Jeff had not been made as welcome there as they had been in the Hunkpapa village, this band of Teton Sioux had seemed friendly enough, if a little reserved.

The white men were tramping beside the creek, Clay and Jeff on the south bank, the other men on the north side, when suddenly Clay paused and peered ahead, squinting a little. The sun was bright overhead, but the thick growth of the pines caused shadows to cluster beneath the trees. Clay thought he had seen something up ahead, but he could not be sure.

Then he heard the unmistakable flutter of an arrow in the air, followed an instant later by the grisly thud of an arrowhead against flesh. On the other side of the stream, the trapper called Tompkins gasped and stumbled, then cried, "Oh, God, boys, I'm kilt!" He dropped his rifle and his possibles bag and pawed feebly at the shaft of the arrow protruding from his chest for a few seconds before he pitched forward onto the ground. The impact of his fall drove the arrow into his body, ripping through his back, leaving the arrowhead to stand bloody and defiant above the corpse.

"Get back!" Clay shouted to Scott and Curry. At the same time, he was lifting his Harper's Ferry rifle and searching for a target. Again he saw a flicker of movement in the shadows.

Clay lashed out with his foot. The kick slammed into Jeff's thigh and knocked him to the side. Clay dove in the other direction. Between them, an arrow slashed through the air. Holding tightly to the rifle as he landed heavily on the ground, Clay rolled over, brought the stock of the weapon to his shoulder, and fully cocked it. He caught a glimpse of a figure under the trees and pressed the flintlock's trigger.

The blast of the rifle echoed from the slopes around them and mingled with the cries of the attackers, who dashed out from their cover beneath the trees. At that distance Clay couldn't be sure which band of Indians they were, but it was obvious their intentions weren't friendly. He got to his knees, jerked one of his pistols from his belt, cocked it, and sent another ball into the charging men. Jeff was firing, too, as well as Scott and Curry, and the deadly volley spilled two of the Indians and made the others turn and seek shelter again.

"Come on!" Clay ordered. "Let's get out of here before they regroup!"

He jumped to his feet and stepped over to grab Jeff's arm, pulling his brother upright as well. The other two trappers were retreating back along the north bank of Ten Sleep Creek. Clay and Jeff dashed along the opposite side, the creek running cold and swift in between.

Clay estimated that at least a dozen men had been in the group that had jumped them and killed Tompkins. Two of them had been downed, but that still left ten. Not good odds, but not impossible—if Jeff and he and the others could find a suitable place to make a stand.

He remembered a spot several hundred yards upstream where Jeff and he had been forced to climb over a deadfall. A fallen tree near the bank had caught brush carried along by the stream, forming a barrier of sorts. It would not be the best place in the world to fort up, Clay thought, but it was sure as hell the closest. He called over to Scott and Curry, who were ahead of him and Jeff, "Get on this side of the creek! There's a deadfall up ahead!"

Not wasting their breath to acknowledge his words, the two men angled into the creek and splashed through the icy water, joining Clay and Jeff on the south side of the stream. Clay could see the deadfall up ahead now, but the Indians were close behind. Arrows whistled past their heads.

Clay glanced over his shoulder and saw that one of the attackers had drawn ahead of the others and was closing in on the fleeing men. He was only about ten yards back, close enough that he could have stopped and put an arrow into any of them with ease. But from the twisted expression of rage on the man's painted face, Clay surmised that he wanted the trappers to die a more cruel death. He had cast his bow aside and was reaching for his 'hawk.

"Keep going!" Clay panted to his companions, then stopped as suddenly as he could. The Indian could not slow down in time, and as Clay whirled around and dove for the warrior's legs, they collided with an impact that left Clay breathless. The Indian sprawled over him. Clay rolled quickly to the side and jerked his own 'hawk free. He knew he had to dispose of this man in a hurry. If he did not, the other Indians would catch up to him, and he could never fight off all of them.

He lunged toward the fallen warrior, who was on the edge of the stream. The man was trying to get up, but Clay's knees landed in the middle of his back and drove him down again. Clay heard ribs crack under him as the Indian let out a grunt of pain. Before his opponent could throw him off, Clay lifted his 'hawk and brought it down with all his strength on the back of the man's head.

The 'hawk made an ugly sound as it crushed the warrior's skull. The man stiffened, then went limp and dropped into the mud at the edge of the creek. Clay rolled off the corpse and sprang to his feet. The kill had been quick, all right, but not quick enough to prevent the other Indians from drawing close to him. An arrow plucked at his sleeve as he turned and ran after Jeff, Scott, and Curry.

They had reached the deadfall and ducked behind it, Clay saw. He was still some fifty yards from it, and the Indians were closer to him than that. His arms pumping at his sides, heedless of the beating his moccasin-clad feet were taking on the rocks of the bank, Clay raced for his life toward the makeshift shelter as the Indians closed in on him.

A rifle spoke suddenly, and Clay saw smoke blossom from behind the deadfall. Jeff and the other trappers were making their presence felt again. There was another shot, and Clay heard one of his pursuers cry out in pain.

The shots made the Indians slow down slightly, and that was all the advantage Clay needed. He reached the deadfall, put a hand on the rough trunk of the fallen tree, and vaulted over. As he sprawled behind it, one of the men fired again.

Jeff leaned over his brother, an anxious expression on his face. "Clay! Are you all right?"

Clay nodded, rolled over, and pushed himself to his feet. As he crouched behind the brush, he drew his unfired pistol and leveled it at the charging Indians. He was about to press the trigger when he suddenly eased off and exclaimed in surprise, "Those are Tetons!"

"Are you sure?" Jeff asked beside him.

"Look!" Clay pointed. "That's Wind-in-Hair, the chief of that Oglala village that's not far from here!"

He was right, and Jeff, Scott, and Curry all recognized the Oglala leader now. Wind-in-Hair was in the forefront of the group, his face contorted in a killing rage. The Oglala came on, seemingly determined to kill all the white men.

With no time to ponder what might have turned the peaceful Oglala into murderous warriors, Clay aimed his pistol and fired. Luck was with him, and the ball burned a path along the side of Wind-in-Hair's thigh, spinning the chief to the ground but not seriously injuring him.

Jeff and the other two trappers fired again, but they followed Clay's lead and shot to wound now, if possible. Several more of the Oglala staggered, burned by the accurate shooting of the mountain men.

Wind-in-Hair was lifted to his feet by a pair of his men, and with a series of shouted curses, he led the band in a quick retreat. The trappers took advantage of the respite to crouch behind the deadfall and reload.

There was no longer any need for the weapons, however, for the Oglala vanished around a bend in the creek. After twenty minutes Clay said, "I reckon they're gone. We put up more of a fight than they wanted."

"What in the world got into them?" Scott asked. "Them Oglalas have always been friendly."

Jeff added, "That's what I was wondering. They acted like they wanted our hair."

"They did." Clay grunted and shook his head as he looked at the spot where the Oglala had disappeared. "I don't know why either. But I sure as hell intend to find out."

The four men went downstream again, keeping a close eye out for trouble along the way. When they got back to the place where Tompkins had been killed, they found his body untouched. The ground was too stony to dig a grave, but they were able to place the corpse in a small gully and cover it with large rocks. That was the best they could do; at least animals would not be able to get at the corpse.

That task done, they set out for the Hunkpapa village of Bear Tooth. If anybody could give them an explanation for the unexpected hostility of the other Teton band, it was Bear Tooth, Clay reasoned. Very little went on in this part of the woods that the chief did not know about.

It took them two days to reach the village, and when they finally trudged up to the tipis of Bear Tooth's people, the sun was low above the mountains to the west. Lookouts had spotted them approaching, and several of the Hunkpapa came out to meet them, including Proud Wolf. The youngster clasped Jeff's forearm in greeting. "We did not expect to see you again so soon, my friend. But we are glad you are here, as always."

The boy's English was steadily improving because of his dealings with the white men, Clay thought. He wished they were bringing better news. If other bands of Teton Sioux were growing hostile toward the trappers, the incident with Wind-in-Hair and his warriors could be just the beginning of a dark, dangerous time in these mountains.

Proud Wolf must have seen something in the expressions of the white visitors because he frowned and said, "Something is wrong. What is it? Tell me, Jefferson Holt."

Jeff explained, "We had a run-in with some other Tetons. Wind-in-Hair's bunch. They killed one of our friends and did their best to put us under, too."

Muttered exclamations of shock and disbelief ran through the small crowd of Hunkpapa who had gathered around. Clay noticed that Shining Moon was not among them. Bear Tooth and the subchief, Elk Horn, were not present either.

"We must tell Bear Tooth of this," Proud Wolf said. "This is bad, very bad. Since the white men came to the land of the Hunkpapa and Oglala and the other Teton tribes, they have been our friends."

"Then you don't have any idea why Wind-in-Hair and his men jumped us?" Clay asked.

Proud Wolf shook his head, and when Clay peered around at the other Hunkpapa, they looked equally baffled. "We will find out," Proud Wolf declared. "Come. Tell Bear Tooth what has happened."

The group of white men proceeded to the chief's tipi, the Hunkpapa closing in around them as they walked. Clay noticed that Scott and Curry, not knowing these people as well as Jeff and he did, looked decidedly nervous.

One of the older warriors went ahead to tell Bear Tooth of their presence, and by the time they reached his tipi, Bear Tooth had emerged and was standing in front of it, arms folded across his chest and the usual calm expression on his face. Clay could see worry lurking in his eyes, however.

Elk Horn was standing slightly behind and to the right of Bear Tooth, a scowl on his face as he watched the white men approach. Clay had figured out in the course of their visits to the village that Elk Horn had little use for the white men and stayed away from them as much as possible. At a time like this, though, when something was amiss, his chief would expect him to stand nearby.

The entrance flap of the tipi was pushed aside, and Shining Moon appeared. She was as lovely as ever, Clay saw, and he felt the quickening pulse that the sight of her always brought. Her expression was solemn as she looked at the visitors. Clay met her eyes for a moment before she looked away, and he saw the worry there.

"There has been trouble," Bear Tooth said by way of greeting. His words were a statement, not a question.

Clay nodded anyway. "That's right, Chief," he said. Quickly, he sketched for Bear Tooth the details of the brief battle, and the chief's expression grew even more grave as he heard the story.

When Clay had finished, Bear Tooth shook his head. "I know Wind-in-Hair. He has no hatred for the white men."

"We know him, too," Jeff said, "and we thought the same thing until he and his warriors came at us firing arrows."

"You are certain they were Oglala? I would expect such a thing from Blackfoot or Arikara."

"They were Oglala," Clay said firmly. "We saw Wind-in-Hair himself."

Bear Tooth took a deep breath and said nothing for a long moment as he considered the situation. Finally, he declared, "I will send a runner to Wind-in-Hair's village. We must know why the Oglala would try to kill our white friends."

"Has to have been some kind of mistake," Clay remarked. "We need to know what so we can set it right."

Bear Tooth nodded sagely. "We have fought many wars against the Blackfoot and the Arikara. We do not need to fight a war against the white men, too."

"That's our feeling also," Clay assured him. "Whatever the cause of the trouble, we want to put a stop to it."

For the first time since their arrival, Bear Tooth allowed a smile to touch his face. "You will stay with us until the runner returns from Wind-in-Hair's village?"

"Sounds good to us, doesn't it, boys?" Clay asked his companions.

Jeff agreed enthusiastically. Scott and Curry seemed less convinced but were willing to bow to the judgment of the Holts. After all the months in the mountains, Clay and Jeff had probably covered more ground and knew more about the Indians than anyone else west of the Mississippi, except for John Colter.

Clay would have appreciated Colter's presence right then. They could have used his experience in dealing with the Indians. But the Virginian, who had still not returned from the mission he had been given by Manuel Lisa, was somewhere in the mountains southwest of the fort, spreading the word about the white men and their desire to trade for beaver pelts.

Before he'd left, Colter had confided to Clay that he intended to make a huge circle through the Rockies and probably wouldn't be back until sometime in the fall.

Clay and Jeff were given the tipi where they usually stayed, and another was set aside for use by the other two trappers. "Will all of you eat with me tonight?" Bear Tooth asked. Clay accepted on behalf of himself and his companions, trying to hide his slight disappointment. He had been hoping that Shining Moon would prepare supper for Jeff and him, as she usually did. If that had been the case, he might have been able to get a few minutes alone with her.

Maybe later, he thought. There would probably be other chances to talk to her during the visit. One thing was certain—he did not intend to leave the relative safety of Bear Tooth's village until they had discovered the reason the other Teton band was suddenly after their scalps.

He had other important matters to consider, though, and what he had to say to Shining Moon was one of them. She had been on his mind constantly of late, and they had to get things straight between them.

And as those thoughts crossed his mind, Clay found he was just as nervous as he had been when the Indians were after them. Maybe even a little more so.

After the white men had gone to their tipis to rest for a short time before joining Bear Tooth for the evening meal, Proud Wolf stepped up to the chief, crossed his arms, and looked up into Bear Tooth's face. Bear Tooth was his adopted father, yet Proud Wolf felt the respect that any Sioux brave would feel for his chief. He was also more than a little in awe of Bear Tooth, who in Proud Wolf's mind was the mightiest warrior the Sioux had ever known.

Bear Tooth was preoccupied with the disturbing news about Wind-in-Hair, but he smiled tolerantly at the lad he had taken into his family. "You wish to speak to me, Proud Wolf?"

The boy nodded. "I would like the honor of being the runner who goes to Wind-in-Hair's village."

That brought a slight frown to Bear Tooth's face. "This is a job for a warrior."

"I know." With effort Proud Wolf maintained his dignified pose and let the chief draw his own conclusions.

Elk Horn, still standing nearby, spoke up. "We cannot send a boy to perform a warrior's task," he said scornfully.

"Wait," Bear Tooth said. He looked intently at Proud Wolf. "Do you believe you can do this?"

"Yes. I can run from the time the sun rises in the morning until it sets in the evening without growing tired. I know the trails and all the ways of the forest. I can carry your message to Wind-in-Hair, and I can return with his answer to you. Faithfully will I do all these things, if you will allow me the opportunity."

There was still quite a crowd gathered around Bear Tooth. As Proud Wolf finished speaking, Elk Horn gave a contemptuous chuckle, and some of the young warriors in the group echoed it.

Bear Tooth stopped the laughter by giving the men a stern glance. Putting a hand on Proud Wolf's shoulder, he declared, "You will be our runner. When the sun rises tomorrow, you will go to the village of Wind-in-Hair and ask him why he tries to kill the white men. Bring his answer back to me."

Proud Wolf was almost overcome by emotion. His throat was as choked and full as if he had tried to swallow a stone. He managed to nod solemnly, and Bear Tooth squeezed his shoulder. With that, the chief turned away in dismissal.

To show his excitement by dancing would be improper, Proud Wolf knew. But that was exactly what he felt like doing. Bear Tooth was entrusting him with a very important mission, placing the same confidence in him that he would have in a veteran warrior. After this, the boy thought, no one would belittle him again, despite his size.

Soon everyone would know that even though he was small, Proud Wolf was a Hunkpapa warrior!

That evening Shining Moon helped serve the meal to the four white trappers, guests of the chief, as they dined with him in his tipi. Bear Tooth's wife and one of his daughters also served, but Clay had eyes only for the lovely young woman who had occupied his thoughts for many months. As usual, Shining Moon was reserved. He saw no sign of the proud, headstrong young woman she professed to be.

After the meal Bear Tooth and the Holts discussed the situation that had brought them there, but they came to no conclusions. "A runner will leave for Wind-in-Hair's village in the morning," Bear Tooth told them, without revealing the identity of the messenger. "When he returns, perhaps we will know why this evil thing has happened."

"I hope so," Clay said sincerely, "because we sure want to make things right with Wind-in-Hair. We had to kill several of his men before we knew they were Oglalas. I reckon he'll hold that against us, even though they were doing their best to kill us."

Bear Tooth's expression was grim. "It will not be easy to set things right. But we must try."

The white men could not argue with that.

To allay the nervousness of Scott and Curry, Clay and Jeff walked with them to their tipi after the meal with Bear Tooth. "Don't worry," Jeff told them. "We're safe here, and if anybody can get to the bottom of this, it's Bear Tooth."

"Maybe so," Curry said. "But I'll be damned glad when I'm back behind the walls of the stockade at the fort."

Scott nodded his agreement.

Clay and Jeff bid them good night and returned to their own tipi. It was no surprise to find Shining Moon waiting there for them.

Jeff looked at her for a moment, then at Clay, who stood expressionless just inside the entrance of the tipi. Shining Moon was sitting on the far side of the dwelling. Jeff put a hand up, rubbed his jaw for a second, then said, "I'm not very sleepy yet. Think I'll take a little walk around the village, maybe talk to Proud Wolf awhile."

"You do that, little brother," Clay said, grateful for Jeff's sensitivity.

Shining Moon did not say anything until Jeff had ducked back out through the entrance flap. Then she looked up at Clay and said, "Your brother did not have to leave."

Clay took a deep breath. "Reckon he thought it would be easier for me to say what I've got to say without him around."

"You wish to speak with me, Clay Holt?" Despite the words, he could tell that she was not really surprised.

"That's right." He stepped closer to her, wishing his nerves would calm down. He had never felt quite like this before. "I reckon you know what's been on my mind."

Shining Moon shook her head no but said nothing.

She was not going to make it easy for him, Clay saw. He took a deep breath. If that was the way things had to be, it was fine with him. He would speak his mind and not hold anything back.

"I've been watching you for a while now, Shining Moon—ever since Jeff and I started coming here to your village, in fact. You've taken good care of us. A man couldn't want a better cook. You've mended our buckskins, helped us with the plews, done everything that anybody could have asked."

"You are pleased with Shining Moon?"

The ingenuous question made Clay's frustration and impatience grow. "Dammit, of course I'm pleased!" he said sharply.

Her chin lifted, and her own voice was curt as she said, "That is why you curse at me, then?"

Clay sighed and rubbed a hand over his face. He

was no good at this sort of thing, and a part of him regretted ever starting the conversation. Now there was nothing left for him to do except plunge ahead.

"I'm sorry I said that. Didn't mean any harm. It's just sort of—difficult for me to tell you what I really want to say."

"And that is?"

He thought he heard a hint of mockery in her tone as she asked the question, and for the first time he began to get an inkling of why the young men of the village tended to shy away from her. She was clever, and she had little patience for fools. Unfortunately, Clay thought, that was exactly what he was making of himself.

He looked at her, meeting her dark eyes squarely, and said, "Shining Moon, you're a beautiful young woman, and I reckon I'm falling in love with you."

Her face lit up. "You—you mean this, Clay Holt?"

"I'm not in the habit of going around lying."

"I know," she said softly. She got to her feet and took a step toward him, and although he searched her eyes intently, he could not determine what she was feeling. He thought he saw some happiness there, but it was more than tempered by a look of regret.

"I know you are an honest man," she said. "I have seen this in you. You and your brother. If all white men were like you, no trouble would come between your people and mine."

She had not yet laughed at him or told him that what he suggested was impossible. That gave Clay some hope, and he reached out and put his hands on her doeskin-clad shoulders. Her eyes looked up into his. He was a strong man, but there was a limit to what he could resist.

And he had just reached that limit.

His mouth came down on hers. Shining Moon seemed to melt against him, her body molding to his. His arms enfolded her, drawing her even closer. The sweet, wet warmth of her lips jolted Clay to his core, awakening sensations and emotions he had not been sure he even possessed. He had kissed plenty of women before, many quite expert in pleasing a man, but never had it been like this. *Never*.

Had he not already been sure he was in love with Shining Moon, he would have been now. He prayed that she was experiencing the same thing he was.

Finally, when the kiss ended, she asked in a whisper, "This thing you do is strange, Clay Holt, but —I think it is good. Do you wish me to be your woman?"

"More than anything else in the world," he replied.

"Then that is what you shall have."

A thought suddenly occurred to him that made him frown slightly. "Wait a minute," he said. "You're not agreeing to this because you think it's what Bear Tooth would want you to do, is it?"

"Do you really think I would allow even Bear Tooth to dictate to me in a matter such as this?"

The tartness of her answer caused him to grin. "No, I reckon not." He reached up and stroked his fingertips along the softness of her cheek. "I should have told you a long time ago, when I first started realizing how I felt."

"I knew."

"But you said you didn't!"

"I did not speak the truth." Now there was definitely a mischievous gleam in her eyes.

As Clay realized what had happened, he was not sure whether to kiss her again or turn her over his knee and spank her. She had watched him fumbling around for the right words and probably enjoyed every second of it. She was a minx, all right.

"Oh, what the hell," he muttered to himself. Then he kissed her again. No point in getting angry.

Not when there were so many other, better ways to spend their time.

Jeff Holt had not been gone long from the tipi he and Clay shared when he ran into Proud Wolf. He had been hoping to find the youngster, so this was a stroke of luck.

Proud Wolf was walking along rapidly, his head down, but the large fire in the center of the camp cast enough light for Jeff to see that the boy's face was creased in concentration. Jeff put out a hand and stopped Proud Wolf with a touch on the arm.

"Slow down there," Jeff said, smiling. "You look like you've got a lot on your mind."

Proud Wolf looked up at Jeff and smiled briefly before his expression became solemn again. "Bear Tooth has entrusted me with an important mission," he told his white friend. "Tomorrow I go to the village of Wind-in-Hair to learn why he and his warriors attacked you."

Jeff tried not to show the surprise he felt. That was indeed a vital job the chief had given Proud Wolf; the future of this part of the country might depend on it. But so did Proud Wolf's self-confidence, and at the moment Jeff was more concerned with that.

"I'm sure Bear Tooth thinks you'll do a good job," he said. "I do, too."

"I will do my best. The young warriors of this village will see that Proud Wolf deserves to be one of them."

"As far as I'm concerned, that's already true." Jeff fell in step beside Proud Wolf as the lad resumed his walk across the village. "Where are you headed now?"

"To see the medicine man of our people. He will search the visions for me and see if my mission will succeed."

Jeff was not sure that was such a good idea. He knew how much stock the Hunkpapa put in their visions and their medicine men. It was all well and good to talk to such an individual—if the message he conveyed was an encouraging one. But if the medicine man told Proud Wolf he was destined to fail, the young man would be more likely to give up before he even got started, or so it seemed to Jeff.

He had to admit, however, that he did not know everything about the way an Indian's mind worked, much less that of Proud Wolf's.

"Mind if I come along with you?" Jeff asked.

"I do not mind, if it is agreeable to North Star. He has very strong medicine. He has seen many visions and can speak with the spirits."

Jeff did not say anything. The Hunkpapa had a right to their own beliefs, even though he himself might not put much stock in things like visions and spirits.

With Proud Wolf leading the way, they went to a small tipi on the outskirts of the village. The hide that had been stretched over a pole framework was lavishly decorated with drawings, even more so than the usual Hunkpapa dwelling.

An old man sat cross-legged in front of the entrance flap. Without looking up at Proud Wolf and Jeff as they came to a stop in front of him, he said, "You have come to seek the wisdom of the spirits." He looked and sounded as if he had been expecting them.

"Yes, Grandfather," Proud Wolf said, using the term as one of respect, rather than relationship. "I wish to know if they will bless my journey."

"Come inside." The old man rose from his sitting position with a grace that belied his years and turned an intent gaze on Jeff.

Even though it was difficult to see North Star's face in the gloom, Jeff could feel the power of his eyes.

"You are a friend to Proud Wolf?" the elderly man asked.

"Yes. He is like a younger brother to me." And that was the truth. Jeff had come to regard Proud Wolf almost in the same way he did Edward and Jonathan. The Hunkpapa who had made Clay and him welcome here were like family now.

"Then you may enter," North Star declared.

Jeff followed the old man and the boy into the tipi. A small fire was flickering in the fire pit. North Star circled it and sank down by the flames, and as he did, he motioned for Jeff and Proud Wolf to sit down as well. They settled themselves on the ground and watched intently as North Star closed his eyes, rocked back and forth slightly, and began to chant in a soft voice. Jeff could not understand what the medicine man was saying, but he felt a small shiver go through him anyway. He sensed that this was the beginning of a powerful ritual.

Of course, a rational man had no business believing in such things, he told himself.

After a few minutes of chanting, North Star drew a small leather pouch from a pocket of his buckskins and opened it. He took a pinch of something from the pouch and tossed it into the fire. The flames changed color, burning a bright green for a moment. North Star took out another pouch and upended it on the ground in front of him, pouring out a jumble of sticks, rocks, feathers, and what looked like small pieces of bone. That was exactly what they were, Jeff decided as he looked closer. The medicine man leaned forward, frowning in concentration as he studied how the contents of the medicine bag had fallen.

Jeff glanced over at Proud Wolf. The boy's features were taut with anticipation. The outcome of the medicine man's conjurings was very important to him.

Abruptly North Star announced, "I see great trouble ahead for you, young one."

Proud Wolf stiffened even more. That was not what he had wanted to hear, Jeff knew. He had been hoping that North Star would speak of glory and success.

"There will be trouble for all our people," the medicine man continued. "Blood shall flow like the rivers of the earth, and the women shall weep. The dead shall cover the fields like flowers."

Jeff had to clamp his jaws firmly shut to prevent himself from lashing out angrily at the old man. What kind of thing was this to tell an impressionable youngster? Proud Wolf was facing probably the most important day of his life so far, and here was this old man filling his head with lurid predictions of blood and death. It made Jeff furious.

Proud Wolf was equally shaken, although he did not seem angry as he said, "This is what you see about the mission I am to go on?"

"I cannot say," the medicine man declared. "The signs and portents are too strong. I cannot tell you to what they refer. I know only that such things lie in the future for our people."

Proud Wolf took a deep breath. "Then it may be the visions do not concern my task."

North Star shrugged slightly.

Proud Wolf got to his feet. "I will succeed," he said, his voice stronger now. "And the vision will be proven wrong." He turned and stalked out of the tipi.

Jeff had not expected him to do that, and he was left sitting there facing the old medicine man across the fire. North Star smiled faintly at him. "The young think nothing is beyond their reach," North Star said quietly. "They do not believe the future, even when it is shown to them. So they strive against what is to be."

"Maybe he's right." Jeff pushed himself up. "I mean no offense, North Star, but it seems to me that what folks do is a lot more important in determining the future than a heap of sticks and old bones."

The medicine man just smiled faintly. Jeff turned and left the lodge, then went looking for Proud Wolf.

He caught up to the boy as Proud Wolf was walking angrily through the village. "Hold on," Jeff said, putting a hand on Proud Wolf's arm. "There's no need to get so upset. The old man was just babbling."

Proud Wolf stopped in his tracks and swung to face Jeff. "That is what you believe, white man," he snapped. "We may be friends, but we are not brothers. I will always be Sioux, and you never can be." He took a deep breath, and Jeff could see that not only was there anger in his expression, but fear lurked there, too. "The visions are never wrong."

"You said you would prove that this time they are."

"That was the talk of an angry little boy. A man knows the truth and must face it."

"So you're giving up before you ever start?"

Proud Wolf took a deep breath. "No. I will do my best. I will fail, but I will know that I tried. My chief will know, and so will my people."

Jeff put a hand on his shoulder. "Maybe this is the time you prove the visions wrong. Has to happen sometime, I reckon."

"Perhaps you are right. We shall see." Proud Wolf glanced over Jeff's shoulder as something else caught his attention.

Jeff turned to see Clay and Shining Moon emerging from the tipi where he had left them. They walked with their heads close together, speaking softly.

Jeff grinned as he turned back to Proud Wolf. "Looks like you and me may wind up related after all. Then you really will be my little brother."

"No," Proud Wolf said. "This cannot be."

"Well, why in the world not?" Jeff asked, startled that the boy would react this way. Maybe he was a little jealous; Shining Moon was the only blood relative Proud Wolf had left, and it could be that he did not want anyone coming between his sister and him.

"It is as North Star said. There will be much trouble."

"I don't see why. Clay's in love with your sister. Shoot, I've known that for a long time, probably before he even realized it himself. I think it's a good thing. He needs somebody to help him forget all the bad things that have happened in his life."

Jeff could tell just by looking at Clay that he had finally spoken his heart to Shining Moon. Jeff remembered how much it had helped to have Melissa to turn to in times of trouble.

The thought of his wife brought on a pang of longing and regret. Not a day went by that he did not miss Melissa with a pain deep in his heart. Come fall, when Manuel Lisa and the trappers went back to St. Louis, Jeff intended to go, too. Maybe enough time had passed so that he could return safely to Ohio and be reunited with his wife. He had not discussed the situation with Clay, figuring that his brother would probably want to stay on the frontier. With the developments that seemed to have taken place between Clay and Shining Moon, that was more likely than ever.

"You do not understand." Proud Wolf's anxious words cut through Jeff's thoughts of home. "I wish that Clay and my sister could be together, too. But it cannot be so. There is another."

Jeff gave him a puzzled frown. "Another? I'm not sure I know what you mean."

"Today, just before you and Clay and the other white men came to the village, Elk Horn went to Bear Tooth—and asked that my sister be his woman."

CHAPTER EIGHTEEN

In the evening we learned, by means of a Snake Indian who happened to be at this place, that one of the old men had been endeavoring to excite prejudices against us, by observing that he thought we were bad men, and came here, most probably, for the purpose of killing them.

—from ''The History of the Lewis and Clark Expedition''

Jeff Holt spent a great deal of the night tossing restlessly, wondering how to tell his brother what Proud Wolf had explained to him earlier.

Elk Horn, whom they had come to know was second only to Bear Tooth in the leadership of the people, was attracted to Shining Moon and had finally decided that she would be his wife. As was customary, Elk Horn had gone to Bear Tooth, Shining Moon's adoptive father, and presented him with three horses in exchange for his daughter's hand in marriage. Shining Moon had attended the meeting between Bear Tooth and Elk Horn, but she had not been allowed to voice her opinion of the arrangement Elk Horn desired. Nor had anything been settled. Bear Tooth had said only that he would consider the matter and announce his decision later.

Jeff had learned all of this from Proud Wolf, who had heard the details from his sister. It complicated things tremendously, taking what should have been a cause for happiness and making it a problem.

Clay was an outsider; there was no getting around that fact. Added to it was Elk Horn's position in the tribe. It would be difficult for Bear Tooth to deny his subchief anything that he wanted within reason. And it was certainly reasonable that Elk Horn should want Shining Moon. She was one of the most beautiful young women in the village.

Not only that, but if it came down to a decision between one of the Hunkpapa and a white man, Bear Tooth would almost have to decide in favor of his fellow clansman. Shining Moon had known all this when Clay revealed his love to her. She should have said something, Jeff thought bitterly as he stared up at the conical tip of the dwelling above him.

Maybe she was not planning to accept Bear Tooth's decision. Maybe she loved Clay so much that she would defy her father. That would certainly lead to trouble. Already, Elk Horn had no use for the white men. Such a stand by Shining Moon would only increase his hatred.

And the worst part about it was that Jeff had been unable to bring himself to tell Clay about any of this. Clay was happier than Jeff had seen him in years, and there was only one explanation for that—Shining Moon. If anybody threatened to take that happiness away from him, things could get bad in a hurry.

That left Jeff lying in the dark, wondering what the devil he was going to do next.

Proud Wolf left before the sun rose the next morning. Clay was not sure how long it would take the boy to reach Wind-in-Hair's village and then return, hopefully with an explanation of why the formerly peaceful Oglala had turned hostile. Two days would be required for the journey, at the very least.

That was all right with Clay. As long as they were waiting for the message Proud Wolf would bring, Clay had a good excuse to stay with Shining Moon.

She was still a model of propriety whenever anyone else was around. When they were alone, however, she demonstrated that she had just as much passion burning within her as he did. Their kisses left both of them shaken to the center of their beings, and it would have been all too easy for them to go ahead and make love. Clay had gently indicated that he wanted to wait, however; more was involved than the simple slaking of a physical need.

Life got complicated, he realized, when one fell in love.

Something else was bothering Shining Moon, too, Clay could tell, although he realized he could never fully fathom her mind. She was in the habit of keeping things to herself. When he asked her if something was troubling her, she merely smiled enigmatically and made no reply. That disturbed him, but he was feeling such relief and excitement that their friendship had finally grown into something stronger that he did not spend a lot of time worrying about it.

Life on the frontier was always hazardous and a little tentative, he told himself. Best to enjoy the good things while you had a chance.

Jeff had something gnawing at him, too, Clay thought, but again, he had too much to be happy about to dwell on his brother's problems. Jeff was probably just missing Melissa and home. In another couple of months Manuel Lisa would head back down the Yellowstone to the Missouri and then on to St. Louis. Jeff could go with him and then make the journey back to Marietta. Whether he would ever return to the frontier or not, Clay could not have said. It would depend on what Jeff found in Ohio. Certainly, if the threat from the Garwoods was gone, Clay would not blame his brother if Jeff stayed and took up farming again.

As for himself, he would never be happy doing that. Not now that he had lived in the wilderness again and had seen even more of its beauty and majesty. Not now that he had found someone to share all of it with him. . . .

One day passed and then another, and still Proud Wolf did not return. There was no cause for concern yet; no one had really expected the youth to get back so quickly. But as the third day dragged on, both Clay and Jeff had to admit they were getting a little worried. Jeff spent most of the day playing cards with Scott and Curry, who seemed more relaxed now about staying in the Hunkpapa village. Clay preferred Shining Moon's company, but she was also anxious for Proud Wolf to return safely. They comforted each other as best they could, talking in vague terms about the future.

Not long before dusk, a shout went up from the edge of the village. Proud Wolf had emerged from the trees and was jogging steadily toward the tipis clustered along the bank of a small brook. Several warriors went out to meet him.

Clay had been talking quietly with Shining Moon when he heard the news. He took a step forward when he saw Proud Wolf, intending to go meet the boy, but Shining Moon stopped him with a light touch on his arm. "My brother will speak first with Bear Tooth."

Clay nodded in understanding. Proud Wolf had been given this mission by the chief and would be expected to deliver his report to Bear Tooth first. Clay wanted to be nearby when that happened, though, so he slipped his hand into Shining Moon's and started toward the chief's dwelling.

Jeff got there about the same time, followed by Scott and Curry. What the youngster had found out would have a direct bearing on their future in the mountains.

Most of the village, in fact, gathered around Bear Tooth's lodge to await Proud Wolf. Bear Tooth came out, followed closely by Elk Horn, who glowered at Clay. Clay knew the subchief did not like him, but Jeff was the only one who was aware of the reason behind Elk Horn's hostility.

The waiting Hunkpapa formed a corridor for Proud Wolf that led to where Bear Tooth stood, arms folded, features expressionless as usual. As Proud Wolf walked past him, Clay thought the youngster appeared a little haggard. That was to be expected. Proud Wolf had run hard and fast, pushing himself to the limit for hours on end. He might be bearing bad news as well.

Proud Wolf came to a stop in front of Bear Tooth, who barked a question at him in the Hunkpapa tongue. Without waiting to catch his breath, Proud Wolf began to speak, his voice revealing his weariness.

Clay tried to understand Proud Wolf's report, and he looked grim as he heard the words "killed by white men" and "women attacked." He could not translate everything Proud Wolf said, but he understood enough to know that the trouble was worse than he had feared.

Jeff could tell the same thing from the reaction of the Hunkpapa listening to the boy's report. Angry glances were directed toward Clay and him and the other two trappers. Elk Horn's expression, none too friendly to begin with, darkened even more. Something was very wrong.

Shining Moon's fingers tightened on Clay's arm. He glanced at her and saw how shaken she was. An angry muttering began around them.

Finally, Proud Wolf fell silent. Bear Tooth put his

hands on the young man's shoulders and spoke. The chief was congratulating him on a job well done, Clay knew, and despite Bear Tooth's concern, his pride for Proud Wolf's accomplishment was evident. After this day, it was doubtful that Proud Wolf would ever again be the target of gibes and belittling comments from the other young men.

After turning away from Proud Wolf, Bear Tooth caught the eyes of Clay and Jeff and summoned them to him with a brusque gesture. Shining Moon stepped back from Clay's side, and the Holts, trailed nervously by Scott and Curry, went over to face the chief.

"You have heard the message Proud Wolf brings to us?" Bear Tooth asked.

"Some of it," Clay replied. "Couldn't follow all of it, though."

"It is bad, as we had feared. Wind-in-Hair says that white men have attacked his men, killing them with firesticks. White men have also raped Oglala women and slit their throats. Wind-in-Hair asks that all Teton Sioux join him and his warriors in killing every white man we can find, so that the others will leave this country and the Oglala and the Hunkpapa and the other Teton tribes can live in peace again."

Clay studied Bear Tooth's stolid features, trying to decide if the chief believed the story or not. It was impossible to tell. Finally, after a few seconds, Clay said carefully, "Wind-in-Hair is a chief of the Teton Sioux and an honorable man. He would not lie. But he could be mistaken. The white men from our fort want only peace with the Indians. You are our friend, Bear Tooth, and we are yours."

Bear Tooth nodded slowly. "What you say is true, Clay Holt," he admitted. "But you and your brother are not the only white men in these mountains. Do you say that you know the hearts of all the men who came with you? Some could have evil in them."

Clay had to agree with the chief. "It could be. Our leader, Manuel Lisa, has told us all to be friends with the Indians and treat them fairly. Some men do not always do as their leaders tell them, though." That might be a hard concept for the Hunkpapa to grasp, Clay knew. The words of their chiefs were law. But he still had to try to salvage this situation.

Jeff spoke up. "We've heard that other white men are in the mountains, too, Chief, besides the ones who came with us to the fort. They call themselves free trappers, and they work for themselves. Could be they're the ones who are causing problems—if Wind-in-Hair's not mistaken about what he told Proud Wolf. Seems to me it's more likely the Blackfoot or the Arikara are the ones behind the trouble, though."

"The Oglala know well the ways of the Blackfoot and the Arikara," Bear Tooth pointed out. "They would not be mistaken for white men. No, I must believe Wind-in-Hair."

That pronouncement caused a chill to go through Clay. He and Jeff and the others were right smack in the middle of several score of Hunkpapa. If Bear Tooth decided to go along with his fellow chief's request and join the war on white men, Clay thought, things could get dicey in a hurry.

"I give you my word," he said to Bear Tooth, "that my brother and my friends and I have never harmed one of your people—except when Wind-in-Hair jumped us, and we didn't have a choice."

Bear Tooth said nothing. But judging by the looks on the faces of many of the warriors surrounding the white men, Clay feared for his life and the lives of the other trappers. The sun had not yet set, but the air seemed suddenly colder.

He and Jeff and the other two had rifles and pistols with them, loaded and primed. They could put up a fight if they had to, but the odds against their escaping from the village were just too heavy. Besides, innocent women and children, including Shining Moon, could be hurt if a brawl started.

Elk Horn was fingering the hilt of the knife at his waist. He spoke up, saying, "We must do as our brothers ask! We must kill the white men!"

He took a step toward Clay.

Tensing, Clay set himself to fight. He was damned if he was just going to stand there and let Elk Horn cut him down.

"No!" Bear Tooth's voice rang out, putting a stop to the violence before it could get started. "There will be no bloodshed here today!" The chief stepped over to Clay and faced him squarely. "I have smoked the pipe of peace with you, Clay Holt. We will talk." He turned and swept his gaze over the rest of the crowd, giving orders in a ringing voice.

Clay could follow enough of the sharply spoken commands to know that Bear Tooth was instructing his people not to molest their white visitors. Heaving a sigh of relief, Clay exchanged a glance with Jeff, then followed Bear Tooth as the chief ducked through the entrance of his tipi. As Clay passed Elk Horn, he saw the disappointment—and the hatred—smoldering in the eyes of the subchief.

While Clay disappeared into the tipi with Bear Tooth, Jeff turned to Scott and Curry and said in a low voice, "We'd best stay close by here, in case Clay needs us. Besides, I reckon it's just about the safest place around here right now."

The other two trappers nodded in anxious agreement.

Inside, Bear Tooth sank to the ground and motioned for Clay to join him. Clay wished that Shining Moon were with him, but he knew this discussion had to be between only Bear Tooth and him. What was said might mean life or death for the dozens of white men back at the fort and in the surrounding mountains.

"You can speak freely now," Bear Tooth told him. "Do you believe Wind-in-Hair was lying when he gave the message to Proud Wolf?"

"Well, as I said, Chief, I think Wind-in-Hair is an honorable man. I'm sure he spoke the truth, as far as he knew it."

"But you do not believe white men have been attacking the Oglala?"

Clay took a deep breath. "None of the white men I know would do such a thing, and Manuel Lisa would never approve of it. But I can't speak for all white men in these parts."

Bear Tooth nodded. "That is what I believe as well. There are renegades among every race. But my people may not be as quick to understand. To many of them, if one white man commits evil against our people, then all white men are to blame."

"You can convince them that's not the way it is, can't you?" Clay leaned forward.

"I cannot promise."

"Then what can we do?"

For the first time since Proud Wolf had arrived with the bad news, Clay detected a trace of a smile on Bear Tooth's face. "I was hoping that you might have some ideas about that, Clay Holt."

Clay regarded the chief for a moment. "I do. The only way the Oglala and the other Teton Sioux will believe that my friends and I had nothing to do with those atrocities is for us to find out who's behind them. And put a stop to them, once and for all."

"And how would you do this?"

"I don't know just yet," Clay admitted. "I'll have to think on it. But I can promise you one thing, Bear Tooth." His expression was fierce as he patted the stock of his Harpers Ferry rifle. "When we find the men who've been doing this, we'll stop them. Permanently."

The short, wiry man walked alone down the trail that led along a wooded ridge. The village of Wind-in-Hair was nearby, and he would reach it soon. He had his .69 caliber flintlock musket primed and loaded, cradled in the crook of his left arm, but he did not seem overly apprehensive about being in the middle of the wilderness, less than half a mile away from a village full of hostile Teton Sioux. He was, in fact, rather relaxed. The plan was proceeding just as he had worked it out.

Duquesne had left his men behind because he knew it would impress the Oglala more if he strolled into their village by himself. Besides, it was possible, though unlikely, that some of the Oglala might recognize one or more of his men. After all, some of the Indians had been permitted to escape when Duquesne's men ambushed them. The plan would not have worked otherwise. There had to be witnesses to go back and tell the others about the murdering white men.

Duquesne hoped that at least some of the inhabitants of Wind-in-Hair's village spoke French. He could handle English well enough, and he even knew enough of the Teton Sioux language to get by in an emergency, but if he could speak to them in French, it would reinforce his claim that he had nothing to do with the men who had killed their warriors and raped and killed their women.

Duquesne's men all spoke English, despite the French heritage many of them shared, and they had been under strict orders to use no other language while they were going about their work. Fluency in English had been one of the requirements when he set about recruiting them.

That, and a willingness to kill ruthlessly, cold-bloodedly, and eagerly.

He was quite pleased with the results. He had wound up with a mixed crew of Frenchmen, Englishmen, and Scots, all of whom took his orders without question—they knew *he* was the most cold-blooded and ruthless of them all. With their cooperation, the opening move in his campaign to force the Americans out of the Rocky Mountains had gone quite well. He had heard rumors that warriors led by Wind-in-Hair himself had already fought with a small group of American trappers. And this was just the beginning, Duquesne told himself. Before he was through, it would be worth the life of any American to be west of St. Louis.

Duquesne spotted the familiar cone-shaped dwellings of the Oglala through the trees. He didn't know if they would have lookouts posted or not, but he was counting on their curiosity to allow him to enter the village. A lone, small white man would surely not represent much of a threat.

Duquesne approached the village and, as he had expected, was not challenged, although a group of warriors waited for him, confirming his suspicion about sentries. He watched the waiting Oglala closely as he walked toward them, deliberately casual in his pace and bearing. He lifted his right hand and extended it palm outward in the universal sign of peace. Several of the men held bows with arrows already nocked; others clutched tomahawks or knives. They could riddle him with arrows or fall on him and hack him to pieces in a matter of moments. It was no surprise they were willing to wait and indulge their wonder at this foolish white man.

He stopped when twenty feet separated him from the lookouts. His palm still out, he greeted them in French. For a moment he was afraid none of them understood him, but then one glowered at him and growled in surly tones, "Why are you here, white man? Do you not know we kill white men now?"

Duquesne smiled. "You kill Americans," he said, still in French. "I am not one of them."

The Oglala warrior spoke swiftly to one of his companions, a sturdily built man with a bandage on one leg. This man nodded solemnly, and Duquesne decided he was Wind-in-Hair, the chief of this band. The one who spoke French leaned forward and spat contemptuously. The spittle did not reach Duquesne's feet, but the meaning of the gesture was plain enough.

"All white men are same," the warrior said.

"You are wrong. I hate the Americans just as much as you do. That is why I have come to help you fight them."

"Why would you fight your own people?"

"I am French, not American," Duquesne repeated proudly. "I am a voyageur. Men such as I have come to these mountains for many moons. I have spent many winters in the mountains north of here, in the land called Canada. Like you, I wish to drive the Americans from this land so that your people and mine can live in peace once more."

After a few seconds of quick discussion in the Oglala tongue, the words flying too quickly for Duquesne to keep up with them, the first man turned to him once again and said, "You speak the same tongue as the man from the north who told us about the Great Spirit. This man was wrong about many things; still he was friend to the Oglala."

"As I wish to be," Duquesne said quickly. "I have heard how the white men from the fort have committed great wrongs against your people. That is why I have come to you now. I wish to give you the means to take your revenge!"

That final word seemed to communicate itself better to the Indians than anything else he had been saying. It drew an immediate reaction. The men talked among themselves, and Duquesne could see the angry looks on their faces.

His plan was working. He could sense it. Wind-in-Hair grasped the shoulder of the translator and talked rapidly for a moment. Then the man turned back to Duquesne and asked, "How would you help us?"

Duquesne had fished in mountain streams before. He knew when a fish had taken the bait and when it was time to set the hook. He did so now by grasping his musket, one hand on the stock just behind the trigger, the other on the barrel, then thrusting the weapon into the air over his head. "With this!" he said.

That gesture brought more muttering from the assembled men.

"With one firestick?" the translator asked scornfully.

"No. With many firesticks."

That got their interest, just as he had intended. When the talk had died down again, the translator asked, "You have many firesticks?"

"Not with me, no. But I can get them, and I will give them to the Oglala in return for beaver pelts and the promise that you will use the weapons only against the Americans."

"How will we know which white men are Americans?"

"You can recognize the ugly sound of the tongue they speak," Duquesne pointed out. "And you know many of them by sight, since they have been in this country for many seasons, pretending to be friends with you and the other Teton Sioux so that you will not be suspicious when they betray you. None of them can be trusted." Duquesne came down hard on that point. "All of them must be killed or forced to leave these mountains. Only then will your people know peace again."

He could see the look of agreement on the faces of many of the men as they glanced at Wind-in-Hair to see what his reaction would be. Even though Duquesne had convinced most of the warriors, he knew his plan would not work unless the chief himself went along with it.

Wind-in-Hair strode forward, limping from the wound on his thigh. Duquesne did not move as the chief came up to him, planted himself only feet away, and looked intently into his eyes. Wind-in-Hair would see only sincerity there, Duquesne knew. He was well practiced at hiding his evil.

After glaring at him for a moment that seemed far longer than it was, the chief nodded abruptly and reached out. Duquesne took a deep breath and placed the musket in Wind-in-Hair's hands. He was convinced he had won over the chief, but this was still a nerve-racking situation. The Indian could turn the musket on him and kill him, and there would be little Duquesne could do to stop him.

Instead, Wind-in-Hair's leathery face creased in a humorless smile, and he turned to face his warriors. With a whoop, he flung his arms up, holding the musket over his head much as Duquesne had a few minutes earlier. The warriors screeched back at their chief, shaking their bows, 'hawks, and knives in the air. This demonstration sent a chill through Duquesne, but at the same time, he felt a surge of exultation. He had done exactly what he set out to do.

And although this was just the first step, there was no doubt in his mind that he would be successful.

The American trappers were doomed.

"We'll start back to the fort first thing in the morning," Clay said to Jeff, Scott, and Curry when he emerged from Bear Tooth's tent. Night was falling, and that was the only reason the white men were not setting out for home immediately.

"What else did the two of you decide?" Jeff asked.

"I promised Bear Tooth we'd try to find out who's been attacking the other clans around here, and that we'd put a stop to it when we do. In return, he's pledged that we'll be safe here tonight and while we're on our way back to the fort."

Curry scratched his beard and looked worried. "That safe conduct, that's only good where his bunch is concerned, ain't it?"

"That's the best I could do. We'll keep our eyes open. We ought to be able to make it back without any trouble."

Jeff said, "What's this going to do to the trapping business?"

"It's going to play hell with it for a while," Clay replied bluntly. "Word of the trouble is going to get around, and the other Teton tribes will be after us every time we get too far from the fort. God knows what's going on up in Crow territory. If some white renegades are attacking the Teton tribes, I reckon it's a safe bet they'll stir up trouble with the Crow, too, sooner or later." Clay's face was grim as he went on, "We're all in for a bad time if we don't get to the bottom of this pretty quick."

He had not even mentioned the worst of it, at least as far as he was concerned. These developments meant that he would have to be apart from Shining Moon. It was unfair, he thought, damned unfair. He had finally gotten up the courage to tell her how he felt—and had discovered to his joy that she felt the same way about him—only to be forced to leave her and return to the fort.

But why did he have to do that? the question occurred to him. Why couldn't she just go back to the fort with him? They could have a wedding ceremony in the village, or whatever the Hunkpapa custom was. He was not sure about that, but there had to be some way of bonding two people together for life. That was good enough for him. He could take Shining Moon back to the fort with him as his wife.

The more he thought about it, the more the idea appealed to him. He would still have to convince Shining Moon, however.

"You boys go on back to your tipi," he told Scott and Curry.

Curry asked skittishly, "You sure that's safe?"

"It's the safest place for you to be tonight, that's for damn sure," Clay said. "Jeff and I will be staying close to home, too. Like I said, we'll pull out at first light."

"I'm keepin' Ol' Leadspitter handy," Scott vowed.

Clay could not argue with that. He did not intend to let his rifle stray very far from his hand either.

As the two trappers moved off, casting nervous glances around them, Clay looked at Jeff and asked, "What happened to Proud Wolf?"

"Shining Moon took him back to their tipi," Jeff said. "He was pretty played out. She was going to give him some stew and see that he got some rest."

Clay wanted to talk to Shining Moon as soon as

possible, but he would not interrupt her while she was caring for her brother. "Come on," he said to Jeff. "I'd just as soon we stayed out of sight as much as we can tonight. No need in stirring up any more bad feelings."

Already, they were being given unfriendly stares by many of the village's inhabitants. The crowd that had gathered to listen to the message Proud Wolf brought back from Wind-in-Hair had broken up, but dozens of Hunkpapa were still standing close by. Men, women, and children were all regarding the Holts suspiciously. Clay could understand why Scott and Curry were jumpy. He was nervous himself.

The only thing that had saved them so far was the fact that Bear Tooth was a wise, patient leader. If some hothead like Elk Horn had been in charge when Proud Wolf brought the news of white atrocities against Oglala women, no doubt Clay, Jeff, and their companions would be dead by now, their hair decorating the tipis of their killers.

Clay and Jeff reached the tipi they had been using, pushed aside the entrance flap, and stepped inside. To Clay the dwelling seemed emptier than it should have. It was amazing, he thought, how much Shining Moon's presence changed the place. Without her it was just ugly pieces of smoke-stinking hide lashed to poles.

Twigs and bark had been laid in the fire pit for kindling, and Clay knew that was Shining Moon's handiwork. She had prepared the fire before Proud Wolf's return with the bad news. Jeff knelt beside the pit and used flint and tinder to get the small blaze going. The light from the crackling flames dispelled the gloom of twilight and should have made the tipi seem cheerier, but it did not have that effect on Clay. Sitting, he stared broodingly into the fire.

Jeff sank down on the ground and watched his brother for a moment. "Clay, I've never known you to stare into a fire before. You know it'll blind you for a little while."

Clay looked down, swept the coonskin cap off his head, then rubbed his temples wearily. "You're right," he admitted. "I reckon I've got so much on my mind I wasn't thinking clearly."

"This trouble between us and the Oglala, you mean?"

"That," Clay nodded, "and something else." He took a deep breath and made a decision. Jeff deserved to know what he was planning. "It's about Shining Moon—"

The entrance flap was thrust aside, and she stepped through the opening, stopping short as she heard Clay speak her name. "What is about Shining Moon?" she asked, giving Clay a faint smile.

Clay lithely rose. "It can wait a minute," he told her, wishing that Jeff were not there so he could speak privately with the young woman. However, given the current mood of the village, he was not going to ask Jeff to leave. Whether he was embarrassed by it or not, his marriage proposal was going to have a witness. But before he got to that, he asked, "How's Proud Wolf?"

"Very tired," Shining Moon said, "but he will be all right. He is sleeping now."

"Good. I reckon he's mighty pleased with himself."

"He did what his chief told him to do. Any warrior would be proud of that. But he is very upset about the words he brought back from Wind-in-Hair. He does not believe his white friends would do such evil things as Wind-in-Hair said."

"I'm glad to hear that," Jeff said. "Proud Wolf knows us well enough to realize it's all some kind of bad mistake."

"As do I," Shining Moon agreed. She stepped closer to Clay. "When I came in, you were speaking my name. . . ."

She was not going to let him pass off the issue, and to be honest, he did not want to. He stepped over to her and rested his big hands on her shoulders. She looked up at him, her gaze both curious and slightly apprehensive, as if she were anxious to know what he was going to say but also a bit frightened by the possibilities.

"Jeff and I are going back to the fort first thing in the morning," Clay began. "I don't know how long it'll be before we can return here safely, but it's liable to be a while. I know one thing, Shining Moon. I don't want to be away from you that long. I don't think I could stand it."

"And I want to be with you," she murmured softly. "But if it is not safe for you to be here, you must go. My heart would die if anything happened to you, Clay Holt."

"I feel the same way." Lord, this was hard! He took a deep breath and hurried on, "That's why I want you to go back to the fort with us. I want to marry you, Shining Moon, and I want to marry you now."

He heard the startled exclamation from Jeff but did not turn to look at his brother. All of Clay's attention was focused on Shining Moon. He saw the sudden shimmer of tears in her eyes and thought for one joyous instant that she was crying with happiness; but then her features contorted in pain, and she sagged against him, sobs racking her body. Clay put his arms around her and held her tight. Something was very wrong.

Jeff got to his feet and moved beside them. He put a hand on Clay's shoulder and said hesitantly, "I was about to tell you when she came in, Clay."

Clay jerked his head around to stare at his brother. "You *know* what this is all about?" he demanded.

Jeff's expression was grim. "Elk Horn has asked Bear Tooth's permission to take Shining Moon as his woman."

A surge of anger shot through Clay. "Elk Horn?" he repeated. "That surly bastard?"

Shining Moon was able to speak through her

tears. "He—he is a mighty warrior and the subchief of the tribe. Bear Tooth will give him what he wants."

Cupping her chin, Clay tilted her head back slightly so that he could look down into her eyes again. "What do you want?" he asked.

"You know the answer, Clay Holt. I want to be with you."

"Then why are you even worrying about Elk Horn?" Impatience and frustration put an edge on his voice. "You told me once you wouldn't let Bear Tooth tell you what to do with your life. If that's still true, you don't have anything to worry about."

Shining Moon drew a deep, ragged breath. "When I told you that, I did not think that you—that you wanted me to become your woman for life. I thought you wanted me only for—for pleasure. If you had asked me then, I would have come to your blanket. I would have been with you for a short time, and I would have been content with that. At least I would have had your memory. Because I knew the first time I saw you, Clay Holt, that I loved you."

Clay's face felt warm, and he was having a little trouble breathing. The words Shining Moon had spoken had shaken him clear through. "I reckon I loved you, too," he whispered.

"Then why did you never take me to your blanket?"

"Because I wanted more than that, dammit!" He passed a hand wearily over his face. "Deep down, I reckon I knew I wanted whatever we had between us to last forever."

She pressed her face against his shoulder and began to sob again. Clay stroked her hair and glanced at Jeff, who had sat down again and was looking the other way, giving them as much privacy as he could under the circumstances. Clay appreciated that gesture, but right now, he needed all the help he could get to straighten out this tangled mess.

"Jeff," he said, "what do you reckon we ought to do?"

With a shake of his head, Jeff said, "I can't tell you that, big brother."

"Dammit, Jeff—"

Shining Moon lifted her head and broke in on Clay's angry words. "He is right, my love. Only I can settle this, and there is only one thing I can do." She met his eyes squarely. "I will remain here and become the woman of Elk Horn."

Clay felt as if a punch had just been slammed into his gut. He wanted to reel backward. Instead, he tightened his grip on Shining Moon. "What?"

"You know what I say is true," she said, her voice growing cool now. "I am Hunkpapa, not white. I belong here with my people, not closed up in some white man's fort."

"You wouldn't be staying at the fort forever," Clay argued. "Sooner or later, things'll settle down, and there will be peace between your people and mine again. Then both of us could live wherever we wanted. Part of the time at the fort, part of the time here. The rest of the time we'd be out trapping beaver. It could work out just fine, Shining Moon, believe me!"

"I cannot," she said, her voice taut. "And I cannot go against the will of my father, my chief."

"Has Bear Tooth said you have to marry Elk Horn?" Clay asked quickly.

She shook her head. "Not yet. But he will—".

"Not if I go to him first and ask for you myself!" He started to pull away from her, as if he intended to stalk out of the lodge and go to see Bear Tooth that very instant.

She clutched his arm. "No! You cannot do that! Already, many warriors in the village say you and Jeff and the others should be killed. It will only make things worse if they know that a white man wants me for his own. Not even Bear Tooth would be able to keep them from killing you!"

Clay did not believe that; Bear Tooth's command

of his people was very strong. But the rest of what she had to say made sense. He hesitated.

"You must stay here," she pleaded, "out of sight for the rest of the night. And tomorrow, you must go back to the fort as quickly as you can. It is no longer safe for any of you in these mountains."

"She's right, Clay," Jeff said quietly.

Clay blinked several times, his features a study in confusion. Finally he said, "Dammit, why do the two of you have to be so reasonable?" He turned back to face Shining Moon, his expression growing bleaker. "You don't want to be my wife?" he demanded.

She managed to shake her head. "I cannot. And I no longer wish to."

"You're sure of that?"

"I pledge you my word on it, Clay Holt."

"Well, that's all there is to it, then, isn't it?" He started to reach out to her again, but he let his hand fall to his side before his fingers touched her. "If that's the way you want it, I won't argue with you anymore." He turned and strode over to his blanket. "Think I'll turn in and get some sleep. It was a long day, and tomorrow'll be even longer."

He lay down, rolled into his blanket, and turned his back to the other two occupants of the lodge. Nothing more was said. After a few minutes, Clay made his breathing fall into a rhythmic pattern, as if he were asleep. Actually his eyes were open, and he was staring at the wall of the tipi.

It seems as if the Holts are born to trouble, Clay thought. Here they were in the middle of a Teton Sioux camp, surrounded by savages who wanted them dead. Jeff's wife was hundreds of miles away, and he might never see her again. As for himself, the woman he wanted no longer wanted him, and at this moment, that depressed him more than anything else.

Yet, as bad as things had gotten, he was absolutely convinced that they would get even worse.

*　　*　　*

Along toward morning, something disturbed Jeff's slumber. He was a light sleeper most of the time, but that night he was even more on edge. As he opened his eyes, he saw a figure moving stealthily out of the entrance of the tipi. The embers of the fire cast enough of a glow for him to make out the soft doeskin dress worn by Shining Moon.

Jeff glanced at Clay. He had been well aware that his brother was only shamming sleep earlier in the night, but now Clay's snores were the real thing. Shining Moon's departure had not roused him.

Quickly Jeff threw back his blanket and got to his feet. He hurried to the tipi's entrance and pushed through the flap. There, in the faint light of the stars, stood Shining Moon, about five feet from the tipi.

He stepped out and let the flap fall shut behind him. The village was quiet; somewhere a dog growled, but that was the only sound Jeff heard other than the usual night noises. His voice little more than a whisper, he said, "Shining Moon?"

She turned sharply. "Oh! I did not mean to disturb you, Jeff Holt. I am sorry."

"Don't be," he said, moving closer to her. "I don't reckon it would hurt for you and me to talk a little."

"Talk—about what?"

"You and my brother." Jeff paused, then said, "He loves you, you know."

"And I—I love him."

"If that's really true, then why don't you—"

"Go with him?" she finished. She shook her head. "I cannot. Even if I wished to, I cannot."

A suspicion began to lurk in the back of Jeff's mind, and he gave voice to it. "Because if you said you were going back to the fort with Clay, Elk Horn would challenge him, would want to fight him for you. Is that it?"

"It is the way of the Hunkpapa."

"And you're afraid Clay would be hurt, maybe killed." This time it was a statement, not a question. "You really do love him, don't you?"

"Of course."

"You love him enough to stay here and marry another man, just because you think Clay might be hurt if you don't."

"You think I am an awful woman," Shining Moon accused.

"No," Jeff said softly. "I don't think that at all. But I do feel sorry for you."

She turned abruptly to him, her graceful movements suddenly reminding him of the great panthers he and Clay had spotted a few times in their travels through the mountains.

"I do not want your pity," she said. "And I do not want you telling your brother any of the things we have said. Do I have your word on this, Jeff Holt?"

He hesitated before answering. If Clay knew her real motivation for refusing him, he would probably go and challenge Elk Horn himself. Clay was more than hotheaded enough to do that. With all the trouble that already existed between the white men and the Teton Sioux, a fight over a Hunkpapa woman would only make things worse.

Especially if Clay defeated, perhaps even killed, Elk Horn. Jeff knew that might happen.

"I won't say anything," he promised. "And I'll see to it we leave in the morning like we're supposed to. But I hope you know what you're doing, Shining Moon."

"I pray to the Wakan Tanka it is so," she said simply.

CHAPTER NINETEEN

There are crimes which may be committed without a breach of our present laws, and which make it necessary that some further restrictions than those contained in the present licenses of our traders should either be added . . . or else be punished by way of a discretionary power lodged in the superintendent, extending to the exclusion of such individuals from the Indian trade. . . .

First, that of holding conversations with Indians tending to bring our government into disrepute among them, and to alienate their affections from the same.

Second, that of practicing any means to induce Indians to maltreat or plunder other merchants.

Third, that of stimulating or exciting, by bribes or otherwise, any nations or bands; or against the citizens of the United States; or against citizens or subjects of any power at peace with the same.

—MERIWETHER LEWIS, from "Essay on the Indian Policy"

Shining Moon was gone the next morning when Clay woke up and if Jeff knew where she was, he did not say. Instead, he urged Clay to join him in getting their gear together quickly. Curry and Scott were ready to go; they had been at the tipi of the Holt brothers when dawn was still a gray shadow in the sky to the east, urging them to get moving.

When the four trappers were ready to leave, Bear Tooth himself accompanied them to the edge of the village. Once again the white men were the targets of many angry, suspicious glares from the other Indians.

"Do not linger," Bear Tooth advised them. "I have instructed my people that you are not to be harmed on your journey to the fort, and I have sent runners to the other villages of the Sioux asking that they honor my pledge as well. I cannot be certain that they will do so."

"We understand, Chief. And we appreciate what you've done for us. You have our word that we'll do everything we can to see to it the day comes when the white man and the Hunkpapa can live together in peace again."

"Let it be so, my friend," Bear Tooth replied solemnly.

As Clay turned away he let his eyes sweep one last time over the assembled crowd. He could not spot Shining Moon anywhere. Elk Horn was much in evidence, however. He was standing near Bear Tooth with his arms crossed and hatred burning in his eyes.

He knows, Clay thought abruptly. *He knows about Shining Moon and me.*

A shiver ran through him. He was not afraid of Elk Horn, but he knew he and the others would have to be mighty careful on their way back to the fort. Elk Horn might view this journey as a perfect opportunity to dispose of a rival, in spite of Bear Tooth's edict guaranteeing their safety. If Elk Horn did ambush them, he could always blame the attack on some other group of Teton.

"We'd best get moving." Clay shifted his pack slightly on his back. "We've got a lot of ground to cover, and we're wasting daylight."

The four white men trudged away from the Indian camp. They had gone about a hundred yards when a faint shout made them pause and look back. A slight figure was running after them. It was Proud Wolf, Clay realized as the young man drew nearer.

Proud Wolf clasped Jeff's arm at once and said, "You were leaving without bidding farewell to your friends?"

Jeff said, "Sorry. I didn't figure it would do your new standing in the tribe any good to be saying good-bye to us. Most of your friends think we're the enemies now."

"Proud Wolf knows better," the youth said. "You will be back, and everything will be all right again."

"I hope so. I really do." Jeff squeezed the young man's shoulder.

Clay said good-bye to him as well, and then Proud Wolf stood there watching as the white men walked away. Clay hoped the boy's gesture of saying farewell would not cause him trouble.

Setting a good pace, the group walked all morning, finally reaching a small creek that would eventually lead them to the Big Horn. When they had been through that area before, they had cached a couple of canoes in a clump of brush near the stream. When Clay and Jeff checked, the birchbark craft were still there and in good shape. Traveling by water would get them back to the fort that much sooner, and Clay figured that if they wanted to risk paddling at night, they might even reach it by the next morning.

That was what they did. Trying to navigate the river in darkness was chancy, but so was staying in the wilderness an hour longer than they absolutely had to. With Clay guiding them from the forward position in the front canoe, the four trappers glided along the Big Horn during the night and, not long after dawn the next morning, spotted the impressive log fort in the confluence of the rivers ahead of them.

"Doesn't look like Elk Horn's going to have a try at us," Jeff commented. "Reckon he didn't want to go against Bear Tooth after all."

"Can't blame him for that," Clay replied. "But if Elk Horn's lying low now, it's just so he can hit us that much harder in the future. He's got a grudge against white men, and he's not going to give it up until he figures he's won—which will mean running all the whites out of the territory."

"He'll never be able to do that," Jeff said, frowning.

"Nope. But he can see to it that a lot of people get killed while he's trying."

They fell silent, concentrating their efforts on paddling instead of talking, and less than a quarter of an hour later they were grounding the canoes on the bank of the river near the fort.

A shot was fired inside the stockade, no doubt by a lookout announcing their arrival, and before they could reach it, the gates swung open and a small group of men marched out, led by Manuel Lisa himself. The sturdy-looking Spaniard had a grim expression, and as he reached out to clasp Clay's hand in greeting, he said, "I will wager you had trouble while you were out, yes?"

"Sure did. Pretty bad trouble, too. Tompkins has gone under, and the rest of us nearly followed him." Quickly Clay explained how they had been attacked by Wind-in-Hair's warriors, then told what they had learned at Bear Tooth's village.

Lisa said, "Our men killing the Teton and raping their women? Impossible!"

"Not really," Jeff put in. "We don't know what all the men do when they're away from the fort. And there're probably some free trappers in the mountains we never see."

"You've heard about other trouble besides what

we ran into," Clay guessed as he noted Lisa's serious expression.

"Yes, I am afraid so. Two days ago, one of the men returned here. The group he was with had been ambushed, and he was the only one who survived. He ran here with the Oglala following him, and he made it even with an arrow in his back." Lisa's mouth tightened into a thin line. "He died a few hours later, but not until after he had brought word to us of the trouble. I knew when he insisted the Oglala were responsible for the massacre that something was badly wrong. You gentlemen have confirmed it."

"We've got to put a stop to whoever's stirring up the tribes of the Teton Sioux," Clay said. "Otherwise, we won't ever be able to work in these mountains again."

"I fear you are right. Come, let us go inside. We must decide on a course of action."

They could really do very little, however, and that was the conclusion they came to after several hours of discussion. Lisa agreed to question all his men about the atrocities committed against the Oglala, but if any of the trappers in the group were responsible, they would not be likely to admit it. If free trappers were the ones doing the killing, Lisa's group would have great difficulty proving it.

"We will continue trapping," Lisa finally decided. "We will travel in large groups, and only one or two groups at a time will leave. That way we will not be spreading ourselves too thin to defend the fort—its security must not be compromised. Keep your eyes open, gentlemen, not only to protect yourselves, but also in hopes of discovering who is to blame for this dreadful situation. Only by doing that can we put things back as they were."

Lisa was not saying anything that Clay and Jeff did not already know all too well. They would go along with the decision of their leader and hope for the best. Right now, that was all they could do.

* * *

Without his new friends Proud Wolf was lonely. Although Jeff and Clay had visited the Hunkpapa village only sporadically, Proud Wolf had looked forward to their visits and had been sad when they left. The most recent departure was the saddest of all, since there was a chance they might never come back.

He knew his sister was upset, too, although she did not say anything to him about it. To Shining Moon, he supposed, he would always be a little boy. But he knew his sister loved Clay Holt and that her love had been returned.

After it was announced that Elk Horn would take Shining Moon as his wife, Proud Wolf went to the dwelling he and his sister shared and demanded of her, "Why have you done this, my sister?"

"I have done nothing," she replied. "Elk Horn asked Bear Tooth for me to be given to him, and as my chief and adopted father, Bear Tooth has the right to do as he pleases. There is nothing for me to decide."

"But if you had told Bear Tooth you did not want to be with Elk Horn, he would not have forced you to accept," Proud Wolf protested. "It is Clay Holt you care for."

Shining Moon would not meet his eyes. She merely shrugged and went about her business.

Proud Wolf stared at her, his frustration growing. Suddenly a thought occurred to him, and he said, "You did this to protect Clay Holt, did you not?"

She looked sharply at him. "You will not repeat that to anyone," she commanded sternly.

Proud Wolf knew he had stumbled onto the truth. His sister cared so much for Clay Holt that she was trying to protect him by driving him away. Elk Horn's hatred of white men in general and Clay in particular was well-known, as was his skill as a warrior. Given the slightest excuse, Elk Horn would challenge Clay to meet him in battle, and the subchief would not hesitate to kill the white man if he got a chance.

"You are a very brave woman," Proud Wolf said softly to his sister.

"And you are a foolish young man—most of the time." She smiled slightly and touched his hand. "Leave me now. Go hunting with your friends. Do whatever you wish. But do not waste your time hoping that Clay and Jeff will return. Fate and the Wakan Tanka have stolen them away."

That was hard for Proud Wolf to accept, but perhaps his sister was right. As much as he missed his white friends, life had to continue. Still, over the next few weeks, Jeff and Clay Holt were never far from Proud Wolf's mind.

Word arrived in Bear Tooth's village that more men had been killed, more women molested by roving gangs of white trappers, not only in Teton country but to the north as well, where the Crow lived. A flame was growing on the frontier, a flame of anger and hatred that threatened to explode into a blaze that would consume every white man in the area. Proud Wolf had already heard Elk Horn say on more than one occasion that the Hunkpapa should not wait but should move in force against the fort of the white men. If the fort was overrun and burned to the ground, the white men who survived would be easy to track down and kill.

Proud Wolf felt sickened by such war talk, but he could do nothing to stop it. None of the warriors would have listened to him, not even Bear Tooth. Despite the way he had fulfilled his task as runner to Wind-in-Hair's village, he was, after all, still a boy. Helpless rage seethed inside him. He had to be able to do something.

Then the Frenchman called Duquesne came to the village.

A stir of excitement went through the camp when scouts brought news that a lone white man was approaching. Elk Horn was all for ambushing him and killing him right away, before he had a chance to escape, but Bear Tooth overruled him and counseled caution.

"This man must have a great deal of courage," the chief decided, "not to mention an important message for us. Otherwise, he would not risk his life by coming here alone."

Proud Wolf was among the crowd waiting eagerly when the white man walked into the village. The stranger stopped some yards away from the group of armed warriors. He lifted his voice and called out in French, "I am looking for the warrior known as Bear Tooth."

This was the first time Proud Wolf had heard French spoken since the missionary had left the tribe, several years before. The stranger's voice was level, calm, and seemingly unafraid, and it was matched by his casual demeanor. A moment after he had spoken, Bear Tooth stepped forward and said, "I am he whom you seek. I am called Bear Tooth. What do you want with the Hunkpapa?"

"I am Duquesne," the small, bearded man said. "And I have come to help the Hunkpapa in their fight against the invaders of their land."

"You speak of the white trappers?"

"The Americans, yes. They are the ones killing your men and using your women, are they not?"

"So it is said," Bear Tooth replied carefully. "There has been no trouble among our people."

Duquesne smiled, but it was not a particularly pleasant expression. "Then fortune has truly smiled upon you and your people, Bear Tooth. The Americans have brought death and suffering to many of your brothers in other villages."

"We have heard this talk," Bear Tooth admitted.

Elk Horn spoke up. "But still we wait!" he said angrily. "We wait instead of joining our brothers in fighting the hated whites!" A murmur of support ran through the crowd of warriors, making Proud Wolf uneasy as he stood among them. He did not like the turn this conversation was taking.

Duquesne patted the stock of the muskets cradled in his arm. "I have many firesticks," he said. "I will give them to the Hunkpapa of Bear Tooth, and then to other Teton and the Crow, as I have given them to the Oglala of Wind-in-Hair. Soon the mountains and the valleys will run red with American blood, and I ask you to join in this battle!"

Whoops of approval went up from many of the warriors, including Elk Horn. Bear Tooth frowned at him, but this time the subchief did not shrink under the stern look from his leader. Elk Horn was caught up in a frenzy of hate, as were most of the other men. As Proud Wolf looked around nervously, he sensed that events were slipping beyond Bear Tooth's control.

Someone had to put a stop to this—now.

Proud Wolf stepped forward, his small stature making it easier for him to slip through the press of warriors facing Duquesne. As Proud Wolf emerged from the shouting group, he pointed a finger at the diminutive Frenchman and called out in as loud a voice as he could muster, "You lie!"

That quieted the others down, and they stared at him, surprised by his temerity. Proud Wolf gulped down his fear and went on. "The white men have always been friends of the Hunkpapa and the other Teton. The stories about them doing evil are lies!"

Duquesne regarded him coolly. After a moment, he said, "You know this for a fact, do you, boy?"

"I know my friends would not harm the Teton," Proud Wolf replied boldly. He could feel Bear Tooth's eyes on him, but he did not look around to see how the chief was reacting to his bold action.

"If you're so fond of the Americans, boy," Duquesne said, a faint sneer on his face, "maybe you should go live with them."

"I am Hunkpapa, and my place is here," Proud Wolf shot back. "But I will not stand by while you lie."

"And I will not waste my time arguing with a boy." Duquesne turned his attention back to Bear Tooth. "What is your decision, Bear Tooth? Will you accept my help and let me give you firesticks to fight the Americans?"

Elk Horn urged Bear Tooth to agree, but the chief stood silently, his face masklike. Finally, he said, "I will think on this," then turned and stalked away.

When he was gone, Elk Horn and several others crowded around Duquesne, talking quickly in their native tongue and examining his musket. Proud Wolf hung back, not wanting to get any closer to the Frenchman. Something about Duquesne made Proud Wolf uneasy. The man was evil; Proud Wolf was convinced of that.

The others could not seem to see what he could, though. Urged on by Elk Horn, they considered the Frenchman an instrument of vengeance against the white men, delivered to them, no doubt, by the hand of the Wakan Tanka. To the Hunkpapa way of thinking, there was no point in trying to fight what fate had decreed would be. They were meant to take the firesticks and kill white men with them; otherwise, Duquesne would never have come here.

Proud Wolf felt as if everyone in the world had gone mad except him. He turned and hurried toward his tipi, hoping to find Shining Moon there. At least she would be reasonable, he told himself.

He had gone only a few steps when he felt something like the touch of a spider brush the back of his neck. When he stopped and turned, nothing was there. Several yards away, though, the man called Duquesne was looking at him, eyes narrowed with dislike and suspicion, and Proud Wolf knew that he had sensed the man's scrutiny. After glaring back for a second, Proud Wolf turned and stalked away. As he left he heard Duquesne telling Elk Horn and the other warriors how they should attack the Americans' fort, just as Elk Horn had suggested earlier.

A shiver ran through Proud Wolf. Jeff and Clay would surely be killed in such an assault.

Shining Moon was sitting in the tipi, mending a doeskin tunic, when Proud Wolf entered. At least that was what she was supposed to be doing; she did not seem to be concentrating on the task.

"There is an evil man in the village," Proud Wolf said.

"I know. I heard some of the things he was saying. This is a sad day, my brother. Soon there will be much bloodshed and death." Her voice was dull, resigned.

"We must do something to stop it!"

At her brother's outburst, Shining Moon looked up. "What can we do? A woman and a boy—who will listen to us?"

"Elk Horn said our warriors should attack the fort. Now this man Duquesne tells them the same thing and promises them muskets with which to kill Americans." Proud Wolf paced back and forth, his anger making it impossible for him to remain still. "Someone should warn Jeff and Clay and the other trappers!"

For the first time, a flicker of interest shone in Shining Moon's eyes. "What you say is true. They should know of this man—Duquesne, you called him? They should know he is traveling through the mountains, spreading lies about them and trying to goad the tribes into war."

Proud Wolf thumped a fist against his chest. "I will tell them," he declared.

Shining Moon did not seem surprised by her brother's announcement. She knew him well enough to understand the way his mind worked. "It is a long way to the fort of the white men," she cautioned.

"I know. But I have been there before, and I remember the way. I can reach it in two days."

"Perhaps I should go with you."

"No," Proud Wolf said. "I can travel faster alone."

"That is so." Shining Moon got to her feet and put her hands on her brother's shoulders. "Go, then, and warn our friends. But take care as you do so."

Proud Wolf nodded. Already he was consumed

with the idea of this new mission. "I will leave today, as soon as I tell Bear Tooth."

"No. We cannot tell Bear Tooth."

"But he is our leader," Proud Wolf said, confused. "It is his right to know what his people do."

"Not this time," Shining Moon insisted. "Bear Tooth is undecided about the white men. He may decide that Elk Horn is right, that Clay and Jeff and the others are our enemies. He must not know you are trying to help them."

Proud Wolf could see the reasoning in what his sister said, but it still bothered him to think about doing something behind the back of their father and their chief. On the other hand, he did not want to take a chance that Bear Tooth might forbid him from journeying to the fort.

"I will do as you say," he told Shining Moon. "I will leave now, taking only what I have to for the trip. If anyone asks you where I am—"

"I will tell them you have gone hunting," Shining Moon finished.

Since Proud Wolf had few friends among the Sioux, it was not unusual for him to go into the woods on his own, spending days at a time away from the village. He had been on such a trip, hunting by himself, when he first encountered Clay and Jeff Holt and saved them from the Arikara. Since the advent of the trouble between the white men and the Indians in recent weeks, he had not gone hunting, but no one would be concerned if his absence was discovered.

He slung a quiver of arrows over his shoulder and picked up his bow. His knife and 'hawk were already tucked under the narrow belt around his waist. Again Shining Moon warned him to be careful, and Proud Wolf agreed, but he would not let caution slow him down; it was important that he reach the fort as soon as possible. He hesitated, unsure of whether to hug his sister good-bye or not. He was, after all, a warrior, he told himself.

Then, acting on impulse, he threw himself into

Shining Moon's arms and hugged her tight around the waist. "I will be back, my sister."

"I know," she said, and her confidence in him made a warm glow begin inside him. Without another word he ducked out of the tipi and ran toward the edge of the village.

This will be a great adventure, Proud Wolf thought. But he also knew that this was no child's game. It was deadly serious business.

He carried with him one of the last hopes for preventing a long and bloody war between white man and red.

Duquesne saw the boy go. The Frenchman was hunkered on his heels next to a campfire, sharing strips of dried venison with the subchief called Elk Horn. Duquesne had sensed right away that Elk Horn wanted the Americans out of the mountains every bit as much as he did. Of course, Elk Horn's feelings were based on a personal hatred, while Duquesne's motivation was strictly monetary. Fletcher McKendrick was paying him well to get rid of the American trappers, and that was what he intended to do.

If he could cause a great deal of bloodshed and suffering in the process, then so much the better.

When he noticed the young man who had spoken against him leaving the village, Duquesne felt a sense of alarm. The boy was carrying a bow and arrows, and he moved with a sense of purpose. Duquesne's eyes narrowed in thought.

Could it be that the boy planned to go to the Americans to warn them of his presence?

So far, Duquesne was fairly confident that Manuel Lisa and his men did not know he was in the area traveling among the Indians and inciting them to greater violence, promising them weapons to use against the Americans. Lisa had a reputation for shrewdness. If he learned what Duquesne was doing, he might also figure out that Duquesne was backed by one of the rival fur companies from the far north. Duquesne himself did not particularly care if such a discovery was made, but he knew McKendrick would not be pleased by such a thing. The Scotsman wanted to keep his own involvement, and his company's, out of this matter. Besides, every bit of information Lisa had in his possession made it that much easier for the Spaniard to plan for future trouble.

Those thoughts flashed through Duquesne's mind, leading him to an inescapable conclusion: He had to stop the boy.

Maybe he was wrong, he thought as he stood up. Perhaps the lad was just leaving the village to hunt. In that case, he would die for nothing. But he would die, either way. Duquesne had already determined that.

"Where are you going?" Elk Horn asked, his French rendered with an atrocious accent that grated on Duquesne's ears. "Bear Tooth has not decided yet."

"And how long will he take to decide?" Duquesne asked.

Elk Horn shrugged. "He is chief. He does things in his own time."

"And I am a chief among my people. I will return for Bear Tooth's decision another day." The Teton respected strength, Duquesne knew. It might help his cause if he did not appear overly deferential to Bear Tooth. Besides, it was important to stop the boy from getting to the fort, if that was indeed where he was bound.

Elk Horn seemed reluctant to let him leave, however. "You are sure you have many firesticks for us?" he asked.

"Yes. And plenty of powder and ball, enough to kill all the Americans."

Solemnly, Elk Horn nodded. "It is good. When you return, bring them with you."

"But what if Bear Tooth decides not to join his brothers in attacking the fort?"

"Bear Tooth will do what is best for the Hunkpapa," Elk Horn said quietly. "Or he will no longer be chief."

Ah, Elk Horn was indeed a man much like himself, Duquesne thought in triumph. Elk Horn saw the situation as an opportunity to wrest control of the tribe away from Bear Tooth. That would be fine with Duquesne. He had a feeling he could work better with Elk Horn. He could understand the man's hate and ambition much easier than he could fathom Bear Tooth's honor and caution.

"I understand," Duquesne said. Then he turned and headed for the woods, following the same path the young man had taken. The boy had a good lead already, but Duquesne was confident he could overtake him.

And when he did, there would be one less obstacle in the Frenchman's path to riches.

Proud Wolf ran along the trails that led through the forest, up and down ridges, along narrow, bubbling streams, around the rocky upthrusts of bluffs and hills. This was a good land, he thought, a land of great beauty. He would not let it be spoiled by fighting and death.

By late afternoon he was nearing the Big Horn River, with another half hour's travel to go before he reached it. Once he got there, he would camp for the night, then follow the river all the way to the fort the next day. With luck, he would reach the fort by nightfall.

He hoped Clay and Jeff would take his warning seriously and not consider him some foolish boy who could not be believed. Proud Wolf did not think that would happen, yet he worried all the same. Despite his size, he had always responded to the challenges in his life, but he feared that sooner or later a task would prove to be too big for him, and then he would fail. He prayed this would not be the time.

Those thoughts were going through his head as he trotted along a ridge thick with brush and trees. The slope to his right was steep and rocky, while the one to the left fell away more gradually. At the base of the steeper slope was a small creek, which had carved a channel in the side of the hill so that a bluff partially overhung the water. That creek eventually merged with the Big Horn, but Proud Wolf knew its course was so twisting and meandering that to follow it would add several miles to his journey. He would make better time cutting across country.

Suddenly a rustling in the brush caught his attention, and he slowed his pace, not wanting to stumble over a grizzly foraging for food. Some of the white men had started referring to the large, dangerous bears as "Ol' Ephraim," for reasons Proud Wolf had not been able to fathom. Whatever the beasts were called, he did not want to run into one.

The beast that stepped out of the bushes in front of Proud Wolf was human, though, not a grizzly. The youth stopped in his tracks, startled to see Duquesne standing there. The Frenchman held his musket ready to use. He regarded Proud Wolf with a suspicious squint and asked in French, "What are you doing here, boy?"

Proud Wolf thought the question might have been more appropriate coming from him. Duquesne was the interloper here. Instead of answering, Proud Wolf stood in stony silence, watching him.

"Wouldn't be heading for the American fort, now would you?" Duquesne prodded. There was no friendliness in the man's grin, and Proud Wolf thought it only made him uglier. "Wouldn't be thinking of warning those bastards what me and Elk Horn and the other savages got planned for them, would you? That wouldn't be a smart thing to do."

Proud Wolf tried not to show his surprise that Duquesne had figured out his intentions so easily. He was more convinced than ever that Duquesne was not only cunning, but also thoroughly evil.

Not to mention at home in this rugged land. It could not have been easy for Duquesne to get ahead of him, since the Frenchman had been in the village, talking to Elk Horn, when Proud Wolf left. And the youth knew he had not been traveling slowly either. Duquesne must have taken some shortcuts and set a blistering pace for himself to enable him to catch up to his quarry.

"I left the village to hunt," Proud Wolf said, hoping his voice did not reveal his nervousness. "I want no trouble."

"I have been watching you, boy. You're not hunting. You're heading for that fort, as fast and as straight as you can. I know damn well what you've got in mind. You're going to warn the Americans." He started to lift and cock his musket. "I cannot allow you to do that."

Too late, Proud Wolf realized what was about to happen. The scrawny Frenchman was actually going to shoot him! Proud Wolf threw himself to the side as the musket roared. He had the speed and reflexes of youth, but he had hesitated a split second too long. What felt like a fist of fire slammed into his side, knocking him off his feet. He felt himself spinning and falling, and then he landed heavily on the steep slope. The agony in his side was so great he barely felt the impact as he began to roll down the side of the ridge, crashing against rocks and boulders. He was so dazed from his wound that he could not even try to stop his fall by grasping at bushes or trees. He just tumbled on, out of control.

Abruptly the earth seemed to fall out from under him, and he felt the bite of the chilly stream as he splashed into it. He hit his head on the shallow, rocky bottom. The cold of the snow-fed creek did not revive him but seemed instead to pull him farther down into a great void, waiting hungrily to receive him. He felt the current pluck at him and vaguely heard the sounds of someone scrambling down the rugged hillside above him.

Then he surrendered to the lure of the darkness and let it embrace him.

*   *   *

Picking his way carefully, Duquesne climbed down the ridge. He had reloaded and primed his musket before starting down, and now he held it ready just in case the boy was not hurt as badly as he had seemed to be. *Why couldn't the damned redskin have fallen down the other side of the hill?* Duquesne asked himself. It would have been much easier to check the body that way and make sure the boy was dead. Duquesne could not take a chance on leaving him alive.

The young Indian's face had been ridiculously easy to read, Duquesne reflected, but his intentions had come to nothing. The Americans would remain unaware of Duquesne's presence, and soon it would be too late for anyone to stop him. The Indians, Teton and Crow alike, would be worked into a fever pitch until they exploded in a frenzy of killing that could only be sated by American blood.

By next year, Duquesne thought, the only men trapping beaver in these mountains would be the ones working for Fletcher McKendrick and the London and Northwestern Enterprise. And he himself would be in Montreal, perhaps, enjoying the fruits of his labors.

Duquesne slid down the last ten feet of the slope and dropped from the bluff that overhung the creek, his moccasins splashing in the water. He had not seen exactly where the Indian had gone into the stream, but he knew it had to be somewhere around there. He crouched, ready to fire, his keen eyes searching up and down the creek. He paid particular attention to the shadowy area underneath the bluff.

The boy was nowhere to be seen.

Duquesne had seen the ball from his musket rip through the lad's buckskin tunic and enter his side. The rapidly spreading bloodstain had been clearly visible, even during the boy's tumble down the slope. He had been too badly hurt to get up and run away when he reached the bottom. And even if the shot had missed, the fall itself should have been sufficient to badly injure him.

Cursing, Duquesne tramped several yards up and down the creek. No sign of his victim.

He knelt and studied the water. The stream was fairly shallow, but it was deep enough to float a body, especially a dead one. The current might have caught the Indian's corpse and carried it downstream toward the Big Horn. That would be a mixed blessing, Duquesne thought. On the one hand, he hated to leave without knowing for certain that the boy was dead. But he was fairly sure his shot had been a fatal one, not to mention the other injuries the boy had surely sustained in the fall. And if the body was found with a gunshot wound, it would be just one more piece of evidence that white men were killing Indians. Duquesne could turn the whole thing to his advantage.

He was pleased. Like it or not, the body was gone, and he had to proceed from there. He would camp somewhere close by, then return the next day to Bear Tooth's village for the chief's decision.

Duquesne left the creek without looking back.

Proud Wolf had not planned to hide from the Frenchman. He had been unconscious when the swiftly flowing water had carried him into the little crevasse. Sometime in the dim past, an upheaval of the land had split the base of the ridge, forming a narrow opening. While the main body of the creek foamed past the gap, some water eddied in and created a quiet pool. Above this haven, the chimneylike crevasse eventually narrowed down to nothing, closing up some thirty feet beyond the spot where the boy floated. His head had happened to bob up to the surface of the water when he was forced through the opening, and that was all that had saved him from drowning.

By the time Proud Wolf's eyelids finally fluttered open, many hours later, night had fallen, and darkness surrounded him. At first his stunned brain assumed he was dead and that instead of the promised afterlife, death was really nothing but an endless black void. As time passed, however, he became aware of how badly he was hurting.

All pain ended with death, did it not? If a man's spirit left his body, nothing remained to experience such agonies as the ones that gripped him now.

No, he decided, if he hurt this badly, he must still be alive. And if he was still alive, there was hope.

For a long, timeless time, perhaps minutes or seconds, perhaps hours, Proud Wolf lay in the water, gathering his strength. Finally he lifted his arm and reached out with his fingertips in an effort to discover what lurked in the darkness around him. He touched stone, smooth and slick with dampness and mossy growth. His explorations were slow and time-consuming, but gradually he became aware that he was in a narrow gash in the rocky slope of the hillside. The water around him had to come from the creek.

He remembered Duquesne, remembered the evil look of triumph on the Frenchman's face when the rifle in his hands blasted. Proud Wolf let out a groan, pain and anger mingling in the sound. He would not die, he vowed. Dying would be letting the Frenchman win, and Proud Wolf could not stand that thought.

He found a rock wall behind him; therefore, he reasoned, the way out had to be in front of him. He began edging in that direction. The pain in his side was sharp and piercing, but it did not seem quite as bad as it had earlier, the cold water having numbed it somewhat. But his muscles were stiff and did not want to work at first. That was the danger of the chill. It would have been easier just to lie back and rest—but that way lay death, and Proud Wolf was aware of it. Now that he was moving again, he had to keep going.

The current grew stronger, and he knew he had emerged from the little grotto where he had been for hours. Tilting his head back, he saw the stars overhead and almost wept for joy. The creek was too shallow to swim in, but when he tried to crawl on hands and knees, his head slipped under the flow and he had to jerk it back out. Rising to his knees, he lunged and flopped across the creek toward the grassy bank on the far side, like some sort of grotesque fish.

Falling on the bank, he drew in great ragged gulps of air. The pounding of his pulse was louder than the thunder of a summer storm, but it slowed, finally, as strength flowed back into his body.

He seemed to be drawing warmth from the ground. His muscles relaxed. It was a deceptive feeling, though, and he knew it. He was too badly hurt to reach the fort. His only hope was that someone would find him and help him.

One of the trails used by the trappers was not far off, perhaps half a mile or so. In his current condition, that might as well have been a hundred miles—a thousand!—but it was the only chance Proud Wolf had. Of course, the white men were not nearly as evident in the woods since the trouble had begun. Even if he did reach the trail, it would be sheer luck if someone came along and found him before he died.

But luck was all that Proud Wolf had left.

He rested for a time, and then as dawn was beginning to glow in the eastern sky, he crawled to a nearby tree, grasped its trunk for support, and pulled himself to his feet. Staggering from tree to tree, he started through the woods toward the fort.

CHAPTER TWENTY

The white bears have now become exceedingly troublesome; they constantly infest our camp during the night, and though they have not attacked us . . . yet we are obliged to sleep with our arms by our sides for fear of accident, and we cannot send one man alone to any distance, particularly if he has to pass through brushwood.

—from "The History of the Lewis and Clark Expedition"

Clay Holt hated nothing more than being cooped up, and he found it especially galling to be stuck inside the fort's stockade when he could see the mountains rising proudly on both sides of the valley. The rugged upthrusts of rock seemed to call out to him every time he saw them.

He had never been one to disobey orders, though —at least not without a good reason—and after Clay,

Jeff, Scott, and Curry had returned from Bear Tooth's village, Manuel Lisa had decreed that all would stay close to the fort for a couple of weeks. That would give things time to settle down a bit, Lisa hoped. Once the time had passed, trapping expeditions could resume, but only with large, well-armed parties of men.

That was all right with Clay as long as he was included in the first group to go out. Since Jeff and he had as much experience in the wilderness as any of the men, and more than most, Clay fully expected them to be tapped for the job.

That was exactly what happened.

Twelve men set out from the fort on a clear autumn day, with Clay nominally in charge of the group. Lisa had allowed him some leeway in picking the men to go with him. Jeff was one of them, of course, and the other ten were all veteran frontiersmen by this time. Each man carried a rifle—either a Model 1803 Harper's Ferry like Clay and Jeff owned or a .45 caliber Kentucky flintlock—two flintlock pistols, and plenty of powder and lead. The Sioux would think twice before attacking such a formidable bunch. The trappers, however, would not be looking for trouble; they were under strict orders from Lisa to avoid making contact with the Indians if possible.

Clay knew the situation was gnawing at the Spaniard. Indians had stopped coming to the fort with beaver plews to trade. Although the storage buildings were nearly full and the trapping season was winding down, there were still pelts to be taken. Lisa needed to make a huge profit from this sojourn to be able to come back the next year. The fur trade had only a foothold in the Rockies, and Clay sensed that its success was important not only to men like himself, but also to the entire nation. Some politicians back in Washington City insisted there was no real reason, economic or otherwise, to explore the western half of the continent. It was up to men like Manuel Lisa, John Colter, and Clay and Jeff Holt to prove them wrong.

As the twelve mountain men clad in buckskins

left the fort and paddled along the Big Horn in birchbark canoes, such considerations were not really on their minds. Clay and the others were just glad to be doing something again.

They followed the river until late afternoon, when Clay waved them in to the bank. "We'll cache the canoes here," he announced after all six craft had pulled up to the shore, "push on into the woods for a while, then camp for the night. There're several little creeks east of here we can work for a few days."

So far they had not seen any Indians, but Clay ordered two men to keep a lookout while the others concealed the canoes in the thick brush near the river. That done, the group shouldered their packs and walked into the woods, following Clay and Jeff.

A faint trail remained from the last time they had trapped in this region over a month ago. The beaver should be plentiful again, Clay thought, and if they had any luck, it would not take long to accumulate a good load of pelts.

Just before sundown, the trappers reached a small clearing that would make a good campsite.

"Are we going to have a fire, Holt?" one of the men asked.

Clay said, "I don't want to risk it. A cold camp is better than losing your hair."

The others agreed. They had plenty of dried, salted meat with them, as well as hard biscuits. They would not go hungry.

"We'll each stand watch," Clay said as they sat down to eat. "Two men at a time, and make sure you stay awake. Chances are we won't run into any trouble—but I don't want to count on that."

Clay felt a bit uncomfortable being in charge, but the men looked up to him and respected his decisions, and Lisa had had the faith in him to give him this responsibility. He wouldn't let any of them down.

After the men had eaten, they rolled into their blankets, all except the two who would take the first guard duty. Clay had assigned himself and Jeff the third watch, since it was the most disruptive of a night's sleep.

Clay dozed off rapidly, his slumber deep and dreamless, as it usually was in the wilderness. It seemed that he had barely closed his eyes when a mental alarm jogged him awake. He sat up, rubbed his eyes for a moment, then reached out to prod the shoulder of his sleeping brother.

"Our turn to stand watch, Jeff," Clay said quietly.

Jeff stirred, then rolled over and pushed himself into a sitting position.

The two of them got up and went to relieve the men who had stood the previous watch, one posted on either side of the camp. As Clay approached his man, the trapper stiffened, then said, "Oh, it's you, Clay."

"Any trouble, Henry?"

"Nary a sign of Indians or any other kind of skulkers. A big varmint came by a while ago. I reckon it was either Ol' Ephraim or maybe a painter."

Clay knew that grizzlies and mountain lions usually stayed away from human scent, especially the smell of white men. Only when wounded or starving would the wild creatures attack a man.

He put a hand on Henry's shoulder. "All right, thanks. You go lie down and get some sleep now."

"I sure will," the man replied. He slipped off in the shadows and joined the others in the center of the clearing.

Clay found a good rock to sit on—it was rough and uncomfortable and would help him stay awake. He rested the butt of his rifle on the ground beside his feet and waited quietly, not making a sound. There was no moon, and high, thin clouds obscured the light of the stars. A man's eyes were not much use in a situation like this, Clay thought, but his ears could make up for it. He listened intently to the night sounds.

Hearing nothing out of the ordinary, he relaxed a little, then suddenly stiffened. Something was not right. A moment later he realized what had warned him—faint, irregular footsteps coming toward the camp, and the insects that normally sang at night were falling silent. Someone was approaching.

Clay stood as still as if he had been carved from wood, although his breath plumed a little in the cold night air. He wished he could call out to alert Jeff, but by doing that he would also warn whoever was approaching. All he could do was wait. Noiselessly, he cocked his flintlock and slipped his index finger through the trigger guard. With his other hand he lifted the barrel.

The footsteps were closer and louder now. Leaves and branches crackled. If the interloper intended to approach in stealth, Clay thought, he was making a sorry job of it. Unless the intruder was hurt . . .

Or maybe it was a trick. Clay stepped silently away from the rock where he had been sitting, and taking shallow breaths, he curled his finger around the trigger of the rifle. He waited. A slight, dark shape detached itself from the deeper shadows of the trees and stumbled toward him.

"Hold it or I'll fire!" Clay called, knowing that his voice would alert Jeff and rouse the other trappers, too.

The figure stopped its shambling progress but continued to sway back and forth. A voice that Clay barely recognized croaked, "C-Clay Holt? Is that y—"

Then the young man plunged forward, falling to the ground.

"Proud Wolf!" Clay leapt toward the fallen youth. Behind him came voices, exclaiming in confusion. Jeff raced across the clearing to join his brother as Clay knelt beside the lad who had been their best friend in Bear Tooth's village.

"He's hurt," Clay said grimly as he lifted Proud Wolf's head and rested it on his leg.

Jeff turned to the other men and ordered, "Somebody make a torch. We're going to need some light."

"That's a redskin, ain't it?" one of the trappers

asked, his voice gruff from being jerked out of a sound sleep. "You ain't plannin' to help him, are you?"

"He's a Hunkpapa, and he's our friend," Clay snapped. "Besides that, he's just a boy. Now do as you're told, dammit!"

Proud Wolf stirred a little at Clay's sharp words. "Not . . . boy," he whispered raggedly. "Proud Wolf is . . . warrior."

"Sure you are, son," Clay told him. "Just take it easy, and we'll tend to you. What the hell happened?"

"Frenchman . . . shot me."

Clay glanced up at Jeff, but he could not see his brother's face in the darkness. "Frenchman?" he repeated. "Who the devil's he talking about?"

"Don't know," Jeff said. "I'd sure like to get my hands on the bastard, Frenchman or not."

A torch was lit and brought over to the spot where Proud Wolf lay with the trappers clustered around him. As the flickering glow touched the lad's face, Clay grimaced. Proud Wolf was as pale and haggard as an old man on the verge of death. The buckskin of his tunic was ripped on the right side, just above his waist. Moving the clothing aside, Clay saw the ugly wound.

"Somebody shot him, all right," Jeff said.

Clay checked Proud Wolf's back. "Punched a good-sized hole in him, but the ball went on through. That's good. I didn't fancy the idea of digging it out. Looks like he's pretty busted up. Somebody gave him a hell of a beating."

"What do we do now?"

"We'll patch up those holes, wrap him up so he'll stay warm, then try to get some food and water down him. That's about all we can do for him tonight. In the morning we'll make a litter so we can carry him back to his people."

"That ain't why Lisa sent us out here, Holt," one of the men objected. "We're supposed to be trappin' beaver, not nursemaidin' some heathen."

"Like I said, this boy's our friend," Clay replied,

and this time his words had a tone of cold menace to them. "We're going to do everything we can for him, and I'm not in the mood to argue. Any of you don't like it, you can head out on your own in the morning. Fair enough?"

"Sure, sure," the trapper agreed sullenly. "I wasn't tryin' to cause no trouble."

Proud Wolf was unconscious now. Clay slipped his arms around the youngster and gently lifted him, then carried him back to the center of the clearing. "Use that torch to get a fire started. We'll have to risk the light."

Soon a small blaze was crackling, and Proud Wolf was lying beside it in Clay's blankets, the wounds in his side crudely but efficiently bandaged. While that had been going on, the boy had roused briefly from his stupor and mumbled several words, but nothing that Clay and Jeff could understand. One of them sounded like "cane."

Clay and Jeff sat beside the boy's still form, and Jeff asked in a whisper, "You reckon he'll make it?"

"I don't know," Clay said honestly. "But if being bullheaded counts for anything, I'd say he's got a chance. No telling how far or how long he walked before he happened to run into us. One thing's for sure—he'd have died if we hadn't found him."

Clay was thinking of Shining Moon as he fell silent. He did not want to have to tell her that her brother was dead. He tasted bitterness in the back of his throat at that thought.

Jeff broke into his grim musings by saying, "What do you think will happen when we show up at Bear Tooth's village? Could be he's decided to go to war against us by now."

"Could be," Clay agreed. "But I don't see that we've got any choice. We're a little closer to the village than we are to the fort, and besides, if anybody can take good care of the boy, it's Shining Moon and that medicine man, North Star."

"North Star . . ." Jeff echoed. "He said he saw death in Proud Wolf's future."

"Comes to everybody, doesn't it?" His voice softened as he looked at Proud Wolf's ashen features and went on, "For some it comes too early. Like Ma and Pa."

Neither of them had mentioned their parents' deaths for a long time, but memories of their murders were still fresh enough to be painful. It seemed to Clay that trouble had been dogging his heels ever since he'd come back from the West with Lewis and Clark. Maybe it would have been better, he thought, if something had happened to him the first time he traveled through the Rockies. Maybe if he had died then, his death would have prevented some of the trouble with the Garwoods. His mother and father might still be alive, and so might Luther and Pete Garwood. Now Proud Wolf was lying on the verge of death, and for all Clay knew, he was partly to blame for that, too.

For some, death came too soon. Perhaps for others, it came too late.

Proud Wolf was still alive when the sun rose the next morning, and to Jeff's stubbornly optimistic eye, the boy even looked a little stronger. He was able to drink more water and eat a little crumbled-up biscuit.

Clay used his tomahawk to cut down a couple of slender saplings. He hacked off the branches, wove them together with some he had cut from other trees, then lashed them to the saplings to form a litter. "I reckon we can carry him on this," he said to Jeff when the task was finished. "How's he feeling?"

"Better, I think. He drank some water and ate a little."

"Say anything?"

Jeff shook his head. "Nope. I'm not sure he was awake enough to really know where he was or what was going on."

Several of the men came up then, standing nearby until Clay asked, "What is it, boys?"

"Well, we're just not sure about goin' to that Hunkpapa village," one of the men said slowly. "I reckon we spoke kinda out of turn last night, and we're sorry the boy there got hurt. But we don't figure it's a good idea to put ourselves in the hands of them Hunkpapas right now."

Jeff started to object, but Clay put a hand on his shoulder and stopped him. "Could be you're right. That's why I don't want you going with us," Clay said.

Jeff glanced at him in surprise, as did the other men.

"Proud Wolf's our friend," Clay explained, "and Jeff and I are going to do everything we can to help him. But that's our responsibility, not yours. Besides, if the Sioux see a dozen men coming toward their village, they're liable to start shooting arrows before they know what's going on. If it's just the two of us carrying the litter, I reckon they'll wait to see what's what."

One of the trappers spoke up. "And then they'll lift your hair, sure as hell."

"I don't think so. But even if they do, we've got to take that chance. We can't just let Proud Wolf die without trying to save him."

"Is your brother speaking for you, too, Jeff?"

"Damn right. What he says makes sense."

Clay continued, "You men head on east, just like we planned. There's ten of you; that's a big enough bunch to handle most any trouble you might run into. Go ahead and trap up and down those creeks, and if we don't find you before you're ready to head back to the fort, then go without us. We'll get back as soon as we can."

"Well, if the two of you are sure . . ."

"We're sure," Jeff assured them.

The others got their possibles bags together and prepared to leave. Proud Wolf was still wrapped in blankets when Clay and Jeff carefully lifted him onto the litter, then grasped the poles that extended at each end of the conveyance. "Easy, now," Clay cautioned as they straightened, then lifted the litter off the ground.

After calling farewell to the others, the brothers headed southeast toward the Hunkpapa village. The woods were so thick that it was not long before the other white men were lost from view. Moving slowly and carefully so as not to jostle Proud Wolf, the Holts carried him through open valleys, up ridges and hills, and across the tiny rivulets of water so common to that area. Much of the way was rugged, and it was not easy keeping the litter level. Occasionally Proud Wolf groaned.

By the middle of the day Jeff's arms ached from carrying the unaccustomed burden. Clay and he set Proud Wolf down and paused long enough for a quick, cold meal. Again the boy took a little nourishment, but not much.

The optimism Jeff had felt that morning was fading. It was hard to believe that anybody could be hurt as badly as Proud Wolf and survive for long. But just as Clay had said, the young man was stubborn, and Jeff planned to cling to that hope, just as Proud Wolf was clinging to life.

The day wore on, the afternoon seeming twice as long as the morning. By nightfall they were still several miles from Bear Tooth's village. As they paused again Jeff asked, "Do we push on in the dark, or will we have to make camp for the night?"

In the fading light of dusk, Clay studied Proud Wolf's drawn features and said, "I don't know if he'll make it if we wait, Jeff. I reckon we've got to push on."

Jeff agreed. They ate again, rested their arms and blistered hands, then picked up the litter and continued on their way.

Darkness slowed them down, as Clay had predicted. Jeff had gone beyond weariness to numb exhaustion, but he kept plodding along, holding up his end of the litter. Clay set their course, and Jeff was thankful for his brother's uncanny sense of direction.

Alone in the gloomy woods, Jeff was sure he would have been lost in a minute.

Finally Clay paused and said, "I see campfires up ahead. I reckon that's the village." A moment later several dogs set up a frenzied barking, alerting the camp of the men's presence.

When Jeff and Clay stumbled up to the cluster of tipis a few minutes later, they found more than a dozen warriors waiting, weapons at the ready. Women and children peered curiously from the openings in the tipis. Bear Tooth stood in front of the warriors, and even his normally stoic features displayed astonishment at the sight that greeted his eyes.

"Bear Tooth, we have bad news. Proud Wolf has been hurt," Clay said.

A startled cry came from behind the group of warriors. A figure pushed through them and ran forward, and Jeff recognized Shining Moon. As the two men lowered the litter to the ground, she went to her knees beside it and cradled the head of her injured brother.

"You see it with your own eyes now!" The harsh words came from Elk Horn, who had moved up beside Bear Tooth. "You see what the Americans have done to Proud Wolf! Do you still say we should not kill them all?"

"Don't be a damn fool," Clay snapped. "If we'd shot the boy, would we have brought him here?"

Jeff noticed that Elk Horn's accusation had been directed at Americans, rather than white men in general. He met Clay's eyes in a quick glance and saw that he had taken note of that, too.

For the first time Bear Tooth spoke. "North Star! You will care for the boy. His sister and the other women will help you. Save his life if you can, and guide his spirit into the Great Beyond if you cannot."

The medicine man nodded and hurried forward, trailed by several women. They picked up the litter and carried it toward North Star's tipi. Shining Moon walked along beside it, one of Proud Wolf's limp hands clutched tightly in her fingers.

Bear Tooth looked at Clay and Jeff. "What happened?"

"We found him not far from the Big Horn," Clay said. "He stumbled into our camp last night. Somebody'd shot him, and he looked pretty beat up, too. I don't know exactly what happened to the boy, Bear Tooth, but I give you my word Jeff and I and our friends didn't have anything to do with it."

"Lies!" Elk Horn insisted, pushing forward, 'hawk in hand. "More American lies! I say we kill them now!"

"No one will die," Bear Tooth decreed sharply. "Not until we see whether Proud Wolf lives or not."

Elk Horn pointed his 'hawk at Clay and Jeff. "Then if the boy dies, they die! That is fair. Or has Bear Tooth forgotten what justice is?" Contempt dripped from his voice.

Jeff caught his breath and watched to see how Bear Tooth would react to the insult. He perceived a subtle change in the atmosphere, a sense that he and Clay were in more danger than before. Something had been going on in the village that he knew nothing about. The men seemed solidly behind Elk Horn now.

"If Proud Wolf dies, the white men will be killed," Bear Tooth said. "In that manner the Wakan Tanka shall show us who lies and who speaks the truth."

Elk Horn accepted the proposal. He gestured to some of his supporters. "Take their weapons," he ordered. Bear Tooth did not contradict the command.

The Hunkpapa swarmed over Clay and Jeff, snatching their rifles, pistols, knives, and 'hawks. Both of the Holts were shoved around roughly in the process, but they had the sense not to put up a fight. The slightest excuse was all the warriors needed right now to kill them.

When they were unarmed, Bear Tooth said, "Take them to the tipi they used before. They will stay there until we see if Proud Wolf will live. Until that time, no one is to harm them." He looked intently at Elk Horn. "Do you understand that?"

"I understand." Elk Horn's eyes narrowed. "Perhaps they will still be alive to see Shining Moon become my woman tomorrow."

Clay stiffened, his face turning red with rage.

Jeff hissed under his breath, "Easy, big brother. We'd best keep cool heads."

Bear Tooth's expression was grim, and Jeff sensed that Elk Horn had finally pushed things too far. The ambitious subchief had given the chief an opening. "There will be no ceremony," he declared.

Elk Horn's face flushed. "It has been arranged—"

"Shining Moon's brother is badly hurt. She will be busy caring for him." Bear Tooth shook his head firmly. "Elk Horn can take her as his woman some other day."

With that, he motioned for the men guarding Clay and Jeff to take them away. The brothers were marched over to the tipi and prodded inside.

As they sank wearily onto the ground, Clay said, "I'm going to kill that bastard Elk Horn one of these days."

Jeff said, "Bear Tooth may save you the trouble. I reckon now we wait."

"Yep," Clay agreed. "Proud Wolf's got three lives riding on him now."

Clay had hoped he could snatch some time alone with Shining Moon, but over the next two days he did not even see her from a distance. According to Bear Tooth, who came to the tipi occasionally to let them know that Proud Wolf was still clinging to life, the woman was not leaving her brother's side even for a moment.

"Shining Moon loves her brother very much," Bear Tooth said during one of his visits. "She is a good woman, and she will be a fine wife for the man who marries her."

"I thought she was promised to Elk Horn," Clay said, cautioning himself not to let the chief's words give him too much hope.

Bear Tooth shrugged eloquently. "A man can make plans, but sometimes the Wakan Tanka has other plans."

Clay was not sure what Bear Tooth meant by that. He told himself to be patient. Right now, he had to worry about staying alive.

"What's been going on around here, Bear Tooth?" Jeff asked. "Things seem a little different from when we left. Your people were pretty well up in arms then, and they're even more angry with the white men now."

"With the Americans," Bear Tooth said, making the same puzzling distinction as Elk Horn. "After you left, a man named Duquesne came to the village."

"Duquesne . . ." Clay mused, remembering the muttered words Proud Wolf had spoken in his delirium. "Would this Duquesne be a Frenchman?"

"Yes," the chief said. "He told us he had heard that American trappers were killing Teton warriors and raping our women. He promised us muskets, many muskets, if we would promise to use them against the Americans."

"Son of a bitch," Clay said softly. He looked over at Jeff and saw that his brother was thinking the same thing he was. Turning his attention back to Bear Tooth, he said, "Chief, right after we found Proud Wolf, before he passed out, he told us it was a Frenchman who shot him."

Bear Tooth's dark eyes narrowed, and his forehead creased in thought. "You are sure of this?"

"We both heard him," Jeff said.

Bear Tooth was sitting cross-legged on the ground with the Holt brothers. He leaned back slightly, the look of intense concentration still on his face. "There is much to think about," he said solemnly.

"This fellow Duquesne," Clay said. "What did you tell him?"

"He left without waiting for my answer, then came back the next day. I told him I had not decided. He was angry, but he said he would be back another time. Since then we have not seen him."

Jeff commented, "It's a good thing you stalled him. He was bound to be lying."

"I was not—stalling, as you say. I have not reached a decision. Elk Horn and most of the other warriors want me to take the guns and join with the other Teton tribes in an attack on the white men's fort."

Clay was more concerned by this information than by anything that had come before. If Duquesne could convince the different bands of Teton to join together and if he supplied them with guns and goaded them into a killing frenzy, then Manuel Lisa and the men at the fort were doomed.

"You don't believe the Americans are really behind the trouble, do you, Bear Tooth?" Clay asked.

For a long moment the Hunkpapa chief did not answer. Then he said, "I do not want to believe this is so. But we have heard many stories of the evil being done in our land. Our warriors are angry. They cry out for vengeance. Soon there will be no stopping what is to come. Not even a chief may deny the wind."

Clay knew what Bear Tooth meant. The wind of which he spoke would be a red one, a red wind that would sweep through the mountains and hills and valleys and wipe the white newcomers from the face of the earth.

And the only one who might be able to stop it, Clay thought, was a young boy who at this moment lay unconscious, on the brink of death.

Clay and Jeff stayed close to the tipi, venturing out only when Bear Tooth accompanied them. Each day a woman brought their meals. That was the extent of their contact with the Hunkpapa.

Around noon on the third day after their return to

the village, the entrance flap of the tipi was thrust aside, and Clay glanced up idly, expecting to see another of the women with food for them.

Instead Shining Moon stood there. Her features, though still lovely, showed the strain she had been under. Clay sprang to his feet, followed closely by Jeff. For an instant Clay feared that Proud Wolf had finally succumbed to his injuries, but then he saw Shining Moon smile.

"North Star says my brother will live." Her words were calm, but her voice trembled with happiness and excitement. "Proud Wolf wishes to see you."

Clay let out an exultant whoop, which was echoed by Jeff. With a bound, Clay swept Shining Moon into his arms and hugged her tightly. "That's wonderful!" he exclaimed.

Jeff also hugged her, once Clay finally let go of her. He said, "We want to see him, too."

"Proud Wolf is still very weak," Shining Moon cautioned. "You must not make him too tired."

"We'll be careful," Clay promised. "We've got to ask him some questions."

"Bear Tooth is with him now. They talk about many things."

Jeff pushed the hide flap back so that the three of them could leave the tipi. As they stepped out into the midday sun, Clay glanced around and saw that Jeff and he were still the targets of hostile glares from some of the men. Others looked less unfriendly, though, and more confused. Already word was spreading in the village that Proud Wolf would recover.

They walked quickly to the tipi of the medicine man, Shining Moon flanked by the Holts. No one tried to stop them, not even Elk Horn, although Clay saw the hate-filled expression of the subchief as they passed him. As they stepped into North Star's tipi, Clay smelled a pungent, unfamiliar aroma. No telling what plants and herbs the medicine man had used on Proud Wolf, he thought.

Proud Wolf was wrapped in a buffalo robe, propped up so that he was half sitting. His face was gaunt from his ordeal, but his cheeks were tinged with color again, and his eyes sparkled with the vitality that Clay and Jeff remembered so well.

Bear Tooth knelt beside the boy while North Star and two women stood to one side of the tipi. Shining Moon went to her brother, and Bear Tooth motioned for Clay and Jeff to join him, saying, "This warrior wishes to speak with you."

Proud Wolf beamed at his adopted father's words. Trying to make his voice solemn and dignified, he said, "Greetings, Clay Holt. Greetings, Jeff Holt. It is good to see you again."

"You don't know how good it is to see you, Proud Wolf," Jeff said. He reached out and squeezed the youngster's shoulder. "How are you feeling?"

"I am ready to take my place again as a warrior of the Hunkpapa, but North Star tells me I must rest for a while first. Soon I will be roaming the forests and the mountains, as I have done in the past."

Clay said, "I'm sure you will. Right now, we need to find out just what happened to you."

Bear Tooth spoke up. "Proud Wolf has already told me that the Frenchman called Duquesne tried to kill him. He was on his way to the fort of the white men to warn them when Duquesne shot him."

"He was trying to persuade the Hunkpapa and other tribes to attack the fort," Proud Wolf told them. "He is an evil man."

"You're right about that," Clay said grimly. He looked at the Indian leader. "Jeff and I have been thinking, Bear Tooth. Could be this Duquesne is the one who's really behind all the trouble your people have been having."

"You mean instead of the Americans . . ."

"It could be men working for Duquesne who have been attacking the Oglala," Clay suggested. "Think about it. He stirs up the tribes, puts the blame

on us, then gives the Teton guns and points them at
the fort. It's a pretty devilish plan."

Jeff added, "But it sure does explain a lot of
things."

Bear Tooth said slowly, "Your words have the
ring of truth. But why would Duquesne do this
thing?"

Clay had to shake his head. "Reckon he's got
some reason of his own."

Proud Wolf said fervently, "You must find him
and kill him. He is like a grizzly that has tasted blood
and gone mad."

"You should not worry about such things," Shining Moon told him firmly, putting a hand on his
shoulder as he tried to sit up straighter.

"Your sister's right," Clay said. "You've done
your part, Proud Wolf. You've proven that Duquesne
can't be trusted."

Bear Tooth stood up. "Come," he said to Clay and
Jeff. "I will speak to my people. Shining Moon, you
come as well."

After telling Proud Wolf to get some rest, the
three of them followed Bear Tooth out of the tipi to the
center of the village. The chief raised his hands over
his head and called out in his native tongue, demanding the attention of everyone in the village. When they
had gathered around him, he gestured for Clay and
Jeff to come forward. Putting a hand on the shoulder
of each brother, he spoke loudly for several moments.

Clay could not follow all of the speech, but he
understood enough to know why there were looks of
surprise on the faces of many of the listeners. In fact,
Elk Horn seemed downright stunned, Clay thought.

"What's he saying?" Jeff asked anxiously.

"Just hold on," Clay replied, a tingle of excitement growing in him. He thought he had an idea of
what Bear Tooth was leading up to.

Finally the chief said to them in English, "I have
told my people that you two are now our brothers.
Even though Proud Wolf is not blood of my blood and

flesh of my flesh, he is my son, and you have saved his life. For this, Bear Tooth and the Hunkpapa can never repay you. As long as the rivers flow, you will have a home in our land."

Clay felt humble and grateful. "Thank you, Bear Tooth. There can be no greater honor for us."

"I will return your weapons to you and send runners to all the tribes so they will know you are brothers to the Hunkpapa. None will bother you in the future."

"What about our friends?" Jeff asked. "Do you believe now that they didn't have anything to do with hurting your people?"

"I believe this in my heart," Bear Tooth said somberly. "But we must have proof to convince the other tribes." Then with a wave of his hand, he said, "That is a matter for another day. This day, there is one more thing we must do." He turned to Shining Moon and extended a hand to her. "You are my daughter, and I grant you a boon. Of all the warriors of our people, including these two new ones, who would you have for your man?"

Elk Horn gave a howl of outrage before Shining Moon could answer. He sprang forward and shouted, "No! She has been promised to me!"

"Shining Moon may choose," Bear Tooth said coldly.

Clay's heart was beating wildly in his chest. Before, he had been an outsider, and even though Bear Tooth had liked him, he would not have given his permission for her to marry him. Now he had been welcomed into the tribe, and evidently he had just as much right to marry a Hunkpapa woman as any of the other men. He looked over at Shining Moon and saw the smile on her face. He knew what her decision would be.

"I choose Clay Holt," she said.

Elk Horn screeched again and leapt at Clay, his hand plucking his knife from its sheath. Clay tensed to defend himself, but Bear Tooth struck first, slamming an open-handed blow into Elk Horn's chest as he thrust a leg between the subchief's ankles. Elk Horn spilled to the ground before he could reach Clay, and Bear Tooth dropped to his knees beside him, whipping out his own knife and holding it to Elk Horn's throat.

A tense silence hung over the village for several seconds. Then Bear Tooth lifted his blade and stepped back. "You have disgraced yourself," he said harshly to Elk Horn. "No longer will the young men follow you. No longer will you be welcomed in my dwelling. If you try to attack our brothers again, you will be banished from the village!"

Elk Horn was trembling with anger as he awkwardly got to his feet, but he bowed his head and choked out, "It will be as Bear Tooth commands."

Elk Horn turned and stalked away, his head down, not meeting the looks of scorn of the other Hunkpapa.

Bear Tooth turned back to Clay, who had slipped an arm around Shining Moon's waist and drawn her against him. "In time, you will marry Shining Moon," Bear Tooth said to Clay. "But now, we must decide what to do about the man Duquesne."

Bear Tooth was right, Clay thought. Someone had to put a halt to Duquesne's plans, or the whole frontier might soon be awash with blood. Clay glanced at Jeff, who nodded and put a hand on his brother's shoulder.

"We'll stop Duquesne," Clay promised.

PART IV

The uncontrolled liberty which our citizens take of hunting on Indian lands has always been a source of serious difficulty on every part of our frontier. . . . When the Indians have been taught by commerce duly to appreciate the furs and peltries of their country, they feel excessive chagrin at seeing the whites, by their superior skill in hunting, fast diminishing those productions to which they have been accustomed to look as the only means of acquiring merchandise; and nine-tenths of the causes of war are attributable to this practice.

—MERIWETHER LEWIS,
from "Essay on an Indian Policy"

CHAPTER TWENTY-ONE

You had to hand it to Bear Tooth, Jeff Holt thought as he sat in the chief's tipi. The Hunkpapa leader was a shrewd man. With the single, well-timed stroke of accepting the Holts into the tribe, Bear Tooth not only had made it possible for Clay and Shining Moon to be together, but had also eliminated Elk Horn as a possible rival for leadership of his band. By giving in to his rage, Elk Horn had provided Bear Tooth with the excuse he needed to humiliate him and destroy any support he might have had from the other warriors. Even the most hotheaded young men would not align themselves with Elk Horn now.

Most folks back home would probably consider Bear Tooth an ignorant savage, but from Jeff's vantage point the chief seemed to be as cunning and refined as any of the politicians in Washington City.

Clay was sitting to Jeff's right, and Bear Tooth

was across the fire pit from them. They were discussing the problem of what to do about the murderous Frenchman.

"If Duquesne has men pretending to be American trappers so that they can cause trouble with the Teton tribes, they've got to have a hiding place around here," Clay said. "If we can find it, maybe we can get the proof you need to convince the other tribes not to start a war."

Bear Tooth said, "You would search for this hiding place?"

"Seems like that's the only thing we can do."

"It's a big country around here," Jeff added, "but we know it pretty well by now."

"There would be danger," Bear Tooth pointed out. "My people will not harm you, but warriors from other bands of Teton could. They might not know that you have become our brothers."

Clay said, "Reckon that's a chance we'll have to take."

Shining Moon spoke up from the side of the tipi where she was kneeling, her legs tucked under her. "There would be less danger if one of the Hunkpapa went with you, Clay Holt."

Bear Tooth had not been too eager to allow a woman, even his daughter, into the tipi while he and the Holts were deciding what to do, but Shining Moon had been respectfully insistent. Now that she and Clay could be together, she did not want to be apart from him for a single moment.

"Are you saying I should send a warrior with our new brothers, Shining Moon?" Bear Tooth asked.

"No. I will go."

"Now, wait just a minute—" Clay began.

"I know this land as well as any warrior," she pressed on. "From the time I was a child I roamed the mountains, the hills, the valleys. I have paddled a canoe up every river and creek. You know these things I speak are true, Bear Tooth."

"Perhaps," he admitted grudgingly. "But a

woman does not travel with warriors on an important mission."

"You're right, Bear Tooth," Jeff said, "but Shining Moon's presence might make us less noticeable. A couple of trappers traveling with a Teton woman . . . Anybody who's up to no good wouldn't think we were much of a threat."

"Blast it, nobody's asked my opinion!" Clay snapped. "Shining Moon's going to be my woman, and I won't allow this, no matter what the rest of you say. It's just too damned dangerous."

Jeff saw the sudden flash in Shining Moon's eyes. He had seen that same look in Melissa's eyes on a few occasions, usually to his regret. He knew that his brother had just made a mistake.

Shining Moon spoke sharply to Bear Tooth in their language, and the chief listened impassively. Jeff thought he saw a hint of amusement in the Indian's eyes, though.

Clay said irritably, "Slow down, dammit. I can't keep up when you're talking that fast."

She gave him a look as cool as an autumn night. "If I had wanted you to know what I was saying, Clay Holt, I would have used your tongue."

Clay was about to say something when Bear Tooth said, "I will explain what Shining Moon has told me, Clay Holt. She says that she is not your woman yet, and this is true. She says also that she is a Hunkpapa and that she does not wish to see any harm come to her people. If they go to war against the Americans, death and suffering will result on both sides, and Shining Moon would like to stop this from happening. Her words are honorable."

"I reckon," Clay said. "But that doesn't mean I have to like them."

"No. But your brother is right. I think it would be a good thing for Shining Moon to accompany you on your search for Duquesne. When you find him, you will come back here, and the Hunkpapa and the

Oglala shall deal with him. Shining Moon will be in little danger."

"You can't be sure—" Clay broke off his protest when he saw the stubborn look on Bear Tooth's face and the sly smile on Shining Moon's.

"You've been outfoxed, big brother," Jeff told him.

"Looks like it. All right. She can go with us." He turned to Shining Moon. "But you've got to go now and get some rest. You've been sitting up with Proud Wolf for nearly three days. We'll wait and leave in the morning."

Shining Moon's face was drawn with weariness, and she could not deny her need for sleep. As she stood up to leave, she said, "Do not try to slip away from the village without me, Clay Holt. If you do, I will follow you."

"You'd better believe her, Clay," Jeff advised after Shining Moon was gone. "I reckon she's one lady who means what she says."

"I reckon I'm starting to understand that," Clay said.

Before leaving the village early the next morning, the three of them said good-bye to Proud Wolf, who was disappointed he could not go with them. "I will be able to travel soon, if you would wait," he complained. "Proud Wolf could help you find these evil men."

"We know you could," Jeff said, "and we wish you were going with us. But there's just not enough time to wait."

"Yes, you are right, Jeff Holt." Proud Wolf reached up from the robes where he rested and clasped Jeff's hand. "May the Wakan Tanka guide you."

He shook hands with Clay as well. Then Shining Moon embraced him. Tears sparkled in the eyes of the brother and sister as the little group took its leave.

Bear Tooth also wished them luck and bid them

farewell, and most of the village turned out to watch them go. Clay looked for Elk Horn in the crowd but did not see him. The humiliated former subchief was probably sulking in his tipi.

As they set out Clay had to admit that, deep down, he was glad Shining Moon was coming with Jeff and him. He would be able to spend more time with her this way, even though that time would be arduous and perhaps even dangerous.

He knew the hiding place used by Duquesne and his men could be almost anywhere in this vast land. Yet there were certain considerations that might narrow down the area they would have to search. The hideout could not be too close to an Indian village, or the risk of discovery would be too great. Also, it had to be near water. And if it were completely isolated, it would take too long for the renegades to reach safety after their raids. Bear Tooth had called in his best hunters and scouts, and they had discussed all of this with Clay and Jeff. The consensus was that the northern reaches of the Big Horn Mountains, around the headwaters of the creeks that eventually merged to form the Tongue River, would be a likely area. Clay and Jeff had been through that region before and knew it was rugged country, with plenty of places for someone to hide.

For nearly a week Clay, Jeff, and Shining Moon traveled along the western edge of the Big Horns, sticking to the foothills and not challenging the heights. Clay had to admit that Shining Moon did not slow them down. If anything, her presence allowed them to make better time, for she knew shortcuts. Her claim of knowing that part of the country well was proven every day.

Clay and Jeff did some trapping in each creek they came to, in order to appear to be a fur-gathering expedition. The pelts they took were a little better now. Winter was still long weeks away, but already the beaver were beginning to put on thicker coats of fur.

The real purpose of the trip was never far from their minds, however, and all three watched closely for any sign of strangers. So far they had seen no one, not even Indians, and once again Clay was struck by the size of this country. Even though the Teton Sioux and the Crow were numerous, they were still far too few to fill up the vast territory.

Those foot-dragging politicians back East are crazy, Clay thought one day as he stood on a rise and looked west across the broad Big Horn valley to the Absaroka range and the main upthrust of the Rockies beyond.

The Shining Mountains was a fitting name indeed. Washed with sunlight, the perpetual snow sparkled on the peaks in the clear air. The sky overhead was the deep blue color of a mountain pool. To Clay, the frontier country was worth more than all the flatlands in the East put together.

Despite its dangers, this was his home—and it always would be.

"Clay!" Jeff called from down the hill. "Come here! Shining Moon's found something!"

Clay looked down the slope to where Jeff was waving. Clutching his rifle, he trotted down the hill. As he got near to them, Shining Moon pointed to a narrow track beaten in the grass. The trail looked fairly fresh, and it led deeper into the foothills.

"This path was not here the last time I was here," she said. "Perhaps the men we seek made it."

Clay knelt down next to the trail. "Could be," he said after a moment. "Doesn't really look like a game trail. Could your people have made it?"

"I do not think so. The Hunkpapa use game trails, or they change their path so as not to leave tracks like this." Although her face remained solemn, Clay detected a trace of amusement in her voice as she went on, "This is the kind of trail white men leave."

Clay straightened and looked along the path to where it wound into the foothills and disappeared. "We'll follow it."

With a trail to follow, they abandoned the pretense of trapping and covered the ground as quickly as they could. When night fell, they had to stop for fear of losing the path. On other nights they had risked building small fires, but that night Clay opted for a cold camp.

The terrain became even more rugged as they continued to follow the trail the next day. Here, almost in the shadow of the Rockies, the Big Horns did not seem very impressive, but they were still good-sized mountains. As the land rose and became rockier, the path they had been following faded and was gradually lost.

Clay stood glaring in frustration at ground that was too hard to hold a track.

Jeff seemed equally discouraged. "What do we do now?" he asked.

Before Clay could answer, Shining Moon pointed to the east, deeper into the mountains, and said, "We keep going. The way is there."

"How can you know that?" Clay asked.

"Shining Moon knows." Her tone seemed to say that she would tolerate no argument.

Clay and Jeff looked at each other, and Jeff shrugged. "Might as well," he said. "We've come this far."

Clay agreed. He did not know what instinct had prompted Shining Moon to choose that direction, but he shared it; his gut told him they were still on the right path. They spent the day climbing higher into the mountains.

Late in the afternoon Clay looked back to the west and caught a glimpse of water shining in the sun. "Must be the Big Horn," he said to his companions, pointing to the distant river. "It's what, fifteen or twenty miles across there?"

"I reckon so." Jeff rubbed his bearded jaw as he stared at the river. "I hope the boys up at the fort are all right. They could have already been attacked, and we wouldn't know anything about it."

Clay's expression was grim as he gazed to the

north, toward the direction of the fort. Jeff was right; their mission might have already failed.

No point in dwelling on that, he thought. They had to push on. If there was still a chance to put a stop to Duquesne's scheming, they wanted to take advantage of it.

The three travelers did not pause until nightfall, when they ate another cold supper and then debated whether to keep going or camp for the night.

Shining Moon helped them come to a decision by suddenly reaching out and grasping Clay's arm. She pointed in the gathering shadows and said, "Smoke."

Clay and Jeff turned to where she was looking, a little higher in the mountains than their current position and perhaps half a mile to the south. Narrowing his eyes, Clay thought he saw a thin thread of smoke, almost invisible in the gathering gloom. Jeff confirmed that he saw it, too.

"Pretty smart," Clay said. "They light a fire at dusk, when the flames and smoke are harder to see. Probably put it out as soon as they've cooked themselves some supper."

"It might be some of our boys or some free trappers," Jeff pointed out. "Maybe even some Indians."

Shining Moon shook her head. "Not my people."

"And not ours, either." Clay was not sure how he knew, but he was certain they had found their quarry. "That's Duquesne's bunch." He straightened, tightly grasping his primed and loaded rifle. "Come on."

Shining Moon led the way, with Clay behind her and Jeff bringing up the rear. As the darkness deepened they had to proceed more slowly, picking their way up the rocky slope. It was impossible to see the smoke any longer; either the fire had been put out, or the smoke was now indistinguishable from the night sky. Shining Moon had fixed its location in her mind, however, and she led them unerringly toward it.

They climbed onto a ridge that overlooked a steep-sided canyon, and Clay felt a surge of excitement when he saw the small campfire below. The narrow, grassy glen was about a quarter of a mile long and half that wide. It came to an abrupt end against a wall of rock. Although the sloping sides were not too steep to climb, it would be difficult to negotiate them, and impossible to do it silently. Anyone attempting it would surely set off a small rockslide. That left only one good entrance to the valley, where a twisting passage led through the rocks at the near end. As a hiding place, the canyon was as close to perfect as anyone could have found in the mountains. There was even a small trickle of water flowing out from under the cliff at the far end of the hollow, forming a pool there.

At least thirty men were in the canyon, many of them gathered around the fire. All wore buckskins. Some sported coonskin caps; others wore beaver hats or floppy-brimmed felt hats. Rifles and pistols were everywhere. The aura of menace surrounding these men was almost palpable, Clay thought. Some were passing jugs of whiskey, and their harsh laughter was clearly audible. So was the babble of voices, some speaking French, others English.

"Did you ever see such a band of rogues in your life?" Jeff whispered to Clay.

Before he could answer, Shining Moon's fingers clutched his shoulder, and she pointed with her other hand. "There! That one is Duquesne!"

Clay saw the man she was indicating, a small, bearded, unimpressive individual. "That little fellow?"

"Yes. When you are closer, you can see the evil in his eyes. Then he does not look so small."

Clay was more than willing to take her word for it. He was about to motion for the three of them to slip back down the slope on the far side of the ridge from the canyon, so that they could figure out what to do next, when a familiar name came floating on the night air.

". . . the fort of Manuel Lisa," he heard one of the renegades say.

"Wait a minute," Clay breathed to his companions. "Let's try to hear what they're talking about."

Sound carried well in the clear mountain air. As they crouched at the top of the ridge, listening so intently that it seemed a physical exertion, they began to understand more and more of what was being discussed below them.

Duquesne was stalking back and forth, and it was obvious that he was upset about something. He was speaking in heavily accented English to one of the men, probably his lieutenant from the way Duquesne was addressing him.

"I tell you, Cyrus, we can wait no longer for these damned savages to do our work for us!" Duquesne exclaimed.

"Then what do ye think we should do?" the man called Cyrus asked in a Scottish burr.

"If the Indians do not fall into line soon, we will have to attack the fort ourselves!"

"The boys will not like that," Cyrus responded dubiously. " 'Twill be dangerous. That fort is well made, and the Americans are damned good shots."

Wearily Duquesne rubbed his temples. He said something too faintly for Clay to make it out, but Clay had a feeling from the tone of voice that Duquesne was agreeing with Cyrus's objection. He went on, ". . . must do something to speed things up."

"Jacques came in with a report," Cyrus said. "There be a bunch of American trappers heading back up the Big Horn to the fort."

Duquesne abruptly ceased his nervous pacing. "That is a wonderful idea, *mon ami*!"

Cyrus scratched at the red hair underneath his coonskin cap. "I did not have an idea—" he began.

Duquesne ignored him. "We will dress as Indians —we have those clothes we have taken from the ones we killed—and we will attack these trappers. One or two will escape to take word back to the fort that the Teton tribes are finally on the rampage. Then, we stage one more attack on a Teton village. That will be enough to fan the sparks into a flame, *certainment!*"

Clay heard only part of what Cyrus said next: "lucky . . . might work." But it was enough. Clay felt his heart pounding in his chest. His eyes had adjusted well enough to the darkness by now that he could discern the expressions on the faces of Jeff and Shining Moon. Both looked worried, and he knew they had drawn the same conclusion.

Duquesne spent several minutes talking to one of the other men, most likely the man Jacques, who had been mentioned by Cyrus. He had evidently just returned from a scouting trip and brought with him the news of the party of trappers heading up the Big Horn. Clay and Jeff both knew those men would be the same ones who had come into the wilderness with them over a week earlier. Now, with all the pelts they could carry in their canoes, they were going home. But they would never reach the fort alive if Duquesne had his way.

Down in the canyon, Duquesne lifted his voice to address the entire company of renegades, giving them orders to prepare to travel: "We will be leaving tonight so that we may be ready tomorrow to ambush those trappers when they paddle up the river." He spoke to Jacques again for a moment, then went on, "We must reach the river by the middle of the day in order to intercept them."

He was asking them to make a long, hard march in the darkness, Clay thought, but there were no complaints from the renegades. That told Clay something about Duquesne right there. That hard-bitten bunch of killers held him in such respect that they readily agreed to his wishes.

Despite his unimpressive appearance, Duquesne had to be the cruelest, most ruthless man down there. Remembering what Proud Wolf had said about the way Duquesne shot him, Clay could easily believe it.

As the renegades prepared to move out, Clay motioned for his companions to slip back down the slope with him, on the far side from the valley. They moved carefully so as not to dislodge any small rocks that could tumble down the hillside and raise a commotion.

When they could talk more freely, Clay said, "I know we'd planned to go back to Bear Tooth's village once we'd found out where Duquesne was hiding, but there's no time for that. Not with our friends from the fort paddling upriver right into an ambush."

Jeff said, "Yes, we've got to warn them first. Then we can call in the Hunkpapa to help us get rid of Duquesne and his men. Might even get the rest of the trappers to join up with Shining Moon's people and work together to get rid of the ones causing all the trouble."

That idea appealed to Clay. "The two of you head for the river. Find the boys and warn them what Duquesne's up to."

"What'll you be doing?" Jeff asked.

"I'm going to stick close to Duquesne. If you don't manage to hook up with the trappers, I'll be nearby when Duquesne tries to ambush them. I can let off a warning shot, maybe get those bastards in a cross fire. At least our boys would have a fighting chance."

"And you would surely be killed!" Shining Moon protested. "Clay Holt, you cannot do this thing. It is too dangerous!"

"Dammit, there's no time to argue." Clay took hold of Shining Moon's shoulders and pulled her to him, then brought his mouth down on hers in a passionate kiss. When he finally pulled away, he said more tenderly, "I love you, Shining Moon, and I know you think I'm sending you away because of that, but I'm not. You can find your way through these mountains in the dark a lot better than either Jeff or I could. But I can't send you alone."

"I'll stay here and keep an eye on Duquesne," Jeff offered without hesitation. "You go with Shining Moon."

Clay shook his head. "You've grown up into a

hell of a man, little brother, but I'm still a better shot than you, better all around in a scrape. If somebody's got to jump Duquesne's bunch from behind, I'd stand a better chance of coming out alive."

That might be true, but what he was talking about still amounted to suicide. Yet it might not come to that if the unsuspecting trappers could be warned of the ambush in time.

Jeff sighed. "All right. I reckon you're making sense, as usual. Like you're fond of saying, though, I don't have to like it."

"Neither do I." Shining Moon caught Clay's face between her hands and kissed him again, then whispered, "Do not die, Clay Holt."

He embraced her again, then released her and shook hands with Jeff. With Shining Moon leading the way, she and Jeff left quickly, slipping off into the darkness and leaving Clay crouched there on the slope. He watched them until they had disappeared in the shadows, then crawled back up to the top of the ridge to keep an eye on Duquesne and the other men. They were nearly ready to pull out, Clay saw. Wherever they went, he would be right behind them.

That was what he was thinking when something slammed into him from behind.

For long days and nights, Elk Horn had been watching Shining Moon and the two hated white men. He was carrying his bow, and slung over his back was a quiver of arrows. At his waist were his knife and 'hawk. He wished he had one of the muskets promised by Duquesne, but such was not the case.

No matter, Elk Horn told himself. It would be much more satisfying to kill the Holt brothers with his bare hands.

At night he had squatted in the darkness, observing from the shadows as Clay and Shining Moon talked together in quiet, intimate tones around the campfire. He had seen the way they sometimes touched each other when they were walking, quick

brushes of fingertips against an arm or a shoulder that
spoke volumes about how they felt for each other. Elk
Horn had even seen them kiss; the sight made his guts
churn as if he had eaten tainted buffalo meat. Elk
Horn was able to suppress his hatred by reveling in
the knowledge that vengeance which waited for the
proper moment was even sweeter.

Once he saw, however, that the Holts were splitting up and Shining Moon was going with Jeff, Elk
Horn knew he could postpone his revenge no longer.
He had not been close enough to learn who the
strange white men in the canyon were, and he did not
care. All he wanted to do was kill Clay Holt, then go
after Jeff and Shining Moon. He had hoped that Shining Moon could witness Clay's slow, painful death,
but he realized that was not to be.

As she and Jeff moved off in the darkness, Elk
Horn crept closer and closer to Clay, moving silently,
until he was near enough to raise his knife above his
head and spring!

Clay must have heard the faint scrape of a foot on
rock, a sound so soft he was not even consciously
aware of it. He jerked his head to the side as Elk Horn
crashed into him, and the blade in the Hunkpapa's
hand rang on the rocks beneath them as the killing
thrust missed. Clay grabbed Elk Horn's wrist and
tried to heave the burly warrior's weight off him.

There was no doubt in Clay's mind about the
identity of the shadowy attacker. He could smell the
bear grease rubbed into the man's hair and knew his
opponent had to be an Indian—and Elk Horn had the
best reason to want him dead.

Clay twisted again as Elk Horn struck at his face
with a clenched fist. The blow scraped along Clay's
temple with enough force to make lights dance in
front of his eyes. He brought up his right leg and managed to hook his foot in front of Elk Horn's left shoulder. With a grunt of effort, Clay kicked the warrior
away from him.

Elk Horn rolled over twice and came up in a crouch. He snarled like a maddened animal as he tensed to throw himself at Clay.

Clay was dimly aware of startled shouts coming from the canyon where Duquesne and his men were camped. Already the battle between him and Elk Horn had made enough noise to alert the renegades.

Now, as Elk Horn lunged again, Clay met his charge as best he could, but he was a little off-balance. He fell on the crest of the ridge, the breath whooshing out of his lungs as Elk Horn's weight came down on top of him. The two men rolled several feet down the slope toward the canyon floor, setting off a small rock-slide before they came to a halt. The falling stones bounced and rattled on down to the canyon, giving away the location of the struggle to the Frenchman and his group of killers.

Clay had no time to worry about that. He blocked another thrust by Elk Horn's knife, but this time the blade ripped the buckskin of his sleeve and laid open the flesh beneath in a searing gash. Clay drove a punch to Elk Horn's face and felt the Indian's nose flatten under the blow. Elk Horn howled in pain. Clay tore out of his grip, scrambled to the side, and came up on his knees as he drew his knife from its sheath.

Elk Horn slashed back and forth with his own blade as he attacked again, forcing Clay to duck backward against the hillside. There was nowhere else to go. He snapped a kick at the warrior's belly and felt it connect. Elk Horn staggered, but still he came on. He reversed his hold on the bone handle of his knife, then brought it slashing down toward Clay.

Clay rose to meet him, and a fiery pain drew a line across the top of his left shoulder. At the same time, he thrust his own knife upward. The blade slipped past Elk Horn's flailing left arm and penetrated the warrior's torso. At first the knife went in smoothly, seemingly unhindered by the flesh it was rending. Then the blade grated against bone, stopping for a second before it drove even deeper into Elk

Horn's chest. Elk Horn gasped, his breath foul in Clay's face, and then he went limp. His weight sagged against Clay.

With a grunt of effort Clay shoved the corpse off him. His shoulder ached where the Hunkpapa's blade had slashed it, and he could feel blood soaking his shirt. He started to push himself to his feet.

Shapes emerged from the darkness, and a rifle muzzle suddenly dug itself painfully into Clay's throat, forcing him back down. As he lay on the rocky slope, pebbles pressed uncomfortably into his back, he saw figures looming over him and knew that Duquesne had come to investigate. In fact, the little Frenchman was the one who had prodded him with the rifle and now had its muzzle resting lightly on Clay's chest.

"Someone bring a light," Duquesne snapped brusquely. He chuckled, and his tone sounded more cheerful as he went on, "I want to see what we have caught. Perhaps its pelt will be worth something, no?"

CHAPTER TWENTY-TWO

If British merchants were prohibited from trading . . . American merchants . . . would be enabled, most probably, to become the successful rivals of the Northwest Company in the more distant parts of the continent; to which we might look, in such case, with a well-founded hope of enjoying great advantages from the fur trade. But if this prohibition does not shortly take place, I venture to predict that no such attempts will ever be made, and that consequently we shall for several generations be taxed with the defense of a country which to us would be no more than a barren waste.

—MERIWETHER LEWIS, from "Essay on an Indian Policy"

Clay's hands were tied and his weapons stripped from him, but his legs were still free. Of course, there was no place for him to run—not surrounded by killers.

Duquesne stood before him, one side of his bearded face garishly lit by the red of the campfire flames.

Clay understood now what Shining Moon had meant about Duquesne's eyes. Once you had looked into them and seen the viciousness there, you forgot all about how small the man was. Evil had no size.

"So you refuse to tell us who you are or why you were spying on us, eh?" Duquesne said. "No matter. I care nothing for that savage you killed, either, but both of you shall be of use to me." He turned to two of the renegades who stood nearby, pointing their rifles in Clay's general direction. "You men will stay here with this one. Keep him alive for now—if you can. If he tries to escape or causes trouble, go ahead and kill him. You understand?"

The men nodded. Neither looked the least bit upset at the prospect of killing Clay.

"When we are through with the trappers, we will raid Bear Tooth's village," Duquesne went on, speaking now to the lieutenant called Cyrus. "The damned savage should have given us an answer by now. I do not trust him. He and his people will pay for not cooperating with us."

Clay felt a wave of horror wash over him. If Duquesne was not stopped, all those people—and many more innocent men, women, and children—might well die.

"When we are through, we will kill this American and leave him there, as if he fell in the attack," Duquesne told Cyrus. "The other Teton will be more convinced than ever that the Americans are to blame for all their grief. The war will come, my friends. I am sure of it."

Two other men came up carrying Elk Horn's body, which they had brought down from the ridge. Duquesne motioned for them to place it on the ground at his feet. When they had done so and stepped back, Duquesne pulled a pistol from his belt, cocked the loaded weapon, and fired it into the chest of the corpse, the lead ball obliterating the fatal knife wound Elk Horn had received from Clay.

Clay jumped a little, startled by the unexpected roar.

Duquesne said in a satisfied voice, "There. We will take the redskin with us and leave his body on the bank of the river where we ambush the Americans. When Lisa's men come to retrieve the bodies of their fallen comrades, they will find this dead Indian as proof that the Teton attacked them." He glanced up at Clay. "Perfect, is it not?"

Clay only clenched his teeth. Nothing he could say would convey the depth of the contempt he felt for the voyageur.

Duquesne sneered, laughed again, and turned away. "Come," he called to his men. "We must go now."

Led by Duquesne, the renegades filed away from the fire and out of the canyon. Clay had a chance to count them now. There were fewer than he had first estimated—twenty-six, minus the two left behind to guard him. That left twenty-four men to ambush the trappers carrying pelts back to the fort.

Still better than two-to-one odds. Clay bit back a groan of despair. His friends were heading into sure death and disaster, unless Jeff and Shining Moon managed to get to them first and warn them.

He had been trying to avoid thinking about Shining Moon. The chances that he would never see her again had increased with his capture by Duquesne. *Damn Elk Horn!* Clay thought.

Elk Horn had paid for his hatred and his obsession with his life, but he had probably cost Clay his own life in the process. Clay smiled grimly. Elk Horn might have considered that a fair trade.

One of the guards suddenly thrust a leg behind his feet and then slammed a rifle butt into his chest, knocking Clay over backward. He landed heavily on the floor of the canyon. "Ye don't have anything to smile about, mister," he said in a coarse British accent. "Pretty soon you'll be dead, eh?"

Clay looked up at the men standing over him and gave in to curiosity that had been plaguing him ever since he had figured out that someone was trying to pit the Americans and the Teton tribes against each other. "What the hell are you Englishers doing here, working for a Frenchman?"

The other man shrugged. "Don't much like taking orders from a bloody Frog, but Duquesne's paying good wages. He ain't told none of us what he's up to. Keeps that to himself, he does. But if I had to guess, I'd say 'tis something to do with the beaver. There's fur companies in London'd look at this country with a bit of envy. Teeming with beaver, it is."

"Shut up, Nick," the first guard snapped. "Why're ye blathering on to this scut? He'll be dead soon."

"Well, maybe he wants to know what he's dying for, Donnie. I don't see that it's doing any harm."

Clay was in no mood to listen to them squabble. Awkwardly he pushed himself into a sitting position.

Both men immediately jumped back and leveled their rifles at him. "Here now!" Nick exclaimed. "Don't be trying nothing funny now!"

"How much harm can I do like this?" Clay asked, pulling against the bonds on his wrists. He had already tested the strength of the knots and knew that he would not be able to slip out of them.

He looked over at the fire. An iron pot sat in the embers at its edge. He nodded toward it and asked, "Is that food?"

"Aye," Donnie said. "Stew."

"Would ye like some?" Nick asked.

His companion said, "We don't have to be feeding him! Duquesne's going to kill him tomorrow or the next day. Won't hurt him to go hungry 'tween now and then."

"Won't hurt none to feed him, neither." Nick

turned to Clay and said, "I'll fetch ye a cup of the broth."

He ambled over to the fire, put his rifle on the ground, and found a tin cup in a jumble of gear. He dipped it into the pot of stew, straightened, then returned to Clay.

The rifle was left behind by the fire.

Clay saw that and felt his heart begin to slug a bit harder in his chest. It was possible, even probable, that Jeff and Shining Moon would not reach the trappers in time to prevent the ambush by Duquesne. The odds would be much better if he could somehow escape and go after Duquesne. At least his friends from the fort would have some warning that way. He was going to have to make an escape attempt sometime, and better sooner than later. He had already decided to seize the first opportunity, no matter how scant it might be.

This was it, Clay realized.

"Can't cut you loose," Nick said as he approached, "but I think ye can hold the cup well enough to manage. That all right with you?"

"Sure." Clay moved onto his knees, again awkwardly because of his bonds.

Nick leaned toward him, the cup extended in both hands.

Clay took the cup, then lunged forward, flinging the contents up toward Nick's face. The hot broth splashed into the man's eyes, blinding him and making him let out a bellow of pain and anger. Clay rolled into his legs, knocking them out from under him. Nick fell on top of him.

"Dammit, get out of the way, you bloody fool!" Donnie screeched, dancing around and trying to get a clear shot at Clay with his rifle.

Clay twisted, fumbling for the ax tucked behind Nick's belt. It was not a crude stone 'hawk such as the Indians carried, more suitable for bludgeoning than cutting, but rather a keen-edged steel instrument. Clay jerked the ax free, feeling the blade cut across the ball of his left hand and hoping he would not slash his wrists before he managed to cut the ropes. Then the bindings caught on the edge, and he worked them back and forth for a couple of frenzied seconds.

He felt some of the strands part, but not all. Nick squirmed away, rolled over to face him, and lifted himself on one hand while he groped for his pistol with the other. "You bloody bastard! You burned me!"

Clay's shoulders heaved as he struggled to cut the remaining strands of rope. He knew that in another instant both Nick and Donnie were going to shoot him.

He threw himself backward as the two renegades fired. One of the balls thudded into the ground beside him, but the other ripped across Clay's left side. Pain lanced through him, but with it came the important realization that both men had discharged their weapons. Nick's rifle was by the fire, several yards away, and Donnie did not have a pistol.

Clay had a few seconds' grace, which he put to good use. He slashed at the bonds again and felt them part all the way. Ignoring the pain in his side and the sticky wetness that seemed to be running from it, he shifted his grip on the ax he had taken from Nick. His arm went up and back, then flashed forward. The throw was perfect, the ax completing a single revolution before its blade smashed into Nick's head with a soggy thud. The man went over backward, arms splayed out at his sides.

Donnie screamed curses at Clay and ran forward, jerking a knife from his belt as he came. Clay was getting dizzy now, but he forced himself to move. He rolled to the side, and the charging renegade dove past him. Clay scrambled up and dashed toward Nick, who was either unconscious or dead, the ax still protruding from his forehead.

Before Clay could reach the weapon, Donnie tackled him from behind, and Clay felt the gash of steel on his right thigh. He tried to twist away, but his muscles were not obeying him as quickly and smoothly as they usually did. He managed to grab Donnie's wrist and turn the next slash of the knife away from him.

They rolled over and over, Clay desperately hanging on to the Englishman's wrist as they went, until they bumped against Nick's corpse and came to a halt. With his free hand Clay groped at the body, hoping to find something else he could use as a weapon. His fingers brushed the smooth grip of a hunting knife.

Donnie had not noticed what Clay was doing. As the world swam dizzily before Clay's eyes, he grasped the knife, tugged it loose, and plunged the blade into Donnie's side. The man shrieked as the steel tore into him. Clay shoved with all of his remaining strength. Not tempered as well as it should have been, the blade snapped and broke off.

But it had already done its work. Donnie went limp, his own knife falling harmlessly to the side.

Clay rolled the dead man away from him. He had to make sure Nick was dead, too. Although dizzy, he checked the other man. The ax blade was deeply imbedded in his forehead, and blood had seeped from his ears, nose, and eyes.

Clay closed his eyes. What was left of his strength deserted him, and he stretched out full length on the ground next to Nick's body. He knew he had to get up, gather all the weapons he could find, and get started after Duquesne. He had to ignore the wound in his side, the knife cut on his thigh, and the earlier injuries from the fight with Elk Horn.

All right, he told himself sternly. He had lost some blood, but not enough to stop him. He could tell the lead ball had only dug a deep furrow across his ribs; it was not lodged in his body. He could keep moving. He had to, but only after he had rested a bit—

That thought went through his head, and then Clay Holt was out cold.

When the sun rose, Jeff estimated that he and Shining Moon were still a good ten miles from the Big

Horn River. During the night they had not been able to proceed very quickly through the rugged foothills, despite Shining Moon's familiarity with the terrain. The possibility that they might not reach the river in time to warn the trappers had begun to gnaw at Jeff's mind. All they could do was push on and hope for the best.

They were sliding down a steep slope covered with thick foliage, the branches clawing at Jeff's clothes and skin, when Shining Moon suddenly grasped his arm and hissed, "Get down! Do not move!"

Jeff dug in his heels and grabbed the trunk of a stubby bush to stop his descent, then waited to find out why she had called such a sudden halt. Breathing shallowly, she crouched beside him. The sun washed the slope where they hid, and already Jeff could feel its warmth chasing away the chill of night.

A few seconds later he heard the faint clip-clop of horses' hooves. He gave Shining Moon a look of puzzlement, but she gestured for him to be quiet. She lifted her head just enough to study their surroundings, then motioned for him to do the same.

Through the screen of leaves he saw a dozen Indian braves riding along a trail at the base of the slope. Their faces were painted in colors and patterns unfamiliar to Jeff, as were the markings on their buckskins. As he and Shining Moon lowered their heads, he asked her in a whisper, "Your people?"

She shook her head. "Blackfoot."

Jeff's face set in grim lines. He knew that this was a long way from the usual stomping grounds of the Blackfoot, but like the Arikara, they staged an occasional foray into the territory of the Crow and the Sioux, looking to raid, plunder, and kill their traditional enemies. In addition, the Blackfoot hated white men and had ever since that encounter with the Lewis and Clark expedition Clay had told him about. If the warriors down below knew that Jeff and Shining Moon were there, they would be in great danger.

Jeff's jaw clenched. Trying to slip past the Black-foot would just get them killed, and then the warning to the trappers would go undelivered for sure. They would have to wait until the Blackfoot passed, which would delay them that much longer.

Then Jeff heard the Indians talking among them-selves and ventured another look. To his dismay he saw that they had stopped for some reason and were dismounting. He did not think their calling a halt had anything to do with Shining Moon and him; they had not even been down where the Blackfoot were, so they could not have left any tracks. But regardless of the reason, he and the woman were stuck there until the Indians moved on.

Every second seemed like an eternity. Yet some-how they managed to stay in the brush—crouched, motionless, silent—for the hours that passed before the Blackfoot got on their horses again and rode away. When the Indians were finally gone, Jeff wiped sweat out of his eyes and stood up. Shining Moon started on down the hillside, and he followed her.

As they walked they chewed strips of dried, salted buffalo meat, and occasionally they stopped to drink from one of the many streams they came to. By mutual agreement they had stepped up the pace and were trotting through the open areas now. For too much of the time, however, the terrain was too rugged to allow that. They had to slow down to keep from twisting an ankle or falling and breaking a bone on the rocky ground. Jeff tried not to pay too much attention to the sun as it followed its inexorable path upward in the sky, but he found his eyes straying to it quite fre-quently. Suddenly, during one such glance, he real-ized that the sun was almost directly overhead. It was nearly noon.

Jeff bit back a groan. Duquesne had intended to reach the river by noon with his men so that they could set up their ambush. The murderous Frenchman probably had his killers in place by now, and they would just be waiting for the American trappers to paddle into the sights of their rifles.

His legs were like lead, but Jeff forced them to keep moving, to continue carrying him west toward the Big Horn. They had to reach the stream soon. Surely they had come far enough by now—

Shining Moon caught his arm at the top of a rise and pointed. Water flickered brightly in the sun. "The river," she said.

Along that stretch, the Big Horn ran relatively straight between brushy banks. The hill where Jeff and Shining Moon paused, panting for breath, was about a hundred yards from the water. To the north a rocky bluff thrust out almost to the edge of the river itself.

Jeff looked to the south. "There they are!" he exclaimed, pointing toward the small convoy of five canoes being paddled up the river by buckskin-clad men. He could see the beaver hides, piled in each canoe between the pair of trappers wielding paddles. As he and Clay had speculated, this was indeed the group with which they had left the fort.

Shining Moon grasped Jeff's arm, her fingers digging painfully into his flesh. "Look on the bank, on this side!"

Jeff studied the thick growth and began to see the men concealed there, hiding behind bushes, trees, and rocks. Duquesne's men were ready. The first volley would wipe out at least half the trappers, maybe more.

Jeff lifted his rifle and cocked the primed and loaded weapon. It would be a long shot, but maybe he could drop one of the ambushers. At any rate, the explosion of black powder would warn the men on the river that something was amiss.

"By the Wakan Tanka!" Shining Moon suddenly cried. "Clay Holt!"

Even as she spoke, a pair of shots erupted.

Jeff saw a man standing at the top of the bluff overlooking the river. In each hand he held a smoking pistol. As Jeff watched in amazement, Clay tossed the empty weapons aside and snatched up a rifle from the ground at his feet. The long-barreled flintlock roared, and one of Duquesne's men screamed in pain as he staggered out of his cover to the edge of the river, then fell in with a great splash.

Clay was on the opposite side of the renegades from Jeff and Shining Moon, but even at that distance, Jeff could see the bloodstains on his brother's buckskins. Thrusting aside his worry for the moment, Jeff let out a whoop and turned his attention back to Duquesne's men. Sighting in on one of them, he cocked the rifle and pressed the trigger.

It was impossible to see through the smoke and tell whether or not his ball had hit anything.

Jeff reloaded the flintlock. Beside him Shining Moon snatched the pistols from his belt. As he went to one knee to steady his aim, she fired first one pistol, then the other. The range was too great for her to hit anything, but the shots made it sound as if they had a larger force.

Out of the corner of his eye Jeff saw the canoes angling toward the far bank of the river, the burst of gunfire having warned them that something was wrong. There was a ragged volley from Duquesne's men, but it had been fired in haste as they came under attack, and the lead balls splashed harmlessly into the water.

Clay was still firing, and over the continuing explosions, Jeff faintly heard his brother shout, "Duquesne!" There was no time to wonder how Clay had gotten hold of so many guns or how he had turned up just at the right moment. Instead, Jeff squeezed off another shot with his own rifle.

The trappers grounded their canoes and scrambled out of the craft, then ducked behind cover. They could tell that the hostile fire originated from the brush on the other side of the stream, so they unlimbered their rifles and began firing. Some resistance came from Duquesne's men, but not much. Even though they had the superior numbers, they had lost the element of surprise and were pinned down in a three-way cross fire—Clay to the north, Jeff and Shining Moon to the south, and the intended victims across the river to the west. All poured lead into the stretch of riverbank where the would-be ambushers were concealed.

To Jeff time seemed to slow in a haze of acrid black powder smoke. He loaded and fired, loaded and fired, until the actions were automatic. He could see more and more of Duquesne's men sprawled on the ground now. The gunfire was taking a deadly toll.

Suddenly Jeff spotted a figure running through the brush, fleeing from the cross fire that was decimating the renegades. Shining Moon saw the man, too.

"Duquesne!" she exclaimed. "He is getting away!"

Jeff shifted his aim and squeezed the flintlock's trigger. "Did I get him?" he shouted, the eerie echo of his own voice telling him he was becoming momentarily deafened by the continuous crash of gunfire.

"No! He is still running!"

Jeff could not afford to leave and go after Duquesne. Somebody had to keep the pressure on the Frenchman's lackeys. Maybe Clay—

Jeff glanced toward the bluff as that thought started through his mind. Clay was gone.

How it was possible for him still to be moving after everything that had happened, Clay did not know. Maybe the power of a person's rage could keep him functioning when he should have long since collapsed.

All he knew was that he would not let Duquesne get away if he could help it.

When he had slowly regained consciousness back at Duquesne's camp, his first thought had been the last one on his mind before he passed out: He had to get to the river and warn his friends. His muscles were stiff, he was injured, but he was able to move. He had gathered up his own weapons, as well as those of the men he had killed, loaded and primed them all, then slung the powder horns and shot pouches over his shoulder. Weighted down with this miniature arsenal, he had trotted out of the canyon, every step sending pain through him. He had ignored it and kept going.

Instinct alone had guided him, and he knew he might get hopelessly lost in the night. He had had to take that chance. He could not stand by and let Duquesne's ambush succeed without at least trying to stop it.

The stars had allowed him to keep his path headed in a generally westerly direction. He knew he would hit the Big Horn sooner or later if he kept going that way, and he knew that when the sun came up, he would be able to adjust his course even more.

The hours that followed had been a hellish nightmare of pain and effort that he never would forget. By the time the sun had come up, he felt as if he'd been running forever, and he could tell that he was still nowhere near the river. He had paused only to slake his thirst every now and then, but other than that he had kept running.

Then, abruptly, he had reached the bluff overlooking the river, and it had taken him by such surprise that he'd almost run right off the brink. He had stopped himself in time, looked around, and spotted the canoes coming up the river. A flicker of movement in the brush along the near bank had caught his eye, and when he had looked closer, he'd seen the men hiding there.

He was in time.

He had allowed that exultant thought to run through his mind for only a second. He had to focus on turning the tables on Duquesne. He pulled a brace of pistols from his belt and fired. . . .

And now, with the battle nearly over, Duquesne was fleeing like the dog he was. Clay left the rifles on the bluff, loaded and primed a couple of the empty pistols, and summoned up the willpower to make his aching legs run again, this time after Duquesne. He followed the bluff until the slope along its side became gradual enough for him to negotiate it. His heart pounded heavily in his chest as he half ran, half slid down to the forested benchland where Duquesne had disappeared.

Clay did not believe fate would allow Duquesne to escape. Something, some mysterious destiny, had guided him to the river and allowed him to reach it when his injuries should have prevented such an accomplishment. Jeff and Shining Moon had made it, too; Clay had seen them on a hill to the south and felt a pang of excitement and pride at the way Shining Moon was joining in the fight. Surely the power that had brought him and his brother and the woman he loved here in time to foil the ambush would not permit Duquesne to escape unpunished.

The sound of someone crashing through the brush came to Clay's ears, and he followed the noise. That had to be Duquesne. Branches slashed at Clay's face as he forced his way through the undergrowth, but he ignored the pain. He had gotten quite good at ignoring pain by now, he thought fleetingly. When this was over, he might collapse, but not until then.

Suddenly the noise that he had been following stopped. Duquesne was not running through the brush anymore. But if that was the case, then where was he?

The faint crackle of a leaf to his left made Clay dive to the ground. A gun blasted, so close it seemed almost in his ear. Twisting on the ground, Clay angled one of his pistols toward the sound, cocked it, and squeezed the trigger. The flintlock bucked noisily in his hand.

He could not tell if he had hit anything or not. As he tried to scramble to his feet, his right leg gave way unexpectedly beneath him, and he fell. Clay grimaced as he looked down at the leg and saw the fresh, spreading bloodstain. Duquesne's shot had hit him after all. In the heat of the moment he had not even felt the ball tearing his flesh.

He heard the sound of running footsteps. The cords of his neck standing out from the strain, Clay tried to lift himself to go after Duquesne, but his leg would not support him. He uttered a bitter, heartfelt curse as he collapsed again. The footsteps faded.

Providence, fate, destiny . . . whatever you wanted to call it, Clay supposed that it only went so far.

A few minutes later he heard someone calling his name. Recognizing the voice as that of his brother, Clay lifted himself on one elbow. "Jeff! Over here, Jeff!"

There was an anxious expression on Jeff's face when he came running up. He dropped to one knee beside Clay and exclaimed, "My God! How bad are you hurt, Clay?"

"Not as bad as it looks. Some of this blood on me belonged to a couple of other fellows. I'm shot in the side and leg, though, and I can't go after Duquesne any more. You'll have to find him."

Jeff frowned for a moment, then shook his head. "I'm taking you back to the river. Catching up to Duquesne can wait for another day."

Clay started to protest, then fell silent. Jeff was making sense. Duquesne was gone, and it would be a waste of time to chase him now. Besides, Clay thought as he summoned up the ghost of a grin, it would be good to see Shining Moon again. Even though it had been less than a day since they had parted, he felt as if he had been away from her for months.

"Reckon you're right," he said to Jeff. "Give me a hand up, and we'll get started."

Jeff helped Clay to his feet and then put an arm around his waist. Leaning on each other, the brothers walked toward the river.

When they got there, Shining Moon broke away from the group of trappers and dashed over to meet Jeff and Clay. She threw her arms around Clay and held him tightly. "I was so afraid I would never see you again," she whispered.

"I plan on being around for a long time yet. And there's going to be peace between your people and mine now, so we won't have to worry about that, either." He stroked her raven hair, taking comfort and strength from the warmth of her body pressed against his. A man could endure a hell of a lot, he thought, as long as he had a woman like this standing with him. And that was the way it would be with them from now on.

A handful of Duquesne's men had surrendered to the American trappers. The others were either dead or gone, having fled into the wilderness. The survivors would not cause any trouble, Clay reflected as he sat on a rock while Shining Moon patched up his wounds as best she could. Scattered through the woods, alone, with limited ammunition and powder, the remnants of Duquesne's forces probably would not survive to regroup, and even if they did, they would probably light out for the far north and home rather than come up with any more deviltry.

He would feel more certain of that, though, if they had managed to kill or capture Duquesne himself.

"We will go to my village," Shining Moon told Clay and Jeff. "Bear Tooth will hear the truth about the troubles that have come to our land, and he will see that all the other Teton tribes know the truth as well. Soon everyone in the mountains will know of Duquesne's evil."

"There's proof right there," Jeff said, pointing to Elk Horn's body, which Duquesne's men had brought with them. "That shows he was intending to lay the blame for this ambush on the Hunkpapa."

"We'll take the word back to the fort, along with these prisoners," one of the trappers said. "I reckon ol' Lisa will spread the news, too." The man's whiskery face creased in a grin. "It'll be good to know the mountains are safe again—except for grizzlies and panthers and such."

Clay watched the canoes shove off, heavily laden now with prisoners as well as plews. A wave of weariness washed over him as he tried to stand up. He sank back down on the big rock and said, "Reckon I'd better rest awhile before we start back. Ought to be safe enough now. The danger's over."

"Yes," Shining Moon agreed. "The danger is over. Come."

With his brother supporting him on one side and his woman on the other, Clay limped over to a grassy spot under a tree. Jeff and Shining Moon lowered him carefully to the ground.

"You get some sleep, big brother," Jeff told him. "We'll be here when you wake up."

"That is a promise, Clay Holt," Shining Moon added, taking his hand warmly in hers.

She was still holding it when he went to sleep.

CHAPTER TWENTY-THREE

The liberty to our merchants of hunting for the purpose of procuring food, in ascending and descending the navigable water-courses, as well as while stationary at their commercial posts, is a privilege which should not be denied them; but as the unlimited extent of such a privilege would produce much evil, it should certainly be looked on as a subject of primary importance. It should, therefore, enter into all those compacts which we may think proper to form with the Indians of that country, and be so shaped as to leave them no solid grounds of discontent.

—MERIWETHER LEWIS, from "Essay on an Indian Policy"

It had been months since the man called Duquesne had left Fort Rouge. Fletcher McKendrick was beginning to despair of ever seeing him again. He vondered if Duquesne had taken the money from the London and Northwestern Enterprise fully intending not to honor their agreement. That would not really fit what McKendrick had heard about the man, but the canny Scot knew not to put anything past anyone. Betrayal was always a possibility.

If that turned out to be the case, Duquesne would regret it. McKendrick had a long memory, and sooner or later he would even the score with the little Frenchman.

In the meantime, the company's directors back in London were becoming more and more impatient. McKendrick had received several letters from them, each demanding in increasingly stronger language to know when he would have some progress to report. The Hudson's Bay Company and the North West Company were both growing, and unless the London and Northwestern soon gained a foothold in the American Rockies, it would never be able to catch up to its larger competitors.

McKendrick was sipping a mug of ale in the small tavern one late autumn day and mulling over such dark thoughts when he heard a commotion outside. He glanced toward the door in idle curiosity, figuring that the disturbance was nothing more than a couple of trappers fighting over a dog or a woman. He was shocked when the door burst open and a haggard figure was ushered into the room by several of the company's trappers.

The man's beard was long and tangled, his features gaunt, and his eyes sunken deeply in his head. His clothes were in tatters, and he looked as if he had been lost in the wilderness for weeks. He staggered a little as he walked.

And McKendrick realized to his shock that the man was coming toward him.

"You're McKendrick?" the stranger rasped in a voice grown hoarse from disuse.

"Aye," the Scotsman said. "What do ye want with me, man?"

"I was with Duquesne," the man said.

McKendrick's eyes widened in surprise. He got to his feet quickly and grasped the stranger's arm. It felt thin and brittle under McKendrick's fingers. "What's happened to him?" McKendrick demanded.

"Dead, for all I know." The man let out a moan and started to collapse. McKendrick held him up. "For God's sake, guv'nor, let a man sit down and buy him a drink."

McKendrick signaled for ale to be brought, then carefully helped the stranger onto the bench next to the table. He waved the other trappers away, motioning for them to leave the room. He did not know what this man would have to say, but he wanted his ears to be the only ones hearing it.

"Tell me all about it," McKendrick said as he sat down himself.

Between great swallows of the ale that was brought to him, the man did just that, telling of Duquesne's efforts to cause a war between the Indians and the American trappers at the fort in the valley where the Yellowstone and Big Horn rivers met. He shuddered as he spoke of the ambush that had gone wrong and the battle beside the river.

"My God," McKendrick breathed. He leaned forward and asked intently, "Do the Americans know who Duquesne was working for?"

"I don't think so," the man replied. "I believe was the only one he took into his confidence. I was his second-in-command."

"And ye say he got away, too?"

The man shook his head. "I don't know. Not many of us did, and as far as I know, I'm the only one who made it back up here."

McKendrick leaned back, a little relieved. It was vitally important that the Americans not know who was behind Duquesne's efforts because even if Duquesne was dead, there were other men McKendrick could hire. He could try again. His employers in Lon don would not like the extra delay, but he could do nothing about that.

Manuel Lisa and the Americans, he vowed, had not seen the last of Fletcher McKendrick.

"Drink up, laddie," he told the gaunt stranger. "Plenty more where that came from."

Nearly a month had passed since the carnage on the Big Horn. Winter would be setting in soon. Clay Holt still had a slight limp from the wound he had received from Duquesne, and he could already tell that the leg was going to ache in cold weather, a reminder that would stay with him for the rest of his life —as if he needed to be reminded of Duquesne's villainy.

All of Clay's other wounds had healed, and he felt back to normal for the most part. As he walked across the open space in the center of the stockade at the fort, a cold breeze blowing in his face to offset the warmth of the afternoon sun, he actually felt good. Shining Moon was beside him, and she was all he really needed.

But in addition, the fort was full of his friends that afternoon, and laughter filled the air. The fur season was over, and for the past few days trappers had been coming to the fort. Most of them were Lisa's men, who had spread out over the territory for one last sweep of the creeks and rivers once it was clear they no longer had anything to fear from the Indians; but there were also visitors, free trappers who had come to the Rockies to make fortunes of their own. Bear Tooth, Proud Wolf, and some of the other Hunkpapa were there, too, as well as some Crow braves who had brought their families with them. Manuel Lisa had spread the word that everyone was welcome at the celebration to mark the conclusion of the highly successful first season of trapping in the valley of the Yellowstone.

Clay saw Jeff leaning against one of the posts that held up the awning over the porch of the fort's main

building. The fort had taken on a solid, respectable
look, Clay thought. A town might even grow there
someday, he mused, if enough folks came west. And
once they discovered how successful Lisa had been in
his daring endeavor, they would come. The lure of
money, of independence, would prove irresistible, and
there was nothing any short-sighted politicians could
do to stop it.

The vast frontier had been opened at last. The
people would come.

But some would be heading east, at least for a
while. Manuel Lisa and a party of men would start
back down the river, bound for St. Louis, within a
week. Among the men going with him would be Jeff
Holt. Others would spend the winter at the fort.

Clay and Shining Moon would be part of that
group. They even had a small cabin of their own,
which was fitting for a married couple, Clay thought.
The ceremony had taken place while he was recovering from his wounds at Bear Tooth's village, along
with a ritual formally welcoming him and Jeff into the
Hunkpapa tribe. They were Clay's people now, his
family.

But Jeff's family was back in Ohio, and Clay could
not blame him for wanting to go there.

He and Shining Moon stepped up onto the porch
beside Jeff, who was watching the carousing. The
mountain men had spent a long, dangerous summer
in the Rockies, and they were making up for it now
with whiskey guzzling, bawdy songs, wrestling
matches, and shooting competitions.

"Quite a party, isn't it?" Clay asked.

Jeff nodded. "Lisa says he intends to hold one
every year about this time. It sure drew folks in from
all over." With a glance over at Clay, he asked, "Did
you know Colter's back?"

"No!" Clay exclaimed. "Where is he?"

"He was around here a little while ago, telling tall
tales about some of the things he saw while he was
out tramping across the country. From the sound of it,

he found hell's back door. Claimed to have come through a valley where the ground smokes and steams all the time and the air stinks of brimstone. Said that in some places the stuff bubbles right up through the earth, and in others water and steam shoot straight up into the air a hundred feet or so." Jeff grinned. "I don't put much stock in the story myself, but you've got to admit it makes a good yarn. I just didn't know old John had that much imagination."

"Neither did I. Reckon they can call the place Colter's Hell." He looked across the clearing. "Say, here he comes now. What's he carrying?"

John Colter was indeed strolling toward them, a large pouch made of buckskin dangling from his hand. The lean Virginian smiled and waved in greeting as he came up to them.

"Howdy again, Jeff." Colter extended his hand to Clay. "Good to see you, Clay. I've heard about your troubles this summer. Sounds like you were busy."

"Reckon you could say that," Clay commented dryly. "John, this is my wife, Shining Moon."

Colter touched the floppy brim of his hat and nodded to Shining Moon. "Pleased to meet you, ma'am. You've got yourself a good husband here, but I wouldn't count on bein' able to keep him at home much. He likes to wander around, sort of like me."

"That is fine, Mr. Colter," Shining Moon said. "I will go with him when he wanders."

"She means it, too." Clay gestured at the bag Colter was holding. "What's that you've got there?"

"Found it out in the woods the other day while I was comin' in," Colter said. "Thought you boys might be interested in it, and now that I've heard what went on around here while I was gone, I know you will be."

Clay and Jeff looked at each other and frowned, unsure of what Colter might be getting at.

"Well, let's see it," Jeff said.

"Sure." Colter undid the drawstring at the top of the pouch, then upended it.

A human head fell out, then bounced once on the ground before coming to rest with its eyes staring hideously, sightlessly, up at the sky.

"Duquesne!" Clay stiffened.

Beside him, Shining Moon recoiled in horror. Jeff took a deep breath.

"Thought it might be him," Colter said, unbothered by the grisly sight of Duquesne's head lying on the ground. "I figure he ran into some Indians who'd heard about how he was really responsible for all those raids on their villages. Reckon they had some fun with him for a while, then killed him and stuck his head up on a pole. That's how I found it. Barbaric, ain't it? But then, considerin' whose head it is, maybe he had it comin'."

"I don't know," Jeff said slowly. "I'm not sure even Duquesne deserved that."

"But if anybody ever did . . ." Clay left the thought unfinished.

Colter bent over, grasped the hair on the head, and put it back in the pouch. "I'll be seein' you boys," he said.

They watched him walk away with his gruesome trophy, and Clay shook his head—which he was thankful was still attached to his shoulders. "Reckon that finally puts an end to it."

"Holt!"

The angry voice was familiar, and the bitter memories it brought back flooded through Clay.

Jeff said harshly, "My God! It can't be!"

But it was, Clay saw. Stalking toward them were two men in buckskins. Both of them wore beards now, but they were still recognizable as Zach and Aaron Garwood.

"You'd better step back, Shining Moon," Clay said quietly.

"What is it, Clay Holt? Who are these men?"

"We knew them—a long time ago."

It was shocking how long ago that seemed. All the tragedy brought on by the Garwoods seemed far n the past. And it was not fair for them to reappear now, by God! Clay thought. He had made a life for himself in the mountains, and the Garwoods had no right to intrude on it.

But they *were* here, and they would have to be dealt with. Clay glanced over at Jeff, and the two of them stepped down off the porch and walked forward to meet Zach and Aaron.

The Garwoods came to a halt a few feet away. They carried all the accoutrements of trappers, and it was obvious they had come to the frontier to seek their fortunes. Knowing Zach Garwood, though, Clay thought they probably had another reason, too. They had probably been hoping to find Jeff and him so that they could finally settle the score for Luther and Pete.

Zach fingered the hilt of his hunting knife and said, "Figured we'd run into you boys at this little get-together. Nice to see somebody from back home, ain't it?"

"Not necessarily," Clay snapped. "We don't have anything to say to you, Zach. You'd best move on, both of you."

"Now, that's not very friendly. Here Aaron and I come all the way out here, just hopin' to find the Holt brothers again, and this is the way you act when we do find you. Some folks might be offended by that attitude, Clay." Hate burned plainly in Zach's eyes despite his smile.

"I don't give a damn whether you are or not."

"Clay and I don't want any trouble with you," Jeff put in. "We don't want anything more to do with that stupid, senseless feud. We came out here to put all of that behind us."

"Like you put my brothers in the ground?" Zach's voice was taking on an edge now, an unpleasant keening that revealed the depth of his hatred and madness. His hand tightened on his knife, but he had still not pulled the weapon.

"Just back off, Garwood." Clay took a deep breath. This was insane. The celebration continued all around them, the other trappers unaware that a beast every bit as dangerous as a wounded grizzly was in their midst. "There was a lot of bad blood between us in the past, but that's over now."

Zach's mouth twisted in a sneer. "It'll never be over as long as there's one goddamned Holt still drawing breath." He yanked his knife from its sheath. "Take the other one, Aaron!"

"No," Aaron Garwood said.

Zach stopped his lunge before it began. Surprised by his younger brother's defiance, he stared at Aaron.

Aaron was trembling slightly. Not from fear, though, Clay decided as he watched intently. What Aaron was feeling was anger, pure and simple.

"This has always been your fight, Zach," Aaron said, "ever since you—you did that to Josie. I know you said she was lying, but I don't believe you anymore. It's your fault, Zach. All the bloodshed, all the suffering on both sides." Aaron's voice was steadily climbing as he finally vented emotions that had been simmering inside him for months. "You started it by yourself. You can damn well finish it that way!"

With that, he turned and walked off, back stiff and straight, not looking behind him.

Zach was wide-eyed, shaken by his brother's desertion. For years, Aaron had done as he was told, but no longer. Zach was alone.

His pride would not let him back down. Clay realized that as Zach turned toward him again.

"You and me, then, Holt?" Zach growled.

Clay's mind was still somewhat stunned by the implications of what Aaron had revealed. "It was you? You attacked your own sister?"

"Hell, she was a slut," Zach spat. "If she'd lie with a Holt, she sure as hell wasn't too good for me."

Clay shook his head and stared at Zach in contempt for a moment. Finally, he turned away, muttering, "A man like you isn't even worth killing."

Zach let out a wild shriek of rage that finally drew the attention of everyone else in the fort. He sprang toward Clay, sunlight glinting off the knife in his up-raised hand.

"Look out, Clay!" Jeff shouted, grabbing for one of the pistols in his belt.

Clay spun around, unslowed by his recent injuries, well aware that Zach was coming after him. His own blade flickered in the sun as it flashed out of its sheath. The ring of steel meeting steel filled the air as Clay blocked Zach's thrust. Clay reached out with his other hand and grasped Zach's wrist, tugging hard on it as he slipped a foot between Zach's ankles.

Zach went down, thrown off-balance by Clay's maneuver, but he caught Clay's shirt with his other hand and pulled Clay to the ground with him.

The other mountain men hurriedly formed a circle around the struggling pair. No one had to be told that this was a battle to the death.

Jeff and Shining Moon stood to one side, both tense and worried but unwilling to interfere. Jeff held the pistol ready just in case he needed it. He glanced around to see where Aaron was, but the younger Garwood seemed to have disappeared.

Clay and Zach rolled over and over, hands locked on wrists, each man trying to hold off the other's blade. The only sounds in the clear mountain air were their harsh breathing and grunts of effort. The first man to make a slip would die.

Suddenly Zach inhaled sharply, then released his breath in a long, shuddering sigh. He slumped to the ground.

Clay pulled his knife free from Zach's body, wiped the blood from the blade on his dead opponent's buckskins, and wearily got to his feet.

Shining Moon sprang forward to throw her arms around Clay as he limped away from the body. Jeff was beside them a split second later, grasping Clay's arm.

"I'm all right," he assured Jeff and Shining Moon. "Just nicked up a little here and there." He glanced grimly over his shoulder at Zach, who lay on his back, empty eyes turned toward the sky. Quietly Clay said, "It damn well better be over now."

When he turned away, he met the eyes of Aaron Garwood, who came striding up in time to hear his comment. Aaron looked past him at Zach, then turned to nod solemnly at Clay and Jeff. "It is over," he said. "And I wish to God it had never started."

Then he went, for the last time, to tend to his brother.

Jeff had a lump the size of one of the mountains in his throat. At least that was what it felt like as he stood on the bank of the Yellowstone with Clay and Shining Moon and watched the last of the pelts being loaded onto the keelboats that had brought the trappers there.

"Well, I reckon we'll be shoving off. Lisa doesn't want to waste any time getting back to St. Louis." He managed a grin. "I suppose he's anxious to see how much money he's going to make off this expedition."

Clay extended his hand to his brother. "You say hello to Melissa for me. Hell, give her a hug for me— when you get around to it."

"That's right," Jeff said. "The hugs are all going to be from me for a while."

He was silent for a moment. Then he said, "Clay, about the farm. I'm planning to see that it's tended to and the taxes are paid on it. I don't rightly think I could live there after what's happened, but I think Ma and Pa would want the property kept up."

"That's fine by me," Clay said quietly. He took a deep breath. "I reckon you still don't know if you'll be back next spring or not."

Jeff shook his head. "I just can't tell you, Clay. It all depends on what Melissa wants to do, on what I find when I get back home. I'd like to come back, but I just . . ."

"I understand," Clay said. And he did, completely. He would not have been able to leave Shining Moon, and he could understand now why Jeff would not want to leave Melissa once he was reunited with her. "Doesn't matter where you are. You'll still be my brother."

Jeff's expression brightened. "Maybe I'll go on back to Pennsylvania, get the kids, and bring them and Melissa back out here. How'd that be? Get all the Holts in one place again, instead of spread out all over the country."

"That would be mighty fine."

The Holt family had been through so much, had been split asunder by fate and Zach Garwood's evil. It would be nice, Jeff thought, to reunite them out here on the frontier, where there would be room for everyone, room to grow.

Jeff hugged Shining Moon and told her good-bye, then exchanged one more look with Clay and hopped up onto the keelboat. The current tugged at the vessel, anxious to bear it back toward civilization. In a matter of moments, the boats were shoved away from the shore, and with shouts and waves, Manuel Lisa and his crews floated down the river and out of sight around a bend.

Clay and Shining Moon watched until Jeff and the others were gone.

In a soft voice, she said, "He will be back."

Clay's arm tightened around her shoulders. "I know," he said. He understood now.

Wherever there were frontiers, there would be Holts.

Wagons West * Frontier Trilogy
Volume 2

EXPEDITION!
by
Dana Fuller Ross

After the Lewis and Clark expedition unlocked the vast wilderness of the American West, an influx of adventurers set out to explore the wonders of the new land. Among them were men and women of science, eager to record for the world the plant and animal life native to the region and to document the strange, awe-inspiring natural formations rumored to exist.

It is just such a group that Clay Holt encounters as he and his Sioux wife, Shining Moon, and their companions trap beaver along the Yellowstone River in the spring of 1809. Under attack by Blackfoot are a Harvard professor, his daughter, a Prussian artist, and the buckskin-clad men who have led them there. Stranded on a small island midstream, they futilely try to defend themselves, and only because of the expertise of Clay Holt and his group does the expedition survive. The grateful professor persuades Clay to assume leadership of the expedition—but the outraged buckskinner who held that position before will not rest until he gets revenge.

Clay's brother Jeff Holt is hundreds of miles away, returning to their home in Ohio to resume married life with his bride, Melissa. But when Jeff reaches the house, he is greeted not with kisses but with musket balls, and he comes face-to-face with the disheartening news that Melissa is gone—and he has no idea where to begin his search for her.

Read on for an exciting preview of *Expedition!*, the second book in the Frontier Trilogy, on sale February 1993 wherever Bantam paperbacks are sold.

The paddle in Clay Holt's hands bit smoothly into the waters of the Yellowstone River, sending the birchbark canoe gliding over the placid surface. The Yellowstone ran narrow and fast in places, but here it was wide and peaceful, sparkling with a blue and white shimmer in the midday sun.

Springtime in the mountains was Clay's favorite time of year. The sun was warm during the day, and the nights were cool enough for a man to sleep well, rolled in a buffalo robe . . . especially when that robe was shared with a woman like Shining Moon. A man could search the world over, Clay had often thought, and never find a better, more beautiful wife.

They made an impressive-looking couple. Clay was dressed in a buckskin shirt and trousers, along with high-topped fringed moccasins and a coonskin cap. His Harpers Ferry rifle lay at his feet in the canoe, where it would be easy to reach in case of trouble.

Shining Moon, a young Hunkpapa Sioux woman of some twenty summers, also wore buckskins, but her dress was decorated with porcupine quills painted different colors and arranged in elaborate patterns. She wore a hunting knife and like her husband had placed a rifle at her feet. Shining Moon had been an invaluable help, leading Clay and the others unerringly to creeks and small rivers teeming with beaver.

As a result Clay's canoe was heavily loaded with beaver pelts—plews, as the mountain men called them —as was the canoe being paddled by Proud Wolf, Shining Moon's brother, and Aaron Garwood, the fourth member of this partnership. Their canoe followed the one carrying Clay and Shining Moon.

It was still early in spring, but Clay and the others had already trapped enough beaver to make it necessary to visit the fort established by Manuel Lisa at the junction of the Yellowstone and Big Horn rivers, where they could sell the pelts. The previous year Clay and Jeff had worked for the Spaniard; this year Clay had decided to go it alone except for his wife, her brother, and their friend Aaron.

The past six months since he and Shining Moon

were married in a Sioux ceremony had been like an extended honeymoon. His brother Jeff might choose to remain in so-called civilization, but not Clay. This was his home now, and he would be happy to spend the rest of his life in the Shining Mountains.

Suddenly the sound of gunfire came floating to their ears, followed an instant later by bloodcurdling cries.

"What in blazes!" Clay twisted around to look at Shining Moon.

She shook her head. "I do not know. It comes from upstream."

Clay could tell from the anxious expressions of Proud Wolf and Aaron that they also heard the ominous noises. He pointed to the shore again, urgency in his gesture.

The prow of Clay's canoe struck the grassy bank, and he leapt out, rifle in one hand, and after Shining Moon had stepped out, reached back to haul it onto dry land. Proud Wolf and Aaron beached their canoe and joined Clay and Shining Moon.

The gunfire from upstream continued, sporadic blasts punctuated by shouts and cries. A battle was going on, no more than a few hundred yards away.

"What do you reckon that's about, Clay?" Aaron asked as he gripped his flintlock rifle. He had been in the mountains less than a year and was not totally at home there yet; given his nature, he might never be, in such rugged surroundings.

"Don't know," Clay replied, "but I intend to find out. You and Shining Moon stay here, Aaron. Proud Wolf and I will go have a look."

Proud Wolf's chest swelled, and he smiled broadly. At eighteen the Hunkpapa Sioux was still young and his body was undersized, but he had a warrior's heart and spirit. He admired no one more than his brother-in-law Clay Holt, and to accompany Clay on a dangerous chore appealed to him.

"You should take me," Shining Moon said quietly. She had never been one to accept meekly a decision with which she disagreed, even if it came from her husband. "I can move as silently as the wind and without the exuberance of youth."

"You are only two summers older than me, sister," Proud Wolf reminded her.

"Two summers can sometimes be a great deal of time."

"Proud Wolf goes with me," Clay said. "He can keep quiet enough when he wants to, and I want you and Aaron covering our back trail, Shining Moon."

She nodded, realizing that Clay's decision had been based on logic rather than his feelings for her. He knew all too well that nothing got her dander up more quickly than sensing that he was trying to be overprotective of her.

A fresh flurry of shooting exploded upriver. Somebody was burning a hell of a lot of powder, Clay thought as he and Proud Wolf made their way along the shore. Thick brush thronged the bank, in places growing all the way to the river. Clay was grateful for the cover it provided.

They were almost on top of the battle before they got sight of the conflict. The gunshots were louder now, and as Clay parted the screen of brush to peer through it, he saw that some of the combatants were less than fifty yards away.

In the middle of the river was an island, little more than a sandbar with a few trees and bushes growing on it. On that island, their backs to the shore where Clay and Proud Wolf crouched, were some two dozen white men, trying to fight off a band of hostile Blackfoot warriors on the far bank. Clay recognized the Blackfoot markings by the beadwork on their moccasins—a design ending in three prongs, which designated the three tribes that comprised the Blackfoot: the Siksika, the Blood, and the Piegan. The warriors were raking the island with arrows and musket fire, and as Clay and Proud Wolf watched, one of the white men crumpled, bending almost double over the arrow that had been driven through his midsection. Several more lay motionless on the sandy island.

"Damn!" Clay swore. "Those pilgrims are in a bad way."

"They have more guns, but the Blackfoot are many. They will attack the island, I think."

Clay agreed with Proud Wolf. The island was separated from the far shore only by a narrow strip of shallow water. The Blackfoot would wait, content to thin the ranks of the island's defenders before charging across those shallows to overrun the white men. Clay searched for any sign of canoes but did not see any. The white men must have been on foot; when they'd been jumped by the Blackfoot, they must have retreated onto the island, pinning themselves down.

"What will we do?" Proud Wolf asked quietly.

Clay looked over at him and saw that the young man was almost jumping out of his skin with eagerness to join this fight. The Sioux and the Blackfoot were ancient enemies, and Proud Wolf would like nothing better than to spill some Blackfoot blood. Clay had no love for the Blackfoot, either. He had first clashed with them during the journey with Lewis and Clark, and he knew them to be a treacherous bunch.

But when you got right down to it, this was not his fight, and he hated to risk the lives of his wife, brother-in-law, and friend to help a group of men who had blundered into a bad situation.

At least that was what Clay tried to convince himself of for all of ten or fifteen seconds. Then he said, "I reckon we'll pitch in and do what we can to help. The way the river bends here, I think we can get our canoes up to this side of that island almost before the Blackfoot see us coming."

Silently, Clay and Proud Wolf retreated through the brush until they reached Shining Moon and Aaron Garwood. Clay explained tersely what they had witnessed, and Aaron said, "We're going to help those folks, aren't we?"

"I don't see as we've got much choice," Clay replied. "Don't reckon I could live with myself if we went off and left them there to die."

"Nor could I," Shining Moon said, "not at the hands of the Blackfoot." Her eyes were aflame.

Quickly, Clay outlined his plan, which was simple. They would approach the island from the deeper channel of the river and throw their four flintlocks into the battle on the side of the whites. Shining Moon got into the canoe while Clay pushed it into deeper water. Likewise Proud Wolf shoved off from the bank in the other canoe with Aaron. They made sure their rifles were primed and loaded, then took up the paddles and propelled the canoes toward the bend.

They rounded the bend and saw a haze of black-powder smoke hanging in the air over the island and along the shore. Flintlocks still boomed, and arrows hummed in the air. Clay bent his back even more to the task of paddling. Though he could see only a few Blackfoot warriors, he figured they outnumbered the defenders on the island two to one.

Four more rifles would not make a great difference, or at least one would not think so. But Clay had confidence in his own marksmanship, along with that of Shining Moon, Proud Wolf, and Aaron. If they could reach the island and make every shot count, the Blackfoot might decide the price they would have to pay to continue the attack was too high.

Over the gunfire and the splashing of the paddles, Clay heard a sudden cry of alarm, echoed seconds later by other warriors. He saw a musket ball splash just ahead. As long as the aim of the Blackfoot stayed that far off, he was not worried. If they had a chance to get the range, though, he and the others might be in trouble.

More lead missiles peppered the surface of the river near the canoes. Clay ignored them and kept paddling. A few seconds later the sandbar loomed ahead to the right, between the canoes and the far shore where the Blackfoot hid in the trees. Clay dug down with the paddle and sent the canoe grating onto the sandy beach. He and Shining Moon leapt out with their rifles as Proud Wolf and Aaron arrived nearby, also unhurt by the gauntlet of musket fire.

Some of the island's defenders had seen them coming. Buckskin-clad bearded men jumped up and ran toward the newcomers. They would have been better off fighting the Blackfoot than greeting the reinforcements, Clay thought.

Then he realized that a greeting was the last thing these men had in mind. Without slowing, one slammed into Clay, knocking him off-balance. Clay caught himself before he fell but had no chance to regain solid footing before another man slashed at him with a rifle butt. Clay blocked the blow, but this time he went down under the impact. A few feet away Shining Moon cried out in alarm as another man knocked her roughly aside and sprang into the canoe.

"Hey!" Aaron yelled as he and Proud Wolf were the victims of a similar assault. "What the hell are you doing?"

One of the bearded men paused long enough to throw him a hideous grin. "Gettin' out o' here, sonny!"

Clay got to his knees and saw at least half a dozen men piling into each canoe, fighting one another for space. They were making a desperate attempt to escape, stealing the canoes and abandoning the others to their fate. Clay's instincts cried out for him to put a shot in the middle of the ungrateful lot of them, but from the corner of his eye he saw a Blackfoot emerge from the shelter of a deadfall on the shore—and train his musket on the fleeing men.

Throwing himself down on his belly, Clay brought his rifle to his shoulder, thumbed back the cock on the flintlock, and settled the sight on the chest of the Blackfoot warrior. He fired at the same instant as the Blackfoot. Clay's shot caught the warrior in the chest and sent him sprawling backward.

Clay glanced over his shoulder and saw that both canoes were in the river now, riding low in the water with too many passengers. They were not even paddling but were content to let the current carry them downstream.

The boats were awash within moments, however,

not only overloaded but also perforated by balls from Blackfoot muskets. From the island, Clay saw them sinking and uttered a heartfelt curse. When the canoes went down, they would take all the supplies and a season's worth of pelts to the bottom of the river.

He could do nothing about it, Clay realized bleakly. Supplies and pelts meant nothing if he and the others were killed. Clay helped Shining Moon to her feet, and together they ran toward a clump of small trees where several defenders were clustered. Aaron and Proud Wolf ran to a brushy thicket nearby.

Clay and Shining Moon threw themselves to the ground beside the other defenders. Musket fire still rattled and popped around them. Clay's eyes widened in shock as he realized that one of the whites was a woman. A young woman, at that, with strawberry-blond hair underneath a hooded cloak. An older, round-faced man hovered beside her, one arm over her protectively. Neither of them seemed to be armed, but the men with them, all buckskin-clad frontiersmen, were firing toward the shore with pistols and rifles.

Clay reloaded with fast, practiced ease, then rose up to get a bead on one of the Indians. The Blackfoot was showing only a few inches of shoulder behind a tree, but that was enough. Clay's rifle roared, and the warrior went staggering, his right arm dangling from a shattered shoulder.

"Good Lord!" cried the round-faced man sheltering the young woman. "That's quite some shooting!"

Clay put the rifle on the ground and jerked out his pistols. They did not have the range of the long gun, but in his hands they were accurate enough to down a couple more Blackfoot. As he crouched, he glanced toward the river and saw that both canoes had sunk, leaving the would-be escapees floundering in the water. Some were floating facedown; others struggled back toward the island.

Clay swallowed the revulsion he felt for those men. There would be time later to deal with them—if he came out of this mess alive.

The bestselling saga of the Holt family continues
with

The Holts: An American Dynasty
Volume Seven

YUKON JUSTICE
by
Dana Fuller Ross

After a fight with his father forced young Frank Blake
to take to the road, he settled in Sierra, California, to
work in the oil fields. But a company dispute led to
violence, arson, and death, and Frank, aware of the
identities of the perpetrators, found himself running
for his life. After traveling with a circus he headed
north, to the gold-laden Klondike.

Read on for an exciting preview of *Yukon Justice*, Volume Seven in The Holts: An American Dynasty, on
sale September 1992 wherever Bantam Books are sold.

Frank Blake stood staring in the middle of the street. Not even the circus he had worked for could compete with this, he thought. The street near the docks was jammed so closely that horse-drawn traffic couldn't get through. Some drivers had simply dropped reins and left drays, wagons, and hackney coaches standing in the road. The drivers were presumably inside the Northern Pacific ticket office or in the swarm of humanity that surged outside it, trying to get in.

Frank already knew why; for weeks he had heard rumors of a gold strike up north. Today the newsboys shouted the headlines: "Klondike Strike! Gold Ship Docks in Seattle!"

Five thousand people had already been waiting on Schwabacher's Dock at six in the morning when the *Portland* steamed in with sixty-eight triumphant miners and two tons of gold. The *Portland* had been fully booked for her return voyage before she had even docked. Now the whole wharf was a solid mass of would-be prospectors trying to buy passage on anything that would float.

Frank had $254 in his pocket, so he bypassed the Northern Pacific office—the fare posted in the window was being changed from $200 to $250. As he watched, a hand reached out again and made it $300. Next door the sidewalks outside Cooper & Levy Pioneer Outfitters were lined with stacked bales and boxes and hopeful miners. Some looked as if they might have prospected before, but most looked like bank clerks. Frank noted a few enterprising girls from skid-row brothels perched on packing crates, pocketbooks with their fare firmly clutched in their lap.

"Where can a fellow still find fare?" he asked one at random.

The girl smiled at him. She seemed to like his looks. She was a gaminlike waif with blue eyes. "Down at the docks maybe. Try the *Barbry Allen*. She's an awful old scow, but she floats. Tell Luther that Lulie sent you."

"Lulie!" The young woman with her straightened up from the trunk strap she had been tightening. "There's plenty of men going north. You don't have to recruit no more."

The touch of Irish in her voice caught Frank's attention, and he burst out laughing. "I'm the bad penny, Peg," he said helplessly. "You should have known."

She snapped her head around and stared at him. "And what in the blue blazes are you doin' here?" Peggy Dulaney asked, delighted to see her old friend and lover. She flew into his arms, and, laughing, he swept her up and swung her around. "An' you were supposed to be goin' north last year. I thought sure you'd be one o' these fellows comin' in on the *Portland.*"

"Not I," Frank said sorrowfully. "Late as usual."

"Well, *I* mean to make my millions," Peggy told him. "You talked about it all so sure, you got me fired up. But I come to find out that there wasn't no rush to head up there. A laundry's no good without dirty men to wash for."

"So what have you been doing?" Frank asked. "I've thought about you."

"I set up here in Seattle for a while to see which way the wind was gonna blow."

"Now we're going north," Lulie said happily.

"To do laundry?" Frank raised his eyebrows. Lulie did not look like a laundress.

"Lulie's goin' to help me out in the laundry," Peggy said stiffly, as if this was settled in her mind but not in Lulie's. "I got my own business here, or I did have. I just sold out. Did all right, too, without Pa drinking up every blessed nickel."

"Where is your pa?" Frank asked.

Peggy shrugged. "Do you know if he came back to Sierra?"

Frank shook his head. "Not as far as I know, but I never went back, either, after . . ."

Peg nodded, understanding. Her pa was probably dead or would never be seen again.

"I haven't decided what business to go into," Lulie declared, sending a quick glance at Peggy. "I'll see how things look when we get to Dawson."

Without actually moving, Peggy gave the impression of throwing her hands in the air. "Just use your head." She looked as if she didn't have much hope of Lulie's being able to do that. Instead, Peggy turned her attention to Frank. "If you want passage, Luther *might* squeeze you in. But he's planning to beat it out of here on tonight's tide."

A few Seattle residents had consulted returning prospectors before laying their plans, but uncounted hundreds hadn't. The whole adventure had a lunatic cast to it. Squeezed on board the *Barbry Allen*, a leaking oyster boat, Frank watched the hysteria on the docks and the bay full of boats. Ten feet across the water a man was trying to coax a billy goat up the gangway. Entrepreneurs with bizarre schemes had sprung up like mushrooms on shore, their numbers keeping pace with the would-be miners. Hardened from his year on the road, he looked apprehensively at the boats full of preachers, clerks, accountants, cooks, even (someone said) the mayor of Seattle. How were they going to fare? he wondered. They were ready for adventure, cheering as each boat pulled out from the dock.

The merchants of Seattle were stripped clean but made wealthy by the end of the first day. The gold seekers, eyes shining, steamed out into Puget Sound. The *Barbry Allen* would travel north along the Inside Passage, between the continent's edge and the offshore islands, to Skagway or Dyea. Then the passengers would disembark and go overland through White Pass or Chilkoot to the Klondike. The route appeared deceptively short on the map, on which it was difficult to discern that much of the way was vertical.

Luther, the ship's captain, was a big barrel of a man. For a hundred dollars he cheerfully sold Frank a ticket for enough space in which to set down his supplies and sleep on top of them. By the time they made Wrangell on the southern Alaskan coast, Frank had won forty of it back, and Luther had quit playing poker with him.

Despite an almost complete lack of privacy, Lulie had managed to make some money, too, wandering off behind jury-rigged screens that blocked her and her partner from curious eyes.

"You got no sense!" Peggy told her later. "You're goin' to get hurt! That's no way to live."

"I don't go with but nice fellows," Lulie protested.

Frank knew better than to get in the middle of an argument that Peggy was already managing very well by herself, but he listened with fascination to Lulie's saga. She had been working in a Seattle laundry when Peggy had set up her own business. Lulie hadn't liked the work, so she had tried prostitution at night and liked that much better. The money was easier, she said, and some nice fellow was always bringing her a present.

Peggy snorted. "And how long do you think you could have worked on your own before the madams an' the pimps ran you out or had you beat up? Or before some man wanted some favor you didn't like and killed you for it?"

"Nothin' like that's ever happened," Lulie told her.

"It would have if you hadn't left," Peggy said, exasperated. "You aren't fit to be out on your own! You don't know anything!"

"I'm gonna get rich in the Klondike," Lulie said calmly. "Then I won't have to worry."

"You're dumb as a box of rocks," Peggy said, but she was talking to Lulie's back. The girl had already drifted off.

"If you're going to try to reform her," Frank said, "you've got your work cut out for you."

"She's like some half-fledged chicken standin' in the middle of the road, waitin' to get run down,"

Peggy muttered. "I should never have let her come with me." She stared irritably at the passing scenery.

"And how would you have stopped her from joining you?" Frank inquired practically.

"Well, at least I didn't have to let her come *with* me. Now I'll be lookin' after her forever, as if I needed that."

"You've gotten tough in the last year." Frank slipped an arm around Peggy's waist and, ignoring the forty other voyagers on the *Barbry Allen*, nuzzled her ear.

"I haven't gotten tough," Peggy protested. "But I wish I had. I paid my dues with Pa—you know that. I'm entitled to have just my own self to look after." She gave him a sideways glance. "No one else is going to."

"That's right," Frank said good-naturedly. He kissed her earlobe.

Peggy grinned. "Not that I asked you to. I know a man with a wandering foot when I see one. And you leave my ear alone."

Frank stopped, but he didn't take his arm from around her waist. "You feel awfully good, Peg," he whispered. "And who else here is going gold hunting, on her own two wandering feet?"

"I didn't wander out of Sierra," Peggy said flatly. "I was run out of town, same as you. *And* I been makin' an honest livin' in Seattle ever since, not troopin' around with snakes and tattooed ladies."

"We'll see stranger things than that on this road, I imagine." Frank held out one last inducement. "I brought some books, Peg. I'll read to you like I used to. Remember Omar Khayyam? I brought him."

"That might be nice," Peggy mused. "If life gets dull."

It was the closest she was going to get to telling him she'd let him in her bed again. Peggy wasn't Lulie.

The voyage to Dyea—Luther wanted to go there, so that was where his passengers were going—took two weeks. Dyea had no natural harbor. Boats were

anchored offshore, then passengers jumped over-
board, after tossing their belongings into the water.
The cargo had to be dragged across the mud flats.
Frank learned within seconds that if Alaska was an
icebox in the winter, it was a swamp in the summer.
Mosquitoes—big, voracious ones—were everywhere.
As Frank towed one of Peggy's tin washtubs loaded
with flour sacks, he stopped to wonder what on earth
he was doing there. The women were in the water,
too, dragging their trunks ashore and cursing at Luther. They eventually got everything hauled to dry
land, where they stood dripping icy water and staring
despondently at the pile. All around them soaking
Klondikers were doing the same, while the local Chilkat Indians watched with interest. Until recently Dyea
had been their town, with a population of no more
than 250. Now it was overrun by white men.

As the Klondikers stared dismally at the vertical
walls of the mountains rising in the distance, the Indians announced their availability as porters: twelve
cents a pound to carry goods the twenty-seven miles
through the pass to navigable water at Lake Lin-
deman. The only alternative was to carry one's goods
without help, making ten to twenty trips. Many did
just that.

Peggy and Lulie hired Indians, and Frank, because he had won back his forty dollars from Luther,
went along with that scheme. Without ever having
made any verbal agreement, they seemed to be three-
way partners for the trek. Frank wasn't willing to lose
track of Peggy again, and Lulie was part of the deal.

"Why do you want to baby-sit that flighty tart?"
he asked Peggy, who was trudging behind him. Lulie
was three or four paces back, with the Chilkat porters
between them . . . when she wasn't off in the bushes
with one. Peggy didn't answer, and he couldn't see
her expression through the mosquito veiling. Her silence didn't really matter; his had been a rhetorical
question, posed out of boredom.

For the first few miles the trail out of Dyea was an
easy one, and they had walked three abreast, singing

and commenting on the midsummer warmth. Five miles from the tidewater, however, marked the edge of hell. The trail narrowed to a quagmire at the bottom of Dyea Canyon—a chaos of mud, boulders, and the Dyea River, entangled in a thicket of spruce and hemlock. Those who had dragged wagons this far were forced to abandon them now. They whipped their unfortunate teams, used as pack animals, up the trail. Thirteen miles from Dyea, at Sheep Camp, not even horses could conquer the terrain, and the beasts, too, were abandoned there, usually to be rounded up by enterprising Chilkats, taken back to Dyea, and resold. At that the horses fared better than those abandoned at White Pass, where their bones clogged Dead Horse Trail.

It all began with
WAGONS WEST
America's best-loved series by Dana Fuller Ross

❏ *Independence!* 26822-8 $4.95/$5.95 in Canada
A saga of high adventure and passionate romance on the first wagon train to Oregon territory.

❏ *Nebraska!* 26162-2 $4.95/$5.95 in Canada
Indian raids and sabotage threaten the settlers as "Whip" Holt leads the wagon train across the Great Plains.

❏ *Wyoming!* 26242-4 $4.95/$5.95 in Canada
Facing starvation, a mysterious disease, and a romantic triangle, the expedition pushes on.

❏ *Oregon!* 26072-3 $4.50/$4.95 in Canada
Three mighty nations clash on the fertile shore of the Pacific as the weary pioneers arrive.

❏ *Texas!* 26070-7 $4.99/$5.99 in Canada
Branded as invaders by the fiery Mexican army, a band of Oregon volunteers rallies to the cause of liberty.

❏ *California!* 26377-3 $4.99/$5.99 in Canada
The new settlers' lives are threatened by unruly fortune seekers who have answered the siren song of gold.

❏ *Colorado!* 26546-6 $4.95/$5.95 in Canada
The rugged Rockies hold the promise of instant wealth for the multitudes in search of a new start.

❏ *Nevada!* 26069-3 $4.99/$5.99 in Canada
The nation's treasury awaits a shipment of silver just as the country is on the brink of Civil War.

❏ *Washington!* 26163-0 $4.50/$4.95 in Canada
Ruthless profiteers await wounded Civil War hero Toby Holt's return to challenge his landholdings.

❏ *Montana!* 26073-1 $4.95/$5.95 in Canada
The lawless, untamed territory is being terrorized by a sinister gang led by a tough and heartless woman.

❏ *Dakota!* 26184-3 $4.50/$4.95 in Canada
Against the backdrop of the Badlands, fearless Indian tribes form an alliance to drive out the white man forever.

❏ *Utah!* 26521-0 $4.99/$5.99 in Canada
Chinese and Irish laborers strive to finish the transcontinental railroad before currupt landowners sabotage it.

❏ *Idaho!* 26071-5 $4.99/$5.99 in Canada
The perilous task of making a safe homeland from an untamed wilderness is hampered by blackmail and revenge.

❏ *Missouri!* 26367-6 $4.50/$4.95 in Canada
An incredible adventure on a paddle-wheel steamboat stirs romantic passions and gambling fever.

❏ *Mississippi!* 27141-5 $4.95/$5.95 in Canada
New Orleans is home to an underworld of crime, spawned by easy money and ruthless ambitions.

❏ *Louisiana!* 25247-X $4.99/$5.99 in Canada
Smuggled shipments of opium and shanghaied Chinese workers continue to invade the country.

❏ *Tennessee!* 25622-X $4.99/$5.99 in Canada
Unscrupulous politicians lead an army of outlaws and misfits to threaten America's cherished democracy.

LE 13A 7/92